GHOSTS OF
BIRCH LAKE

To Nora —
Best wishes always.
I hope you enjoy the book.

Chri Thibert
Sept. 2016

i

GHOSTS OF BIRCH LAKE

A novel told as oral history

by
CHRISTOPHER TABBERT

**Bristol &
Lynden**

Bristol & Lynden Press
233 Wood Creek Road, Unit 503
Wheeling, IL 60090

www.bristolandlyndenpress.com

ISBN: 978-0-692-70759-3

This book is dedicated to my son,

Alexander Matthew Tabbert,

who spreads light and love wherever he goes.

PART ONE

The time to repair the roof is when the sun is shining.

– John F. Kennedy

Chapter 1

Ray

Chicago, July 1960

My name is Ray Weber. I'm nine years old. I live with my mom and dad in St. Gregory's parish in Chicago. I go to St. Gregory's school, which my mom also went to.

My dad is a building inspector for the city. He goes around to different buildings to make sure they are safe and sound. He is also a precinct captain for the regular Democratic organization, which is called the party. That job is lots of work. He has to help the people in our neighborhood whenever they need something.

One Sunday morning Dad asked me to go outside and get the paper. I found Mrs. Weinschenk and Mrs. Corcoran sitting in our car. They said they were waiting for a ride to church. When I told Dad, he said, "Well, if that don't take the cake. What if I was laid up in bed with a hangnail or something? They'd have sat there all day and it would serve 'em right."

Even though Dad was a little aggravated, he still said he would drive the ladies to church. Then he told Mom, "Ray has to come with, Carol. That way the old gals can't come back later and say I tried to get fresh with them."

In case you are wondering how the ladies got into Dad's car in the first place, it is because he never locks it. "I'd like to meet the fellow who has enough nerve to mess with it," he said.

Whenever there is an election, Dad needs to make sure all our neighbors vote for the party candidates. He has to help the people get to the polls. Some people also need to be shown how to vote when they get there.

My dad and his friends get to march in the St. Patrick's Day parade every year because they work for the city. That is really something. Also, last year when Mayor Daley was running, my folks were invited to a lunch with him. They got to shake his hand and they also got an autographed picture of him for me.

My dad is quite a guy. He is very handsome. Everybody says so. He is a scratch golfer. He is a sharp dresser. He is a good shot with a rifle and an expert fisherman. He was a star center fielder and halfback in high school. I've seen his varsity letters and newspaper clippings. He can shuffle cards and do sleight-of-hand tricks just like a magician. He can shoot pool or darts with the best of them. He bowls around 180 or so. He knows how to drive a speedboat. He is an excellent water skier. When he goes slalom style, which means to go on one ski, he can get his body almost parallel to the water and shoot a giant spray behind him. He can also flick a cigarette butt a good twenty feet with one finger.

My dad served in Europe during World War II. He won the Purple Heart, which is a very important medal. Our friend Don said he got it for falling off of a bar stool in London, but I think Don was only kidding. I asked Dad and he said, "I guess Don's story will do as good as any."

My mom is a housewife. She is very pretty with dark brown hair and eyes. Sometimes she puts her hair in a ponytail and sometimes she puts a scarf around it. But either way she always looks good. She enjoys playing bridge with her girlfriends and also curling up with a good book. She loves baseball, too, so she fits right in with the rest of the family. She is the best mom and she also volunteers to help out at our school and church.

Dad told me how he met Mom. He was riding on the L one day when he spotted her. He didn't get off at his regular stop, but kept on riding to see where she was going to get off. He said, "You can

4

bet your life I wasn't getting off that train until she did." Then he followed her into her office, which was on the seventh floor of the Merchandise Mart building. That is the headquarters of the CTA, where my mom was working in those days.

My dad said by the time he got back on the L and rode back to his stop, he ended up late for work and got chewed out but good. Then he went back to my mom's office the next day and asked her out for a date. He said she looked like just the kind of a girl you would marry.

The Merchandise Mart is known for being the only building in Chicago with its own L stop and post office. The mart was erected in 1930. It was the largest building in the world, if you are talking about square feet, until the Pentagon was erected outside of Washington, D.C.

If you would like to have a real nice vacation, you should do yourself a favor and go to Larry's Lake Aire Resort, which is located up north in Birch Lake, Wisconsin. Our family goes there every year. We are going next month. My Grandpa Mike and Grandma Elizabeth just bought the place over the winter. They used to go on vacation there for umpteen years, and then they decided to buy the place when Grandpa Mike retired. They haven't gotten around to changing the name yet. That's why it's still called Larry's. Larry is the name of the man who owned it before.

My Grandpa Mike is my dad's dad. He is about five-foot-nine and weighs about 165 pounds. That's about the same size as my dad, or maybe a little less. If I picture him, he usually wears an old brown fedora with a red feather, a flannel shirt with the sleeves rolled up, and some gray or tan pants. He also wears a blue windbreaker, especially when we go fishing. Sometimes, if it's very warm out, he just wears a sleeveless undershirt.

Grandpa Mike used to work for the phone company in Chicago before he retired. He fought in France during World War I. He also was a boxer in the service. My dad said he held his own and then some.

There are four cabins for rent at Larry's. You can do many activities there such as swimming, water skiing, and fishing. You can also play croquet, horseshoes, and badminton. At night sometimes we catch lightning bugs in a jar.

Our friend Don is from Birch Lake and he helps Grandpa out. He does a lot of work around the place and he knows how to fix things. He is a good worker and a really nice guy. Dad said Don's job is to be a gofer, but Mom said she would rather call him a handyman or a jack of all trades.

In case you would like to know where Birch Lake is located, it is 361 miles from Chicago, 287 miles from Milwaukee and 135 miles from Minneapolis, Minnesota.

Birch Lake was man-made many years ago when they built a dam so they could float logs down the Chippewa River to the saw mill. Do you know what happens when they build a dam? The water that backs up behind it makes a lake. The low spots on the ground end up under water and the higher spots end up being islands. Grandpa Mike explained that to me.

There used to be a wooden statue of an Indian brave over at the dam. It was carved out of a white pine log back in the 1800s by a man named Luke Lyons, using only an axe and a pocket knife. The Indian brave was known as a good-luck symbol by all the lumberjacks and rivermen for many years. One time he toppled over in a storm and floated all the way down to Jim Falls, which is twenty miles away.

The Indian brave was moved to the town hall park in 1950, when the new concrete dam was completed. I have seen the Indian brave and I would say he is about eight feet tall.

When the new dam was built, Birch Lake got much bigger, but the part by Larry's stayed pretty much the same. The new dam is for generating electric power, not floating logs. When it opened, the newspaper said now the houses that were built out of logs that floated over the old dam are getting their power from the same place the logs came from! Grandpa Mike showed me the article. I think that was pretty neat.

Every year when we go to Larry's I always notice something. When we park the car in the trees behind the cabin and carry our suitcases around to the front, the way the ground slopes down to the lake, the view reminds me of when you come up the stairs at the Cubs game and see the stands sloping down to the field.

Also, whenever we are in the speed boat, the water right behind it gets churned up by the motor and it looks just like foamy root beer.

You can catch all sorts of fish in Birch Lake such as muskie, northern pike, walleye, bass, perch, bluegill, and many others. One day last summer Grandpa Mike took me out fishing and Dad took our picture when we got back. In the picture we are standing on the pier. Grandpa is holding up a string with a whole bunch of little fish on it and I am holding up a giant muskie.

Everybody was very excited because they thought I caught the muskie. But do you know what really happened? Grandpa actually hooked it and reeled it in. All I did was help to land it in the net for him. Then he made believe I caught it. He didn't tell Mom and Dad I caught it, but he didn't tell them I didn't, either.

Even though I didn't really catch the fish myself but only helped out a little, I still like that picture a lot. My dad was so proud when he took it.

In case you don't know this, they have black squirrels up north, but I have never seen any in Chicago. You can also buy fireworks in Wisconsin, which you can't do in Illinois. If you ever go to Wisconsin, you will see lots of places selling fireworks along the road. You probably shouldn't buy them, though, because they are pretty dangerous.

Chapter 2

Don

Birch Lake, July 1960

One time a couple years ago, we were all setting around shooting the shit when Mike said, "You know, this place won't be here much longer the way it's going. That would be a real shame, wouldn't it?"

I don't know if Larry was losing his marbles or what, but you could tell he was letting lots of stuff go.

Just for one little example, there's a light that hangs over the garage door and lights up the space between the garage and the main house. Well sir, when the lightbulb burnt out and I went in the shed as usual to get a new one, there wasn't none.

We always had a clipboard hanging from a nail there, and I was spose to write down the date and whatever item needed replacing. Then Larry would go in town every Saturday morning and buy all the stuff on the list. I don't know how many times I told him I'd buy the stuff and come back with a receipt so he'd know exactly what was bought and how much it set him back, but he wouldn't go for that. Don't get me started.

So anyways I made a note there, *Need ½ dozen 60 watt bulbs*, and left it at that. Saturday rolled around, and Larry didn't get no lightbulbs. I don't know if he even went to town at all. Then we ran out of oil for the lawn mower. Then I needed some screens to patch holes in the screen doors and windows where bugs was flying right into the cabins. I could go on and on. It was just typical stuff you'd need to keep the place up, but the list kept getting longer and Larry never bought nothing. Whenever I reminded him, he'd get his nose out of joint. "Don't worry about it," he says. "I'll get around to it in my own time."

Finally I just went and bought all the shit out of my own pocket. I never even asked him to pay me back. It was worth it to save myself the aggravation of standing around with my thumb up you know where and watching everything go to hell right in front of my eyes.

You know how you can tell when a place has really went to pot? I mean if you didn't notice a hunnerd other things like I was just talking about, then you'll know for sure when you see there's weeds growing on the roof! That means there's enough dirt piled up in the rain gutters and between the shingles to grow plants with.

That's exactly what happened at Larry's after the old boy started slipping even worse and his kids took over the place. There was weeds growing on the roofs of the cabins, the garage, and even the main house. I hated to see that. When you consider how nice we used to keep the place up, it was a goddamn shame. The worst part was I couldn't do nothing about it. After I worked there on and off for twenty-some odd years, Larry's son Henry told me my services was no longer needed. That was spose to be a nice way of saying I was shit-canned.

After a few months, you couldn't hardly recognize the place. My God, you'd have to walk through knee-deep grass and weeds just to go from the house to the garage. You'd be liable to get bitten by a snake or something.

You can bet your bottom Larry wouldn't of stood still for it if he actually knew what was going on. But the poor guy doesn't hardly know his own name by now, much less any of this other stuff. I guess that's a blessing when you stop and think about it. Also on the bright side, his kids saved theirself the buck and a quarter an hour it would of costed 'em to keep me on.

I ain't gonna lie to you. When Mike and Mrs. Weber turned around and bought Larry's, I was as happy as a pig in shit or however you want to say it. The idea of them being up north all year round—well, I just can't get over it. Mike has all sorts of ideas for improving the place and he encourages me to come up with my own ideas. We been mapping out a whole plan. We're making a list of all the projects, figuring how much they'll cost, and putting a schedule together.

I couldn't of asked for anything better. Between Mike and Mrs. Weber, they make a guy feel right at home. And how.

Chapter 3

Carol

Chicago, July 1960

Jack enjoys being a precinct captain. Or rather I should say he enjoys the status the job confers upon him. He likes being viewed as an important man. He certainly looks the part, I'll say that. He is always presentable, smells good, knows which fork to use (most of the time), and he keeps the "dese," "dem," and "dose" to a minimum.

As much as I hate to think this way, though, I've always doubted whether he is very well suited for the job. I mean for the actual work the job entails, which boils down to 1) ingratiating himself to all our neighbors by doing favors for them, 2) making it clear that the favors are done not out of the kindness of his heart but in exchange for votes, and 3) seeing to it that all these debts, if you will, are settled on election day.

It's the first one that would give you pause if you knew Jack at all. He is not a back-slapper or a glad-hander by any means. His normal tendency is to be somewhat aloof. But as precinct captain, he has to inject himself into people's lives in very obvious ways. He has to extend congratulations for every birth or baptism or graduation or wedding or housewarming, offer get-well wishes to people in the hospital, and attend every wake and funeral.

He can also fix traffic tickets or other minor legal entanglements for certain constituents. Or he might help someone fill out the paperwork to get a relative into the United States. He might even try to find a job for a family man who's out of work.

"I have to get these people to vote for me," Jack said, "not the candidates. Most of 'em wouldn't know the candidate if they tripped over him." He has to be at people's beck and call more or less constantly. If someone has a broken sidewalk in front of the house, or a dead tree in the parkway, or a streetlight out, or rats in the alley, or Heaven knows what else, they'd never think to call the city government—Streets and Sanitation or the Forestry Department or what have you. They come to Jack, and their problem becomes his problem. It might seem strange that people call an agent of the party to get action from the city, but in practical terms there is no difference between the two.

Jack rather resents the people who come to him time and again for the most trivial matters, as if they simply need the attention. A person who comes to Jack with some problem or other twice a week might very well have fewer votes to offer than someone who never uses up more time than it takes to say hello. Jack likens the needier types to "these hypochondriacs who call the doctor's office every time they either have a bowel movement or don't have one."

At election time, Jack is responsible for putting up campaign signs, handing out flyers, ringing doorbells, and canvassing each household to get a few questions answered. Are all people of voting age registered? If they are registered, are they actually planning to show up on election day? Do they need a ride to the polling place? Presuming they plan to vote and can find their way to the polling place, do they intend to vote the right way?

"Say somebody has five registered voters in the house," Jack said. "I tap him on the chest and I tell him, 'I'm counting on you for five.' If he hems and haws, he better have a damn good explanation. I just stare him down until he comes up with something."

He was just warming up. "And another thing," he said. "If it takes more than thirty seconds for a guy to vote, he's either playing with himself in there or splitting his ticket. I'll come right out and ask him which it is."

12

"Isn't that their own business?" I asked, just playing devil's advocate.

Jack looked at me sort of quizzically, half smiling, as you might look at a child who had asked a naïve question and wouldn't understand your answer anyway, so why bother?

Chapter 4

Ray

Birch Lake, August 1960

One time a few years ago, when I was little, me and Grandpa
Mike were sitting on the pier looking out at the lake. "Want to
know something, Ray?" he said. "In the city, why, you might go
past the same building every day for forty years, and then one day
it's gone. And then, almost overnight, there's a new building
there. But this place never changes. I hope to God you can sit
here someday with your grandson and tell him the same thing."

But when we came up to Larry's this year, a few things were
different. First of all, Grandpa Mike and Grandma Elizabeth own
the place now. That's the big one. We're staying in the main
house instead of one of the cabins.

Grandpa said, "There's plenty of work to do, but we'll get this
place in ship shape before you know it. Why, you'll hardly recognize it when we're through."

And then, if you can believe this, Mom has a two-piece bathing suit. While we were packing for the trip she told me, "We'll
see how this goes over, won't we?"

I would have to say it looks real good on her. Grandpa Mike
thinks so too. He said it's very becoming. I asked Dad what he
thinks of it. He said, "I'm going to tell your mom in private."
Then he winked at me, so I guess that means he likes it.

Mom told me the only one she was a little worried about was
Grandma Elizabeth. She also packed her regular one-piece suit,
just in case, but so far she hasn't worn it.

There's another change at Birch Lake, too. A new man took over

14

the pink store. It was always painted pink as long as anybody could remember, and now the new man has it painted white. But everybody still calls it the pink store out of habit.

The first time we went in there, me and Dad and Grandpa Mike and Don all went. Grandpa said he wanted to introduce Dad and I to the new man running the place. His name is Bill, and he is in a wheelchair. "Glad to know yous," he said. Then he reached out over the counter to shake hands with Dad.

"What can I do you for?" Bill asked us.

"We just need a few miscellaneous items," Grandpa said. He took a paper out of his shirt pocket and looked at it.

"I can't read this note Mother gave me," he said.

"Your arm's not long enough," Dad said.

Grandpa looked at the note again. Then he handed it to Don. "Can you help a fellow out?" he asked.

Don read the note out loud. "Milk, Coppertone, hot dogs and buns, beer, Old Dutch potato chips—make sure to get Old Dutch, it says—charcoal brickets, Eskimo Pies, tannin bells. What in hell is tannin bells?"

He showed the note to me. "I think that says tennis balls," I said.

"Tennis balls," Grandpa said. "For your batting practice, Ray. Because somebody forgot to bring some from Chicago."

The way the pink store is set up, most of the stuff to buy is behind the counter so you can't get it yourself. Bill wheeled himself around and got that stuff and put it all on the counter. Except the charcoal, which I guess he couldn't lift too easily because it was on the floor to begin with.

Then Grandpa said, "Let's also have a pack of baseball cards, Bill. Or better yet, how about two." He had his money out and he was waiting for Bill to tell him how much everything cost.

"Forget it," Bill said. "The cards are on the house." He tossed the two packs onto the counter. "Here you go, Junior."

"His name's Ray," Dad said.

15

"That's awful nice of you, Bill," Grandpa said. "And let's get a paper so Ray can read all the box scores. Have you got the *Chicago Tribune?*"

"Not today's," Bill said. "But I got the St. Paul paper. *Pioneer Press.*"

"I'm sure that'll do," Grandpa said. "And if you don't mind, how about a little box of White Owls while we're at it?"

"Sorry, that's a no can do," Don said. "That ain't on the list."

Grandpa put his finger up to his mouth and winked at Don and I, because he's not supposed to smoke cigars any more.

After we got back in the car, I opened up the baseball cards. I got Jerry Lumpe, Dick Hall, Bob Clemente, Clint Courtney, and Russ Kemmerer in one pack, and I got Earl Torgeson, Pumpsie Green, Don Larsen, Red Schoendienst, and Art Ceccarelli in the other pack. Art was the only Cub I got.

Dad was driving. As he was backing out he said, "How'd this Bill wind up in the wheelchair, I wonder?"

"What I heard, he crashed his motor-sickle," Grandpa said.

"Yup," Don said.

"Lucky he wasn't killed," Grandpa said.

"Maybe," Dad said.

"He was out in Seattle or somewheres when it happened," Don said. "And then he come back here to be closer to his folks."

"Well, it's too bad," Grandpa said. "A young fellow crippled like that."

"Is he a married man?" Dad asked.

"I believe he is," Don said.

"Jesus," Dad said.

Everybody was quiet for a minute or so. Then Dad said, "I suppose he'd be easy prey to a holdup out here, wouldn't he? In that wheelchair?"

Don said, "Oh, I wouldn't be surprised if he don't have some backup under the counter."

"You think so?" Dad asked.

"Sure," Don said. "Why not?"

"What does that mean?" I asked.

Grandpa said, "Maybe he's got a pistol handy, Ray."

"Or maybe a shotgun," Don said. "I hear he's spose to be quite a man with guns. A real deadeye."

"Is that right?" Dad asked.

"That's what they say," Don said. "He was spose to be a sharpshooter in the war. Picked off Germans like nobody's business. Of course that wouldn't matter none in that little place. You couldn't hardly miss."

"No, I guess not," Dad said.

Chapter 5

Carol

Birch Lake, August 1960

I wasn't sure what to expect when we went to the lake this year, the first year of the new Weber administration at Larry's.

Jack has been up there a few times to help out and came back each time saying that the renovations were coming along "slow but sure."

The occupancy rate is something else again. "You have to figure it'll take a while to build up the word of mouth again," Jack said. "Thanks to that bunch of morons." He meant Larry's kids, who ran the place into the ground during their brief stewardship. One time I joked that they should change the name to the Last Resort. I don't know if the others didn't hear me, or didn't get it, but none of them laughed. Maybe they did get it but just didn't think it was funny.

When we first pulled in this year, I didn't notice any particular changes. But as soon as we stepped into the main house, I understood. The interior is much improved. Just about everywhere you look there's new paint, new curtains, new light fixtures, even some new pieces of furniture and appliances.

At first I thought that was backwards, because wouldn't you work outside while the weather was nice and then tackle the inside of the house over the winter? Not if you were Mike Weber, you wouldn't. Of course you would do the inside of the house before anything else, for Elizabeth's sake.

Mike said that he and Don had a few more projects inside, and then they would work on the outside of the house in the fall. The improvement program for the cabins, the beach, the boat launch, and the rest of the grounds is scheduled to begin next year. Mike and Don walked us around and pointed out all the different spots that'll be fixed up or redone completely. It was touching, really, to see how excited they are about their plans.

Ray got to spend lots of time with his grandpa, which he always loves. The two of them are thick as thieves. They went out fishing by themselves a couple times, and they never came back empty-handed. Jack and Don went along another time, but they went in one boat while Mike and Ray remained together in the other.

The guys came up with a game in which Mike, with his back to the lake, pitched tennis balls to Ray. Jack and Don stood waist-deep in the water serving as outfielders. Whenever Ray really got hold of one and knocked it over their heads, he got quite a thrill. So did Mike.

We also had a croquet match, which Mike called the First Annual Birch Lake All-American Croquet Championship and Regatta. He even got Ray to make a poster to that effect. I'm not sure where the regatta part was supposed to come in, but it did have a nice ring to it. We drew names out of a hat to choose the teams. Jack ended up paired with his mom, Ray with Don, and Mike with me. (Mike later told me that he had fixed it so we'd be teammates.)

At one point during the game Jack had a chance to send Don's ball for a buggy ride. You could see he meant to put that ball into the next county. He got set up and swung with all his might, but he did not hit his ball into Don's. He hit the side of his foot. No one laughed out loud.

Mike and I won the croquet championship, with Ray and Don second and Jack and Elizabeth third. Mike went into the garage and returned shortly with homemade gold, silver, and bronze medals that looked a lot like the tops and/or bottoms of soup cans. The medals were duly awarded in a brief ceremony.

After the medal ceremony, we grilled some steaks with corn

on the cob and baked potatoes in tin foil. Then we all sat at the water's edge having a libation or two, and I tell you it was a wonderful feeling. I don't mean the warm glow from the drinks, although that probably contributed. I mean the feeling that we all belonged exactly where we were in time and space.

Jack and I held hands, which we don't do often enough these days. Mike and Don regaled us again with their plans for turning Larry's into "the damndest resort anybody ever seen," in Don's words. The rest of us, even Elizabeth, egged them on. Mike said there was no reason we couldn't have a nice little nine-hole miniature golf course. Don said why not make it eighteen, with a beer garden to boot? Ray suggested go-karts. And on it went. By the end of the discussion, you'd have thought that the Larry's of the future would be nothing less than a northwoods version of Disneyland.

Don offered to take Ray over to the pink store for ice cream. Naturally, the moment they left, the conversation turned to Don himself.

After the usual encomiums such as "Salt of the earth" and "He'd give you the shirt off his back" were tossed out there, Mike took the floor. "What I respect about Don," he said, "is that he's had to fight like hell for everything he's gotten in this world. And it ain't much at that."

"You don't have to feel sorry for him, Dad," Jack said. "I always figured he was happy in his own way."

"I don't know," Mike said.

I felt like chiming in. "Well," I said, "it's very obvious he loves all three of you. He sees you as his family."

Elizabeth liked that one. She patted my free hand.

"It's the least we can do," Mike said. "The least anyone could do."

"You're too modest," I said.

"Well, he's been through an awful lot ever since he was a kid,"

Mike said. "But he seems pretty well squared away now."

"Anyone can see he loves working with you around here," I said. "He's in his glory."

"Even so," Mike said, "I worry about him now and then. He must be lonesome, don't you think?"

Then another county heard from, as they say. "I gather he had a pretty tough time of it after his wife left," Elizabeth said.

"Terrible," Mike said.

"You know," Jack said, "I always wondered if that little gal didn't marry him just so she could get to the States and then drop him like a hot potato."

"Oh my gosh, Jack," Mike said. "Don't say that."

Wasn't it Shakespeare who said what's done cannot be undone? I guess by the same token, what's said cannot be unsaid. I'm afraid I won't be able to look at Don from now on without thinking about what Jack said. I'll probably never get it out of my head, no matter how hard I try.

Chapter 6

Ray

Chicago, September 1960

I guess you could say I follow all sports. I like playing them and watching them. My dad and I root for the Cubs, Bears, and Blackhawks.

We watched the Olympics on TV just about every night. Did you know Wilma Rudolph of the U.S.A. is the fastest woman in the whole wide world? She won three gold medals. She is a Negro lady. The *Tribune* said the people in Rome call her the Black Gazelle. Rafer Johnson of the U.S.A. won the decathalon, which means he is the world's greatest athlete. He is also a Negro. The U.S.A. basketball team also won the gold medal. Dad said it will be a cold day when they ever lose one game, let alone the gold medal.

The U.S.A. won 34 gold medals and 71 medals all totaled, but the Russians won more. That was too bad.

Even though I like all sports, baseball is definitely my favorite. This year I played in Little League at Winnemac Park. I was on the Orioles. I was hoping to get on the Cubs, but that didn't work out. I played second base most of the time and also pitched once in a while. My dad was the coach of our team. We ended up winning eight games and losing ten.

I'm a big Cubs fan. My favorite player is Ernie Banks, the Cubs shortstop. Ernie was elected Most Valuable Player of the National League last year and the year before. He is a Negro.

My dad is also a Cubs fan and so is Grandpa Mike. Grandpa Mike's dad, my great grandpa, was a Cubs fan too, but I never met him because he passed away before I was born.

We were watching a game on TV recently when the Cubs made an error in the bottom of the ninth and let in the winning run. Dad was wearing loafers, and he took one of his shoes off and threw it at the TV! Mom told him, "You'd be that much madder if you had broken the TV."

When Grandpa was about my age, the Cubs won the World Series two years running, in 1907 and 1908. "You talk about a ballclub," he said. "For Pete's sake, you had Tinker, Evers, and Chance. Of course you've heard of them. Johnny Kling, Harry Steinfeldt. And pitchers? How about Three-Finger Brown, Ed Reulbach, and Orval Overall? Now there's an unusual name for you, Ray, Orval Overall. What a team they had! It's a wonder they ever lost a game."

Grandpa said he never realized how spoiled he was in those days. He said if somebody told him the Cubs wouldn't win the Series again for fifty-some years, he would've told them they must have a few screws loose.

Did you know the Cubs used to win the pennant every three years when my dad was a kid? They won the pennant in 1929, 1932, 1935, and 1938. But they didn't win the Series.

Have you ever heard the story about how Babe Ruth called his shot during the World Series back in 1932? They say he pointed to the stands in center field and then hit a home run right to the same spot! Grandpa Mike was at that game and he told me the re-al story. "Don't kid yourself, Ray," he said. "The Babe never did any such thing. He wouldn't dare. If he did, why, old Charlie Root would've loosened him up all right. He would've spun the bill of his cap around for him and knocked him on his can."

Grandpa and Dad were listening on the radio when Gabby Hartnett hit the home run that won the pennant in 1938. I bet that was pretty exciting. Dad was fourteen years old back then.

The Cubs also won the pennant in 1945 but they lost the Series to the Detroit Tigers. Do you want to know something interesting? Dad told me Grandpa could've gone with some of his bowling buddies, but he didn't think it would be right to go without Dad—because Dad was overseas in the service. Grandpa said he would wait until the next time so Dad could go with.

My mom's side of the family are all White Sox fans. If you can believe this, the Cubs haven't had a winning season since I was born. But on the other hand, the Sox have never had a losing season in all that time. Mom said, "You should seriously consider switching sides."

"Oh, I don't think I could do that," I said.

"Well, how about this?" Mom said. "You could say the Cubs are your favorite National League team and the Sox are your favorite American League team. That way you could root for both."

I told Mom I would think about it.

The Sox won the pennant last year. My Grandpa Foley took Dad and Grandpa Mike and my Uncle Tim to a World Series game against the Dodgers at Sox Park. Sister Constance let us listen to a couple innings on the radio. The Sox won that day, but they ended up losing the Series four games to two. Dad said, "Just between us four walls, it was a darn good thing the Sox lost. If they won, we'd never hear the end of it."

Dad promised to take me to the first home game the next time the Cubs are in the Series, school day or no school day. I can't wait.

Chapter 7

Carol

Chicago, September 1960

Now with the election fast approaching, everyone is wondering when JFK will make an appearance in Chicago. He's already campaigned downstate and in the suburbs any number of times without setting foot in the city. "Daley is waiting until the time is just right," Jack told me. "And then, when everybody's practically wetting themselves, he's going to pull out all the stops. You wait and see."

Last night we watched the debate between Kennedy and Nixon on TV. It's amazing when you think about it. Two men running for the greatest office in the world, and here we and millions of our fellow citizens could see them and hear them live. It's really a wonder. And do you know what else? They came out smiling and shaking hands. Whether they like each other or not, at least they have the decency to be civil.

They are both very young men. I suppose you could say Nixon has more experience, having been Vice President all this time, but there must be more to it than that. "I'm sure Nixon is a fine man," I finally said to Jack and Ray, "but he looks like an undertaker, doesn't he? On the other hand, Kennedy is so handsome and makes a good case for himself."

"Well," Jack said, "I don't know which one is full of more baloney, but I do know which one I'm supposed to be working for." Leave it to Jack. Not exactly a ringing endorsement, but there you have it.

My folks and Ray and I are all in for JFK. After all, isn't it high time for a Catholic man to be elected President? I'd hate to think he could be defeated solely because of his faith.

After Ray went to bed, Jack I were having a drink together when he said something interesting. "Sure, the old man"— meaning Mayor Daley—"would like to get Kennedy elected," he said, "but the one that's really life and death is Adamowski."

Adamowski is Cook County state's attorney. He's a former Democrat and former acolyte of Daley's who has made it his mission to find every skeleton in every closet within the mayor's purview. That means City Hall, the police department, the fire department, the schools, and what have you. My dad says the newspapers keep the following headline on hand so they can use it again and again: ADAMOWSKI WIDENS CORRUPTION PROBE.

"If we don't beat Adamowski," Jack said, "it won't matter how much Kennedy wins by. Daley will cut our nuts off. Pardon the expression."

Chapter 8

Don

Birch Lake, October 1960

One of our improvement projects for Larry's is to get a pontoon boat. Mike figures we can rent it out to people for parties and whatnot, and the rest of the time leave it anchored a ways out from the beach so the kids can swim out there and sun theirself or dive off the back of it or whatever.

I put some feelers out and pretty soon I heard about some guy in Lake Wissota who was trying to unload a used Empress. That's pretty much your Cadillac of pontoon boats. So I got the guy's name, which it turned out was Orville Warnecke, and his address. Then I took a ride out there for a look-see.

I don't mind telling you, the place looked pretty near like a junkyard. Holy cow. You couldn't hardly tell what was left out for the garbage man and what was spose to be for sale. But when I parked and walked up closer, sure enough I seen the boat with a sign taped to it that said:

250$ OR "BEST OFFER"
TAKE AS IS.

This thing needs some work, for damn sure. But it's the right size, about twenty or twenty-two foot. It's also your catamaran style, which is what Mike wants. So I figured I'd go on up to the house and talk to the guy. If you looked at the house, you'd say it just about matched the yard. It seen better days, all right. Of course, I didn't have no call to look down my nose considering I can't tell you my place is a whole lot better.

27

I knocked on the door jamb and this big fat guy in overalls and a baseball cap come to the door. He was a little older, maybe fifty or so. It looked like he was in the middle of eating something or other, because he was wiping his hands on his overalls. And you know what got me? It didn't look like he had nothing on underneath the overalls. Not a shirt or skivvies or socks or nothing. Why would you go to the bother of putting on a baseball cap when you don't even have underwear on? I guess it takes all kinds.

Anyways, he didn't come outside and he didn't ask me to come in. He just stood there looking out the screen at me and wiping his hands.

"Are you Orville?" I says.

"Could be. Depends what you want."

I looked up at him and I seen his cap said DEKALB on top of an ear of corn with wings.

"Well, I'm interested in this pontoon boat over here," I says, pointing back behind me with my thumb.

"I don't blame you," Orville says.

"If you could do me a favor," I says, "just don't sell it to nobody without letting me know."

"Why would I wanna do that?"

"Because then I could try and top their price for you."

"Why don't you just go ahead and buy her now?"

"I gotta check with a colleague first," I says. I thought that sounded pretty good. Then I give him a paper with my number on it. He didn't even have to open the door to take it. He just reached through a hole in the screen.

"Okay now don't forget," I says. "I appreciate it."

I called Jack up long distance in Chicago to let him know what I was thinking. I didn't catch him the first couple times, but Carol give him the message and then he finally called back.

"You know how your pa says he always wanted a pontoon boat?" I says.

"If you say so."

"Well he does," I says. I felt like saying, Come on and get your head out of you know where. "I found a pretty nice used one and I wonder if we can go half and half on it."

"Why don't you just let my dad look it over and decide if he likes it?"

"I want to surprise him." I says. "Buy the thing and fix it all up and then give it to him for Christmas or his birthday or something."

"Hell, Don," he says. "Why do you have to make everything so complicated? I was just there three weeks ago. Why didn't you bring it up then?"

So then I thought okay, here we go. Sometimes Jack will argue with you just for the sake of arguing, and other times he'll agree with you just to shut you up. You can't never tell which it's gonna be from one time to the next.

"Jack," I says. I didn't say nothing else except Jack.

I was just about ready to start in persuading him when he says, "I guess we can do that. Yes, all in all not a bad idea. My dad might get a kick out of it."

Well, I'll be a monkey's uncle. I was surprised he didn't want to argue about it, but I didn't tell him that. I just said, "That's the stuff. You're a good man."

Mike couldn't hardly believe it when Jack called one day and says he was coming up for the weekend.

"He said he'd like to help out with some chores around here." Mike says. "Don't get me wrong. It'll be swell to see him, but..."

I knew where he was headed. "But this election is spose to be the biggest thing since MacArthur broke wind," I says. "So how can he get the time off?"

29

"You took the words right out of my mouth," Mike says. "I don't understand it either. But he says he'll be glad to get away."

Of course, I didn't admit it was me who asked Jack to come up.

"Well," Mike says, "I'm sure he knows his business better than we do."

I wasn't around when Jack rolled in late Friday night, but later on Mike told me all he done was fill himself up with his ma's leftovers and then went straight to bed. Jack had it fixed with his ma that her and Mike was gonna take a field trip out to the cheese factory in Conrath on Saturday around noon. As soon as his folks headed out, Jack drove over to my place and then we went off to see Orville Warnecke. We took my truck along with a trailer I borrowed from my neighbor. We couldn't use Mike's trailer for fear he'd figure something was up.

The plan was to bring the boat back to my ma's place, and then I'd work on it in the garage whenever I had the time. Since I already give the boat a good once over, I assumed we could wrap the deal up pretty quick once we got there. But everybody knows what happens when you assume.

It's about forty-five minutes to Lake Wissota. During the ride we seen and heard a few flocks of geese heading south. You can usually hear geese before you see 'em. Jack told me about all the goings-on with the election. It was pretty interesting. I never realized some of the stuff that goes on in politics. I guess most of your Sunday school teachers wouldn't neither.

Finally we pulled up in front of Orville's. "Holy Jeez," Jack says. "What the hell is this?"

Then we walked into the yard and I pointed out the boat. "There she is," I says, "the *Queen of the High Seas*. Or whatever your pa wants to call her. Maybe *Queen Elizabeth*, after your ma."

Jack looked at the sign with the price on it. "Two hundred and fifty, my ass," he says. "When you told me the price I pictured something in better shape."

"Don't worry about that," I says. "I'm sure we can talk him down."

"We better," Jack says. "Well, let's have at it."

We went up to the house and before we could knock or anything else, here come this giant black dog from who knows where like a bat out of hell. He got up on his hind legs and started scratching at the screen like mad with his front paws, and all the while he was barking like nobody's business. I think you'd call this guy a Doberman. Me and Jack kept our distance. We figured the dog was gonna fly right through the screen any second.

Then Orville Warnecke come out from another room acting like nothing happened. "Oh, he won't bother you," he says.

"He's already bothering us," Jack says.

"That's enough out of you, Bruno," Orville says and pulls on the dog's collar. "Just calm down and leave these fellas be." I always thought it was funny when people talk to a dog like it's a person. Like it can really understand English. But maybe they're onto something after all, because the dog did calm down a bit. He kept on snarling at us but he got back down on four feet anyways.

"I brought my colleague this time," I says to Orville.

"That's fine," Orville says. Then he squeezed out of the screen door and shut it before the dog could get out. Thank God.

Orville was wearing the same outfit as before, dirty overalls with nothing underneath and a DeKalb corn cap. "All right, Bruno," he says through the screen. "That's a good boy."

"I didn't know you had a dog," I says.

"I don't think he was here the last time you come," Orville says. "He must of been over by my ex's place."

Jack kind of snorted. Then he says, "You got shared custody of the dog, did you?"

Orville didn't say nothing to that. He took his cap off, scratched his bald head, and put the cap back on again. Then he says, "Well, let's talk turkey. Do you fellas want the boat or not?"

I was just about to answer when Jack says, "Not at two fifty we don't."

"Is that so?" says Orville.

"Well," I says, "we figured we might try and bargain with you."

"Is that so?" says Orville again. "Go on and make your offer then."

Me and Jack should of talked all this over before we got there. God knows we had plenty of time in the car. As it was I had no idea what he was liable to say or do.

"One seventy five," Jack says.

Orville looked at him and didn't say nothing right away. He had his hands in his pockets and he was sort of leaning back on his heels. Then he says, "I don't believe you're being serious. You know that? You're wasting my time and yours."

Jack looked at me. "Aw shit, Don," he says.

So then I was on the spot. See, I was thinking about how happy Mike would be if we got this boat for him. But Jack was thinking of it as a contest he had to win.

"What do you think, Orville?" I says. "Where are you at?"

"You already know where I'm at," says Orville. "Two fifty."

Then Jack chimes in again. "We could maybe do two hundred," he says to me for Orville's benefit. "If we really wanted to bend over backwards."

"I'd say two twenty five's more like it," Orville says.

"Look, we're only talking about the boat," Jack says. "We're not asking you to throw in the house and the car and the dog on top of it."

"Oh, you'd never get my dog for any price."

Well sir, we didn't wind up buying the boat from Orville. In fact we was lucky to get out of there without his dog tearing us limb from limb.

I was pissed off at Jack for queering the deal, but I can't say I was surprised. Sometimes he does things you'd think are the opposite of what he means to, just to try and prove a point. It seems like he can't help hisself. I don't blame him too much, because God knows I done the same thing myself plenty of times.

On the way back to Larry's, Jack says. "I sure could use a cold beer." I was thinking along the same lines myself. I pulled into the first bar we come acrossed. It was called the Star Lite Tap.

I thought I knew every last dive bar and roadhouse in the area, but if I was ever in the Star Lite Tap before I couldn't tell you when. Anyways, it looked like a nice enough joint. We went in and bellied up to the bar. There was a football game on TV.

We were about halfway through our first beer when Jack elbowed me and says, "Speaking of which." That's what he always says when he spots a cute gal. I looked around and seen he meant the waitress. It was a blonde gal with a nice figure, from what you could tell with her back to us. Nice legs for sure.

"I see what you mean," I says.

This gal was waiting on some guys at a table. One of 'em said something to her and then she said something back that made 'em all laugh.

"Very promising from this angle," Jack says. "But could easily be a false alarm. I bet you the next beer she's a butter face. Good from far but far from good."

"Okay, you're on," I says. We shook on it.

One of the guys at the table said something else and this gal laughed. Then she turned around with a big smile on her face and Jack says, "I owe you a beer."

And then I took a good look and pretty near keeled over. Because who do you spose it was but the one and only magic Jeannie.

33

Chapter 9

Jeannie

Birch Lake, October 1960

When I was a kid of sixteen, seventeen, I served root beer and hot dogs at the A&W. I had to wear a short little skirt and put up with the wolf whistles and that. I didn't really mind. It was like water off a duck's back. In the first place, I didn't know any better. And I figured it was worth it if I could save up enough money to get the heck of here. I planned to be as far away as possible by the time I was twenty or twenty-one.

I'll never forget the first time I had that conversation with my mom, God rest her soul. She asked if I was thinking of the Twin Cities or Milwaukee or what. I said, "Are you kidding?"

I guess I shouldn't have said it that way. I didn't mean to hurt her feelings. It wasn't her fault. Just goes to show you how she looked at things, which was way different.

If anybody told me that by the time my age doubled, I woulda graduated (if you can call it that) to serving beer and liquor just a couple miles up the road, still in a short little skirt and dealing with all the rest of it, I would've swore they must be nuts. But you don't have to know much to know things don't always work out according to your plans.

I didn't plan on getting pregnant when I was eighteen. I didn't plan on my father throwing me out of the house over it. I didn't plan on Mom passing away from cancer when she was only fifty-two. I didn't plan on my husband ending up in a wheelchair when he was thirty-seven.

I could go on and on, but you get the idea.

Bill always laughed when I told people he was a lumberjack. "I don't know where you been," he said, just joshing. "We call it a logger nowadays." So I kept on saying lumberjack just to get his goat a little bit.

We got married as soon as Bill got out of the service, and we didn't hang around here long after that. Both of us were the type to take our chances living someplace else. First we moved to Calumet, Michigan, and soon we made it all the way to Port Angeles, Washington. Now that's about as far away from Birch Lake as you can get without going to Alaska or Hawaii or something. The lumber business was going great guns out there, and the fellas could make pretty good money. Just like in our part of Wisconsin way back when.

We had a nice little place off the beaten path, and we were getting by okay. Bill was making out well enough so I could stay home and take care of the kids without having a job on the side. It wasn't exactly what every little girl would dream of, but it wasn't bad. It wasn't bad at all.

And then Bill had his accident. Crashed his motorcycle through no fault of his own. Some jackass turned left smack dab into his path as if he was invisible. Paralyzed from the waist down. If you think it was horrible, congratulations. You're right. I can't begin to tell you. Just try and imagine how horrible you think it was and then start multiplying. Bill was always such a big bear of a man who could do anything physical, and now all of a sudden he was practically helpless. That was the most pitiful thing about it to me.

So it was back to America's Dairyland for us with our tail between our legs. We found a place outside of town, not too far from my in-laws. I don't know what we'd do without them. My mom is gone, God rest her soul, and we don't exactly see eye to eye with my father.

I got hired on at the Star Lite Tap, and Bill bought the famous pink store from his uncle. The first thing he did was have it painted white. "If you think I'm gonna sit all day inside of a pink building," he said, "why, you've got another guess coming." He tries to get people to call it the Pine Creek Store, which was its real name all along, but they won't do it. Everybody keeps calling it the pink store. Boy, does that make him mad!

One time just after he took over the place, I was in there with him and the phone rang. "Good morning," he said, "Pine Creek Store. Bill speaking."

The person on the other end must've said something like, "Sorry, I was trying to reach the pink store."

"Yes!" Bill said. "This is the Pine Creek Store."

The person on the other end still didn't get it.

"I'm telling you, this is the place you want. Pine Creek Store."

The caller was still not getting it.

Well, it went on and on from there. Poor Bill just couldn't win. That would've been a good one for *Candid Camera*.

The Star Lite Tap is on River Road, not far from the Ranch Supper Club. By the way, Bill always liked the Ranch. Who doesn't like a nice relish tray?

You'll pass by the Star Lite if you're heading out of Birch Lake on the way to Chippewa Falls or Eau Claire. It's a typical watering hole for our neck of the woods. You could probably picture the place yourself without even seeing it. There's a pool table, a couple dartboards, a pinball machine or two, a jukebox, and one of those bowling games where you slide a metal puck at plastic pins. Behind the bar they have a great big sign that says FREE BEER TOMORROW. I guess that's sort of cute.

We get a mix of farmers in overalls and guys from the paper mill, along with an occasional truck driver who's just passing through. Or maybe lost.

When I got hired, the first thing they told me was to take off my wedding ring and I'd make way better tips. But I didn't think I could do that.

Well. Who do you think showed up the other day but a couple of ghosts. Jack and Don.

I didn't see them right away. It was a Saturday afternoon. I don't know what time exactly. I was pretty busy. They must've came in while I was occupied one way or the other. They were sitting at the bar so they had their backs to me while I worked the room. They might've been there a while without me knowing it.

As it was, they saw me first.

I was coming back to the bar with a tray of empties and all of a sudden Don spun around on his barstool and yelled, "Hiya, stranger!"

I looked up and recognized him right off. Then I noticed Jack sort of peering over Don's shoulder at me. This sounds crazy, I know, but I wasn't sure it was him at first. I would've known Don anywhere. But Jack, who I mooned over and pined for and dreamed about longer than I'd care to say? With him it took me a moment to register. Somehow he didn't look quite like I imagined he would. But it was him, all right.

I dumped my tray. Thank God it was only empties.

I didn't know if I should shake their hands or hug them or what. Meanwhile Don jumped up and started trying to help out by picking up the broken bottles, but all he did was cut his finger. Pretty bad, from the looks of it.

"Shit!" he said. "Pardon my French." He turned around to ask for a towel or a napkin or whatever, and when he did, Jack and I ended up facing each other about three or four feet apart.

"Of all the gin joints in the world," I said. Sometimes when I can't think of anything else to say, I'll toss out a movie line.

Jack had no clue what I was talking about. He didn't say, "Here's looking at you, kid." He didn't say, "We'll always have Paris." He didn't say anything at all. But he did take a step forward, grab my hand, and kiss the back of it. I'm not kidding you.

Chapter 10

Ray

Chicago, October 1960

Sister Theresa told us a very sad story that happened recently only a block or two from our school. A lady was at home doing her housework when the doorbell rang. She ran downstairs to see who it was, but nobody was there. So she went back upstairs and the same thing happened again. And then it happened again and again.

Some teenagers were ringing her door bell and then hiding. This is called playing ding-dong ditch.

These naughty teenagers didn't realize the poor lady had a heart condition. When her children came home from school they found their mom dead at the bottom of the stairs.

So you see it wasn't just a harmless prank after all. I wonder how those teenagers would feel if that happened to their own mom.

I would never play ding-dong ditch.

We were doing tongue twisters in class the other day. Sister started off by saying the Peter Piper one. You know. "Peter Piper picked a peck of pickled peppers. A peck of pickled peppers, Peter Piper picked. If Peter Piper picked a peck of pickled peppers, where's the peck of pickled peppers Peter Piper picked?"

Then she called on Peter Cullen. She said, "Peter, since you have the same name as the boy in the story, would you like to go ahead and say it for us?"

Peter Cullen asked Sister, "What is a peck?"

"Never you mind about that," Sister told him. "Just go ahead and say the tongue twister. It's good practice for public speaking."

So Peter Cullen said the tongue twister. He made a couple mistakes, but he did okay. Then he said, "I still don't know what a peck is."

Brian Drummond whispered to me, "No, but we know what a pecker is."

Then Sister said the woodchuck one. "How much wood could a woodchuck chuck if a woodchuck could chuck wood?"

You'll never guess what Peter Cullen did then. He raised his hand and said, "Six?"

Everybody laughed. Then Sister said, "I can see it's no use trying to do something fun with you children. Therefore, we'll just go back to our regular lesson."

Sister always tells us the easiest way to tell the difference between right and wrong. If you are thinking of taking something that doesn't belong to you, or saying a swear word, or smoking a cigarette, or looking at a dirty magazine, or spitting on the sidewalk, or picking on a smaller kid, or making fun of somebody who is maybe a little slow, just imagine that Mom and Dad and Sister and Father Fahey and President Eisenhower and everybody else you know is watching.

If there is anything you would be ashamed to try and do with all those people watching, then you know you shouldn't do it in the first place. And also we should remember that Jesus is always watching, even when nobody else is around.

A bunch of us were playing kick the can after school when a car came down the street. I kicked the can before I saw the car, and the can bounced into the street and banged off the guy's fender.

It was kind of a hot-rod type car with a shiny red paint job. Somebody told me they call that color candy-apple red. All of a sudden the driver slammed on the brakes and jumped out of the car. I would say he was around twenty or twenty-five. He started screaming, "Who did it? Who did it? Which one of you fucks hit my car?"

I was the one who did it, but it was by accident. I didn't say anything, and neither did anybody else.

But then this guy grabbed ahold of Kevin Drummond. Maybe because he was the closest or he was the biggest, I'm not sure. He threw Kevin down and pushed his face into the curb for quite a while.

We didn't know what else to do except just stand there and watch, but finally this guy let go of Kevin. Then when the guy was getting back in his car, Kevin was bawling but he yelled out, "My dad's a policeman and he'll get you!"

The guy said, "Aw, let him try. Send him over and I'll fix him too." Then he spun his tires and drove off.

Do you want to know something? Mr. Drummond isn't really a policeman. He's a fireman, but I guess Kevin thought a policeman would seem scarier.

My dad always says if somebody ever gives you a hard time, you need to make sure and remember their license plate number. So when he got home I told him the whole story and gave him the license number.

"You did good, Ray," Dad said. "You did real good."

My mom was there too. "Jack," she said. "Don't get too carried away now."

A couple days later at supper Dad said, "I have some news for you, Ray. You can tell your buddies something for me. Tell them this punk who rubbed the Drummond kid's face on the curb won't be bothering you boys in the future. As a matter of fact, I'd be very surprised if he comes anywhere near this block ever again."

Chapter 11

Carol

Chicago, November 1960

Kennedy seems to have captured people's imagination in a way that I haven't seen before. You can almost feel the excitement in the air.

Jack might be the only person in my circle of acquaintances who's unimpressed. Frankly, I think he's had his fill of the whole business. His job is grating on him. He even took off a whole weekend at the height of the campaign and went up to Birch Lake. I'm sure he wasn't supposed to do that, but I sympathize with him. He's been getting it from all sides.

Well, it'll all be over in a few days now.

You know, Jack was right when he said that Daley would wait until the very last moment to bring Kennedy to Chicago. Only when the suspense and buildup had become almost unbearable, Daley finally announced that JFK would be the guest of honor at a torchlight parade and rally the Friday night before election day. His honor added that the event would be televised live from coast to coast on NBC. As if that weren't enough, he also said it would be "the greatest spectacle in the history of the United States."

The parade was to start at Michigan Avenue and Madison Street downtown and head west on Madison for a rally at Chicago Stadium. Jack and a bunch of the guys in our neighborhood each received a letter telling them to report to ward headquarters at 4:30 p.m. on Friday. They would then take buses to various locations along the parade route. Jack's group was assigned to cheer the motorcade from the corner of Madison and Franklin. "Attendance will be taken," the letter said, "and your ward commit-

41

teeman will personally receive each and every man aboard the buses."

In Jack's opinion, Daley set up the whole elaborate production not to get Kennedy elected President of the United States, but to get Dan Ward elected state's attorney of Cook County! "He even got Kennedy's old man to pay for everything," Jack said. "Incredible."

A couple days before the big event, my dad called and said he had tickets for the rally inside the Stadium. "You could bring Ray," he said. "Not every youngster gets to see a future President in person."

Dad said we three—himself, Ray, and I—could save a seat for Jack at the Stadium, and he could join us as soon as he was able. But Jack wasn't wild about the idea. He was inclined to go through the motions on the parade route and get it over with as soon as possible. And what's more, he wanted to take Ray with him. "Think about it," he said. "Any kid would rather see the parade than the speeches."

"Okay," I said. "I'm not going to argue with you. But maybe we should ask Ray what he wants to do."

"Well, I already invited him to the parade. I don't want to go back on it now."

"How about this?" I said. "Take Ray with you to the parade, and then you both can meet up with us at the Stadium."

That also wouldn't work, for reasons known only to Jack. I let it go in order to keep the peace, while also agreeing to go to the rally with my dad.

On the morning of the event, the *Tribune* said, "Chicago Democrats will blow their stacks Friday evening in a mammoth salute to Senator Kennedy." You can always rely on the Trib for stuff like that.

It rained steadily all day, and it was still raining when the time

42

came for Jack and Ray to leave. But Jack still insisted that Ray should go with him rather than come with my dad and me. I bit my tongue and kissed them both goodbye, then waited for my dad to come and pick me up. I was tidying up in the kitchen when I heard someone coming in the front door. At first I thought it was Dad, but he had said he was coming over at half past five—and when he says he will be somewhere at a certain time, that means not a minute before or a minute after. Furthermore, he wouldn't simply walk in without knocking or ringing the bell.

And then I heard "Mom?" so I knew it was Ray.

Well, it turned out that there were only enough seats on the buses for the assigned party workers and no one else. They had it figured to the exact number of fannies in the seats. So Ray had had to walk back home in the rain.

I wish Jack had thought the whole thing through before putting Ray in a position to be embarrassed like that. I tried to keep my emotions in check in the hope that Ray would do the same—and he did, the brave boy. If he was hurt or upset, he never let on. Was I proud of him! I hugged him, not hard enough to give myself away, and sent him to his room to change into some dry clothes. Just then the doorbell rang, and it was my dad. "I've got good news," I told him. "Ray is coming with us after all."

"So Jack thought better of taking him out to stand in the rain, did he?"

I just smiled and didn't answer.

The Stadium was packed to the rafters. Daley would've seen to that in any case. Hanging over the stage were three enormous photographs of Daley, JFK, and LBJ—in that order! Can you imagine? You really had to give his honor credit for having a lot of gall, if nothing else. Each of these photos must have been thirty feet high and twenty feet wide. I kept wondering where you would go to get something like that made, and how in Heaven's name you would get it from there to the Stadium.

On the floor, every second or third person had a cardboard sign stapled to a yardstick. There were hundreds of these signs with a few (slightly) different slogans printed on them. CHICAGO WELCOMES KENNEDY. WIN WITH KENNEDY. LEADERSHIP FOR THE 60'S. AMERICA NEEDS KENNEDY. WELCOME JACK.

The people on the floor bounced their signs up and down and swirled them around, while the people in the balconies chanted, "We want Jack! We want Jack!" There was nothing spontaneous about it, of course. My dad got hold of a WELCOME JACK sign and gave it to Ray. Our seats, folding chairs, were right along the red carpet that Kennedy would take to get to the stage. My dad pointed out to Ray the tunnel from which JFK would make his entrance.

Suddenly the Frank Sinatra song "High Hopes" came on over the P.A. "Oops, there goes another rubber tree plant!" The place went up for grabs, and there was JFK in the flesh. Daley was beside him with Eunice and Sargent Shriver right behind, and there was a circle of Andy Frains around the four of them.

Kennedy was mobbed. He couldn't get to the stage because people had swarmed into the aisle in front of him. Really, it was pandemonium. And then to make matters worse, the lesser dignitaries—aldermen, commissioners, union bosses, and the like—started coming out of the tunnel behind JFK, and they were pushing forward as if they were afraid of missing something. Kennedy was literally being shoved toward the stage by the people well behind him who were surging forward. I was afraid for Eunice because she was the only woman in this rolling tide of humanity, and she's just a little thing, but she seemed to hold up okay. She's a real trouper.

When "High Hopes" was over, "Anchors Aweigh," the Navy song, came on. The crowd became truly hysterical at that point. In all the noise and confusion, the line veered toward us just then. And wouldn't you know it, JFK ended up face-to-face with yours truly. I mean, I could've probably smelled his after-shave lotion if I'd put my mind to it. I stuck out my right hand for him to shake, and he took it with his left for a second or two and then continued on.

And that's how I met John F. Kennedy, if you can call it that.

Something funny happened when they got to the stage. When Daley went up to the podium, he got an ovation that must have gone on for six or seven minutes. "Reminds me of Stalin," my dad said to me from behind his hand. "Nobody wants to be the first one to stop clapping."

After a fashion, Daley finally held up his hands to ask for quiet. It's interesting to contemplate what might have happened if he hadn't done so. Would the applause have continued indefinitely, for hours and even days, until the applauders exhausted themselves and started to drop, one by one by one, and finally the arena was silent?

Daley introduced Kennedy, who acknowledged the candidates for governor and senator and then began his own speech. "I come here tonight," he said in that distinctive Boston accent of his, "in the closing days of this campaign, to ask for your help. I ask (pronounced 'ahsk') you to join us." You should have heard the cheer that went up for that one. It was pretty standard stuff, but Ray and I were already believers. We yelled as loud as anyone.

So far so good. There was a problem, though, which we didn't realize at the time but found out about later. What with the parade running a little long, the mob scene that broke out when Kennedy entered the Stadium, and the prolonged ovation for Daley, the hour of live TV time ran out just as Kennedy started speaking. NBC cut away to whatever program was scheduled to come on next. As a result, people all across the country missed the climax of JFK's speech. They missed the rousing call to action for election day and beyond that was supposed to be the sum and substance of the whole event. Oops.

When my dad dropped Ray and me off at home, Jack was still out. I assumed (and not incorrectly, as it turned out) that he and his cronies had adjourned to Sully's Tavern after the parade. Ray still had his WELCOME JACK sign with him, and he had a cute idea. He propped it up between two cushions in the sofa, so Jack would see it when he came in. Then Ray went to bed, and I went myself soon after.

The next morning at breakfast, Jack thanked us for the sign.

"Don't thank me," I said. "That was Ray's doing."

"Is that right?" Jack said. "Well, thank you, buddy. That was very nice."

"You're welcome, Dad," Ray said. "I'm glad you liked it." What a sweet, generous, and forbearing boy! The good Lord hit a home run when He made that kid.

"You'll never guess what happened, Dad," Ray cried. "Mom shook hands with Kennedy!"

Jack looked up from the sports section. "Is that right?" he said. I'm not sure what he would have said next, because just then he had a sneezing fit. He seemed to have caught a cold.

Chapter 12

Don

Birch Lake, November 1960

So the election come off and Jack's man won. I'm happy for Jack as far as that goes, but I can't say I voted for Kennedy. He'd of lost Wisconsin anyways, even if I'd of voted for him.

As soon as the election was over, Jack said he was coming up for the beginning of deer season. That's the weekend before Thanksgiving, in case you don't know.

The funny thing is, I don't think Jack gives a flip about deer season one way or the other. Him and Mike used to come up for the first weekend of the season five or six years running. In all that time, I only seen him shoot a deer once.

Here's what happened. The three of us was going along the edge of this old logging road, and we seen a doe pop out of the woods and start acrossed in front of us. I bet she wasn't more than a hunnerd yards away. We all froze and tried not to draw attention to ourself.

Just then a bunch more deer come out of woods. I'd say six or seven all together, including a pretty good size buck. A couple of the little guys still had their spots. They all done the same thing. Climbed up out of the ditch and onto the road, then back down and into the woods on the other side. But for some reason the big boy stopped before he got there and sort of looked around. A real nice buck, an eight-pointer.

Mike whispered, "Go ahead and take him, Jack."

Well sir, Jack went ahead and fired, and sure as shit he hit that buck right below the shoulder. Man, it looked like a straight kill shot. This guy went down like a ton of bricks, and we figured that was all she wrote.

Me and Mike just got done slapping Jack on the back when damned if that buck didn't get up and stagger off into the woods.

"Okay," Mike says. "Now we got a problem."

"Shit," Jack says. He looked me right in the eye, and we both knew the exact same thing. Nobody was going nowhere until we found that buck and made sure he was done for. Hell could of froze over first, far as Mike was concerned.

We followed the blood trail as far as we could, and after that we just made it up as we went along. I couldn't tell you how far we walked or how long it took. For all I know, we was going in circles the whole time. But by God, we finally did find that poor buck just before dark.

Jack seen him first. He was lying down in some leaves and he looked like he was dead. Jack ran ahead of me and Mike. When he got there, he put his hands on his knees and bent down to take a real good look. Then, all of a sudden this buck turned his head! I don't know if he could still hear Jack or see him or what, but I do know this much. He scared the living hell out of Jack.

Jack screamed and jumped back like he was on a trampoline or something.

Mike went ahead and finished that buck off. And I never seen Jack shoot a deer since. I mean even if one practically sauntered up right in front of him. You know what I think? I think he don't mind the shooting part at all. But he does mind cleaning up after himself. If he gets a kill shot, he'd still have to field dress the deer, which is a pain in the ass even if you know what you're doing. And if he don't get a kill shot, then he's liable to have another experience like the one I just got done telling you about. Chasing a half-dead deer all over hell and back. I think he'd just as soon not bother with it either way.

To each their own, I say. So what if Jack only wants to walk around in the woods with a flask full of schnapps, get some fresh air, and have a few beers afterwards? There ain't nothing wrong with that, if you ask me. More power to him. And more deer for the rest of us.

Chapter 13

Jeannie

Birch Lake, November 1960

When Jack and Don showed up at the Star Lite out of the blue that Saturday in October, it was the first time I saw either of them since before the war. What a hell of a thing, when you stop and think about it.

It was late afternoon or early evening, still light out, and the two of them were talking about the World Series. Don said he didn't know which team to pull for. On the one hand the short-stop for the Yankees was a Wisconsin boy, from Wausau I think he said, and also a fellow Polack. That was Don's word, not mine. But on the other hand, the second baseman for the Pirates was also a Polack, so that's why Don was torn.

That's the kind of stuff those guys talk about. I guess it isn't any more or less interesting than most of the conversation you hear in a bar.

Unlike Don, Jack wasn't torn at all. "My money's on the Yankees," he said. He sounded so sure of himself. I was glad, because it meant he was the same old Jack I used to know.

After we got to talking, they gave up their barstools and moved over to one of my tables. They each had a burger and a few beers. The three of us got caught up on eighteen years in a few sentences each. The *Reader's Digest* version of our adult lives.

Jack's living in Chicago, as he always has and always will. He has some big job down there from the sound of it. He's married to a nice gal and they have a nine-year-old son named Ray. "Greatest kid you'd ever meet," Don said. Jack said he's spending more time up north because his folks just bought Larry's Resort and he's helping them fix it up.

Don is divorced, poor guy, working at the Sinclair station, still helping out at Larry's, and doing a few odd jobs like plowing snow on the side. A jack of all trades and a master of none, he said.

And I'm back in Wisconsin, not by choice, with my husband and three kids: Julie (age sixteen), Jerry (fourteen), and Debbie (eleven).

We chatted a while, and then Jack and Don took off and left a tip that was way too big. Afterwards I didn't think a whole lot about it. It was fun to see them and they seemed glad to see me, but I tried not to get too worked up over it. After all, there was a lot of water over the dam since I was with Jack. Let's be realistic. I mean, my gosh, we were just kids at the time. After you get a little older and life kicks you around a bit, you wise up. At least I hope so. You don't keep on living in a fantasy world.

If I was really honest with myself, I'd have to admit it wasn't much more than a schoolgirl crush on a boy who was unavailable in every way. I understand now I was part of Jack's life at Birch Lake, and that was it. Whatever he was doing the rest of the time, it didn't include me. Summer vacation, Birch Lake, and me all went together. His life in Chicago, his real life, was something totally different.

You live and learn, right? And here's another thing that kind of got me. It turned out the Yankees lost the World Series. When I heard that, I was disappointed. Isn't that weird? It wasn't because I know or care anything about baseball. It was because Jack said the Yankees couldn't lose, and he was wrong.

Whenever deer season comes along, or any hunting season for that matter, it's a tough time for Bill. Here's something that he loved so much and was so good at, such a big part of his life, and it's been taken away from him.

With the type of injury Bill has, there's really no good way to get him out in the woods where he can hunt. Obviously, his wheelchair wouldn't do him any good. You'd need a bunch of guys to carry him out there and sort of prop him up somewhere. Even if they could manage it without doing more damage to him, he'd never put up with it.

Bill's friend Steve offered to take him out and drive him around the old logging roads so they could look for deer. God love that Steve. He really means well. I thought it would be a good way for Bill to at least get out and do something different for a change.

"Why don't you go ahead and go with Steve?" I asked him. "It might be fun."

He wouldn't hear of it. "If you think I'm gonna sit on my ass and take pot shots from a moving vehicle, well..." He didn't finish.

"But what if you didn't shoot?" I asked. "What if you just went out and looked for deer?"

"I don't see the point in that."

"What about this?" I said. "What if we got you a nice camera and you could take pictures of the deer?" That was a darn good idea, if I do say so myself.

"I don't know what to tell you," Bill said, and that was that.

I'm not all that religious, but don't they say the Lord helps those who help themselves? Maybe Bill should get cracking one of these days.

I was still feeling sorry for Bill, and for myself, when Jack and Don stopped in at the Star Lite again. This was opening day of deer season, and the place was hopping pretty good.

"Hey, you!" Don said. "How come every time we see you you're in a bar?"

I was really glad to see those two. I pointed them to a high-top table in my station. I noticed they weren't in their hunting outfits, which practically everybody else in the place was, so I asked about that.

"Oh," Don said, "somebody didn't want to go out because it was sort of a damp and chilly day." He cocked his head toward Jack.

"My," I said. "A fine couple of cavemen you fellas woulda made."

"We've evolved enough to come in out of the rain," Jack said. "And we thought this was as good a place as any to take shelter."

Did I already mention I was really glad to see those guys again?

Chapter 14

Ray

Chicago, December 1960

Grandma and Grandpa Foley came over to our house for Christmas Eve. After dinner, me and Dad and Grandpa took the L downtown to look at all the Christmas lights and decorations.

There are some pretty neat windows at Marshall Field's. For example, they have elves skating on a frozen pond, having reindeer races, working in Santa's workshop, and stuff like that. They also have one where Santa is sitting in his shirtsleeves smoking his pipe and going over the nice list and the naughty list. Grandpa Foley said, "I heard you made the nice list again, Ray. Congratulations."

When we got back home, there were some presents around the tree. They weren't from Santa, because he hadn't came yet. They were from the rest of us.

I opened my gift from Grandma and Grandpa first. It was a baseball glove. A real nice one, a Rawlings. Too bad it's a lefty. I think maybe Grandma and Grandpa got mixed up because I bat lefty but I throw righty. Anyways, I didn't say anything because I didn't want to hurt their feelings. I just thanked them. Maybe we can take it back and swap it for a righty one of these days.

I got Mom a matching hat and scarf, which me and Dad picked out on Clark Street. They are plaid with red and green. Christmas colors. Mom loved them.

Dad got Mom a little statue of a boy and girl that look like they are from the old country. This type of statue is called a Hummel, which Mom has been collecting lately. So far she has a shepherd boy, a little blond girl with ducklings, and the boy and girl Dad

54

got her. Dad also got Mom a pair of tickets to see Johnny Mathis at the Chicago Theatre. Johnny is Mom's favorite singer.

"I wonder who I'll ask to use the second ticket," Mom said. Then she grabbed Dad's hand and said, "Oh, I'm just kidding, honey. Thank you for the wonderful gifts."

Grandma and Grandpa gave my mom a nice leather pocket book. Grandpa told Mom to open it, and when she did there was a check folded up inside. I don't know how much it was for, but my Mom said, "Oh goodness! You really shouldn't have. I mean really." Then she started to cry a little, so I guess she liked it.

Grandma Mike and Grandma Elizabeth came over on Christmas Day. They got here right about the time we were getting home from Mass. We used to always go over to their house on Christmas Day, so it's kind of weird to realize they don't live in Chicago anymore. They had to drive all the way from Birch Lake to visit us. "Well, we made good time," Grandpa Mike said. "The roads were dry, so we had that going for us."

They never stayed overnight at our place before, so Mom was a little nervous about that. She wanted to make sure everything went okay. She made Dad give her a list of all the things Grandma and Grandpa would want to eat and drink, and then she went and bought all that stuff.

Mom and Grandma Elizabeth fixed up some brunch for us, and then we opened our presents.

Mom said I could open my present from Santa first. It was a wood-burning kit. It's pretty neat. You can make all kinds of signs and plaques and stuff. "Here's an idea, Ray," Grandpa said. "What if you made some signs for Larry's with your kit there? Of course, I'd make it worth your while."

"What a great idea!" Mom said. "You know, Mike, I forgot to tell you, but I was thinking maybe we could give each cabin its own name. Wouldn't that be cute?"

"Cute," Dad said.

"And how," Grandpa said.

We all sat around the front room trying to come up with names for the cabins. Mom called it brainstorming. We wrote down a whole bunch of names, and then we voted for the best ones. Dad and Grandma voted, too. We ended up picking some great names.

Everybody was excited. I'm going to get started working on the signs right away.

Then I opened my present from Grandpa Mike and Grandma Elizabeth. It was a giant one, and I really couldn't guess what it was. It turned out to be a golf bag and a set of golf clubs. What a great gift!

"A good walk spoiled," Mom said.

"Pardon?" Grandpa said.

"Oh, nothing," Mom said. "Don't mind me. Just a funny saying."

"We're gonna try your hand at the game, Ray," Dad said.

"It'll be great to have you out there with us from now on," Grandpa Mike said. "Welcome to the club."

I wish next summer would hurry up and get here.

PART TWO

Over the whole northern half of Wisconsin lies a forest wilderness, smelling of pine pitch and brush fires, where rivers thunder
across trap-rock ledges or flow quietly on clean sand beds. The
land is pitted with swamps, hidden ponds, and uncounted lakes,
and wildlife abounds in both the uplands and the lowlands.

— The WPA Guide to Wisconsin (1941)

Chapter 1

Don

Birch Lake, circa 1936

My old man up and disappeared one day when I was just a little shaver, maybe six or seven. At first my ma told us he went to the Twin Cities to look for work. Later on she said nothing panned out there, so he went out west. As soon as he got situated, why he'd send for us lickety split. But she never seemed to know for sure where he was at. One time she might say Denver, another time Phoenix, another time Los Angeles. I figured it must be exciting for him to see all them different places. I kept on asking what she heard from him and when was he going to send for us, and she never really give me a straight answer.

My sister Rosemary is a couple years older than me and has more sense. She clues me in to lots of things I wouldn't figure out on my own. One day she says to me, "You don't know much, do you? Don't you think it's weird that we haven't seen no letters or postcards or nothing from Pa? Why, Mother don't have no more idea where he is than the man in the moon." I ran to Ma bawling and told her what Rose said. She didn't say nothing one way or the other, just sent Rose to bed without supper.

After that I didn't hardly ask Ma about it no more, and she didn't bring it up neither. But one time I overheard her tell a neighbor lady Pa just got swallowed up by the Depression.

Ma does the best she can for us. She has a regular job, thank God, running the cash register at the Woolworth's in town. But it don't pay nowhere near enough to support herself and two kids. She offers to take in washing and ironing for people who come through there, but she don't get many takers because most people, even if they want to give her the work, they can't afford to pay her nothing anyways.

Well sir, she started taking on whatever she could get. For example an old person who was drooling and shitting theirself and didn't have no idea where they was at, Ma would go over and feed 'em, read to 'em, give 'em a bath, launder their undies and whatnot. She might get a couple bucks for a week of that.

You can bet your buttonhole I seen what my ma was doing to herself. I might of been dumb, but not too dumb to know I had to start helping out some way or other. I was maybe eleven or twelve by then. After school, weekends, and all summer long I rode my bike around looking for odd jobs. I didn't care what it was. I'd do it for a dime or fifteen cents. Maybe a quarter for a real big job.

That's how I got in at Larry's Resort. I'd go ahead and do the work and let the other fellow figure out how much it was worth. That suited Larry just fine. He became my best customer in no time flat. He has me mow the grass, pull weeds, rake leaves, bust up beehives, sweep the floors, bait the mousetraps, dig up nightcrawlers so he can sell 'em, bail out the rowboats after it rains, and anything else you can think of.

Larry is a crusty old bastard, if you want to know the truth. He'll give me a good smack once in a while, even since I got a little older and am pretty near as big as him. Not too many people know this, but his name is really Lars. That's what his wife Eloise calls him. They both come over from Sweden. He goes by Larry because he figures it sounds more American.

You know, I never figured out why in hell people would drive seven or eight hours to get here on purpose. I guess the lake is nice enough, but if you live in Chicago or Milwaukee or someplace wouldn't there be plenty of other lakes you could go to closer to home and save yourself the drive? You could go to Lake Michigan anyways if you couldn't think of nothing else. Now at

60

least you're talking about a real lake and not one you can practically spit acrossed.

One of the first jobs Larry give me, Eloise was waddling down to the beach for a swim one day when she stepped smack on a pine cone barefooted. You'd of thought somebody was murdering her, the way she carried on. Larry made me go around the whole grounds and pick up every last pine cone and toss 'em in the woods. Not just around the house and the cabins, but back behind the garage and down by the boat landing and every inch of the whole layout. I picked up hunnerds of them damn pine cones. Maybe thousands. Too bad I couldn't find nobody to buy 'em off of me to make Christmas ornaments or something.

After while I was putting in so many hours at Larry's I didn't hardly need to look for no other odd jobs. So I have to admit that worked out pretty good. Lots of stuff Larry makes me do is pointless, but he's paying for it so who in hell am I to kick? Now and then he'll surprise me by giving me something interesting to do.

How I got to be friends with Jack, well, his folks rent a cabin at Larry's every year. I'm always around, so me and Jack would say hiya or wave to each other, and that was about it for a while. Larry has a rule that the help shouldn't mix with the guests. That's just one more thing about Larry that would make you want to crack him across the puss with a two by four. You could make a pretty long list, starting off with the way he always jingle-jangles the change in his pocket while he's talking to you. I bet he don't even know he's doing it. Man, that'll drive you nuts. That and a hunnerd other things.

Anyways, when Larry says the help he can't mean none other than me. After all, there isn't nobody else working for him. So even after I get done for the day, I ain't allowed to go swimming or play ball with kids my own age who are staying there. I guess that's just Larry's way of reminding me I don't belong with these kind of people, in case I might of forgot.

61

This one day my job was to go from one end of the place to the other and destroy all the ant hills. Not to mention gopher holes if I come acrossed any. A typical project. Larry said if you just stomp on an ant hill or pee on it or pound it down with the back of your shovel, they'll have it built up again by lunch time. So each ant hill I found, I was spose to pour a bucket of boiling water on it, chop it all up with the shovel, and then smooth it out with a rake. Then later on I was spose to come back and put grass seed and water it.

Larry set up this big kettle of water over a fire. I used a ladle to put the water in the bucket. I had a big thick glove on so I didn't burn my hand. It was a pretty hard job because a bucket full of water is pretty damn heavy no matter if it's boiling or not. If it is boiling, the steam comes up your arm and the handle of the bucket is pretty near burning through your glove. And let's not forget most of these ant hills wasn't nowhere near the kettle.

Anyways, I was coming back with another bucket of water when Jack come up alongside of me. "Hey listen," he says. "I've been wondering. Do you go to church every Sunday?"

"Sure do."

"I thought so, because you look like a pretty holy fellow."

"What do you mean?"

"Why, your shirt is holey, your pants are holey, and your shoes are holey. I bet your underwear's even holey." He giggled. You could tell he was awful proud of himself.

I felt my face turning red. "So funny I forgot to laugh," I says. "I hope it was worth your while coming all the way over here to tell me that."

Then Jack frowned, and all of a sudden I was afraid I hurt *his* feelings. Ain't that strange? After all, he was the one who started it.

"Maybe it wasn't that funny anyhow," he says. "Well, either way, when you're done with your chores, you want to play some catch or something?"

"I don't know," I says. "I'm not spose to."

"How come?"

"Just not spose to. Larry won't let me." I wanted Jack to know I wished I could. Just to make sure, I says, "Thanks for the offer, though."

"Okay," Jack says. "See you in the funny papers." Then he went on about his business.

Maybe ten or fifteen minutes later, I was back by the garage getting more water when I seen Jack's ma go up to Larry's house and ring the doorbell. Larry come and pushed the screen door halfway open. They talked a while. Then Jack's ma come over to me and asked would I mind joining the family for a little picnic later on, unless I had other plans. "I already checked with Mr. Larry," she says, "and he agreed it would be all right."

What a hell of a thing. I couldn't believe it.

I never had nobody go out of their way for me like that before. I really didn't know what to think at first. I wondered if maybe they was just fooling—but they wasn't. When the time come I went over there and we had hot dogs, potato salad, watermelon, and pop. After we ate, me and Jack played catch for a while. I didn't have no mitt, so Jack's pa borrowed me his. We played with a regular league ball, a nice new one. I don't think I ever seen a new one before. Jack was way better than me, but I could at least catch the ball most of the time and throw it back to him without bouncing it.

While we was at it, Jack's ma come out and says, "How would you boys like some mores?"

I didn't know what she was talking about. "No thanks," I says. "I already had plenty of supper."

Well, you'd think that was the funniest thing Jack ever heard of. He pretty near busted a gut. "Plenty of supper," he says. "That's a hot one."

"Jack," his ma says. "Be nice."

Then Jack says to me, "Don't you know what some mores are?"

"Afraid not," I says.

So that was the night I found out some mores means a Hershey bar and marshmallow and graham cracker sandwich. I never heard of it before. After I had one, which was pretty good, Jack's ma give me another one. "Now you know why they call them some mores," she says. "Because as soon as you try one, you want some more."

From then on Jack and his folks included me in lots of things they was up to. They always asked Larry first, and he always made me finish my work before I could go. Sometimes he dreamed up a little extra chore to kill another half hour or forty-five minutes. And even after that, he acted like he was being put out when it come time for me to knock off.

Mr. Weber had an idea for getting around that so they could take me fishing. He asked what time I was spose to start in the morning. I said nine o'clock, give or take. "Well that's fine," he says, "because we can have you back from fishing by then. We go out at the crack of dawn."

Who in hell am I to these people that they would bend over backwards for me? I can't understand it.

I went out fishing with Jack and Mr. Weber a few times. Even though I lived my whole life a stone's throw from the lake, I never learned how to fish before. They showed me the ropes and they didn't make fun of me when I screwed up. One day I caught a pretty nice walleye. Mr. Weber took my picture holding up the fish. Later on he mailed it to me.

When their week was up and they was packing the car to go home, I went to give Mr. Weber his baseball glove back. "Why don't you go ahead and keep it?" he says.

I guess that goes to show you the kinda guy he is.

And to show you what kinda guy Larry is, he give me a good going over after Jack and his folks left. Said I was getting too big for my britches.

Chapter 2

Don

Birch Lake, 1937

If you keep going on the gravel road past Larry's house a ways, maybe a hunnerd yards, you'll come to his boat landing. The ramp into the water will be on your right. The woods will be on your left and in front of you. That's where the road circles back on itself, because there ain't nowhere else for it to go, except back where it come from.

One day me and Jack was poking around in the cattails over there, shooting at frogs or turtles or whatever with his BB gun, and we found an old logging trail we never seen before. It was behind a giant tangle of weeds and bushes. It curved away from the shore and up a little rise back into the woods.

"Let's see where it goes," Jack says.

"You betcha."

We followed this trail. We went along half a mile or so, and then we come upon an old run-down building.

You might call it a cabin if you wanted to be nice, but really it was a shack. Maybe ten by ten foot, more or less, and only one room. There was an opening where the door would of been, but there wasn't no door. There was a small window, with no glass in it, on the opposite side. The walls and the roof was leaning toward one of the corners, which was caved in part way.

The woods was so thick back there you couldn't hardly see the sky. Plus the skeeters was eating us alive. But that didn't bother Jack none. He kept right on exploring. Then he hollered, "Look at this!" He found another shack, or what was left of it.

And then we seen there wasn't just the one shack, or two. It was a whole camp, maybe ten or twelve shacks all totaled. A ghost camp.

"This place is something else!" Jack says. "What a spot for a hideout. I wouldn't doubt if Dillinger and Baby Face Nelson and some of those guys hid out here."

"Aw, I don't know," I said.

"Hell, they stopped off in Manitowoc, didn't they? Or was it Manitowish? You guys got too many towns that sound alike."

"I think you mean Manitowish Waters."

"Whatever. Isn't that where they had the big shootout with the FBI?"

"That's what I heard."

"How far away is it, would you say?"

"I don't know. A hunnerd miles, maybe."

"See?" he says. "That's plenty close enough for them to pass through this way a time or two."

I always figured them guys had plenty of scratch to hide out in a lot nicer of a place than this. But there wasn't no sense arguing over it.

Anyways, we wandered around a while longer. In some places there was just some planks for a floor and nothing else. In other places there was a pile of boards that used to be a shack. There was heaps of garbage here and there, and some random stuff like a three-legged chair and a busted alarm clock just lying on the ground.

There was an old-fashioned tractor, totally rusted out, with weeds growing up through it. I had to wonder how in hell did that tractor end up there. You have to figure some guy parked it one day and got off and never come back.

We went for a closer look at one shack that seemed to be in pretty good shape yet. The door was still on the hinges, or one hinge anyways, instead of on the ground. So right there that made it the best of the bunch. The door creaked when we opened it, just like in a horror movie. There was a mattress inside, some half-burnt candles, old newspapers and magazines, a few clothes piled in the corner, a chair, and a table, which was really just a scrap of plywood laid on top of a pair of crates. And there was cans of baked beans and dog food.

"Holy shit!" Jack yelled. "Someone's been living here."

We froze there a minute, wondering what to do next. Wouldn't you know it, just then the door creaked open, and we had company. This scraggly-looking fella come in. I swear you could of smelled this guy before you seen him. His hat and clothes was caked with dirt and sweat and God knows what all. His shoes was held together with tape.

When this fella seen us I don't know who was more scared, him or us.

"What're you doin' here?" he says.

We didn't say nothing. We was facing the door, and this fella was standing in the doorway. Jack still had his BB gun. He didn't point it at the guy, but he kind of raised it. Probably didn't even realize he done it.

This guy grabbed the business end of the BB gun and give it a good yank towards himself.

Jack didn't leave go of the gun, so he kind of flew forward and belly-bumped the guy. Now the guy was holding the gun in both hands, but still pointed towards hisself. We just pushed past him and skedaddled the hell out of there.

We sprinted pretty near the whole way back to Larry's. We looked back a few times, thinking the guy might be chasing after us, but he wasn't. It was a good ways to run. I started getting winded about halfway there. Plus Jack is faster than me anyways, so he got there first. When I got back to Larry's, I seen Mr. Weber was setting on the pier smoking a cigar and watching a couple lines he had in the water. Jack was talking to him.

It was that time of day when the sun had went behind the trees and the lake was totally calm. It looked just like a mirror. When I got out on the pier, the conversation was about over. Mr. Weber took a pull on his cigar. "Well," he says, "I'll speak to Larry about it after supper. No sense letting a good supper get cold, is there? Don, I trust you're joining us. I'll drive you home after."

I took him up on it, as I always do when I'm invited. Why not? First off, I eat a lot better than I would at home. Two, my ma and my sister end up with more to eat between 'em with me out of the way. And three, I wanted to stick around and see what was going to happen.

At supper we told a little bit about finding the old logging camp. Mrs. Weber says, "That sounds very interesting for you boys." But Mr. Weber changed the subject, which was fine with me. I wasn't sure we should tell on ourself for barging right into somebody else's place without knocking or nothing.

As soon as Mr. Weber downed his apple pie and coffee and Mrs. Weber started doing the dishes, Mr. Weber got up and went to go see Larry. Jack and I followed right after him, but he told us to stay outside when we got to Larry's doorstep.

After a minute Larry and Mr. Weber come out of the house and went in the shed. Mr. Weber come out with a lantern. Larry had ahold of an axe handle. Then here come Eloise running out the kitchen door in her house dress and slippers. "Lars, shouldn't you ought to call the sheriff?"

"I don't need the sheriff," Larry says. "I got my persuader." As he said that, he held the axe handle in one hand and slapped it into the palm of the other. You could tell Larry was feeling his oats but good.

"Oh goodness," Eloise says. "You boyce be careful. This fellow might be dangerous."

"We'll be fine, for crying out loud," Larry says. "Go on back to your knitting." He thought that was pretty funny, but when he looked around at the rest of us nobody laughed. Then he said something to Mr. Weber which I couldn't make out.

"I'm sure that won't be necessary," Mr. Weber told him.

So that was that. Mr. Weber and Larry went off and told us to stay put. Mrs. Weber made us some popcorn, but I don't think we ate any. We set on one of the picnic tables with our feet on the bench and waited for Mr. Weber and Larry to come back.

"Man, I'd hate to be in that guy's shoes," Jack says. "Believe you me."

"What did you tell your pa?" I says.

"Just told him what happened."

"And what did he say?"

"He just said this guy's gonna have to shove off, that's all."

Mr. Weber and Larry come back after half an hour or so. Larry went to put the lantern and the axe handle away. Mr. Weber set Jack's BB gun down on the picnic table and didn't say nothing.

Then Larry come out talking all kinds of shit about how this guy must of been stealing from him all along and whatnot, and he better not show hisself again, much less bother the wife or anything else, and he knew now Larry wasn't nobody to fool with, and he just got a little taste of it this time, but by God he better keep his distance from now on. You should of heard him.

Mr. Weber puffed on his cigar. He looked at Larry and didn't say nothing. I thought to myself, why doesn't Larry shut his big fat trap? What in hell could this guy have stole? Not much, from the looks of it. Maybe he picked a tomato one time. Who knows?

He wasn't no desperado on the loose like Pretty Boy Floyd or one of them guys. He was only a hobo-type fella that wasn't dangerous or crazy or nothing. He was just tired, if you ask me. He come home to find a couple of nosey kids inside of his place. He didn't like that none—and who would? You couldn't blame him for that, even if the joint was a shit hole. And then to top it off, we pulled a gun on him. How in hell would he know right off it was only a BB gun? When you get down to it, he was minding his own business. And we wasn't.

Another person swallowed up by the Depression.

Chapter 3

Don

Birch Lake, 1939

I'll never forget the time Larry said we was gonna go ahead and make a new sign to put up by the road. I was pretty excited, because this was a way more interesting project than ninety-nine percent of 'em. Also it was about time, if you ask me. The old sign out there looked like some kindergartener made it with his Crayolas.

Larry garbage-picked some sheet metal and some old pallets from someplace or other and told me to figure out how to make the sign from that stuff. It was easy. This sheet metal piece was pretty good size, two foot by a foot and a half, so I figured I could paint the sign on that and use the pallet wood for a frame around it. First I painted the whole thing, front and back, this dark green color. Forest green, they call it. Then I got started working on the lettering. The idea was to paint white letters on the dark green background. I figured that was gonna look real nice.

Larry wrote down what it was spose to say. I used a stencil and marked in all the letters with a piece of chalk. That was just to make sure it looked okay before I went ahead and painted. Even I know you never start painting nothing until you pencil it in first. I stenciled in LARRY'S LAKE AIR RESORT in big letters and then MODERN COTTAGES, INDOOR PLUMBING in medium-size letters and then BATHING BEACH, BOAT LAUNCH, LIVE BAIT in smaller letters. I don't mind telling you, I thought it looked pretty near perfect.

Well sir, it just goes to show you there's always two ways to look at something. It was a damn good thing I didn't start paint-

71

ing right away, because you know what happened? When Larry took a look at it, he had one of the all-time conniptions! He hollered, "Can't you do nothing right?" And then he kicked me right in the ass!

"Look here," he says, and shows me the paper he wrote. "It's spose to say LAKE AIRE with an 'E' at the end!"

"That ain't how you spell it."

"That ain't how you spell it, but that's how I want to spell it! It'll be more classy that way."

I knew there wasn't no point in arguing with Larry once he got that vein sticking out on his forehead. So I went back and added the "E" like he said. Then I made sure to get that row centered again. Finally I wiped the chalk off and went ahead and filled in the letters with paint. Let me tell you, it looked damn sharp.

After I got done painting both sides of the sign, I cut the pallet wood to make the frame. Then I stained it dark brown. We had these two fence posts, and we stained 'em the same color. The idea was to mount the sign in between the fence posts. I put a slot in each of 'em, just the right size so the sign would rest in the slots and be held in place by its own weight. Even Larry had to admit that was a damn good way to do it.

We sunk these fence posts into a couple holes full of wet cement. After the cement dried, we come back and slid the sign into the slots. Larry squirted some glue in there, even though I told him a dozen times he didn't need to. Once we made sure everything was level and all, we was just about done.

The only problem, at first I couldn't figure out how to light up the sign at night without running the electric all the way from Larry's house half a mile away. But Larry actually called the power company and got 'em to run a wire from one of their poles right along the road there. He even paid 'em to do it, which I couldn't hardly believe. Once we had the electric working, I put floodlights on either side to point up at the sign from the ground.

Then I planted some juniper bushes to hide the lights in the day-time.

I guess the whole job took about a week all told. You want to know what Larry had to say after it was done? Alls he said was, "That don't look half bad, Donald."

I'm not one for bragging much, but I don't mind saying that sign will be there until hell freezes over. You better believe it. All you'd have to do is touch up the paint and change the light bulbs about once in a blue moon.

Chapter 4

Don

Birch Lake, 1940

Now that me and Jack are a little older, when we want to go out at night Mr. Weber will go ahead and let us take the family car. Can you believe that?

The first time, he says to Jack, "What do you fellows have planned?"

"Nothing," Jack says.

"Where you going?"

"Nowhere."

Believe it or not, Jack was telling the truth. We really didn't know where in hell we was going or what we was gonna do. But the way he said it, you'd of thought he did know something and just wouldn't say. That's how I got the idea of calling him the Phantom. He comes and goes as he pleases and doesn't tell nobody nothing.

Mr. Weber just said, "Well, be careful and don't make it too late."

His car is really nice. A '39 Buick, in a real sharp light blue color. Man, do I get a kick out of getting behind the wheel of that baby. Me and Jack will take turns driving. We usually end up cruising along the back roads and not really going anywhere in particular. We have a few smokes and shoot the shit about whatever comes to mind.

One time we went into town for ice cream. I said maybe we could see if there was a good movie playing, but Jack nixed that right off the bat. "What are you talking about?" he says. "You want to go and sit in a movie together like a couple queers?"

Jack's always talking about lining up some girls, but there ain't too many around. "The problem with these hick towns," he says, "is they roll up the sidewalks at sundown. Why, in Chicago you can stand on any street corner and pick up all the girls you want."

"Well, it's too bad we ain't in Chicago then," I says.

Just when we pretty near gave up on the idea of finding something interesting to do, we found out the town was having a picnic out on Brunet Island. I asked Jack if he wanted to go. "Why not?" he said. "We got nothing to lose."

Ma and my sister Rosemary already volunteered to work in one of the booths selling taffy apples or some damn thing, so me and Jack was on our own. That was pretty lucky. Then I got the idea to bring some beers from Larry's supply in the garage. He always keeps plenty on hand, so I figured he wouldn't notice a dozen or so missing. I hid 'em on the top step of the storm cellar, and then I grabbed 'em real quick when Jack come around with the car.

When we got to the picnic, of course we had to leave the beers in the car. Then we'd go back every so often and down one apiece and head on back to the picnic. We didn't have no ice, but what could you do? We stuck the beers under the seat so they was in the shade anyways.

They had all these different games, like tossing raw eggs back and forth and the three-legged potato sack race and whatnot. If you wanted to play one, you had to go and sign up first. Each game was going on every half hour or so, and you could sign up as many times as you wanted, as long as they had spaces left.

But here's the thing. Pretty near every game they had was for two people to go in together. Jack didn't want to sign up because he thought it would look like we was spose to be a couple. "We can't sign up together," he says. "We need a couple of gals to go in with us."

So we was on the lookout for some gals. I figured maybe we'd bump into some of Rose's friends, but in the meantime we moseyed over by the beer garden, which we couldn't get in anyways, and the bingo tent, which we could get in. Unfortunately.

"Let's play the bingo for a while," Jack says. I wasn't too sure about that, but I didn't say nothing. It was a dime a card. As soon as we set down, Jack hollered, "I-69! I-69!" Man, did he crack himself up with that one.

Then he says, "Lend me a buck, will you? All I got's a fin." So I give him a buck. Damned if he didn't play ten cards all at once and didn't win nothing.

"Oh, this is bullshit," he says. "This game must be fixed."

"Well, in that case," I says, "maybe we should move along."

Jack wouldn't give up. "Shit," he says. "You know what they say. A winner never quits and a quitter never wins." I borrowed him another buck, and sure enough he blew that. And then I borrowed him another one, and the same damn thing happened again! Mind you, a buck is pretty serious money far as I'm concerned. So now I was out three of 'em with nothing to show for it.

Then Jack asked me for another buck! Being the sap I am, I'd of probably gave it to him. But I was tapped out. Just as well, because otherwise he'd of never quit that game till the cows come home.

Once he realized I couldn't front him any more scratch, he was ready to move along. We went over by the food tent. I figured maybe we could have a hot dog and a corn on the cob, but Jack said, "Let's just sit tight and figure out what's what." Well sir, my pockets was empty, and Jack already said he had a five. I figured he'd cover me the rest of the night, especially since I already floated him three bucks.

"You want to get something to eat?" I asked.

76

"Maybe," Jack says. "Just wait a while." We stood there a while, but we didn't get in line. I figured if I was gonna stand around with my pecker in my hand doing nothing, I might as well go ahead and take a leak. At least then I'd be doing something useful.

I told Jack, "I'll be right back."

He was looking around at this and that. "Okay," he says. "See you in the funny papers."

They had a few outhouses here and there, but between the flies and the stink I don't know why anybody would use 'em. I mean, unless you had a number two coming and didn't have no choice. Or unless you was a girl and had to sit down anyways. If you was just talking number one, you could pretty near go anywhere. I ducked into the trees behind the parking area and done my duty there.

When I went back, Jack was setting on a bench chatting with these two girls, looking just like old home week. I wasn't gone five minutes, and here he's got two of 'em lined up! I don't know how he done it. He had a few beers by then, so that probably helped. But even at that you had to give him his credit. When I come up he said, "Here's another county heard from." Then he introduced me to the girls.

Their names was Lillian and Arlene. A couple of sisters from Bloomer. Lillian was a cute little blondie, not much more than five foot and maybe a hunnerd pounds soaking wet, with some short shorts and nice legs. She would do, and then some. She give her age as sixteen, same as Jack. Arlene was a good half a foot taller and lots heavier. She also had blonde hair, but a duller shade, and a very plain face. Big hands, big arms, big tits, big can, big legs, big feet. She said she was eighteen, which would make her a little older than me.

I had a pretty good idea which one Jack was shooting for and which one I was spose to take.

"Don," Jack says, "I was just telling the ladies here that we should sign up for some of the games together, but first we might as well take a little visit to the car, since we have the beers and all."

"Fresh!" Arlene says, making believe she was offended, but really meaning the opposite.

"Well, time's a wasting, so we better make up our minds soon," Jack says, cheerful as could be.

"How many beers you got?" Arlene says.

"What do you think, Don?" Jack says. "How's our inventory looking?"

I didn't know exactly, but I knew it wasn't good. "Oh, a couple dozen," I says.

"Now you're talking," Jack says. "See, ladies?"

"I don't know if we ought to," Arlene says.

"Suit yourself," Jack says. "But an opportunity like this don't come along every day."

This whole time the cute one, Lillian, just looked around with her big eyes and took it all in. Jack didn't say nothing to her. He said everything to Arlene, because he knew she was spose to be the one in charge, but it was all for Lillian's benefit. You have to hand it to him, boy. He is smart.

"Well, maybe it wouldn't hurt nothing," Arlene says. "Just for a short while, I mean."

"That's the stuff!" Jack says.

And then Lillian finally spoke up. "Ronny'll kill us dead," she says. She laughed when she said it. Arlene said Ronny was their big brother and he drove 'em to the picnic with a few of his buddies.

When we got to the car there was some work to be done yet, because Arlene wasn't sold on the idea of Lillian pairing up with Jack. There was some arguing back and forth between the sisters before everybody got arranged in the car. Of course, I ended up in the front seat with Arlene, and Jack got in back with Lillian.

I reached under the seat and fished out two beers and give 'em to Arlene and Lillian. Ladies first. Then Jack says, "Hey you ain't forgetting your old buddy, are you?"

So I handed him a beer and reached under the seat and got myself one. I realized that was the last one. Then Arlene says, "This beer is warm."

No shit, I thought to myself. That beer's been setting under the car seat for three hours, and we ain't got no ice, and it's pretty near ninety degrees out.

Jack started going to town with Lillian right away. It was unbelievable. You could hear all this slurping and whatnot from the back seat. I couldn't see just setting there listening to that when I had a girl right next to me. Arlene wasn't the best looking, but she could of said the same about me. I shifted over in the seat to get closer to her.

"What do you think you're doing?" she says.

"What do you think I'm doing?" I says.

"Don't you dare try nothing."

Arlene polished off her beer in about two gulps. Then she put her hand out with the fingers curled, like I should just stick another beer right in there. But of course there wasn't nothing I could do about that.

I didn't tell her we was out of beers. I just tried to ignore that issue. I was a little buzzed anyways, so I went ahead and put my arm around her waist.

She elbowed me. Not too hard, but hard enough to get her point acrossed. "Listen, buster," she says, "you damn well better give me another beer, at least, before you start in getting grabby."

I didn't say nothing about the beers one way or the other. "Just wait a second," I says.

"I'll get it myself then!" she says. She got down on all fours and started fishing around under the seat.

"As long as you're down there," I says, "you might as well make yourself useful." I thought that was a pretty good one, but she wasn't paying no attention.

"Some swell party this is," she says.

I figured I didn't have nothing to lose. "Okay, so we ain't got any more beers," I says. "But I can give you a smoke. Why don't you just relax a while and get cozy?"

"Do you got any money?"

"What do you mean, do I got any money?"

"Oh, never mind. I'll take a smoke anyways." I give her a cigarette. When she leaned over to have me light it for her, I reached up and cupped one of her tits in my hand. You'd of thought I stuck a hot poker up her rear end, the way she hollered.

"You are so dead, fuckface!"

"Wait," I says.

"I'm gonna get Ronny! Lil, do you hear me? We're getting out of here. I'm gonna get Ronny."

Lillian didn't say nothing. Arlene got out of the car and slammed the door. Then she opened the back door and tried to pull Lillian out. From what I could tell, Lillian was hanging onto Jack pretty good and wouldn't leave go. She pushed Arlene out. Jack locked the door and rolled up the window.

"Slut!" Arlene screamed. "If you're not coming with me, then you can just go to hell!"

"Jack," I says, "did you hear that? She went to get her brother."

At first he didn't answer.

"Jack, you listening?"

"I heard her all right. Let him come on over here, and see if I care."

Well sir, we had our answer soon enough. Jack didn't even have the words out of his mouth before this guy was at the passenger side of the car pounding on the backseat window.

"This must be Ronny," I says.

"It is Ronny!" Lillian says. "God bless it! Ronny, cut that out!"

I don't know if Ronny was hitting the window with the front of his fist, or with the meaty part on the side of his hand. Either way it sounded like he was liable to break his hand if he kept at it. The frontseat windows was still down, so I went ahead and rolled 'em up and waited to see what was gonna happen next. Jack was just laughing until Ronny started trying to pry the mirror off the side of the car. Then he got out and tore after Ronny.

This Ronny was just a little pipsqueak. Before you knew it, Jack was all over him like nobody's business. He hauled off and knocked Ronny down with the first punch. Then he jumped on top of him and started whaling away. I got out to see if I should try and break it up, but Jack was doing fine so I just leaned up against the car and watched.

Just then, somebody caught me good, right in the mouth. I don't know if this guy thought I was Jack or what. Anyways, I never seen it coming.

I staggered backwards against the side of the car. I was stunned for a second. Then I felt around with my tongue and I could tell I had one tooth broke and another one knocked out altogether. Plus my top lip was cut pretty good. My mouth was full of blood.

I'm not gonna kid you. My mouth hurt like hell. On top of that, I was plenty pissed off at getting sucker punched. I never even seen the guy who hit me. So I got my bearings and looked around, and here this guy was coming at me again! Mister, I popped him square in the nose. I'll be the first one to admit it was a lucky shot. Just a reflex action. This guy dropped like a ton of bricks. He was gushing blood like a stuck pig and crying for his mama and everything else.

By this time, somebody else piled on top of Jack as he was finishing up with Ronny. When it looked like this guy was starting to get the better of it, I ran over there to help out. I pulled this guy off of Jack and wrestled around with him until he sort of lost interest. These farm boys was pretty strong, but so am I.

81

Anyways, if you ever get in a real no-holds-barred fight, strength ain't really the main thing to have going for you. Don't get me wrong, being strong don't hurt any, but the biggest thing is to make the other guy think you don't give a shit. I don't care if you are Joe Louis or what, pretty near everybody is scared of fighting and just wants to get it over with. If the other guy thinks you want to keep going after he wants to quit, then you're in business.

Sure enough, this guy spit the bit and sort of crawled away. I didn't feel like chasing after him, especially since my mouth was throbbing but good by now. Jack got up and dusted hisself off. He went back to see about Lillian. Believe it or not, she was still setting in the car like nothing happened.

This all was going on a little ways off from the main part of the picnic. That was lucky, because otherwise we'd of had to deal with every old jackass who couldn't help poking their nose in somebody else's pudding. I figured we might as well get the hell outta there before Ronny and his friends maybe rounded up some reinforcements.

I says to Jack, "Why don't you go ahead and get back in the car and leave Lillian get out?"

Then here come Arlene hollering "Police!" and swearing at us and yelling for Lillian all at the same time. She was really something, that Arlene. Here she sicked Ronny and the boys on us, and when that didn't work out she couldn't just leave well enough alone.

You know, Arlene probably would of been better off fighting her own battles, instead of having Ronny and the boys do it. I bet she could of held her own all right. She was solid. But I figure a girl, even if she looks like she could play for the Packers, don't want to fight unless it's with another girl. She'd rather set back and let the guys stick up for her, even if they end up taking their lumps. I guess it makes 'em feel more ladylike or something.

"Help, police!" Arlene hollered again. She was carrying on something awful.

"Jack, we better get going," I says. "She's gonna have everybody in the place over here."

"Oh, I wish she'd pipe down," Lillian says.

"I could make her pipe down," Jack says.

I says, "Jack, we really gotta go." I was pretty near begging him by now. Between the fighting and Arlene screeching, we already attracted more than enough attention to ourself. Plus my mouth was throbbing to beat the band. I had blood all down the front of my shirt. Most of it was mine. Then when you add in all the beers I drank, I don't mind telling you I was done. D-U-N, done.

Arlene kept calling for the cops and yelling about indecent liberties and underage drinking and everything you could think of. Finally Jack seen there was no percentage in sticking around there any longer. He kissed Lillian goodnight or goodbye, or whatever you want to call it, and she kissed him back! Even after all that, she kissed him back.

We finally sent Lillian on her way, and I started up the car. Then as I was backing out to turn around, there was a loud thump on the trunk. Arlene had chucked a rock at us! It missed the back window, thank God, but not by much. It turned out on top of everything else, that crazy bitch had an arm on her.

The next day was Sunday, my day off, but I figured I better go over to Larry's and apologize to Mr. Weber.

Of course, when you're trying like hell to avoid somebody, they're sure to turn up like a bad penny. I should of known I couldn't go over there without bumping into Larry. I was riding my bike between the back of his garage and the woods, trying to be invisible, when I almost ran him over. I don't know where he was coming from or going to, but all of a sudden there he was.

I put my head down and said, "Hi, Larry."

"Holy God!" he says. "What happened to you?"

"Walked into a door."

"Really?" he says. "How many times?" He thought that was about the most hilarious thing ever. He just went along laughing and shaking his head and left me alone.

I headed over towards the Webers' cabin. Mr. Weber seen me through the window before I knocked on the door. He come out and the screen door banged behind him. Then we went and set down at one of the picnic tables.

"How you feeling this morning?" Mr. Weber says to me.

"Fine, sir."

"I wouldn't guess it by looking at you."

"How's Jack?" I says.

"He'll live. He's laying down. Did you come over to see Jack or to see me?"

"I come to see you, sir. I want to apologize."

"Apologize for what?" I figured he wanted to know how much my story was going to line up with Jack's.

"For everything, sir."

"That covers a lot of territory," he says.

"For the drinking, to start off with."

"Ah," he says. "Can I ask how you boys got ahold of the beers?"

There wasn't no use lying to him. I told him I took 'em out of Larry's garage.

"Well," he says. He puffed on his cigar a couple times. Where I was setting, I was facing the lake and Mr. Weber was facing me. Behind him the water was sparkling in the sun. If I wasn't hungover, I'd of said it was a beautiful sight.

"You ought to know Jack didn't have nothing to do with it," I says. "It was all my doing."

"You mean stealing the beers?"

"Yes, sir."

"But it seems he helped you out when it came to drinking them."

84

I started to laugh, but then I stopped myself. Then Mr. Weber told me Jack wasn't use to drinking, so it hit him pretty good. I sure wished I would of known that beforehand. I never would of lifted the beers in the first place.

"It's too bad about your mouth," he says. He was rolling his cigar between his fingers. "It must hurt quite a bit. Are you going to see a dentist?"

"I don't know, sir."

"You're a pretty tough customer, aren't you, Don?"

"Well..."

"You gave those farm boys what for, did you?"

"Yes sir, I guess you could say that."

"Three against two, was it?"

"Yes, sir."

"Good for you, Don," he says. "I appreciate the way you looked out for Jack. You're a good friend to him."

"Thank you, sir." I was trying not to cry.

He reached out and slapped me on the shoulder. "You did a stupid thing," he says, "but you faced up to it. That's what separates the men from the boys."

A couple days later I was going about my business, pushing a wheelbarrow somewheres or other, when Larry come up to me.

"Hey Don," he says, "do you remember me borrowing Mike Weber three dollars?"

"No, I don't know nothing about that."

"Well, I didn't neither, but he just give it to me and said, 'Here's that three bucks I owe you.' I don't know."

So then he went off to have a bowel movement or something and I went back to working. After I thought about it for a while, I got it figured out. Mr. Weber wanted to pay Larry for the beers we swiped, but he didn't want to tell Larry we took 'em. So he made believe he owed Larry three bucks and give it to him. Knowing Larry, he probably figured he lent Mr. Weber three bucks one time when he was too smashed to remember. And even if he knew for a fact he never lent Mr. Weber nothing, that wouldn't stop him from taking it.

After everything is all said and done, I'm down two teeth, plus the three bucks I borrowed Jack while he was playing bingo, which I know damn well he forgot all about, and meanwhile Larry's got an extra three bucks he don't need no more than a whore needs the clap.

Chapter 5

Jeannie

Birch Lake, 1941

I never woulda met Jack if I wasn't working at the A&W.

I guess you wouldn't be shocked if I told you there isn't a whole lot to do in the evenings around here. There's the movie theater, and that's about it. If they have a picture you already saw or one you don't care to see, you're pretty much out of luck. There really isn't anyplace else to go unless you just go over to a friend's house to play cards or listen to the radio or whatever. So we were all very excited when we heard the A&W was opening up.

At first I thought it would just be a place to go once in a while to break up the regular routine, but then my friend April said she got hired to work there. She said I should put my name in too. So I did, and sure enough I got hired. I'm sixteen, which is just barely old enough.

The A&W is a drive-in, which is a big novelty. The customers stay in their cars and we take their orders and then bring the stuff back to them on a tray. They call us tray girls, or carhops.

We have a uniform with a brown short-sleeve dress and a little pleated skirt, and an orange apron in the front, and short white ankle socks and white-and-brown saddle shoes. Plus a little orange hat, which we hate. I guess you'd call it a bonnet instead of a hat, I don't know. It's open in the back and we have to pull our hair through this thing.

The first night, we hardly moved our heads for fear these darn bonnets would fall off. It reminded me of how they made us walk with a stack of books on our head in school to improve our posture. The next night we got the idea to pin the bonnet to our hair to keep it on. And the night after that, we got the idea not to wear the bonnets at all. We girls got together and agreed we'd just forget to bring them when we came to work.

Unfortunately that didn't go over with our boss, Mr. Herman. He didn't notice right away when we stopped wearing the bonnets, but as soon as he did he made us put them on again. He said he could see that we needed to have the whole idea of a uniform explained to us. Then he went ahead and did that. We went along with that all right, but he shoulda quit while he was ahead. "You know when you go in a nice hotel?" he said. "What does the bellhop wear?"

I bet there wasn't a one of us girls who ever set foot in a nice hotel. At least nobody that would admit it—because they wouldn't have been there as a customer, if you know what I mean.

"I'll tell you." He answered his own question. "The bellhop wears a little hat as a sign of respect for his guests. And likewise, so do you. Bellhop, carhop. It's the same thing, see?"

We just looked at him and then at each other. Nobody said anything.

"Bellhop, carhop," Mr. Herman repeated. You could tell he thought he was really onto something. "Both have the same job. To hop to it whenever the guest needs something."

April laughed out loud, and in the process she actually snorted. This is a habit of hers that she hates but I find very lovable. Anyways, that was the end of the meeting.

April is such a card. We aren't allowed to chew gum on the job, so naturally that's just what she does every single night. She'll go up to Mr. Herman to ask some silly question, allowing him to show off his expertise on something or other, and she'll be chomping on a huge wad of bubble gum the whole time. She makes a game out of it, to see how long it'll take him to notice. If he doesn't notice after a few minutes, she'll go ahead and blow a giant bubble practically right in his face. Then he'll say, "And what is our policy with regard to gum chewing?" The same thing every time, just like clockwork.

Mr. Herman will stick his hand out for April to put the gum in, and while she's giving it to him with one hand she'll be reaching in her pocket with the other for more gum. This happens at least once or twice a shift. It never dawns on Mr. Herman that April is pulling his leg. The funniest part is I don't think she even likes chewing gum to start with, because I never saw her do it anyplace else except at work. I think she only does it because they told her not to. If they told her to go ahead and chew all the gum you want, well, there wouldn't be any fun in that.

Aside from the little bonnets, the uniforms aren't so bad. At least we don't have to go around on roller skates, like I hear some of the other drive-in places make the girls do. What a darn good way to break your neck. Truth be told, our uniforms are quite flattering if you have a certain kind of figure. We were only open a week or so when one of the fellas back in the kitchen mentioned something interesting. "Did you gals all get poured out of the same mold?" this guy Phil said.

"What do you mean?" I asked.

"Oh come on," he said. "Look at yourselves."

April made a face at me like, How can you be so dumb? And then I realized. All of us girls are sort of tall, blonde or blondish, and not necessarily top-heavy, but what you might call curvy. Myself included. This Mr. Herman is just a little squirt, maybe five-seven and 140 pounds soaking wet, with dark hair plastered down and glasses and a little mustache that isn't filled in all the way. One of these German or Norwegian girls from the farm would practically snap him in two. I mean if it ever came down to it, which isn't too likely.

"I guess Herman knows what he likes," Phil said.

"Well, the feeling isn't mutual," April said. "I can promise you that."

"You don't need to get offended," Phil said. "Anyways, it's good for business."

April blew a giant pink bubble and snapped it loudly against the roof of her mouth. "If that perv ever tries anything with me, I'll knee him right in the nut sack. I'm not fooling."

You can learn a lot from April. I never heard of a nut sack before, but you can figure out what it means if you give it some thought.

Working at the A&W is pretty neat. People came from all over the first few weeks just to see it. Most of our business is in the early evening, especially families with kids or maybe an old grandma and grandpa who want to get out of the house for a change. After dark we get the people in their teens and twenties who are just looking for something to do. The lights are so bright, you can see the glow in the sky from miles away. I always imagine the people are being drawn to the light just like moths.

The job is a little harder than you might think, especially when we have to squeeze between the parked cars with a loaded tray. These frosty root beer mugs we have are big and very heavy. If you've got three or four of them at a time, you have to watch yourself. But no matter how careful you are, you can't help dumping your tray every now and then. When that happens, of course the smart-alecky ones in the crowd will cheer and even honk their horns. Obviously you want to crawl into a hole at that point, but you just have to grin and bear it.

One time I slipped on something and when I went to catch myself I dumped a full tray right on the hood of this fella's car. He was an older man, maybe fifty-five or sixty. He got out of the car and cursed me out. I mean actually using swear words. In front of his wife! And then he ran his hand all up and down the hood to make sure there weren't any dents. My heart was pounding for fear I'd be fired if he found something. So now you know how green I was. Here I was apologizing, when he was the one who was out of line, flying off the handle like he did. I can tell you April wouldn't have apologized. She might've cracked him over the head with one of the frosty mugs. Now that would've made a dent.

Most of the customers are pretty nice, though. It's great having a job where you can be outside and see lots of different people. Some kids I know from school come in, or people from the neighborhood, friends of my folks and that. It's nice to see familiar faces. Plus you can meet new people too. Especially fellas. April says that's the best thing about it. "Why else would you want to work here," she says, "if not to meet some cute guys?" She always seems to end up with the carloads of guys who are sort of loud and rowdy. Mostly they're harmless, just showing off. April takes all the wisecracks and lewd suggestions and gives it right back. It doesn't faze her any. She enjoys it. Myself, I'm usually on the lookout for a quieter type of fella.

I'll never forget one time I was in the bathroom looking over my shoulder into the mirror, you know, to see how my rear end looked in the skirt. Well, April came in just then and caught me at it. Oh my gosh, did she get a good laugh out of that one. I thought she was gonna pee her apron. Ever since then whenever she's walking a few steps in front of me she'll say, "How does my butt look?"

Like I say, it was sort of random how I met Jack. Him and his friend Don came in one night in a pretty nice car. A light blue Buick, pretty new from the looks of it. I guess it was just pure luck they parked in my station.

Do you want to know the date? It was Monday, August 4, 1941. I wrote it down.

Don was driving, so I assumed it was his car. Or more likely his dad's. Don introduced himself and Jack. Then he started in trying to make small talk. He isn't the most handsome fella, the poor thing, but he's a good one for jokes and puns and that. For one example, he said he'd gladly give his left arm to be ambidextrous. He was sort of entertaining, so I played along. They also had Illinois plates, and Illinois people are supposed to be big tippers.

Jack didn't open his mouth. He just sat there looking mysterious. So of course he was the one I was interested in. Well, his looks didn't hurt any. I mean as far as I could tell there in the shadows.

So here's the thing. When Don introduced Jack, he said he was his friend. Not his brother. So then I knew the car didn't belong to the both of them. It had to be one or the other. Since Don was driving, I figured it belonged to him, or his family anyways. But then a little later Don said he was a local guy and Jack was from Chicago. The idea of Jack being from Chicago made him even more interesting to me. I've never been to Chicago and I want to know all about it.

After the guys finished their hot dogs and root beer, I went back to pick up the tray and give them their check. "You know," Don said, "we can't agree on the color of your eyes. Jack here says hazel, but I say green."

"Is that so?" I said. "Well then you guys must be hard up for something to talk about."

"But which is it?" Don said. "We have a bet." I glanced at Jack, and he was looking right at me. That screwed up my train of thought for a second.

"So Don, you said green?" I said.

"That's right."

"And your friend here—Jack, is it?—said hazel."

"Yep."

"Well, I would normally say green," I said, "but I think this brown dress might make 'em look hazel, so I guess maybe you're both right." Then I leaned forward so I could see into the car better. "You don't say much, do you Jack?"

Jack looked at me and sort of smirked. "Depends," he said. That was the first word I ever heard him say. Depends.

Then Don said, "But what about our bet?"

"Maybe you should call it a tie," I said.

"Oh, it can't be a tie," Don said. "There's big stakes involved."

"What stakes?" I said. "If you don't mind me asking."

"Well, the loser has to pay the bill," Don said.

"And the winner?" I asked.

"The winner gets to ask you out for a date," Jack said. The way he said it, he left it up to me to decide if he was kidding or not. If I acted offended, he could just laugh it off and act like he was kidding. But if I didn't act offended, then he'd know I was interested. Wasn't that smart?

I wasn't sure if I should give him the satisfaction, at least right off. "Jeepers," I said. "You guys are pretty sure of yourself. Don't I get any say-so?"

The next night I kept my eyes peeled for the sky-blue Buick with Illinois plates. I had almost gave up when it finally did pull in not long before closing time.

It was in April's station, and she made a beeline over there before I knew it. She wasn't about to miss her last customer of the night. When she came back I asked her if she'd let me take it. "Those guys are friends of mine," I said. "I met them last night."

"What guys?" she said. "There's only one guy in that car. Since he specifically asked for you, you can have dibs on him."

"He asked for me?"

"He inquired as to your whereabouts, yes."

I was excited, but I didn't want to over-do it in front of April. Plus I didn't know for sure if we were talking about Jack or Don. I thought Don could've borrowed the car for some reason.

"Would you say he's good looking?" I asked.

"Are you kidding?" April said. She pointed her index finger to the back of her throat like she was trying to heave. This is terrible, I know, but then I thought it must be Don and not Jack. I have to admit I was a little disappointed.

But when I got to the car, I saw it was Jack after all. I shoulda known. Any question you ask April, she might give you a straight answer, but she'll just as soon give you an answer that's more amusing to her. She doesn't mean anything by it. She's just being April.

My heart skipped a beat. Then, as casually as I could, I said, "Well, look who's here!"

"Hello there," Jack said. "I was in the neighborhood and figured I'd stop in and sample one of your root beer floats."

"Is that all?" I meant is that all he wanted to order. Or pretended to mean that.

"No, not really," he said. "I thought I might as well give you a ride home, too."

Is that so? I thought to myself. This one doesn't waste any time, does he? I just said, "We'll see," and left it at that. You know, I have it on good authority that a girl about my age in Augusta got in a car with a fella she barely knew and was never seen or heard from again. That did pop into my head, but then it popped back out again.

By closing time my mind was made up. I punched out, said goodnight to the girls, and I didn't hesitate. I marched out the door and straight into the car with Jack.

Chapter 6

Don

Birch Lake, 1941

After that first night we met this Jeannie at the A&W, I asked Jack if he was planning on going back again the next night.

I'll tell you this much. I wouldn't of minded seeing that Jeannie again. Not one bit. When I first seen her, I pretty near crapped my drawers. I swear it was like a dream. Tall, blonde, long legs, everything in the right place. When she come up to the driver's side window, you could see her bright green eyes and her big smile and her little name badge. Jeannie. Right away I thought to myself, the magic Jeannie. She's just about the cutest girl I ever seen in person.

Since I was behind the wheel, I was the one she talked to first.

"Good evening," she says.

"Sure is," I says.

"Welcome to A&W. My name's Jeannie. How can I help you gentlemen?"

"I could think of something," Jack says.

"Pardon?" says Jeannie.

"Nothing."

We each ordered a hot dog, fries, and a root beer. That's spose to be the big attraction, the root beer, because it comes in what they call a frosty mug. It's just a regular glass mug they keep in the icebox, but people seem to get a kick out of it.

When Jeannie come back with our order, I watched her every step of the way from the building to the car. What really got me, it wasn't her boobs or the way her skirt swung back and forth or nothing like that. It was the way she carried the tray. Her arm was bent about ninety degrees at the elbow, and her wrist was bent backwards a little bit from the weight of the tray, about the same height as her eyes. Between the position of her arm and the way the light caught it, you could see the shape of her arm was perfect, and the muscle tone was perfect, and the skin was perfect. Man alive.

When it come to paying the bill, Jack handed me a couple bucks and says, "Here you go."

"You don't have to do that," I says. "I'll chip in for my share."

"I'm not doing anything," he says. "My old man gave me the money and said it was his treat for the both of us."

Well sir, that was mighty white of Jack's pa. It was white of Jack too, because I wouldn't of known any different if he just pocketed the money from his pa and didn't say nothing. And you know what else? When Jeannie come back to collect, he let me give her the money like it was mine to begin with.

I was starting to feel pretty good about the whole situation, and even better when Jeannie took the money and thanked us and then stood there alongside of the car like she didn't want to leave just yet. And then she says, "So I take it you fellas are from Illinois?"

She pronounced Illinois wrong, like it rhymed with "boys." That was pretty cute.

"Jack is," I says. I figured that answer worked in my favor, because it meant I'm around all the time, where Jack is only around for one week a year.

I figured that wrong. And how. I really put my foot in it there. Most of the time I don't say a whole lot, but there was one time I said too much. Because before the words was even out of my mouth I realized the question wasn't which of us, me or Jack, was gonna be around for the long haul. The question was which one of us the car belonged to.

Anyways, when I asked Jack if he felt like going back the next night, he hemmed and hawed like you wouldn't believe. After him and his folks had supper and dessert and then played horseshoes for a while, he still said he wasn't sure if he wanted to take a ride into town. I just said the hell with it and went on home for the night.

Later on I found out Jack did go to the A&W that night after all. From then on, whenever he took the car out at night, he went solo. He never told me I wasn't invited. I figured it out on my own.

Chapter 7

Jeannie

Birch Lake, 1941

I went to work at the A&W to make a few bucks and have something to do at nighttime, not necessarily to find a boyfriend. Some of the girls had it the other way around. But even if I wasn't quite as boy-crazy as April, for example, I was interested in meeting a nice fella. Who wouldn't be? Truth be told, the pickings are pretty slim if we limit ourselves to the boys we go to school with.

The first night Jack offered to drive me home in his dad's Buick, I said yes. Well, I didn't actually say anything. I just got in the car. I could hardly believe it myself, because I'm not normally so daring. But then again it's only five or six blocks, so I assumed we'd be there before he got the chance to get too grabby. But you know what? He didn't even ask me where I lived. He just started driving.

"Aren't you going to ask where I live?" I asked. "That might help you get me home."

"Jeez, you're sitting far away," he said. "Don't lean so hard against the door. You're liable to fall out."

That made me laugh. I skooched over to my left.

He drove across the bridge out of town and started heading out on Range Line Road. It's strange, but even though I only live a few blocks from the bridge, I bet that was the first time I saw the water for quite a while. "We stay out this way," he said. "At Larry's. Ever heard of it? It's just a ways further."

"Hey listen," I said. "I really am enjoying it, but I need to be getting home pretty soon or I'm gonna get it."

"That's okay. I just came this way 'cause it's more fun than driving around the block over and over. I'll show you around Larry's another time."

"That would be swell," I said.

He said, "I'll turn around at the pink store." He meant the dumpy little general store at Range Line and County M. The sign says Pine Creek Store, but nobody ever calls it that. Everybody calls it the pink store. If you saw it, you'd call it that too.

He pulled into the parking lot. The store was closed, and there was nobody around. "This is where I buy my smokes," he said. "Speaking of which, do you want one?"

"I better not."

"Suit yourself." He took a pack out from somewhere, and a lighter from somewhere else, and lit up. He has one of those Zippo lighters, and he handles that thing like an expert. It was impressive, the way he made it click and clack just so. Ever since then, I've always gotten a kick out of watching him light up and hearing that sound the lighter makes when he opens and closes it.

I kept looking at the side of his face. Even in the dark I could see he was just as good looking as I thought. Better, even. Dark hair with a nice haircut, a normal nose (I don't know; how do you describe a nose?), a square jaw, big shoulders, and that's about all I could tell until I got a chance to see him in the daylight, or at least standing up.

He turned around and started back towards town. And then, all of a sudden, he kept his left hand on the wheel and leaned all the way over to his right and kissed me, sort of half on the lips and half on the side of my face. Our first kiss, and I didn't even kiss him back because I didn't see it coming.

We were both quiet for a few minutes, and then I tried to start the conversation up again. I asked how long him and his family have been coming up north, and he said since before he can remember. I asked what Chicago is like, and he said it's hard to describe. I asked what he likes to do for fun, and he said the usual.

After we went over the bridge again and back into town, I told him how to get to my house. Or almost to it, I should say. "You better drop me off here," I said, before he turned onto our street. "It's right around the corner."

"Nonsense," he said. "We provide door-to-door service."

"I appreciate it," I said, "but my father will kill me dead if he sees me get out of this car. And then he'll kill you."

"What? He doesn't let you go out with guys?"

"Not in a car, he doesn't. And not even on foot until they come to the front door and introduce theirself."

"Is that right?" he asked. "Well, that's really something. I wonder what he'd think of this."

The second time Jack kissed me, I was ready for it. I think I made it worth his while. Our tongues even touched, but just barely.

I thought if I was looking for a nickel or a dime, I found myself a quarter when I met Jack. He is fascinating to me in every way.

The next night he showed up around the same time. We went for a ride along the backroads again and talked about this and that, and then we parked around the corner from my house and necked for a while. Jack calls that getting better acquainted.

The night after that was shaping up just like the others, with me counting the minutes until closing time and watching out for the sky-blue Buick with Illinois plates, when April came up alongside me. "So," she said. "Are you guys going steady, or what?"

"Oh, I don't know."

"Well, how far did he get?"

"Pardon?"

"Oh, come on. How far did he get? First base, second base..."

"April."

"All the way? Don't tell me he already closed the sale!"

"April!"

100

"A handsome fella from Chicago, and with a nice automobile to boot. My goodness." She's really one of a kind. "I don't understand this withholding of information," she said. "I would tell you. You know I would. If it was the other way around, I would tell you each and every gory detail."

"Oh gosh, April."

"Tell the truth. When you two are smooching, does he look you right in the eyeballs or does he close his eyes?"

Just as I was wondering which one would be the correct answer, here came the sky-blue Buick. Jack barely stopped the car before April was right at the driver's side window. I stayed put and watched. I had no idea what she was up to, but I couldn't stop her even if I wanted to. Nobody can stop her when she wants to do something.

April and Jack talked for a bit. It probably wasn't any more than a minute or two, but it seemed longer. And then she leaned in through the window and kind of hugged Jack around the neck!

She came back to where I was standing with my mouth wide open. "Catching flies?" she said.

"What in the world did you say to him?" I asked.

"I demanded to know what his intentions are."

"Oh, April."

"What? He hasn't peeled rubber out of here, has he?" She waved at the car and smiled. I couldn't tell if Jack was looking or not. "I demanded to know when he plans to take you out on a proper date, and not just drive all around hell and back."

I laughed.

"I don't know what's so funny," she said. You could tell she was trying not to laugh herself. "I told him he hasn't spent a nickel on you yet, except his dad's gas money."

"Oh, gosh. What did he say to that?"

"He said, 'Holy crap, who wound you up?'"

The next night I had my first real date with Jack. I mean the first time we didn't just drive aimlessly through the night and then make out at the end. I wonder if Jack would've gotten around to it on his own, without April pushing him.

Jack wasn't crazy about the idea of stopping by the house to pick me up, and I didn't really mind. I couldn't see how there'd be anything to gain by introducing him to my father just then. I admit I was curious to see if my father would hear Jack was from Chicago and tell him all the big cities are nothing but giant sewers which no self-respecting, God-fearing person would even visit, much less live in. He tells Mom and me that all the time. I wonder how that would go over with Jack.

My father means well, I guess, but he's a hard case. Let me give you an example. Say my grandparents came over for Sunday dinner, and Grandpa happened to say, "My, this roast is delicious!" The rest of us would sort of chime in, you know, agreeing with him. But not my father. He would sit there scowling. You know why? Because you pay good money for a nice roast in the first place, and if the person who cooks it (my mom) isn't a complete moron, well then the roast darn well better be delicious. It's supposed to be delicious, so why get so excited?

Any fella who'd have enough nerve to come to the door and deal with my father deserves a lot of credit. In Jack's case I didn't see the point. Him and his folks were going back home the very next morning, so why in the world did he need to try and impress my father when for all I knew he'd never see him (or me) again?

I agreed to meet Jack at the Palace Theatre. We were going to see *The Mark of Zorro*. We did the date on foot, so we were in line with that part of the rules anyways. Still, I had to hope none of our local busybodies would tell my father he saw us.

I was a little nervous walking over to meet Jack. When he saw me coming, he flicked his cigarette butt into the gutter and gave me a little hug. He paid for the tickets and we went in. I thought the lady in the ticket booth gave us a funny look, but maybe I imagined it. I go to the movies all the time, so she probably recognized my face without knowing my name. As soon as we got inside, Jack said, "Boy, the guy who named this joint sure had a sense of humor."

Then we got in line to get our popcorn and Cokes. Jack looked around at the coming attractions posters and said, "All these pictures already played in Chicago ages ago." I didn't know what to say to that, so I just let it go.

The movie was great. Tyrone Power played Zorro, a masked outlaw who was really a good guy even though nobody realized it. His real name was Don Diego, and he was sort of a Robin Hood type. Even though he was a rich man's son, he tried to help the poor people out. You don't see that every day. He also fell in love with a cute girl named Lolita, who was played by Linda Darnell.

While we were watching the movie I pictured Jack as Zorro and me as Lolita. We held hands at first and then Jack put his arm around me about halfway through. That was nice. In case you're wondering, he didn't do that old trick where the boy pretends to yawn and his arm mysteriously ends up around the girl's shoulder. He just went ahead and did it like he meant to.

There was also a snooty kind of girl in the movie called Inez. Zorro kept flirting with her even though he already liked Lolita. I pictured her to be a city girl like the kind Jack is used to. Basil Rathbone played the bad guy. He's great, isn't he? He's the same actor who plays Sherlock Holmes. Him and Zorro finally got into a big sword fight at the end, but I shouldn't tell you who won because that would give away the whole movie.

Zorro always went around making a "Z" with his sword in walls, curtains, and that. Pretty much everywhere he could think of. That's the mark of Zorro. Get it?

After the movie was over, we got some ice cream cones and went for a walk. How we ended up back at Jack's car instead of at my house, I'll never know! Strange, isn't it?

Jack started out by holding the rear door open for me, like we were supposed to pile in the back seat! But when I hesitated, he laughed and let me in the front instead. I was a little nervous because I assumed the girls in Chicago must know a whole lot more than a country mouse like me. I wondered how much they'd let a fella get away with on their first real date. I wanted to do some things with Jack, but I didn't want to do everything just yet.

We spent some time in the car getting better acquainted. We got acquainted pretty good. Luckily, Jack never tried to go any further than I wanted to, so I didn't have to tell him no to anything. We got to a certain point and then he didn't try go any further. Then we sort of repeated the same stuff for a bit. When I told him I should probably get back to the house, he agreed right away. I think maybe he was even a little relieved.

I promised to write and I made him promise, too. I told him I'd be counting the days until he came back the next summer. I realize that was a little corny. Then we kissed goodnight for real and I headed back to the house not knowing for sure whether I'd see him or hear from him ever again.

It took me a long time to fall asleep that night. I had lots of stuff spinning around in my head. I don't know what time I finally nodded off, but the birds were already starting so it must've been pretty close to sunrise. Jack and his folks were probably already on the road by then.

I had the craziest dream. Jack and I were on some sort of a trip together. I couldn't tell where we were supposed to be, but we kept on looking for a place to stay until finally we found a little motor court or something. Then the next thing you know, Jack and I went all the way! While we were going at it pretty hot and heavy, Jack was clawing my back and my butt and my legs. When I went in the bathroom to look in the mirror (I mean still in the dream), there was a giant "J" scratched into my back.

Isn't that weird?

Chapter 8

Don

Birch Lake, 1941

I skipped school the day after the Japs bombed Pearl Harbor. I went to Larry's and asked him to leave me use his truck so I could go over to Eau Claire and enlist.

Larry being Larry, he give me grief about how I just got done using the truck the day before to take my ma and Rosemary to church. That was beside the point, if you ask me. Here everybody in the whole country was trying to figure out what they could do to pitch in, and he couldn't be bothered to borrow me his piece-of-shit truck for a couple hours.

I guess he was planning on leaving me use it all along, but he needed to give me a hard time just for the fun of it. Anyways, he finally handed over the keys. Instead of saying "Good luck" or "More power to you" or even "Remember Pearl Harbor," alls he said was, "It's icy out. Don't crash." I can promise you he wasn't worried about my life and limb for one second. He was only worried about the truck getting banged up.

When I got to the induction place, there was a long line of guys waiting already. All different shapes and sizes. When I got to the front of the line, I filled out a card with my name and address and all. Then they had me go to the back of another line and wait some more. After while they called me for an interview, as they called it.

This little weasely-looking guy with a bald head and reading glasses was setting behind the desk in a swivel chair. I was standing in front of him because there wasn't no place to sit. He had the card I filled out. He didn't bother to look up while he told me all the things wrong with it. First off, I wasn't eighteen years old yet, and I didn't have no signature from my folks. Two, I wasn't out of high school yet. Three, even if I was eighteen and out of high school already, that wouldn't make no difference anyways, because they wasn't taking nobody under eighteen and a half at the present time.

I don't mind telling you, I felt pretty foolish for even going down there. I hated to turn around and leave because there was other guys waiting behind me, and I figured they heard the whole thing. But just then this guy behind the desk finally looks up at me. "Well, you're a husky enough fellow anyhow," he says. "I appreciate your enthusiasm, son. Just put it back in your pants for now and come back and see us when you're eighteen and a half. I don't expect we'll run out of Japs to kill before then."

So I got out of there without being laughed out.

I figured Larry would pretty near bust a gut when I told him what happened, but he just said, "Better luck next time," and left it at that. As far as my ma is concerned, she don't know nothing about it, so that's one argument we don't need to have just yet.

Chapter 9

Jeannie

Birch Lake, 1941–1942

April's always telling me it's not how much you actually let a boy get away with, it's how he makes you feel that counts. I'm not sure if she means physically or the other way, but I think she probably means both. I couldn't agree with her more. After I saw Jack those few times, I was already head over heels, or ass over teakettle, or whatever you want to call it.

I could picture all kinds of things involving Jack for the future, but the problem was how to live my real life every day knowing I wasn't going to see him. For instance, at work I couldn't be looking down the street every ten seconds expecting to see the sky-blue Buick. I couldn't stop eating or sleeping or going to school or doing stuff with my friends. I couldn't just mope around like a zombie or something.

I didn't write to Jack right away, because I didn't want him to think I was being pushy or trying to smother him or whatever. As if you could smother somebody who's four hundred miles away. I also wanted to keep it as something to look forward to. In a way it seemed like more fun to imagine what I would write to him and what he would write back than to actually do it. But at the same time, I didn't want him to think I forgot about him.

I finally wrote to Jack on September 8. That was the one-month anniversary of our first date, but I didn't mention that in the letter. I kept it short. I tried to make it sound sort of breezy but still let him know I was serious about keeping in touch. I didn't memorize the whole letter word for word before I put it in the envelope, but I do know it started out (I mean right after "Dear Jack") by saying, "What's new in the Windy City?" How embarrassing. I wish I could take that one back.

As soon as I mailed the letter to Jack, the trick was to try and be patient while I waited for him to write back. I didn't want to run to the mailbox every day like some kind of a crazy lunatic. You had to figure it would take a few days or a week for him to get around to writing back. When a week went by, I figured it was a good test for me, stewing in my own juice like that. Isn't there a saying something like "Good things come to those who wait"?

When the second week went by, I started wondering if maybe I should go ahead and try again. After all, my letter could've gotten lost in the mail. It's possible. You have to figure it must happen pretty often, with so many millions of letters going back and forth every day. Or what if I wrote Jack's address wrong on the envelope? Even if I only had one number wrong or misspelled the name of the street, he probably wouldn't have gotten it. Or maybe the people at the post office couldn't read my handwriting.

How about this? What if my letter got through to Jack okay, but his reply had one of these problems I just described? Gosh, it's enough to drive you batty.

Just when I was practically at my wit's end, I got home from school one day and there it was. A letter postmarked Chicago, addressed to me. It didn't have a return address on it, but the writing on the envelope looked just like you'd expect from a fella about my age. Not very neat, and kind of a mix of cursive and printing.

I brought the letter and the rest of the mail inside the house. Then I realized it was a darn good thing I got the mail before one of my folks did. Otherwise I'd have to explain why in the world I should be getting a letter from Chicago. If my father found it, he might've even opened it, read it, and tossed it in the trash without ever telling me.

I ran upstairs, said hello to my mom, locked myself in my room, and plopped on the bed to read Jack's letter.

Dear Jeanie,

Thank you for your nice letter. It sure was swell to hear from you. When you ask what's new over on this end, I would say senior year has been pretty busy so far. Our football team the Calumet Indians are doing alright, knock on wood. We have won 3 and lost 1. Did I ever tell you I play halfback?

Next weekend is our Home Coming game vs Fenger. They are a pretty tough team. I will let you know how it turns out. Wish us luck!

It was swell meeting you this summer and I hope you are doing fine.

Love, Jack

I can't tell you how many times I've read that darn letter. I keep it in my purse and take it with me everywhere I go.

You know what? I started thinking about Jack's school having their homecoming game, and of course that means they'd have a dance the same weekend. Would a handsome, popular fella like Jack, a star halfback, sit at home that night studying his trigonometry? I doubt it. You better believe he went to the dance, and he probably took the head cheerleader for his date. Maybe the two of them were even voted king and queen. I wouldn't be surprised.

The thought of all that practically made me sick. But then again, I guess Jack was entitled to go to his homecoming dance if I already went to mine, which I did with Roger Hagenmeyer. Roger is a nice enough guy, but I only made out with him like a banshee because we were in the dark and I was pretending he was Jack.

I wracked my brain trying to figure out some excuse to get to Chicago. April's big sister Lynn has a girlfriend who goes to college there, and that's about the best I could come up with. But let's say Lynn went to visit this girl. What were the odds of her letting me and April tag along? Even if she did, what were the odds of my father letting me go? And even if that miracle of miracles happened, what exactly would be the plan for getting together with Jack? I might make it all the way to Chicago and never see him anyways.

I keep on writing as often as I can without looking completely pathetic. What I mean is, I write back to Jack again every time I get a letter from him. Take my first letter, for example. I mailed it on September 8, and I got Jack's reply on September 25. So I wrote back to him two or three days later, and then I had to wait for him to respond before I could write again. I always hear back from him, but sometimes it takes a little longer than others.

I never put anything too serious in my letters to Jack. I might mention I'm looking forward to seeing him again or something like that, but mostly I just put a bunch of chitchat about nothing in particular. So does Jack. He kept me up to date on how his football team was doing. One time he mentioned his dad was taking him to the Chicago Bears game and how much he was looking forward to that. It so happened they lost that game—to the Green Bay Packers! But Jack didn't mention that in his next letter and neither did I. That probably wouldn't have gone over very well.

Here's something I noticed. Even since Pearl Harbor, Jack has never said one single word about the war or going into the service or anything like that. He said he was looking forward to Christmas, and his dad was trying to get tickets for another Bears game, and stuff like that. Believe me, everybody around here is just about hysterical at the idea of sending their sons and brothers and boyfriends and husbands off to God knows where and maybe never see them again. I'm deathly afraid for Jack and every other fella who's liable to go. But if he isn't going to bring it up, I don't think it's my place to pound him over the head with it.

When I wrote Jack's Christmas card, I didn't write, I pray to God you and every other fella I've ever known or might ever know is alive to see next Christmas. Nope, I didn't write that. I kept it light. I wrote, *I hope the Bears win the championship game for you. Merry Xmas!*

I got a Christmas card from Jack, too. It was a few days after New Year's, but that's okay. I cherish it all the same. After the printed message about peace on Earth and goodwill toward men and the usual stuff like that, Jack wrote, *P.S. The Bears won!*

In between letters I constantly wonder what Jack is up to. You can pretty well guess when he'll be in class and when he'll be at practice and when he'll be having supper with his folks, all that kind of stuff. I try to picture him doing all those different things, but I can't quite get it. Sure, I can picture what he looks like, how he walks, how he talks, how he smiles. That's easy. But I can't really picture the rest of it.

What exactly is he up to from day to day? Does he have a girlfriend? Is it serious? Does he ever think about me? How often? And if he does and when he does, *what* does he think about me? Now there is the big question. Does he think I'm just a nice girl he killed some time with because he had nothing better to do? Or does he think there might be more to it than that?

So the days and weeks and months go by, and the whole time I keep asking myself all these questions. My favorite one is this: Could Jack possibly be my ticket out of this crummy little town?

111

Chapter 10

Don

Birch Lake, 1942

I graduated from high school on June 8, 1942. I turned eighteen and a half on June 19. If I had my druthers, I'd of gone in the service then and there. But my sister Rosemary come down with pneumonia about the same time. My ma was in a panic. Rose got through it okay, thank God, but Ma begged me to stick around for the summer at least, so I could make a little extra money and help out around the house. I mean she really begged me. When I seen how bad she wanted me to stay, I figured I couldn't do nothing else.

Jack's family come up the first week of August, same as always. By then I felt like I already had one foot in the service. I was itching to go. That was pretty near all I thought about. I was working a ton of hours, and in my spare time I done push-ups and sit-ups till the cows come home. I was trying to build myself up so I could hold my own against the Germans or the Japs.

When I told Jack I was going in the service after Labor Day, he figured I got drafted. "Oh, that's too bad," he says. "Your number came up?"

"No, I'm enlisting."

He looked at me like I had three heads. "What would you wanna go and do that for?"

"Why not?" I says. "Aint got nothing better to do except sit around here blowing farts."

"Yeah, but to volunteer for it? They'll get around to you soon enough as it is."

"I just figured it was high time I done something worthwhile."

"Jesus," he says. "Wait till my old man hears about this! He won't believe it."

"What do you mean? Won't believe it in a good way or bad?" The way he said it, I couldn't tell.

"In a good way or bad? Hell's bells. If he kisses you right on the mouth, don't say I didn't warn you."

I told Jack I seen Jeannie over the winter. One day my ma took Rosemary and me to get some new galoshes. Ma calls 'em rubbers, which I always get a laugh out of. Anyways, we was in the store and we turned down one of the aisles and there was Jeannie and one of her girlfriends. They was looking for handbags or some such thing.

The magic Jeannie. She recognized me right off and give me a little hug. I was proud of that, in front of Ma and Rose. Then she asked did I hear anything from Jack and did I know how he was doing and all. I told her no, I didn't, and it was the God's honest truth because I never hear nothing from Jack between the day him and his folks leave one summer and the day they come back the next.

"Well, you be sure and tell him hello for me," she says.

"I sure will," I says, just being polite.

"You're a prince," she says. And then she kissed me on the cheek!

When I told Jack about it, he just said, "Well, that was nice of her to ask about me." Then he says, "I guess I should probably look her up." Like he never thought of it before!

He swung by the A&W that night or the next and got back in with Jeannie, just like that. Nothing to it.

A couple mornings Mr. Weber took me out fishing early, before I started work. Jack come with us the first time, but the next time he slept in and Mr. Weber took me out anyways. In fact, Mr.

Weber couldn't do enough for me the whole time. He bent over backwards. I was invited to join the family for breakfast whenever I got to Larry's early enough, and then Mrs. Weber always sent Jack out with a snack for me later in the day. When I knocked off, I usually got together with Jack and Mr. Weber for a few beers.

Jack ended up seeing Jeannie every day, far as I could tell. I don't know if she was spose to have a boyfriend or what, but she always seemed to be available whenever it suited Jack. What he did, he usually went out right after lunch to meet up with her. Then he'd come back later in the afternoon after she went to work at the A&W. He'd have supper with his folks and then head out again to pick her up when she got off.

They usually went over to the public beach during the day so they could do whatever it was without the rest of us breathing down their neck, but this one day Jack brought her over to Larry's.

I didn't think anything of it when the blue Buick pulled up, because I figured it was only Jack. But then I seen Jeannie pop out with her blonde hair shining in the sun. She had a sleeveless white top and some beige shorts on and sandals. Jack went in the cabin and come back out in his bathing suit. Then Jeannie done the same thing.

Well sir, to see Jeannie in her bathing suit was really something. That would of been a hard one for anybody to try and get out of their head. Her suit was sort of a reddish color, maroon you might call it, and let me tell you it was flattering and then some.

I was cutting the grass that day, a ways from the beach. I didn't know if Jack and Jeannie seen me or not. It looked like Jack hollered something—probably "Last one in's a rotten egg"—and then the both of 'em ran down the pier and jumped off.

I kept going back and forth parallel to the beach and getting closer with each row. I glanced over that way every so often, but I tried not to be too obvious. Jack and Jeannie was splashing around and playing with a beach ball and having a high old time.

114

After while they got out of the water and lounged around on the pier.

Jack's folks was setting at one of the picnic tables, giving the lovebirds some room. Mr. Weber was reading the paper. He likes to study the box scores line for line. Mrs. Weber was reading a book. They were both having lemonade.

All of a sudden Jack got up and went in the cabin. I thought maybe he had to see a man about a horse, but he come right back out with a sweatshirt and give it to Jeannie. Then he turned around and come over to me. "Hey!" he says. He had to yell so I could hear him over the lawn mower.

"Hey yourself," I says.

Then he yells, "Turn that thing off a second!"

I hated to turn the mower off, because it's always liable not to start up again. Then I have another chore on my hands. So I left it running and we walked a few steps away so we could hear each other. "Hey listen," Jack says. "Would you come over here and talk to us a minute?"

"I don't want to get in your way."

"You ain't getting in anyone's way. Jeannie wants to ask you something."

"Well, if you put it like that."

I didn't know how long it might be, so I had to switch off the mower. Believe me, if Larry come out and found the mower running with nobody there, he would of had one of his typical conniptions. I didn't want it on my conscience if that vein on his forehead popped like a water balloon.

So we went down to the pier, and there was Jeannie setting with her knees pulled up inside the sweatshirt and her arms around her knees. Her hair was still wet, and instead of hanging down the sides of her face like usual it was back behind her ears. And get this. The way she was setting, you could see a little scoop of white at the top of each leg. In other words the bottom of each butt cheek, where her skin wasn't tanned. Man, that was a hell of a thing.

"Hello Don," Jeannie says. "Nice to see you again."

"Likewise, I'm sure." I don't know why in hell I said that. I figured it was a classy thing to say.

"Here's the thing," she says. "Jack and I were talking, and I said my girlfriend Mary Jo is such a good egg, but she doesn't have a boyfriend, and we thought you two might hit it off."

I wasn't sure what to think. I was wondering if she meant the same girl I seen her with over the winter, because that one wasn't bad looking. But I didn't know if I should ask.

"I don't know," I says. "What did you have in mind?"

"See?" Jack says to Jeannie. "I told you. This guy is a stubborn sort of mule."

"Oh, leave him be," Jeannie told him. Then she says to me, "We were thinking maybe we could double date one of these nights."

"I guess so," I says. I didn't know what else to say.

You could tell Jeannie was just trying to be nice, but I wasn't sure if it was such a good idea. I was about to go in the service, and I didn't want to start something I couldn't finish. To be honest with you, I also didn't know if I had the right clothes to wear or the right kind of manners or what. I wouldn't of minded embarrassing myself in front of some local gal just between us, but not in front of Jack and not in front of Jeannie. And what if this Mary Jo didn't like me? I wouldn't of wanted her to give Jeannie a hard time for fixing us up.

"Jeez," says Jack. "Try and contain your enthusiasm."

"Oh, Jack," Jeannie says. "We caught him off guard, that's all." She ran her fingers through her hair and shook her head from side to side. "Don, why don't you take your time and think about it and let us know. Then we'll go from there."

"I'll do that," I says. "I do appreciate it."

"She's a very sweet girl," Jeannie says.

"She's just your type," Jack says. I figured that was spose to mean homely.

I told 'em so long and went back to work. Sure as shit, the mower wouldn't start. I had to drag it back to the shed to work on it. Jack and Jeannie was gone by the time I got the damn thing running again.

I never went out with Jeannie's friend Mary Jo. Jack didn't bring it up again and I didn't neither. And I didn't see Jeannie no more, except in my mind's eye. I seen her there plenty of times. Pretty near every night before going to sleep, in fact.

The last night before Jack and his folks went back to Chicago, Jack went out with Jeannie. Of course. When I knocked off work, Mr. Weber asked me to come over and join him for a libation, as he calls it. We set on the pier and chewed the fat. Mr. Weber smoked a cigar and watched a couple lines he had in the water. The lake was perfectly still, just like a mirror. The sun was going down and there wasn't a cloud in the sky. It was easy to forget there was really a war on. Not some little podunk war either, but a goddamn world war affecting millions of people. It didn't even seem possible.

We had a couple beers apiece. While we was at it, Mr. Weber brought up the subject of Jeannie. "It seems Jack found himself a nice little girlfriend," he says.

"Yes sir, she seems real nice."

"Don't you know her already from school or someplace?"

"No, sir," I says. "I never seen her before we met her at the A&W."

"I see," he says. "I just hope he treats her okay is all." I didn't say nothing, because who am I to say how Jack treats her? How in hell would I know?

After while Mr. Weber fixed up some burgers and we ate 'em at a picnic table with Mrs. Weber. When we was done Mrs. Weber took the dishes back in the cabin, and Mr. Weber said, "Let's

117

go for a little walk." He had a cigar going and offered me one too. I never had one before, but I figured what the hell and took it. Not knowing any better, I inhaled the damn thing and pretty near coughed up a lung before I caught my breath again.

We headed down the gravel drive past Larry and Eloise's house and kept on going. Before you knew it we found ourself out by the road. Once you get to my LARRY'S LAKE AIRE RESORT sign, it's only another quarter mile or so to the Black Bear, which is where we ended up. I was never in there before, except a time or two when Eloise sent me in to try and get Larry out. This was my first time in there as a customer. They have the same kind of knotty-pine paneling Larry has in his cabins, plus all these hunting and fishing trophies on the walls. They don't have a black bear, though—only a painting of one.

There was a dozen or so guys in there hunched over their drinks. I recognized most of their faces, but I didn't know all their names. Mr. Weber bought us a couple beers. "I'm more of a bourbon man myself," he says, "but when in Rome, you know. Or in Wisconsin."

Then he bought a round for everybody in the joint and asked 'em to drink a toast to me! He stood up and says, "To a young man who is going to do us proud in the service of his country." Man, I'll never forget that if I live to be a thousand. Everybody cheered and whatnot. Of course, most of them guys would of drank to pretty near anything as long as they was getting a freebie out of it.

I knew from Jack his pa fought with General Pershing in France. He was proud of it and ought to of been. I asked Mr. Weber what the war was like. He just raised his eyebrows and puffed on his cigar. He didn't say nothing right away. Finally he says, "You're a good man, Don. And a tough son of a gun to boot. I know you'll come through all right."

"Thank you, sir."

"Call me Mike."

I ain't gonna lie to you. That made me feel about ten foot tall.

Chapter 11

Jeannie

Birch Lake, 1942

Isn't it funny when they say somebody lost their virginity, like they just misplaced it or something? I didn't misplace mine. I gave it up on purpose, to Mr. Jack Weber of Chicago, Illinois, on August 6, 1942. That was the night he took me to the county fair in Ladysmith.

It was actually my idea to go to the county fair. I saw an article in the paper about it, and then I cut it out and showed it to Jack.

> The Rusk County Fair, which runs Aug. 6-9 at the County Fair Grounds in Ladysmith, will offer music, entertainment, livestock and horse shows, small animals and fowl, carnival rides on the midway and fireworks, plus many other amusements and concessions. Also featured will be a big band concert, magician, children's shows, antique tractors and farm machinery, and the ever popular demolition derby.

We decided to meet at the A&W, even though it was my night off. I left the house in my uniform and made believe I was going to work. I told my father I had to fill in because one of the girls called in sick. I took along a little bag with a change of clothes in it.

I hated to lie to my father, but I really, really wanted to go to the fair with Jack.

I got to the A&W at half past four. The other girls helped me steer clear of Mr. Herman. It was my day off after all, so really none of his beeswax what I was up to, but just the same I didn't want to see him. I slipped into the ladies' room and changed into the clothes I brought—a sleeveless white blouse, blue shorts, and sandals. Then I waited for Jack over by the back of the building where I could stay pretty much out of sight.

The girls were almost as excited as me, especially April. She was always excited about anything involving fellas. "You look pretty as a picture," she said. "He won't be able to keep his mitts off of you."

I said, "Oh goodness, April." I was hoping she was right, but I was also sort of afraid she was right.

"Jiggers! Here he comes now," April said, and she wasn't fooling. The sky-blue Buick was coming down the street.

Then she yelled, "Places, everyone!"—whatever that was supposed to mean. Jack pulled in, and seeing me standing there with the girls I figured he would hunker down in the car and wait for me. But he got out and came over to say hello to the girls. Then he walked me back to the car with his hand on my elbow and opened the passenger door for me like a perfect gentleman. I was so proud April and the girls were seeing all this.

When Jack got me situated and went back around to the driver's side, I leaned over and pushed his door open for him. And you know what? He said, "I never saw a girl do that before." He didn't say it was good or bad, just said he never saw it before. That was just like him. Lots of times he'll say something or just look at you a certain way, and you can't tell what he means. Or he might say one thing and mean another. He can really keep you guessing.

There's not a whole lot to see between Birch Lake and Ladysmith. You go over a corner of the lake near the beginning and you go over the Flambeau River toward the end. In between there's just a

120

scrubby farm here and there, some billboards, and open spaces with a few stumps mixed in.

I watched the shadow of the car float along the shoulder of the road, and I felt like I was floating myself.

"It sure was nice of you to get out and walk me back to the car," I said.

"Don't mention it," Jack replied. "We aim to please."

"I bet the girls were very impressed."

"I guess it don't take much then." He flicked his spent cigarette out the window.

The fair was interesting. They had some 4H type stuff, giving out blue ribbons and that, and lots of carnival games and rides. And they had the queen and her court, which two out of the three were okay looking, I guess. The queen was called the Fairest of the Fair. I thought that was pretty clever.

As soon as we got to the fair, Jack knew where he was going and there wasn't any two ways about it. I was holding his hand, and he was sort of pulling me along. It reminded me of the way you see a person being dragged by a dog they're supposed to be walking.

First we came to the balloons and darts game. The balloons were taped to the wall, and you threw darts at them. You had to pop at least two balloons out of three throws to win a prize. Jack stepped up there and popped three balloons with his first three shots.

The carnival man said, "Hey hey, it's your lucky day!" Jack did that thing where you clasp your hands together into a ball and shake them once or twice on either side of your head.

"You can take one of them little prizes now," the man said. "Or you can put the points you already got towards a bigger prize."

"I might as well keep going," Jack said. "I wouldn't want any of those prizes anyway."

121

But I did. They had all these different kewpie dolls, including a boy and girl hugging each other. They were precious. I pointed them out to Jack.

"Really?" he asked. "That's what you'd want?"

"Or you could keep on going," the man suggested.

Jack looked at the kewpies, and then at me, and then at the more expensive prizes on the top shelf. They had watches, a rod and reel, a baseball mitt, stuff like that. I could tell he was torn. "Please, Jack," I pleaded. "Would you get them for me?" And then I licked his ear! I realize that was sort of bold.

"Oh, why not?" Jack said. "It's no sweat off my back."

"That's the stuff," the man said. "Give the little lady what she wants." He handed me the hugging kewpies. "I'm sure you'll get repaid somehow, champ." And then as we turned to walk away, the man slapped Jack on the back, and a little cloud of chalk dust went flying up.

Did you know when a carnival man marks somebody with chalk, that's a signal to the rest of them meaning this fella is somebody that can be taken? I saw that in a movie.

I was holding the kewpies in one hand and Jack's hand in the other, and I pulled them all to my bosom. (Lots of people say "bosoms," but they are wrong.) "Thank you, Jack," I said. "I love them."

"I'm glad you're happy," he said.

"Do you know what their names are?" I asked.

Jack didn't answer. He just looked at me and smiled with his mouth closed.

"Jack and Jeannie, of course. And I'm gonna keep them forever."

We kept on going along the row of carnival games. I tried to brush the chalk off Jack's back the best I could without him knowing what I was doing. I didn't tell him about it for fear of hurting his feelings.

Anybody who's ever been to a fair or carnival knows all these games, since they're pretty much the same wherever you go. Jack wasn't interested in most of them, but the one that really got him was a baseball-throwing game. He tried that one over and over. The idea was to knock a little stuffed clown off a table and onto the ground.

I couldn't believe how hard Jack could throw a baseball. The man running the game said he couldn't either. "Gather round, folks!" he yelled. "You can tell all your friends you seen a kid that's faster than Bobby Feller." I was awfully impressed, but I didn't get the idea Jack was showing off for me. It seemed like he was doing it just because he wanted to, not to try and prove anything to me or anybody else. When Jack missed the clown, the ball smacked into the canvas behind it and sounded like a rifle shot. But when he hit the clown, no matter where he hit it or how hard he hit it, the clown just kind of spun around and then popped back up again, still grinning.

"Oh, so close, Rapid Robert!" the man said. "I bet one or two more tries, you'll get him for sure."

This went on for a while. Every so often I asked Jack if we could get some popcorn or go on some rides or whatever, and he said, "Sure, in a minute." I didn't really mind. It was sort of fun to see how engrossed he was in the game and how hard he tried. I enjoyed watching him throw, but I didn't want to spend the whole entire evening at it.

Finally Jack was able to pull himself away from the games and we got in line for the Ferris wheel. As soon as we did, the wind picked up, and these colored pennants they had everywhere started to flutter. Then hot-dog wrappers and stuff started blowing around. I got goosebumps on my arms. I rubbed each arm with the opposite hand.

"What the hell is this?" Jack said. "It ain't supposed to rain tonight." Just as he said that, a giant drop landed right between his eyes. We got on the Ferris wheel with some of these big drops falling now and then. By the time we got off, the drops were smaller but much closer together. Then, before you knew it, it was pouring cats and dogs.

There was an announcement on the loudspeaker: "Ladies and gentlemen, due to the inclement weather, we regret to inform you tonight's fireworks show will not be presented."

Jack pulled my hand close and wrapped it up in his arm. "Come on," he said. "We'll make our own fireworks." We ran back to the car and cuddled up together in the front seat. It was sort of awkward because neither one of us knew exactly what the other one was expecting. Also we were both sopping wet. Water was dripping off our hair into our eyes, rolling down our backs, and making puddles on the seat underneath us. It wasn't quite as romantic as you'd see in a movie.

We passed the time fooling around in the car for a while. Before I lost my head completely, I told Jack we better be heading back before it got too late. I didn't want to be a tease, but I also didn't want things to get completely out of hand right there at the fairgrounds with all those people around. Even if the windows were too fogged up to see into.

The rain let up on the way home. We held hands and didn't talk much. Normally I woulda hated sitting there in those wet clothes, but I didn't mind it this time. I felt like it was something Jack and I had to put up with together, which made it just fine.

We stopped back at the A&W so I could change back into my uniform—or my costume, as Jack calls it—for my father's benefit. Mr. Herman was in the office counting up the receipts, so he was out of the way. I got to put some dry clothes on, but poor Jack didn't. He never complained, though.

Naturally, April and the girls wanted me to fill them in on everything that happened, but Jack was waiting for me so I had to run. He drove me most of the way home and parked the car a ways from my house like always. "Guess what," he said as he switched off the ignition. "I just realized we been out all this time and I didn't get you anything to eat or drink. Plus we hardly went on any rides like you wanted to, on account of the rain. Some swell date."

"Don't say that," I told him. "It was perfect."

We started kissing goodnight, and once we started there was no stopping. After we got pretty far along, we jumped in the backseat and then we really did it. I mean we went all the way! You know, I can't really blame anybody, even myself. I don't feel like I got taken advantage of. I'm pretty sure I wanted to do it as much as Jack did. One thing I do regret, I got so carried away I forgot to ask Jack if he had anything to put on. That wasn't very smart, but I think he pulled out before it was too late.

After we were done, we cuddled for a while. I wasn't sorry or anything, just kind of dizzy. Jack was very sweet. He said, "I hope I didn't hurt you."

"Thank you for being gentle," I said. "That was my first time, in case you didn't know."

"Mine too," Jack said. Now there was a surprise for you. I assumed one of those city girls woulda already gave him the opportunity. I was sort of proud that we both had our first time together.

I got myself dressed again and kissed Jack goodnight (for real this time). Then I watched his taillights get smaller and smaller. That was a weird feeling.

I walked around the corner and got home right at the usual time. I went inside and made sure the screen door didn't slam. Wouldn't you know it, my father wasn't waiting up, so I didn't need to be wearing my uniform after all. Well, better safe than sorry. I tiptoed down the hall past my folks' room. They were both sound asleep.

I went in my room and threw my nightgown on. I got into bed, but just as my head landed on the pillow I remembered something. I got up and looked in my purse for my little hugging kewpies, Jack and Jeannie. I wanted them in bed with me. But I couldn't find them.

If they weren't in my purse, then where were they? Did I leave them on the Ferris wheel? Did I leave them at the A&W when I was changing my clothes? Did I leave them in Jack's car? Or did I drop them on the way from the car to the house? Maybe it sounds crazy, but I couldn't sleep until I at least tried to find them.

I got up and put my robe and slippers on. Then I crept down the hall and through the living room and right out the door. I made sure the screen door didn't slam. I retraced my steps back to where Jack dropped me off. I was lucky because nobody was around, but not lucky enough to find my kewpies.

I couldn't have been gone five minutes, but when I got back home the lights were on and my father was waiting for me.

"Parading around the streets in your nightclothes!" he yelled. "What kind of a daughter am I raising?"

I felt like saying, If you only knew. You'd be amazed.

He took a step toward me. "Do I smell cigarette smoke?"

"Lots of people smoke at the A&W, Dad."

"Lots of people smoke at the A&W. An answer for everything. Do they blow the smoke right into your face and hair?"

Then my father said I was grounded for a week. I called it being under house arrest. I could leave the house to go to work and church, but nowhere else. There wasn't any point in arguing about it, and there wasn't any way to explain what I was doing outside in my nightclothes. You want to know something funny? It was a very warm night, and the only reason I put my robe on over my nightgown was to be more modest out in the street! A lot of good it did me.

I went back to bed and didn't sleep a wink.

Jack took me to the fair on Thursday, the sixth of August. Him and his folks were going back to Chicago on Saturday the eighth. He didn't say yes or no when I asked if I'd see him Friday.

126

I was on pins and needles all day, wondering if I was going to see Jack or at least hear from him. He had my phone number, so he could call if he wanted to go to the trouble. Or better yet, he could just stop by—especially if he found my little hugging kewpies and wanted to return them. He could use that as an excuse to come over. Knock on wood, my father wouldn't be home at the time. I was under house arrest, but I guess I was still allowed to take a phone call or answer the doorbell.

We had a grandfather clock that ticked every single second and then gonged on the hour, so that was just about driving me nuts. It reminded me of a movie where the person is tortured by the sound of clocks ticking louder and louder until they throw theirself out the window or end up in the insane asylum.

Then I started to imagine something terrible happened to Jack, such as maybe he had an accident on his way back to Larry's. Maybe him and my kewpies were inside the sky-blue Buick at the bottom of the lake. If you ever saw the road out there, in some places it's only a few feet from the lake. There's no guardrails or anything. Of course, nobody would think to contact me, of all people, if he was laying in a hospital bed or worse.

I even got the phone book out and looked up Larry's Resort, but I didn't have the nerve to call over there and ask for Jack. I didn't want to be a nuisance. Finally it was time to go to work, and still no word from Jack. So I walked over to the A&W wondering if he was already gone from my life for good.

When I got to work, I searched high and low for the little kewpies but didn't find them. So then I knew they must be back at the fairgrounds or, hopefully, in Jack's car. I mean Jack's dad's car.

April wanted a complete play by play of the night before, but I had to put her off because I just wasn't up to it. I worked the whole shift in kind of a fog and kept on the lookout for the sky-blue Buick with Illinois plates. That car and the boy who drives it already mean an awful lot to me.

Come closing time, Jack still hadn't showed. I was just about to head home when Mr. Herman called me into his office. Oh great, I thought. What can this be about? I went in there and made darn sure to keep the door wide open.

He had the night's receipts spread out on his desk in front of his adding machine. Right next to that were my little hugging kewpie dolls, Jack and Jeannie! Mr. Herman pointed and said, "I believe this belongs to you?"

"Yes!" I exclaimed. "Where'd you get them?"

"A young man dropped it off this afternoon and asked me to give it to you."

I never thought I could say this about Mr. Herman, but I almost kissed him. "Thank you!" I said. I grabbed the kewpies in both hands and turned to leave.

"Wait," he said. "I almost forgot. This goes with it." He gave me a folded-up paper from his pocket. "Very interesting."

The note said: *Found on car seat this morning. Thanks for a swell time. Jack.*

My folks were asleep when I got home. I tiptoed past their room so I didn't wake them, but I doubt they coulda heard anything over my father's snoring. He was sawing logs to beat the band.

My mom is sweet as can be, but always sort of frail and sickly. As terrible as this sounds, I think she's afraid to be herself or even do much of anything, for fear my father will find fault with her. He seems to go out of his way to make everybody as miserable as him. It's really kind of depressing.

And then, all that flew right out of my head and went a zillion miles away. When I reached under the pillow to get my nightgown, a piece of paper flapped out. It said: *A boy name of Jack called this evening. Just to say hello he said. He sounded very nice. Mom.*

There isn't enough room between my bed and the desk for me to turn a cartwheel, or else I would've. I was so glad Jack called.

Tickled pink, as they say. It was just too bad he stopped by the A&W while I was at home and called the house while I was at the A&W.

Chapter 12

Don

Various locations, 1942–1943

The second time I went to Eau Claire to try and join the Army, they didn't turn me down. I guess they wasn't feeling quite so cocky by then. I wished I would of seen the same little weasely guy who turned me down the first time, but he wasn't there when I went back. Maybe it was his day off.

This was in the fall of '42. Rose was all better by then, and my ma finally agreed to leave me go. She didn't like it none, but a deal's a deal. I have to give my ma credit on that one. She went ahead and stuck to the deal. She knew damn well I was champing at the bit, and she didn't fight me over it no more than necessary. Of course, she cried and cried when it come time for me to head out, but you couldn't really blame her for that. I have to admit I might of shed a tear or two myself.

Anybody would call theirself damn lucky to have a ma like her.

I signed up for the infantry. I figured that's where the action would be the toughest. I wasn't gonna try and get off easy.

Uncle Sam sent me down to Fort Leonard Wood in Missouri for boot camp. It might sound crazy, but I didn't hate it all that much. It wasn't really as bad as they make it out to be. It wasn't as bad as I expected, anyways. It was hard work, but I was in pretty good shape so I done okay. Plus it was fall, getting to be winter, so that was good. I hear it's a hunnerd in the shade down there in summertime and humid as a fat guy's armpit.

I ended up getting put in an outfit called the Sixth Infantry. This outfit is nicknamed the Sightseers because they always get around to lots of different places. We got shipped out to Arizona for training on how to fight in the desert. We heard they was planning to send us to Africa to have a go at the Desert Fox.

We trained our ass off on this desert fighting for months. Then they pulled the rug out on us. Just when we pretty near had it down pat, they turned around and told us we was going to take on the Japs instead.

Man, was the guys pissed as hell! Here they thought they was gonna see Casablanca, and then maybe London, Paris, Rome, and have a chance to meet some nice gals to boot, and then they find out they're headed to New Guinea. We never even heard of the damn place before, much less figured on going there. What a kick in the shorts. The guys couldn't believe it.

I might of been the only one who was glad. To tell you the truth, I never was too excited about the idea of shooting some poor German family man to begin with. But a Jap? Now that's something else again, the way I look at it.

We trained in California on hand-to-hand fighting. Then we went to Hawaii to work on jungle fighting. Finally we was ready to go. It was about time, if you ask me. I was in the service almost a whole year already and I never fought nobody except this one loudmouth who got out of line in the barracks.

They say the slogan of the service is "Hurry up and wait." That's about right. Can you believe the first year I was in the Army I never got within four thousand miles of the enemy? I looked it up. Missouri is four thousand miles from France, and Hawaii is four thousand miles from Japan.

After we landed in New Guinea at a place called Milne Bay, the first thing I realized was anybody who use to complain about the heat and humidity back at Fort Leonard Wood didn't have nothing to kick about. This place was just like a steam bath.

Our first camp was on a palm tree plantation owned by the Palmolive Company. Isn't that something? My ma got a kick out of that when I wrote her. She must of pictured it as a pretty nice place. Maybe she figured we was getting free soap and face lotion and whatnot. I didn't tell her all them goddamn trees had to go. Otherwise the Japs would climb 'em during the night and then take pot shots at us when we got up in the morning.

Well sir, I didn't have to worry no more about being too far away from the enemy. The Japs was buzzing all around us like flies on shit.

You know what makes the Japs scary? They don't give a damn about getting killed. I heard that plenty of times before, but I never really believed it until I seen it with my own eyes. In fact, they'll go out of their way to get killed. You almost have to admire it. One of 'em would be setting up on top of a palm tree trying to pick off our guys while they was taking a leak or whatever. There wasn't no way in hell for him to get more than one or two shots off before we seen him and shot him out of the tree. These guys had to know that going in, but it didn't bother 'em none. Sometimes when we knew for sure the guy was out of ammo, why, we'd go ahead and saw the tree down with him still in it.

Like I say, I didn't tell my ma all them nice palm trees had to go. I didn't tell her you couldn't take a step anywheres in camp without sinking ankle deep in muck. I didn't tell her we had to pitch our tent on planks above the ground, because if it was on the ground you'd wake up swimming in leeches as big as your fist. I didn't tell her there's a thousand kinds of bugs and a hunnerd different diseases in the jungle you never heard of back home. I didn't tell her we always had the runs. I mean always.

I didn't tell my ma pretty near anything you do at home and never even think about, like eating good food, or sleeping in a bed, or wearing clean clothes, or turning on the faucet and having water come out (let alone hot water) is hard to even imagine over here.

I also didn't tell my ma if you was unlucky enough to get caught by the Japs, they'd make damn sure you wished you was never born. You know what they do when they got ahold of one of our guys? They tie him to a tree and use him for bayonet practice. That's not very friendly, is it?

I don't figure I oughta go any farther down this trail. There must be plenty of other places you can study up on the war in the Pacific if you want. Alls I know is our C.O. told us the only way to get our ass back home is to win the war, and the only way to win the war is to kill every last Jap.

That'll be a pleasure, if you ask me.

Chapter 13

Jeannie

Birch Lake, 1942–1943

You want to know the topper on this whole thing? I mean the end of my virginity. After I got the third degree from April and the girls umpteen times, I finally let slip what happened the night Jack took me to the county fair.

Then, as the discussion went along, I figured something out. From the questions they were asking, I could tell none of these girls ever did it before! Can you believe that? I'd have never guessed it.

My gosh, to hear them talk, you'd think they were in the habit of doing it like rabbits every time you turned around. Especially April. And then I come to find out I'm the only one who's actually done it and not just talked about it till I was blue in the face.

Well, that's what you get for believing what people tell you.

It took a while, but eventually I got it through my skull to try and be more realistic about Jack. I was counting the minutes when I shoulda been counting weeks and months. Or years, even.

After the night we went to the fair and ended up doing it in the car, we wrote back and forth to each other just like the year before. I usually kept my letters light and breezy, but sometimes I tried to hint at something more serious. If Jack ever picked up on it, I couldn't tell. Still, I had to give him credit for always replying. If he wasn't interested at all, he wouldn't have bothered, would he?

I knew enough not to mention L-O-V-E, unless he brought it up first. That woulda been a sure way to make him head for the hills.

Anyways, Jack and I kept writing the typical letters back and forth about this and that, nothing too unusual. And then one day I got something different.

Dear Jeanie.

Well my number came up. I got a nice letter from Uncle Sam inviting me to report for duty on March 31. Of course, April 1 is April Fools Day but this is no joke. I wont have my breakfast in bed any more. The letter said I am selected for training and service in the Land or Naval forces. I don't know where I will end up but wish me luck. I hope you are doing fine.

Love, Jack

If I never saw Jack when he was as close as Chicago, I sure as heck wasn't going to see him when he was sitting in some foxhole halfway around the world. Hopeless.

Do you know what I did? I took my father's car when he wasn't looking and drove out to Larry's Resort. That was the place I felt like I could feel Jack's presence or aura or whatever you want to call it. It was a raw, blustery day, and nobody was around. I didn't see Jack's friend Don. I think he was already in the service by then. The place wasn't open for the season yet anyways.

I had a screwdriver I borrowed from my father's workbench. There was a tree right next to the cabin Jack and his folks stayed in. The bark was pretty smooth, and I carved "J + J" into the trunk as best I could. I thought if Jack got killed in the war, God forbid, this message would be there from when he was still alive. Too bad the blade sort of slipped on the second "J," so it came out looking like a "J" plus a backwards "L."

Well, it's the thought that counts.

I wasn't looking to meet anybody when Bill came along. Don't they say good things happen when you least expect it?

Bill was on a crew of lumberjacks clearing the vacant lot behind the A&W. The job took them about a week, and Bill and the other guys would come over to use the men's room every so often. I guess this was when they had a number two. Of course, Mr. Herman wanted to charge them for it, so Bill said they'd each buy a root beer when they came over and Mr. Herman could call it square. Then we girls forgot to charge them for the root beers as soon as Mr. Herman had his back turned.

Bill's a big burly guy, kind of a Paul Bunyan type. He's over six feet tall with a big frame and thick reddish hair. He doesn't always shave. He would actually be a little scary if you didn't know him.

The first time Bill asked me out, I turned him down. I wish I could have a do-over on that one. He was so sweet and polite the way he asked. But I still had the idea I'd be cheating on Jack if I went out with somebody else. Here he was off somewhere fighting for our freedom, and I pictured myself being his faithful sweetheart waiting for him to return.

I had written to Jack a few times since his last letter and got no answers. Then finally I got a letter from his mom saying he was in the service all right and couldn't be reached at the address in Chicago. This was the very next day after Bill asked me out! Jack's mom said she'd forward my letters and then Jack could decide for himself whether to respond, but in the meantime there wasn't any sense writing to their home address. She also said I shouldn't feel bad if I didn't hear back right away, because Jack wasn't too good about writing to her either.

So now I had to stop and think about how ridiculous my situation with Jack was. The next day I tried to get Bill's attention when he came over to use the men's room, but he sort of avoided me. I'm sure he was embarrassed that I turned him down. After he went in the men's room, I waited outside the door for him to come out. He couldn't get out without practically bumping right into me.

He was kind of startled when he saw me standing there.

"Hi Bill!" I said.

"Hiya," he said. He was looking at the floor.

"Can I talk to you for a second?"

"Don't see why not."

"Listen," I said. "This is sort of awkward, but when you asked me out the other day, I shouldn't have said no. I was, uh, mistaken. If it's not too late, I'd like to change my answer."

He looked right at me. This was the first time I really got to see his piercing blue eyes. They are really striking. He said, "That'll be just fine with me."

Bill is from Stanley, which I'd never been to even though it's only a few towns over. Hell coulda froze over before we'd have met any other way than the way we did.

The first time he was going to take me out, Bill actually came by the house to pick me up and introduce himself to my parents. Bless his heart. My mom took to him right away, as I knew she would, being a generous type of person to begin with. My father didn't turn cartwheels or anything, but he also didn't throw Bill out of the house or forbid me to go on the date. That was about the best you could hope for.

Before I started seeing Bill, I never heard of guys and girls hanging around together, unless it was a dance or a couples party or something like that. I always thought the guys went one way and the girls went the other way, except when you were out on a date. But with Bill, he invites me to everything he's doing, even if

137

I'm the only girl there. It doesn't matter if they're hunting or fishing or having a barbeque or playing cards or just having a few beers in somebody's garage. No matter what it is, he always goes out of his way to include me. I really appreciate that.

Bill doesn't baby me or treat me like a girly girl. I had to learn how to get a slimy, wiggly worm onto a hook so it couldn't get off. I had to get used to holding onto a slippery, squirming fish while I removed the hook from its mouth. I promise you I've never met a fish that was willing to cooperate, even though they'd be a lot better off if they did.

Anyways, I've gotten to like fishing well enough. I'm sort of proud of myself for trying something I never did before and sticking with it. I've even gotten pretty good at it. I draw the line at ice fishing, though. If you're just looking for an excuse to drink, I don't know why you have to freeze your butt off at the same time.

When it comes to hunting, Bill and his friends aren't too picky. They'll hunt squirrels, rabbits, beavers, pheasants, quail, ducks, geese, wild turkeys, and (of course) deer. I'm probably forgetting a few. They never took me on a snipe hunt, so I'm grateful for that.

You know what Bill says about hunting? He says, "We need to be just as quiet as a frozen creek." Isn't that a great saying?

What's the difference between having a crush on somebody, being infatuated, and really being in love? I already knew how the first one felt. Probably everyone does. The other one is a lot more tricky. I know this much. It didn't take me too long to realize I was definitely in love with Bill. I couldn't tell you exactly when or where or how it happened, but it did. I'm sure of that.

By the time Bill went into the service, I was already pregnant. Isn't that something? I didn't say anything to him before he left, because I wasn't totally sure. I was still hoping it might be a false alarm.

Bill's dad rented out the American Legion hall in Stanley and threw a big going-away party. It was pretty crazy. I never saw anything like it before. You coulda gone swimming in the amount of beer and liquor these guys were putting away. And you know what? It wasn't the younger guys around Bill's age that made the biggest fools of theirselves. It was the older guys, the fathers and uncles and grandpas and that. Bill drank his share, but he didn't get out of hand like these other fellas. I was proud of him for that.

The next night we had our own going-away party, just Bill and I. We didn't go anywhere. We didn't drink anything. We just sat on the front steps of my house and talked. At one point my mom came out and offered us some cake and ice cream. We took it and thanked her, but we didn't eat any. The ice cream melted on the plates, and we went on talking for hours.

We talked about everything you can think of. We talked about what our future together might be like. We both want to move a long ways away when it comes time to set up house together. They call that wanderlust, and we both have it. We both want to have at least a few kids, but we didn't come up with an exact number. It wasn't just talking to hear ourselves talk. Both of us believed each and every word.

Finally, as much as we hated to admit it, it was time to say goodnight. Which meant it was time to say goodbye.

"I want you to know something," I said. "I love you and I always will."

"I love you too," he said. "And I don't say this just for the hell of it."

We kissed for a while, still sitting there on the steps, and then Bill got up to leave. I stood up too, and I ended up standing on one step higher than him. That made us just about the same height. He wrapped his big, strong arms around me. "I'll tell you something else," he said. "We belong together and we will be together, but I can't propose to you now. It wouldn't be fair because there's no way of knowing if or when I'll ever come back again."

"Bill…"

"Don't worry. It's all right. It wouldn't be fair to make you promise to wait around for years, maybe, and then wind up with nothing to show for it. If I come home safe and sound and you still feel the same way, why then you can be damn sure I'll marry you then. And I'll be the proudest guy in the world."

I was sobbing. I couldn't help it. Bill kept stroking my hair and saying, "It's all right, it's all right." Boy, did I ever want to believe him!

Chapter 14

Jeannie

Birch Lake, 1943

You can say what you want about my friend April. She might be silly and flippant and whatever else when it doesn't make any difference, but I'll tell you this much. When there is something really serious or important, she'll come through with flying colors.

A few days after Bill went in the service, April got her big sister Lynn to take me to the doctor so I could find out if I really was pregnant. At first I told April I would just go to the regular doctor in town, Dr. Nordquist, but she said I must be out of my mind. "As soon as you try and schedule the appointment," she said, "the first thing they'll do is call your folks to let them in on it. Before you know it, everybody in town will know. You might as well take out an ad in the paper. And here's the thing. Even if it's a false alarm, everybody will know you *thought* it was for real."

She was right, of course. If it was a false alarm, there was no reason to let my folks or anybody else know about it. And if it wasn't a false alarm, well then everybody would know soon enough anyways.

Lynn finagled some way to borrow the family car, and the three of us drove to Minneapolis to see this Dr. Smith, who Lynn knew about from a friend. She heard Dr. Smith wasn't too strict about what he could and couldn't do.

Lynn had pretended to be my mom when she called to make the appointment, and we were hoping they would take her for my mom when we got there. She put her hair in a bun and wore one of her mom's dresses to try and look older, but it didn't work.

The first thing the lady at the window did was ask if we were accompanied by a parent or guardian.

Leave it to April. She had an answer for that one. "Our dad is still looking for a place to park for free," she said. "He's rather thrifty. I'm sure he'll be here shortly."

"I wish him luck," the lady said. "He might have to walk a few blocks."

"At least it's not raining," April said.

"Yes, well," the lady said. "Go ahead and make yourselves comfortable. The doctor will see Jeannie as soon as possible."

We sat down in the waiting room. It was beyond depressing. The walls were painted a pukey yellowish-green color, and the lighting was bad. There were some potted plants, which were obviously fake. There was a fish tank with three or four fish inside looking very bored. And finally, there was a painting of a sad clown! He had a green derby hat, orange face, red rubber-ball nose, giant blue bow tie, and white circles outlined in black around his sad eyes and frowning mouth. I'm not kidding you.

There was one other woman waiting there. She kept thumbing through a LIFE magazine and didn't say anything or even look up. When it was her turn, the lady at the window called her Mrs. Crandall, not Miss, so I figured that was good news for her—but April thought maybe the lady said that just to throw us off the scent.

Not long after Mrs. or Miss Crandall went into the inner office, April got up and asked the lady at the window for the time.

"Let's see," the lady said. "I have five after eleven on my watch."

April looked at her own watch. "I'm showing six after," she said. "And what time was Jeannie's appointment supposed to be?"

The lady looked at her book. "Ten-thirty."

"Ten-thirty," April said. "So we are now some thirty-five minutes late, or thirty-six. Tell me, does the doctor start even his first appointment of the day on time? Or does he begin each and every day behind schedule?"

I bet this lady did find April amusing but didn't want to admit it. "I really can't speak to that, Missy," she said. "Perhaps you can take it up with the doctor, if you like."

"I think I'll do that," April said.

"By the way," the lady said. "Is your dad still looking for a place to park the car? I'd have guessed he'd have found one after thirty-six—oh, wait, thirty-seven—minutes of looking."

April sat back down. "This really frosts me," she said. "Why is it that you're expected to show up at 10:30—which was mutually agreed upon, mind you—and then you have to wait around until the doctor is good and ready to see you? As if you have nothing better to do. For Pete's sake, they wouldn't even need to have a waiting room at all if they weren't already planning to make you wait. Would they? The very idea of a waiting room would be unheard of."

"April," Lynn said. "That's enough. Just simmer down. Read a magazine."

"That's another thing!" April said. "Why is it that every magazine in these places is six months or a year old? Do they keep all the new magazines in a special warehouse someplace till they're six months old and then ship them out to all the doctors and dentists?"

The lady at the window asked to have a word with Lynn. They whispered back and forth for a bit, and then Lynn came back and sat with us again. "Well, she knows I'm not your mom," Lynn told me. "That one was easy." She chuckled. "She also knows our dad isn't coming. But she said the doctor will see you anyways, so long as we pay for it. Just like we figured."

I finally got in to see the doctor at 11:42. I know that because as soon as the lady said, "The doctor will see you now," April yelled. "Only seventy-two minutes late!"

143

Truth be told, this Dr. Smith gave me the willies right off. I mean, I know you have to get naked in front of a doctor and let him look at your private parts and that, but Dr. Smith was creepy. First he sat in a chair and watched me get undressed. Then it seemed like he was trying to act way too friendly. He was sort of whispering to me the whole time, like he was trying to get romantic or something.

I couldn't tell if all the poking and prodding and rubbing was called for or not. How can you tell? I don't know. The highlight was when he made me pee into a jar. I already expected that, because peeing into a jar is the key to the whole process. Anyways, he watched me do it instead of sending me behind a screen or turning his back at least. Then he sat in the chair again and watched me put my clothes back on.

"We should have the results of your test in two or three days," he said.

"Yes," I said. "That's what somebody told me."

His chair had wheels on it, and he rolled it closer to me. "What else did they tell you?" he asked.

"About what?" I said. "I don't know what you mean."

"Well," he said, "in any case. How would you like to receive your results? I mean, presuming you'd rather I didn't call you on the telephone at home."

I said he could call me at the A&W. I told him the number and he wrote it down.

"Fine, fine," he said. "Now let me ask you this. Suppose your test comes back positive, meaning that you're, uh, expecting. How would you feel about that?"

I was done getting dressed by then. "I don't know," I said. "I guess I'll cross that bridge when I get to it."

Dr. Smith clapped his hands together. "Ah," he said. "A girl who knows her own mind. Very good." He rolled his chair even closer, almost touching my toes. Then he stood up and kicked the chair back to the wall behind him. He put his hands on my shoulders. I tell you, I was just about ready to throw up.

"I'm always here to help you, Jeannie," he said. "If the test were to come back positive, for example, and you felt like you weren't quite up to it, why, there are other measures that could be prescribed."

You can believe me when I tell you I couldn't get out of there fast enough.

I'm sure you can guess what happened next. A couple days later I was working at the A&W when they told me I was wanted on the phone. Sure enough, it was Dr. Smith.

"Hello, Jeannie," he said in that same whispery voice I already hated. "Well, I don't know if it's good news or not, but you're going to be a mom."

"I take it the rabbit died," I said.

"You know, that's funny," he said. "That's a common misconception. In point of fact, the rabbit always dies, regardless of whether the test is positive or negative. You see, the test requires conducting an autopsy on the rabbit."

"Well anyways, thanks for calling."

"Remember, dear, if you have any concerns or you should ever need anything at all—"

I hung up on Dr. Smith. Okay, so I was pregnant. Knocked up. I wasn't surprised at all. Now that it was a real fact and not a "what if," I didn't feel too panicky about it. Sure there would be big trouble when my father found out. Sure it would be nice if Bill and I were already married. But sometimes you just have to shut your trap and play the cards in front of you. I was carrying a little baby inside me that was half Bill and half me. And no matter how hard I tried, I couldn't see how that could possibly be a bad thing.

PART THREE

Love in the young requires as little of hope as it does of desire to feed upon.

– William Faulkner, *Light in August*

Chapter 1

Jeannie

Birch Lake, 1943–1944

When I told my parents I was expecting, my father didn't say, You're my daughter and I'll always love you through thick and thin. We all make mistakes. After all, nobody's perfect except our lord and savior Himself. We'll get through this together, and I'll welcome your baby into the family with open arms. I can't wait to be a grandpa!

That woulda been nice, wouldn't it? I bet that's exactly what Bill would say to a daughter of ours if she found herself in the same predicament. But my father never said any such thing. It woulda never crossed his mind.

My father didn't literally throw me out of the house. I guess he felt more of an obligation as a parent than that. But just barely.

To give you an idea what it was like, I wasn't allowed to have meals at the table with the rest of the family. I was supposed to eat in my own room. My mom could do my laundry, but only if she kept it separate from everybody else's. I wasn't allowed to sit in the front room and listen to the radio, unless I was by myself. If my father came in to read the paper or whatever, I was supposed to scram. I wasn't allowed to be part of any family activities. When they went to church on Sunday, or had a little picnic in the back yard, or were invited over to somebody's house, I was supposed to stay shut up in my room or, better yet, just crawl under a rock someplace.

My mom is one of these ladies whose biggest thrill in life is taking care of her husband. Even if he is a thousand percent wrong and she knows it, she'd never dream of saying so. But don't get me wrong. I love her very dearly. She does whatever she can for me. When my father wasn't around, she acted like nothing was wrong, and she told my brother and sister to do the same. I can't say enough nice things about her. Her only fault is not believing in herself enough.

I ended up spending more and more time at April's. "You're welcome here any time day or night," her mom told me. "There's always room at the inn." At first I just went over there during the daytime to get a break from the atmosphere at home. Then I started staying overnight a couple times a week. Finally, when I started showing pretty good, I stayed there practically all the time. That's what really started people thinking my father had tossed me out. I never bothered to correct them.

If you want to know the truth, I wasn't too concerned about how my folks felt about my situation or how the neighbors felt or how the man in the moon felt about it. The only person whose opinion really counted to me was Bill.

It was horrible to think I couldn't tell him face to face. I couldn't even tell him by telephone. My gosh, a five-minute phone call woulda been a million times better than a whole slew of letters back and forth, because in a letter you can't really get the tone of the other person. Even if somebody is bending over backwards to try and be agreeable, there can still be misunderstandings.

Here's what I think. I think when you write a letter and mail it, it's already dead as far as you're concerned, and it only comes to life again when the other person not only gets it but holds it in their hands and actually reads it. When I folded the letter and put it in the envelope, in my mind's eye I saw Bill's hands holding it.

I love Bill's hands, and I know exactly what they look like. They are large and brown. They have little blond hairs and a few little freckles on the backs of them. The fingers are sort of fat. The right index finger and the left thumb are crooked, because they got broken and never fixed. And the nails are all pretty sad, because Bill bites them when he is not hitting them with a hammer or whatever.

I could see those hands unfolding the letter and holding it with the thumbs on the front side and the other fingers on the back.

I could see Bill's hands holding the letter, but I couldn't tell what they would do after his eyes read it. Would they tear it into confetti and throw it up in the air? Would they wad it into a ball and toss it onto a dung heap? Would they fold it up and put it back in the envelope and slide it into a pocket? Or would they hug it to Bill's chest like it was the baby itself and not just news about the baby?

Well, ladies and gentlemen, the hands I saw in my mind's eye wrote me the nicest letter I ever got.

Dearest Jeannie.

Your letter was dated 5 wks before I got it. God knows how long it will take you to get this. It makes me sick to think of you waiting around to find out how I took the news not to mention you haveing to go thru the whole thing by your self.

I was very stupid to get you in to this position but I will make it up to you. I am the proudest guy in the world to be the dad of your baby and God willing a few more in the future also.

I hope they are not all giveing you a tough time for not being married just yet but you can tell them for me, we are all ready married in our own mind and any body that doesnt like it can stuff it. Also tell them they can look forward to us putting on a

151

swell ceremony when the time comes. If they are nice to you

maybe they will get invited.

I will write to your Dad right away and tell him I'm sorry for

jumping the gun and it wasnt none of your fault.

Please do me one favor and dont ever forget I love you. I will

write more as soon as I can. I hope you get my letters in the right

order. But if you dont I hope you can still make sense out of them.

So long for now.

Your loveing Husband Bill

I'm pretty green and not all that smart, but I know one thing. I know it's very easy for people to write all kinds of stuff in a letter they'd never have enough nerve to say to your face. You shoulda seen this one letter April's boyfriend Johnny sent her. He went on and on about how he couldn't wait to do this and that to her, all these different things I'm not even sure are possible, when they've never even done it before in real life.

Bill doesn't write anything he wouldn't say, and he wouldn't say anything he didn't mean.

I don't have to worry about Bill. I mean, I could worry about him getting killed or maimed, like you would with anybody who's off fighting in the war. But I'm not worried about him ditching me and leaving me on my own with his baby. He never gave me any reason to think that way.

All this time it seemed like I wasn't fish or fowl. I wasn't married, technically anyways, and I wasn't single. I wasn't really living at home and I wasn't really living with April's family. I wasn't a mom yet but I was gonna be sooner than later. Everything was sort of in between. It was pretty awkward.

You know what's sort of funny? How I used to drive myself nuts wondering if or when I was gonna hear from Jack. I mean back before I met Bill. My gosh, even when I did get a letter from Jack, practically all I did then was start waiting for the next one. What a way to live. Of course, when I don't hear from Bill as often as you'd like, it isn't because he's too busy dating cheerleaders and that. There might be a gazillion reasons why I wouldn't hear back from Bill right away, but none of them are silly ones. Lots of them are very scary.

As far as Jack is concerned, I still think about him once in a while. I hope he's doing okay for himself. Whenever I remember to pray at bedtime, I pray for Bill and Jack and Roger Hagenmeyer and all the other fellas in the service. I don't think there's anything strange about that. Anybody would do the same thing.

Dr. Nordquist always seemed satisfied with "our progress," as he liked to say. Whenever I saw him, he said we were following the script line for line. I guess that meant everything was going according to plan. We're just talking about the medical side now. There was no plan for the rest of it. The only plan was to make it through the delivery okay and then keep a roof over our head while we waited for the war to be over with and Bill to come back.

You know, everybody always talks about how brave the boys are, fighting in the war, and that's great. I'm not knocking it. But girls and women also need to be brave in our own way, don't we?

If I give myself credit for anything, it's for not feeling too sorry for myself. My situation isn't all that bad, really. I feel more sorry for Bill. He's the one who was half a world away when his baby was born. He's the one who could be killed any minute and wouldn't get to see his baby until the next life.

Julia May Andressen was born on May 17, 1944, at St. Joseph's Hospital in Chippewa Falls. They asked me which last name to put down on the birth certificate. "Are you kidding?" I said. "Why, her dad's, of course!" That was the first time I ever called Bill her dad out loud.

She was just a little peanut, less than five pounds, but she had all her parts in place and everything working the way it should. Right off you could tell she has Bill's reddish hair. April said maybe I should name her Ginger, but I said we better not because the other kids at school would probably end up calling her Ginger Ale. You have to think about things like that before you name your baby.

I named her Julia because that's my mom's name and May because that's the month she was born in. April's folks named her after the month she was born in, and May comes after April, so there you go! My best friend and my very own daughter. Two spring babies.

Holding Julia in my arms, feeding her, seeing her smile at me (even if it is only gas like they say)—my gosh, there's no way to describe it.

Chapter 2

Don

The Philippines, 1944–1945

I don't mind telling you, we didn't have no walk in the park on New Guinea. Did you ever hear of the Battle of Lone Tree Hill? You can go over to the library and read up on it if you want.

I figure I done my part like anybody else, but I don't want to try and take too much credit. I was in the thick of it a few times on New Guinea, but in the Philippines it seemed like every place I went was already simmering down by the time I got there. They call it a combat zone if the enemy is anywheres nearby, but you usually end up killing time instead of killing Japs. To be honest with you, I can't say for sure if I killed any Japs or not. I fired a few shots at 'em and tossed a grenade every now and then, but I never actually seen how much damage I might of done.

I also never actually seen a Jap take a shot at me, you know, aiming right at me and nobody else—even though they must of from time to time. Sometimes a bullet will hit someplace close by, a tree branch or something, and you don't know if it was meant for you or not. You just duck down and shoot back at wherever you think it come from. Anyways, not knowing if it was meant for you wouldn't make no difference if it hit you. You wouldn't be no less dead.

I don't think people back home can picture this, but if there's a real battle going on, it's so noisy and confusing you don't know your ass from your elbow. You can't hardly tell where your own guys are at and where the Japs are. The Japs might be in front of you, behind you, on your left, on your right, or all around you.

155

You just hope to God you don't kill one of your own guys. I don't know how you could live with yourself if you did.

As soon as I told my ma we was in the Philippines, from then on she asked in pretty near every letter if I met MacArthur yet and shook his hand. I never did, but I probably should of went ahead and told her I did. Wouldn't of costed me nothing, and she would of gotten a kick out of it. Anyways, I wasn't there when MacArthur marched out of the surf in his dress shoes. That would of been something to see. Don't you think it was quite a coincidence all the photographers and newsreel guys happened to be there waiting for him?

Anybody who's ever been in the service will tell you the most aggravating thing is how much time you spend standing around with your thumb up your rear. It really does get old, but being bored silly sure as hell beats getting your head shot off.

The guys are always making up little games or skits or what have you just to have something to do. Of course we aren't spose to gamble, but you couldn't hardly stop it. Some guys will bet on anything you can think of, such as how much time it'll take somebody to drop a load. I mean down to the second.

Stuff you would never dream of doing at home, like setting around and whittling, guys will do for hours on end. You can't blame 'em, because there ain't nothing else to do. One time there was a big rumor Bob Hope was coming. He really did come, but it was about a week after we shipped out to someplace else. By the way, if anybody tries to say anything against Bob Hope to you, do me a favor. Spit in their eye for me and tell 'em I said so.

The war was pretty near over when I met Maricel. How it happened, my outfit had a couple days of R&R in Manila. This one night me and some buddies tied one on pretty good in this dime-a-dance joint. Next thing you know, I woke up in some cruddy rented room.

I was in my skivvies in the bed. My clothes was wadded up on the floor. Maricel was in the bed with me. I could tell she was in her slip, not naked, because I seen her shoulder straps. I didn't know if I already took advantage. If I did, it was too bad I couldn't remember, because it would of been well worth remembering. Believe you me.

She is very pretty. I mean *very* pretty. At first I was just going by her face, because the rest of her was under the sheet. But even at that, you could tell she was way better looking than any girl who'd ever give me the time of day back home. Big brown eyes, jet-black hair, smooth dark skin.

"Sorry," I says. "I was pretty tight last night. I didn't mean to take advantage."

She just laughed. "You didn't do nothing," she says. "You couldn't do nothing."

Then she got up out of bed and made me turn around while she threw her dress on over her slip. It was a sleeveless dress that went about to her knees, kind of orange with yellow flowers on it. You could see some cleavage, but not enough to where she was overdoing it. One of her shoulder straps kept sliding down her arm. That was awful cute.

Maricel ain't much more than five foot tall, maybe a hunnerd pounds if that, with a damn nice shape to her.

Once I set up and shook some of the cobwebs out, we got to talking. I could remember her name without asking, so I had that much going for me. She filled me in on the last hour or two of the night before, the part that was hazy. Her English ain't half bad. She has an accent, but you can understand her pretty good. She told me where I could find my buddies, who were more or less in the same condition. Or maybe not quite. Then she laughed again.

I really liked her laugh. And the look she had in her eyes, like she was smarter than she was letting on. I asked her to have coffee with me after I got dressed, and she said yes.

"One thing I don't understand," I says after we talked a while. "So I passed out. I know that much, anyways. But then why did you stick around all night for nothing?"

"Not for nothing," she says. Then she reached into her brassiere and pulled out a sawbuck.

I must of made a face.

"No, no," she says. "Don't you remember? You made me take it. You said buy me something nice." She laughed again.

"Well, that's fine," I says.

"You want it back?"

I was out ten bucks and didn't even hold hands with her yet, for all I knew. But when you think about it, she could of cleaned me out but good and disappeared while I was sleeping it off. I mean, if she was the type to do a thing like that.

"Naw, I don't want it back," I says. "But there might be more where that come from."

She put both of her hands around my forearm. "I like you," she says. "You are nice gentleman."

"Well, you just stick with me then," I says. "I mean if you want to."

"I will like that," she says. She wrote down her name and address on the inside of a matchbook and give it to me. Maricel Cruz at such-and-such address. I always thought Cruz was a Mexican name, which goes to show you how much I know.

Maricel was the first girl that ever let me do it to her. I don't know why she did, because I never asked her. Alls I can tell you is I'm glad she did. To hear her with her girlfriends and whatnot, you wouldn't think she's talking about the same guy I see when I look in the mirror. You would think she was talking about somebody more good looking, more interesting, more well off, you name it.

Finally I just figured, hell, why question it? If she feels that way, then just thank your lucky stars and go on from there.

Our outfit got to stay in Manila after we got done mopping up around the outskirts, so that meant lots of time with Maricel. After while I figured we were a package deal, like peanut butter and jelly or ham and eggs or whatever. By God, she hasn't gave me no reason to think we couldn't stay together forever. I already figured on asking her to marry me and then take her back home with me. What a hell of a thing, when you think about it.

After V-J Day, all us guys didn't hop right on a boat and go home to a ticker-tape parade the next day. We still had some work in front of us yet. For a while it looked like we'd get sent to Japan to handle the occupation over there, but we ended up going to Korea instead. When it come time for me to shove off, Maricel cried and cried until I decided to go ahead and marry her right there in Manila. I never had any gal cry over me before.

I didn't have to ask for nobody's permission to get hitched to Maricel. Her folks are gone, God rest their soul. She told me they got killed in the war, but I don't know nothing more than that. She won't talk about it. Anyways, the point being we was on our own planning the big wedding. I would of been just as happy going to the nearest justice of the peace, but Maricel said we'd burn in hell for all of eternity if we didn't get married in the church. That would make you stop and think, wouldn't it?

I figured if it was gonna make Maricel happy and get us off on the right foot as man and wife, there wasn't no harm looking for a priest to do the job for us. After all, I'm Catholic myself, even if I ain't as Catholic as Maricel. We found this guy named Padre Felix de los Santos who said he'd marry us in his church for fifteen bucks.

My best man was Archie Matthews, a buddy of mine from the unit. Archie's a hell of a guy. He's from Deer Isle, Maine. Sounds like a nice town, don't it? Maricel's sister Angela stood up with her. There wasn't no organist or nothing like that. There was one altar boy, who took a picture of the four of us and the padre with Archie's camera. Archie tipped him four bits for that.

So that's the story of mine and Maricel's wedding. We got married in an empty church by a padre who kept forgetting our names. We didn't have no reception, just a bottle of champagne Archie brought. We sure as hell didn't have no honeymoon. I wish I could of gave my bride a little better than that.

Chapter 3

Jeannie

Birch Lake, 1945–1946

I hope it isn't too uncouth to say so, but I was pregnant again about ten minutes after Bill got home from the war.

I didn't know it yet when we had our little wedding at the justice of the peace in Stanley. April stood up with me, and Bill's brother Karl stood up with him. My brothers showed up, and so did my folks! I don't know how much arm twisting my mom did on my father, but she got him there somehow. He behaved himself as well as you could expect. I mean at least he shook Bill's hand, for crying out loud. Do you know what he said to Bill while he was at it? You'd never guess. He said, "It's never too late to right a wrong."

It wasn't exactly the wedding I pictured when I was a little girl, but I really can't complain. One good thing was Julie got to be the flower girl. She was about twenty months old. She did a great job. Everybody said she was just precious. The only thing was, we kept trying to get her to call Bill "Daddy," but she wouldn't do it. She kept calling him "Mister."

How many old married ladies can say this? Two of my kids were at my wedding. One was the flower girl, and another was already growing inside me.

Bill's folks invited everybody over for burgers and beer after the ceremony. I guess that was where my father drew the line, because him and my mom didn't come. I felt bad for Mom, because she loves Bill and little Julie very dearly, of course. That's what people like Mom do. They love everybody, but they love certain people even more.

You know what frosts me? You couldn't hardly ask for a better son-in-law than Bill. My gosh, what the heck do you want? He did darn well for himself in the service, and he has the citations to prove it. He came straight home and married me afterwards, just like he said he would. He'd never run out on anything. Whatever happens, he just accepts it and doesn't moan and groan about it. Plus he's always bending over backwards to be nice to my folks and my brothers. Do you think my father appreciates it? If he does, I guess you'd say he's got a strange way of showing it.

We rented a run-down little house not too far from Bill's folks and planned our escape. Bill found the names and addresses of these different logging outfits all around the country, and he started writing to them. The first response he got was from Calumet, Michigan. That's in the U.P. It wasn't as far away as we really wanted, but we had already made up our mind to go someplace else as soon as we could. We both knew you can't start hesitating on something like this, or else you might as well just ditch the whole plan. Neither of us had ever been to Calumet or even heard of it before, but we figured, it might turn out to be as good of a place as any. We decided to give it a try.

This is kind of funny, but Calumet is the name of the high school my old boyfriend Jack went to in Chicago. I wonder if that's supposed to be a sign or an omen or just a plain old coincidence.

One Sunday afternoon not long before we headed off to Michigan, we went out to a picnic grove along the river. It was a gorgeous day. Really, it was fantastic. We grilled up some brats and had a few beers. I was very pregnant by this time, and I don't know if I got a little dizzy from that or the beers or what, but when I looked out at the water, it seemed like it was standing still and we were the ones moving. Isn't that weird?

162

Bill wanted to teach Julie how to skip a stone on the water. "I don't care if it takes all day," he told her. "You need to get one to skip at least three times." He made believe to be very stern and serious about the whole business, but Julie saw through it right away and giggled at everything he said.

First Bill picked up a large, round rock almost the size of his head and threw it into the water. Naturally, it landed with a thud and a giant splash.

"Well," Bill said. "That wasn't any good, was it?"

Julie peed her drawers. I like to think it was from giggling at Bill and not just a coincidence.

"I wonder if a flatter type of stone will work better," Bill said. "What do you think, Mommy?"

"I think that's a swell idea," I said. "Let's try it out."

"Yes, let's do that," Bill said. He picked up a likely stone and tossed it sidearm towards the water. It skipped four or five times before it disappeared. Julie couldn't have been more delighted. "Now we've got it figured out," Bill said. "We just need to find the right kind of stones."

The three of us went around collecting the flattest stones we could find, and then it was Julie's turn to throw. She threw a few herself, as best she could, and then Bill started helping her throw—you know, sort of guiding her arm and tossing the stone for her without letting her know he was. I guess this woulda gone on all afternoon if Julie didn't happen to spot a turtle sunning itself on the river bank. "Daddy, look!" she cried, pointing to the turtle.

She called Bill "Daddy"! Bill and I looked at each other. I wish I knew the right words to describe how I felt.

Bill picked up the turtle and carried it around in his hat until we got home. We ended up naming the turtle Stanley, and of course we've kept him. Actually, I don't really know if Stanley is a him or not. I'm not that interested in checking, even if I knew how. But either way, Stanley means a lot to me. He always re-

163

minds me of the day Julie called Bill "Daddy" for the first time and the way Bill looked at me when she did.

I think that was practically the happiest day of my life. At least so far. I swear I'll never forget it.

Chapter 4

Carol

Chicago, 1946

I went to the same school, St. Gregory's, from first grade all the way through high school, and I accepted everything that was presented to me without question. I made good grades, was devout, never sassed back, even volunteered to help out after school by cleaning erasers or reshelving library books or something.

The sisters often said that each of us had a permanent record that would follow us everywhere, so we might as well make good for ourselves. There was no telling what might happen to someone who made a bad record. They certainly wouldn't amount to much. The sisters always held that over our heads, the permanent record, and why not? It worked for them.

I grew up completely convinced that if you were industrious, reliable, punctual, kept your nose clean, you would get ahead in this world. No need to toot your own horn. People would recognize your value and reward you for it. Hogwash, of course.

When we graduated, it was time to go to work. Without college, you can be a waitress, a maid, a sales clerk, or a secretary. That's about it, as far as I know. Well, there's one other option, which I'm not sure would suit me or vice versa. So I became a secretary at the CTA. My dad has some connections there. If you look reasonably presentable and have enough sense to answer the phone, type, file, get coffee, and mind your manners, then you'll have no trouble making the grade as a secretary—or actually, as a girl. That's what they call us, girls. As in, "Have your girl call my girl to schedule lunch next week."

A lot of these fellows, they look you up and down pretty good. Give you the once-over and not even try to be subtle about it. Some of the girls get their behinds pinched or something from time to time. Sometimes more than that. I hear things from my friends. A lot of it's probably embellished, I don't know. At any rate, I can honestly say I've never had to put up with that sort of thing. I don't know why, exactly, but no one in the office has tried to take any liberties with me. They might be disappointed if they did, because I might as well have VIRGIN tattooed on my forehead.

One of my girlfriends actually married her boss. Rita Grunwald. The man left his wife and three kids for her. That was quite a scandal around the office. If you can fathom this, the poor girl was fired but the man was not. I guess it was supposed to be her fault for enticing him, rather than his for straying. We all thought it was outrageous, but Rita didn't really mind because she was planning to quit anyway once they got married. We had a little going-away party and bridal shower for her at one of the gals' apartment. I lost touch with her after that and never knew if the marriage lasted or not. That was too bad. I always wondered how it turned out.

Most of us take it for granted that we'll quit working as soon as we get married or, at the very latest, when the first baby is on the way. That seems to be a given, even for the gals who are a little bit older and are making pretty good money. Even ones that the rest of us have already written off as old maids talk about getting married someday.

I had a few boyfriends before I met Jack. Nothing too serious. Of course, it all seems very serious when you're going through it, but in reality it was nothing of consequence. Just high-school dances and that kind of thing.

The first time I saw Jack was not the first time he saw me. This I found out later. He saw me on the L and followed me to work.

166

He trailed me right into the Mart and found out which floor I worked on. Cross my heart, I never noticed.

So the first time I saw him, or remembered seeing him at least, was one day I came out of the building with a couple girlfriends, and we were going over to Field's for lunch. It must have been an occasion of some sort, because we usually bring our lunches to work.

It was spring. Well, not quite spring. March. False spring, you might call it—a warm, sunny day and awfully windy. If I recall correctly, it snowed several inches the very next day. When we came out, our skirts were blowing around and we had to try and hold them down.

Jack caught my eye. He was standing off to the side, leaning against the railing along the river. He glanced at us and very nonchalantly flicked his cigarette butt over the railing. I thought, what kind of person tosses a cigarette butt in the river?

A few days later he marched right up to my desk and asked me out. He didn't even introduce himself first. I didn't know what to think. He said that his schedule for Saturday night had unexpectedly opened up.

I was taken aback all right, but at the same time I had to give him credit for having a lot of nerve. He is handsome, too. Anyone would have to admit that. Medium height, athletic looking, big shoulders, narrow waist, dark hair, dark penetrating eyes. He carries himself in an appealing way. There really is something sort of charismatic or magnetic about him. And also I was thinking if I say no, he's going to have to turn around and slink out of here humiliated. Because I imagined that everyone in the room was watching us and listening. Maybe they weren't. But anyway I didn't know how I could say no. I said yes mostly out of politeness. Then I asked what his name was.

When I told the other gals about it, my friend Janice said he'd been hanging around the building for a couple weeks, flicking butts everywhere.

167

On our first date, Jack and I went for chop suey and then we saw *The Postman Always Rings Twice*, with Lana Turner. I gather he's quite a Lana Turner fan, but I found the movie a little too sordid for my taste. I might've preferred to see *The Bells of St. Mary's* for the third or fourth time!

If it was up to me, I'd have guessed the girl's husband would kill the boyfriend, rather than the other way around. I guess that shows you how much I know. On the bright side, John Garfield played the boyfriend, and I've always liked him. Actually, Jack reminds me of Garfield quite a bit. I mean the way they're built, the way they move, and the way their eyes kind of dart around.

Jack picked me up at home. He was very polite and reserved around my parents, and mostly silent while we drove to the restaurant. He did the little things right, such as opening doors and holding the chair for me. He was also impeccably dressed and groomed.

Our conversation over dinner was a little strained at first, but not embarrassingly so. Jack looked around and made some unflattering but accurate remarks about the décor in the place, which was a bit tacky. "Well, let's hope the food's good anyhow," he said. Then he asked me a few questions about myself and my upbringing, and I asked him the same ones.

In case you're interested, here's what was revealed. My folks are Irish immigrants who met soon after arriving in Chicago. My mom was a hired girl in a house that my dad delivered coal to. After they were married, my dad went to night school for years and eventually became a lawyer. My folks have become rather well off over the years, but please don't call them lace-curtain Irish. My mom would be mortified.

Jack's folks are both of German extraction. They met at work. Jack's mom was a telephone operator and his dad was a lineman who reported to the same office.

I have two older brothers and Jack is an only child. I went to St. Gregory's and he went to Calumet High School. We're both Catholic, although he said he and his folks "aren't fanatics about it." I took that to mean they don't always go to Mass. I think maybe they're the kind who only go on Easter and Christmas.

We also established that my family follows the White Sox and his follows the Cubs. You might think that's backwards, given that we're North Siders and they're South Siders, but there you have it. My dad told me once that in the old days it was a given that any Irishman you met was a Sox fan and any German a Cubs fan. Maybe that explains it, even after all these years.

"You're kidding me," Jack said. "You live a mile from Wrigley Field and you're Sox fans?"

I don't know if he was pulling my leg, but he acted as if he really couldn't believe it. At the same time, though, he seemed to see nothing strange about a Cubs fan growing up in the shadow of Sox Park. Being diplomatic, I said, "Well, we follow the Cubs too."

When we got back in the car to go to the show, he opened the passenger door for me, got me situated, and then passed gas, rather loudly, while he was walking around to the driver's side. Having grown up with my brothers and their friends, I understand that guys consider farting to be hilarious. It's sort of a hobby for them. I thought it was sweet for Jack to pass gas outside the car instead of right in front of me. Naturally, I pretended that I hadn't heard. But after we got to know each other better, in an unguarded moment I let slip that I had. As soon as I did, I wished I hadn't, because I was afraid I'd embarrassed him.

I needn't have worried. "Oh, I knew you heard," he said blandly. "You'd have to be deaf not to."

In truth, Jack's roughness is one of the things I like about him. Not the farting or swearing per se, but just a general attitude he has. If you like me, fine. If you don't, too bad. If he thinks someone has insulted me or looked cross-eyed at him, he'll tell that

169

person off in no uncertain terms. It can be a sales clerk, a waiter, a bartender, a ticket taker, a bus driver, a parking-lot attendant, anybody at all. It could be a cop, even.

He's not at all afraid of someone hauling off and taking a swing at him. In fact, he seems to hope they will. Although there have been a few close calls, he's never actually gotten into a fight in my presence. When he's out with his buddies he'll occasionally get into a skirmish, as he calls it, but he's good enough to refrain from that sort of activity when I'm around.

I haven't asked him, but I have the strong impression that Jack had quite a few girlfriends before me. He has a way of looking at women, and they at him, that you can't fail to notice. Furthermore, he was in Italy and France during the war, and I tend to believe the stereotype that all the guys were warmly welcomed by the women they came across over there.

All this being said, though, he was sort of awkward with me, at least at the beginning. Diffident is a good word. He would hardly hold my hand or try a goodnight kiss on our first few dates.

Later on, Jack's mom confided that he'd told her when we started dating that he "wasn't quite sure how to woo such a classy gal." Of course, this implied that he was more accustomed to another type. Mind you, she was quoting him without his being there to defend himself, but I had no reason to doubt her. She seemed to mean it as a compliment, but I wasn't sure whether it really was, or to whom.

Chapter 5

Don

Birch Lake, 1946

After I got shipped out to Korea, me and Maricel wrote back and forth all the time. Her writing isn't the best, but then again mine isn't neither. Come to think of it, the only difference is hers keeps getting better the more she works at it, and mine just stays the same. We can usually understand each other, at least.

Before I forget, let me tell you something about Korea. You can have it, far as I'm concerned. I oughta be thankful I was only there a few months before Uncle Sam cut me loose.

Anyways, it's a damn good thing I went ahead and married Maricel back in Manila, because if I'd of waited and tried to get her over to the States to get hitched, it would of been pretty near impossible. They wasn't none too fired up about letting all these foreigners in after the war, even if they was connected to a service man. So even though we was already married and I had the papers to prove it, I wasn't able to get Maricel into the States until about a year of red tape or whatever you want to call it.

And then one day there she was, running down the gangplank in San Fran and jumping into my arms just like in a movie.

You might think it's pretty corny, but Maricel actually got down and kissed the ground when she got off the boat. I mean after she got done kissing me, or right around the same time. I didn't hardly know what to think, except I realized she was very excited about the whole deal. I was too. Except for the war, this trip to go and pick her up was probably the biggest adventure I ever was on. I don't mind telling you, it cost me a small fortune.

We got on the train in Frisco and took it all the way to Chicago. I tried to explain to Maricel where we was headed so she wouldn't be too disappointed, but I don't know if she understood or not. She kept on listing the different things she seen out the window, and she give each one its own color. The blue Pacific, the red desert, the purple Rockies, the yellow plains, the green valleys, the brown Mississippi, etc., etc. I guess that's just how her mind works.

She got more and more excited all the while, and who could blame her? It must of been just what she always imagined America to be like.

She never seen the white snow and gray slush of northern Wisconsin until later on.

As soon as we got to Chicago, I tried to get ahold of Jack to see if we might be able to get together, but that fell through. Maybe it would of been a little too much for Maricel anyways. Every time she turned around, there was something else to be amazed at. Between the skyscrapers and the lights and the shop windows and the noise and the traffic and everything else, she couldn't get over it. I don't know if she knew it, but she had a vise grip on my arm the whole time. Pretty near cut off the circulation. But I didn't mind.

We had a pretty nice dinner at a place called the Berghoff and spent the night in the Allerton Hotel on Michigan Avenue, which was a little rich for my blood. I should of figured that going in, because Jack recommended the place. They have a bar up on the top floor called the Tip Top Tap. I guess I should call it a cocktail lounge, not a bar. It's pretty swanky. You get a great view of the whole city from up there. Maricel couldn't believe it. She never seen anything like it.

I pretty near had a stroke when I tallied up all the damages for the trip, but what the hell. It's only money, right? After all it was our second honeymoon, so why not splurge a little? Actually, when you think about it we never had any honeymoon to start with, so you couldn't really call this one the second. Either way, it was great. I'll never forget it.

In the morning Rosemary and her husband Walt picked us up at the hotel and drove us back to Birch Lake. Walt even paid for breakfast. That was awful white of him.

Maricel didn't let on, but you have to figure she must of noticed the difference between the train ride from San Fran to Chicago and the car ride from Chicago to Birch Lake. I probably should of done a better job of cluing her in beforehand. You go through a little town every so often, but mostly it's just a farm here and there or a little crick or a grove of trees or something and not much else to see. Maybe if you look real close, you could see a cow dropping a load.

When we got to the state line, Walt pulled over and made us all get out of the car. He took a picture of me and Maricel standing in front of the WISCONSIN WELCOMES YOU sign. That Walt really is a good egg when you think about it. I don't know why I've never liked him.

The farther we went, the less there was to see. And what there was to see was just the same as what you already seen for the last hunnerd miles. Finally Maricel just went ahead and dozed off. The poor kid. How could I tell her we was headed to a place nothing like she pictured? Too rocky to be worth a damn for farming, too picked over to be worth a damn for logging, and too far from anyplace else to be worth a damn at all.

Finally we come to the home stretch. Black River Falls, Merrillan, Humbird, Fairchild, Augusta, Ludington, Cadott. You know what Cadott's claim to fame is? It's halfway between the Equator and the North Pole. Exactly forty-five degrees north latitude. I guess you gotta hang your hat on something. Walt made me wake Maricel up, and we piled out of the car for another picture. Here she was halfway to the North Pole. It was the farthest north she ever was. I mean until we got back in the car again and kept on going.

After while we rolled into Birch Lake. "Home sweet home!" Rosemary says. I don't know if she was fooling or what.

Then Maricel chimed in with, "I love it already." I don't know if I mentioned this before, but her English really isn't half bad.

"Bless your heart!" Rose says to her.

When we got home, I lifted Maricel up and carried her from the car into the house like you're spose to. Walt took our picture again. Maricel is so little, she should of been easy to carry, but I tripped over the front stoop and we both tumbled onto the floor. We ended up doing it right there. I mean after Rose and Walt left.

I don't mind saying that was pretty damn nice. But you know what happened after that? I thought to myself, What in hell do I do now? I hate to admit it, but I really didn't have no idea what to do with Maricel after I just got through dragging her eight thousand miles and done it to her on the front-room floor to boot.

Chapter 6

Carol

Birch Lake, 1947

Jack's folks rent a cabin up at Birch Lake for two weeks every summer without fail. Well, I think it was one week when Jack was younger and then it eventually expanded to two. We'd been dating almost a year when he invited me to spend a week at Larry's with him and his folks. I was flattered because I knew Jack wouldn't have done that if he wasn't serious about our future. I was also nervous, for any number of reasons.

The place is off the beaten path, to say the least. Jack's dad made a little joke about that. "You might think Larry's is in the middle of nowhere," he said. "But you'd be wrong, because you'd have to go a ways to get to the *middle* of nowhere."

After driving seven or eight hours from Chicago, you arrive at the town of Birch Lake. As the old saying goes, don't blink or you might miss it. I think there might be two or three stoplights, if that helps you picture it. At the end of the main drag, you go past the paper mill and across a rickety old bridge over the Chippewa River. Then you follow along the lake shore for a while until the shoreline curves and the road goes straight.

After a few miles on this lonely stretch of road, you see the sign for Larry's Lake Aire Resort (if you come upon the Black Bear tavern, you've gone a bit too far). You turn right at the sign onto a narrow gravel lane and wind through the woods for maybe a mile until you come into a clearing along the north shore of the lake. And there you are.

Larry and Eloise, the owners, live in a two-story frame house which is painted pale green with white trim. There's a little sunroom jutting out of one side that looks like it was tacked on as an afterthought.

The four little cabins are arranged in a crescent facing away from the house, towards the lake. Between the cabins and the house are a few picnic tables, a horseshoe pit, that sort of stuff. There are a good many pine and birch trees on the grounds. And let's not forget the peonies. I never had much of an opinion one way or the other about peonies, but apparently Eloise is wild about them. They are all over the place.

Our cabin, like the others, includes two bedrooms, a small kitchen, a tiny bathroom (you literally have to step into the shower in order to close the door), and a front room with a picture window facing the lake. There's a dining table with four chairs, a coffee table, and a sofa that folds out to provide an extra bed. There's knotty-pine paneling throughout and a linoleum floor that's sort of clammy. The whole place smells a bit off—musty, I guess you'd say.

I was assigned to sleep with Jack's mom in one bedroom while Jack and his dad slept in the other. Our bedroom had a yellowing cartoon taped to the mirror above the dresser. The cartoon showed a bunch of firemen running into a burning house with their hose and axes. The caption said *Don't make an ash of yourself by sleeping in bed!*

The first night we were there, it was pitch black. No moon, no breeze, and too muggy to sleep—at least for me. The rest of them were sleeping like babies. I was lying there listening to the cicadas, to the moths slapping against the window screen, and to Mrs. Weber's snoring. (I don't call her Elizabeth because she hasn't invited me to do so.)

All of a sudden I heard a car crunching up the gravel road and saw the headlights flash across the wall. After the car screeched to a stop, there was the most frightful banging and yelling. I didn't know what to think, so I just rolled over and pulled the sheet up around my neck and tried to ignore the noise. It finally stopped and I drifted off to sleep. Or maybe it was the other way around.

The next morning at breakfast, I asked if anyone else had heard it. "Oh, that was only Larry," Mike said. "When he gets home a little too late, Eloise locks him out and makes him sleep in the sunroom. He hollers for a while, but then he calms down all right."

As soon as we cleared the dishes and Jack and Mike went out fishing, Mrs. Weber said, "What do you suppose the boys would like for lunch?"

I thought to myself, This is going to be some swell vacation.

Mrs. Weber always calls Jack and Mike "the boys," and after a while I found myself doing it too, without even realizing it. The boys began Monday, Wednesday, and Friday with a couple hours of fishing, Tuesday and Thursday with a round of golf. It seems to go without saying that either fishing or golf needs to be done early, before it gets too hot—so regardless of whether it was a fishing day or a golf day, Mrs. Weber and I were up before dawn preparing breakfast. I didn't say so, but I wondered why the boys couldn't help themselves to toast and coffee now and again, especially since Mrs. Weber was in the habit of offering an elaborate hot lunch every day except Thursday. On Thursday the boys had lunch at the golf course.

It was understood that if the fishing trips yielded anything of consequence, what the boys called "keepers," Mrs. Weber and I would clean them, cook them, and serve them for dinner. It couldn't be lunch, of course, because lunch had to be ready by the time the boys landed at the dock. I didn't have the nerve to ask her, but I wondered if Mrs. Weber ever secretly hoped the boys would come back empty-handed.

At any rate, the routine at the lake gave Mrs. Weber and me plenty of time to get to know each other better. Plenty of time and then some.

If it rained, Heaven forbid, all bets were off. Jack and his folks were constantly asking each other whether it was supposed to rain, looked like rain, or was starting to rain. "What'll we do if it rains?" Mrs. Weber might say at breakfast to no one in particular, and no one had an answer. Well, I had an answer that I didn't share. She and I would do pretty much the same as we always did. We would fix the three meals and clean up after each one. The only difference was that the boys would be under foot in the cabin.

It actually did rain one day (thankfully only one) during our week at the lake. A genuine thunderstorm rolled in early one morning just about the time the boys would normally be heading out. We ended up sitting around the kitchen table listening to the weather reports on the radio, in between the pinging of the rain on the roof, and playing spades. I would've just as soon curled up in a corner with a book, but the consensus seemed to be that we should "go ahead and play cards." And then there was more discussion about which card game we should go ahead and play. Eventually, we settled on spades.

On days when it wasn't raining, the boys followed their normal routine in the morning and then, after lunch, Jack and I got to spend some time by ourselves. We'd go for a swim, or take a little rowboat ride, or stroll around the grounds. Maybe we'd play croquet for a while. Sometimes we'd just sun ourselves on the pier or sit and dangle our feet in the water. The water is quite cold, not to mention brown and murky.

Late in the afternoon, the water becomes almost completely still. As the sun starts to sink, the light over the lake is almost uncanny. It's hard to describe, how the cottages and trees across the way are bathed in brilliant golden sunlight while we are already

178

in the shade for the most part. I can see the attraction of the place then. I can understand why Jack and his folks love it.

It was on this trip that I first met Jack's friend Don. Jack had told me a bit about him. He's a local guy from the wrong side of the tracks, so to speak, who's been doing chores around the place for years. I gather that he and Jack have been practically inseparable during Jack's previous visits to Larry's—best buddies for a week or two out of every fifty-two. "You'll love him," Jack had told me on the drive up. "I promise you."

Even as naïve as I tend to be, I knew full well that I was there to be judged, and that Don was one of the judges, along with Mike (he had long since told me to call him that), Mrs. Weber, and Jack himself. They were in their natural habitat, if you will, as comfortable as an old shoe, whereas I could hardly breathe. I lived in constant fear that I would somehow manage to say or do the wrong thing. I imagined a hundred ways I might cause offense, and I reviewed the list in my head over and over. I promised myself I would not use too much hot water, would not take a second helping of anything until everyone else had, would not be too clingy with Jack, would not plop down in someone else's favorite spot on the sofa, would not say one word about flies, ants, mosquitoes, or spiders, and, perhaps most importantly, would not stink up the bathroom.

Mrs. Weber and I were starting to fix lunch the second day when Don and his wife rolled up in an old jalopy. "Hello!" he yelled through the kitchen window. "Here comes trouble!"

"Oh hello there, Don," Mrs. Weber said. "And how are you, Maricel dear?"

Maricel is Don's wife. She's from the Philippines. She is the cutest thing—silky black hair, big dark eyes, nice little figure. She held onto Don's arm in a formal way, just above the elbow, as if they were posing for a picture. She didn't say boo.

"We just come from church," Don said, "and we figured we'd swing by here and see what's doing."

"Well, the boys aren't here right now," Mrs. Weber said. "They're still out fishing."

"Oh fudge," Don replied. "I should've realized."

"You haven't met Jack's girlfriend," Mrs. Weber said. "Don, this is Carol."

"I haven't had the pleasure," Don said, grinning. "And I do mean pleasure! You're so much prettier than Jack let on. I tell you, it never fails. You can't hardly get nothing out of him."

At this point Don and Maricel were still standing outside the screen door peering in at Mrs. Weber and me. It was a standoff until Mrs. Weber finally said, "What's the matter with me? Come on in!" She shooed them over to the table, sat them down, and went to pour some coffee. I started to follow her, but she motioned for me to sit.

It was quite awkward, because after the initial introductions and pleasantries, none of us had anything to say. The best I could come up with was, "I've heard a lot about you, Don."

"Oh, that's too bad!" he said. He nudged Maricel to let her in on the joke, which she didn't seem to get. She just stared at the sugar bowl. "You can't believe everything you hear."

"I assure you it was all very complimentary," I said.

"You see? That just proves my point."

On our last night at the lake, Jack and I went out for a walk before bedtime. The moon was out and full, or darn near full. Everything was still except for the sound of the cicadas and the faint patter of our feet on the gravel. You know how in the movies every scene that's supposed to be in a rural setting at night features crickets chirping one or two at a time? I can honestly say I never heard that particular sound at Birch Lake. Instead there was the literally incessant drone of the cicadas.

We walked the length of the gravel lane all the way out to the main road and back. We held hands and didn't say much. I kept my promise to myself not to mention mosquitoes. All was right with the world.

When we got back to Larry's, we went and sat on the bench at the end of the pier. Jack wrapped his arm around my shoulder and we smooched for a while.

Finally he said, "I should thank you for coming up here this week."

"Thanks to you and your folks for having me," I said. I leaned into him a little more.

"It was a great week, wasn't it?"

He had me there. "Yes, it was," I said.

"And another thing," Jack said. "I realize it took a lot of nerve on your part."

There was my opening. "So how did I do?" I said.

"Pardon?"

"How did I do? Did I pass the test?"

He didn't answer. He wheeled around in front of me, dropped to one knee, and held out the most beautiful diamond ring I could have imagined.

Chapter 7

Jeannie

Calumet, Michigan, 1947–1948

They say winter is pretty rough up here in the U.P., but the other half of the year isn't bad. That would be a pretty funny joke if it wasn't the God's honest truth.

If you don't like cold and snow, then this wouldn't be the place for you. Trust me. I thought I already saw plenty of snow growing up in Birch Lake, but it was nothing compared to here. Our first winter we got 176 inches. What is that, something like fifteen or twenty feet?

Here's the funny part. That's not even an average winter around here. They say they figure on 200 inches anyways. Sometimes they'll even get over 300. I can hardly imagine that. I can't quite picture what it would be like to get twice as much snow as we actually got. As it was, the snow piles ended up higher than most of the buildings. After all, every time they plow the streets, the snow has to go somewhere. I don't think the last of it melted till Decoration Day.

Bill and I like the U.P. well enough. It's pretty wild country, but that suits Bill just fine. He says you could pull off to the side of the road someplace, step into the woods, and walk a straight line for who knows how long without seeing any sign of civilization. You might go fifty miles or more without seeing another person or a house or a man-made object of any kind. Isn't that something?

Bill likes his work and the guys he works with, and he's making pretty good money. He ought to, when you consider how

182

dangerous the job is. I heard logging is the most dangerous job there is, except for deep sea fishing. We're talking about actual jobs now, not crazy stuff like tightrope walking and that. Of course, even if you forget about the danger, it must be darn nasty out there in the cold and snow. As you can imagine, they can't afford to call it off every time the weather goes bad.

Bill's such an outdoor type to begin with, he's never at a loss for things to do around here. For one thing, he gets plenty of exercise digging his car out every time it snows, because we don't have a garage. But he also does lots of other stuff. The same things he's done his whole life, like hunting and fishing, he can do all he wants around here.

They say our winter is the price we have to pay for enjoying the other seasons. And we do enjoy the other seasons. Practically every Sunday when the roads are passable, we drive up to Copper Harbor, which is the end of the line in case you don't know. Somebody told me it's the furthest north you can get east of the Mississippi, I mean while still being in the United States, which I guess is kind of interesting. We have breakfast in a little diner up there and then we relax on the beach or explore the dunes or hiking trails or whatever. It's lots of fun.

Bill recently bought an old Indian motorcycle from the army surplus. It wasn't even running when he got it, but he fixed it up and painted it, and now it looks swell. He really gets a kick out of it. He zips around the back roads for an hour or two whenever he has a chance. Says it clears his head.

Our son Jerry was born here, so he's a native Yooper. Nobody can take that away from him. Lots of people said we were loony to move here while I was as pregnant as you can get, rather than waiting until after he was born. But we wanted to get started on the next part of our life with all due dispatch. That's what Bill told his folks: "All due dispatch."

183

I hate to say it, but Jerry is a little more trouble than Julie was. I wonder if it's because he's a boy. Don't get me wrong, I love him very dearly. He's just fussier than his sister ever was. For example, if he doesn't like what he's having for lunch, he might just grab the bowl and throw it at the wall. Or throw it at me. Well, anyways, I'm sure he'll grow out of it pretty soon.

Back when I used to daydream about getting the heck out of Birch Lake, I promise you I never pictured moving to a place like this. The U.P. isn't too glamorous. It's a rugged place, especially in winter as I already told you. But Bill and I look at it as an adventure we can share with each other and our kids. We have lots of time to spend together without any distractions like you might have if you lived someplace more exciting. Or if you lived closer to your relatives.

I wonder if people that live in hard places like this aren't the best kind of people anyways. You wouldn't think they have much going for them, but they're honest and they get by okay and they don't cry or complain about anything. They'd give you the shirt off their back without you even asking for it. They don't think anything of it. They're just acting the same way they're used to.

Chapter 8

Carol

New Orleans, 1948

Our wedding was marvelous. Jack looked like a million bucks. The only fly in the ointment was that Jack's folks got a flat tire on the way to the church. Mike took off his tuxedo jacket and rolled up his sleeves and changed the tire right in the middle of Western Avenue. He and Mrs. Weber made it to St. Gregory's with about five minutes to spare, and he cleaned up his hands as best he could in the lavatory.

The reception was at the Edgewater Beach Hotel. My dad is a very generous man.

I think my favorite thing about the whole day was when I danced with Mike and Jack danced with my mom at the same time. The orchestra was playing "When Irish Eyes Are Smiling" in honor of Mom, and do you know what Jack did? As the song was about to end, he twirled Mom around two or three times and then he dipped her! Not only that, but then he held her there, well below his waist, for a long moment after the song ended. Everyone sort of gasped, afraid that Mom would end up sprawled out on the floor, but Jack returned her to an upright position as suavely as you please.

Let me tell you, that brought the house down.

We went to New Orleans for our honeymoon. Although it's about a twenty-hour drive, Jack insisted that we drive straight through, stopping only to eat (twice) and go to the bathroom (no more often than absolutely necessary). I honestly didn't understand why it needed to be such a rush job. I was looking at the drive as sort of an event in itself, but Jack didn't see it that way at all. The object for him was simply to get there in the fewest hours, minutes, and seconds possible, as if we were in a race.

They say that getting there is half the fun, but I'm not sure that would apply in this case. At least the car didn't break down. That was a good thing. And we didn't get in a wreck, either, so that was another good thing. But aside from that, the less said about the drive the better. Suffice it to say that Jack and I were thoroughly on each other's nerves by the time we rolled into the Thunderbird Motor Court just outside of New Orleans.

We were friends again after we spent our first night in the room.

We spent most of the next day relaxing at the motel pool and, as it turned out, getting badly sunburned. Everyone told us that we absolutely, positively had to dine at a place called Galatoire's on Bourbon Street, so we drove into town that evening to give it a try. We parked on Chartres, down the street from Jackson Square. There was a sign halfway up the block saying NO PARKING 6PM TO 2AM.

I brought this to Jack's attention—not being bossy, mind you, just letting him know. "It's almost six now," I said. "What do you think, hon? Maybe we'll get a ticket."

"Nah," Jack said, "we won't get a ticket. They wouldn't fool with tourists who come down here to spend good money. That's just for these hillbillies that come in town to have a big night and wind up getting out of hand."

I wasn't too sure about that. Wouldn't the local cops be more likely to fleece the out of towners, rather than their own people? I didn't say anything, though. I just grabbed Jack's hand and we headed off toward Bourbon Street.

We heard Galatoire's doesn't take reservations, which is why we got there rather early in the evening. We hoped it wouldn't be too crowded until later. Well, I guess some other folks had the same idea, because as we approached we saw there was a line out the door and down the block and around the corner onto Iberville.

"Hell's bells," Jack said. "This don't look good." Right away you could see his wheels were turning. He had me hold our place at the back of the line while he went inside to "have a word with the top man." Of course, I had a pretty good idea what he was up to when I noticed him digging into his pocket as he went. Not two minutes later, there was a little commotion at the front of the line, and here came Jack again. I gathered his discussion with the maitre'd had been brief. Some of the people at the front of the line were sort of snickering. As Jack was coming back, embarrassed, to rejoin me in line, I couldn't help thinking of the first time he asked me out. I had said yes only to spare him exactly this kind of indignity.

Jack would've been very antsy waiting in line under the best of circumstances, but of course the failed transaction with the maitre'd aggravated him all the more. "We could always go someplace else," he said. "I mean, if you don't feel like waiting. Why, there must be a dozen other places within a block of here, and probably just as good or even better." That was funny. Of course, it had nothing to do with my not wanting to wait in line at Galatoire's, but it was sort of endearing the way Jack pretended it did.

He made the same insinuation several more times while we waited, but each time I managed to sidestep the issue by pointing out another interesting (to me, at least) balcony with its elegant wrought-iron railing and hanging baskets. At one point a group of young Negro boys showed up and put on an impromptu dance show for a few minutes, accompanied by an older boy on harmonica. Some people on the balconies tossed coins down to the boys, and I even got Jack to contribute a quarter.

187

Finally we got inside and were seated. It had been forty-five minutes, maybe, but I'm sure it seemed much longer to Jack. "Well," I said cheerfully. "Good things come to those who wait."

Jack looked past me, over my shoulder, and said, "Speaking of those who wait."

That was clever of him, because it was the waiter coming—a short, round, balding, and quite obsequious fellow named Armand.

"And where are you nice folks visiting us from," Armand said, "if I may ask?"

"Chicago," I said (at precisely the same time Jack said, "What's it to you?").

"Chicago," Armand said. "Wonderful! And what brings you to the Vieux Carre, if I may ask?"

"It's our honeymoon," I said. I didn't look at Jack just then, but I'm sure he rolled his eyes.

"Your honeymoon!" Armand cried, and slapped his hands to the sides of his face. "Wonderful! Of course, you may certainly have cocktails as well before dining with us this evening, but first I hope you will agree to each have a glass of champagne, with my compliments!"

"Why not?" Jack said. "If you're offering."

Armand scurried off and returned shortly with the champagne. "Here for Madame," he said, "and here for Monsieur."

Jack and I clinked glasses and drank the champagne. Then Jack ordered a couple Old Fashioneds to take the edge off, as he said.

Armand came back with the drinks. "I will give you a few moments to study the menu and wine list," he said. "And it will be my great pleasure to answer any questions you may have upon my return." He scurried off again.

"That one's a little suspect in my book," Jack said.

I knew perfectly well what he meant, but I felt like giving him a hard time. "Suspect in what way, hon?" I asked.

"Are you serious?" Jack said. "If you don't know, I guess there's no use explaining it to you."

In perusing the menu, I had to admit I'd never heard of most of the dishes before, much less tasted them. Jack was in the same boat. Armand, helpful even to a fault, insisted that we have the sweetbreads for our appetizer. "A particular speciality of the chef," he said. "Delicious!" We followed his advice, and we liked the dish well enough. Neither of us had the faintest idea what sweetbreads really are until later.

Armand also recommended the raw oysters, but I didn't have enough nerve to try them—especially after Jack saw some being served at the next table and said, "They look like somebody with a real bad cold coughed 'em up, don't they?"

For the soup, I had the bouillabaisse (excellent!) and Jack had the seafood gumbo. For the entrée, I had a petite filet and Jack had fried shrimp. That was sort of silly, as I think about it. Here we went all the way to New Orleans and ordered entrees we could just as easily have had at home!

Armand grandly delivered our dinners. "It is my great pleasure to present the petite filet mignon for Madame and the crevette frire for Monsieur. Bon appetit!"

Then he leaned over the table so that his head was right between Jack's and mine. "My friends, I don't know if I should tell you this," he said in a stage whisper, "but you are such nice people I can't help myself. Speaking to you confidentially, would you believe Mr. Tennessee Williams wrote *A Streetcar Named Desire* at this very table! He visits us almost every day."

Jack was already chewing on his first shrimp. "Who the hell is Tennessee Williams?" he said.

Our plates were almost clean enough to put back in the cupboard when we finished dinner. I went on and on telling Jack how much I enjoyed it.

"Well, I'm glad you liked it," he said, "but I still don't get what's supposed to be so special about this place. I guess I'll know for sure when I get the bill."

When he did get the bill, Jack made a face but didn't make any further comment. Then we said our goodbyes to Armand, who made us promise to come back again soon.

"That one's really something," Jack said as we stepped out into the twilight. "I hope he'll be able to go on living without us." Then he knitted his brow and stopped in his tracks. "I wonder if he charged us for the champagne. I forgot to check."

For a moment I thought he might turn around and go back, but I'm glad to say he thought better of it.

The sun had set, but the sky wasn't altogether dark yet. The streetlights were coming on. We held hands and walked up Bourbon Street with no particular destination in mind. I can tell you without fear of contradiction that I've never seen any place to compare with the French Quarter. There isn't anything boring about it, that's for sure. I get the impression that nothing and no one is too strange to fit in. There are people dressed outlandishly, behaving the same way, and drawing no particular notice. There are jugglers and mimes, barkers trying to lure you into night clubs and dive bars, pickpockets, women of easy virtue (I assume), drunks holding up lampposts, music blaring from just about every doorway and window, and that's just a partial list off the top of my head.

We ducked into a place called Pat O'Brien's, where there was no cover charge. It's in a very old building or maybe several buildings that share the same courtyard. By then it was dark enough to make the place's many nooks and crannies and meandering corridors seem very mysterious. We got a little table in what we took to be the main courtyard, not far from the fountain. There was a jazz combo with a girl singer who was just launching into "Stormy Weather" when we sat down. Jack seemed to find her bewitching, but I wasn't jealous. I couldn't really blame him. The whole atmosphere was bewitching.

The waitress said we needed to try the "world-famous hurricane, which is the signature cocktail of our establishment." We took her up on it, not once but twice. I was a little wobbly when I got up go to the powder room, so after I got back I told Jack we should get going pretty soon.

"Don't forget we've got some important business to attend to at the motel," I said.

That seemed to register. We kissed. Then Jack paid our tab and we were on our way. We kept to the side streets heading back to the car. The breeze had picked up, and the tops of the palm trees were rustling. The hanging baskets on the balconies were swaying and the gas lamps were flickering. Bourbon Street is busy and sort of crazy, but the side streets are spooky and magical. Enchanted is probably the right word. Walking along them at night is like being in a dream.

We held hands and paused a time or two to share a kiss. On the way through Pirate's Alley, I stopped to buy a bunch of postcards—some to send to the folks back home and some to keep for myself. Then we went along the side of St. Louis Cathedral and ended up back on Chartres.

The cathedral was bathed in bluish white floodlights. "Oh, Jack," I said. "Isn't that lovely? We have to come back tomorrow and get lots of pictures in the daylight." My mom and dad had given us a nice camera as a wedding present, along with lots of color film. I was really excited about that. Neither of us ever had any color pictures before (even our wedding photos, which we hadn't seen yet, were black and white). I wanted to take a whole bunch of pictures on this trip to look at over and over again when we're old and gray.

When we turned down Chartres, my stomach jumped into my throat. Our car was gone. I pointed this out to Jack very gently, almost apologetically.

"Can't be!" he said. "We just got turned around. Probably just ended up on the wrong side of the church."

But we weren't turned around, we weren't on the wrong side of the cathedral, and the car was really gone. After a good deal of back and forth, I finally got Jack to accept those facts. Now, there happens to be a police station only a couple blocks from where we were standing. We had passed it on the way in. Jack cursed a blue streak all the way over there. He announced he was there to report his car stolen and then demanded to know what they were going to do about it.

Well, to make a long story somewhat shorter, it turned out that the car wasn't stolen. When all was said and done, the police were able to tell us what had become of it. It turned out Jack was right when he said the cops wouldn't ticket the car for being in the no-parking zone. They had towed it instead.

Lord willing, I expect to live a good long time. But I don't expect to ever see another human being quite so angry as Jack was when the truth of this situation dawned on him.

Chapter 9

Don

Birch Lake, 1948

When I was a kid, some old timer who had a few told me if you put a penny in a jug every time you get lucky before you're married and take a penny out every time after, you'll never empty that jug until hell freezes over. I always wondered if he was serious or just talking out his pie hole. Do you think lots of married guys would say the same thing?

I don't mind telling you, that sort of bothers me. If that is what a typical married man would say, then I don't know where that leaves me. Because in my case the jug would of been damn near empty before I got married. It wouldn't take no time at all to get it emptied again.

Well, who knows? Maybe that old guy was just pulling my leg anyways.

Even before I got Maricel over here, my ma offered to take us in when the time come. Maybe I should of taken her up on it. At least we'd of had a square meal every night at supper time. But I didn't think that was the way to start off married life, setting back and expecting Ma to take care of us.

I said to myself, what kind of a man can't even put his wife up in a cruddy apartment? Well sir, that's just what I done. Here Maricel come halfway around the world to live in the good old U.S.A., and I put her up in a cruddy apartment above the Rexall.

So then I started thinking, what in hell am I gonna do to try and make some more money? It's not like back in the olden days

193

when I was only trying to help my ma out a little bit. Now I'm on the hook for my own upkeep and for a wife to boot. That little job I had all those years over at Larry's wasn't too bad for a kid who didn't hardly have no expenses and just needed some walking-around money. But when you're a grown man with a wife, you can't be doing some high-school type job and taking shit off of Larry while you're at it and only making pocket change.

I know some guys who work at the mill. Hell, who doesn't? Half the guys in town work there. I grew up with these guys. They told me it wouldn't be no use trying to get in there, because the guys who was already in there before the war and then come back got all the spots taken. Okay, that's fair enough. I wouldn't want to take the spot of some service man who's entitled to it anyways.

I went ahead and took a job pumping gas at the Sinclair station on the outskirts of town. Right now alls I get is the hours nobody else wants. So if somebody says they ain't coming in because they got a bad hemorrhoid or something, then I'm their man. It's a start anyways. Anybody can pump gas, but I also know a little something about how cars work and how to fix 'em. I figure if I just bide my time and keep my mouth shut, I can move up to mechanic and work a regular set of hours.

The Sinclair station give me a dark green shirt and pants to start off with, free of charge, and a patch with my name on it for Maricel to sew onto the shirt. I already have the clodhopper shoes to wear, so I'm all set, far as the costume goes. The whole get-up looks pretty sharp, if you ask me. When I was working for Larry all that time and wearing my own clothes, I wound up looking like a hobo by the fourth of July.

I hope the job at the Sinclair will keep me and Maricel going for a while anyways. I'm gonna keep putting in a few hours at Larry's on the side. Plus I have a truck I bought off of Larry for pretty near nothing, which is just about what it's worth. I'm gonna find an old used snow plow I can put on in the winter and make a few extra greenbacks clearing people's driveways and whatnot.

Maybe if everything comes off according to plan, I'll have enough scratch to get me and Maricel into a little nicer place. I never come right out and asked her, but I don't think she realized at first I wasn't so well off. She might of thought I had a nice house and a boat and all, but now she knows better, whether she likes it or not. She's getting to understand more and more all the time.

My sister Rose tries to help Maricel out by giving her some pointers on housekeeping and cooking and whatnot. I think it's pretty smart the way she does it. She don't come right out with it. She'll say something like, "Now I'm not telling you what to do, Mari. Far from it. But I'll tell you, Walt always likes it when I do it this way. You should try it." I don't know if Maricel picks up on any of it or not. I guess we'll see.

If you want to know the truth about our apartment, I'll tell you. The electric, the plumbing, and the heat act up all the time. After you do your business and flush the toilet, it'll keep running until doomsday unless you go back and jiggle the handle until you get it just perfect. Whenever Maricel lights the oven, it smells like something crawled in there and died. If it rains or snows, we got enough water dripping from the ceiling to take a shower. Plus we got ants. Don't get me wrong. I ain't blaming Maricel. She keeps the place up as good as she can. I guess these ants wander up from the soda fountain or some damn thing downstairs. We can't get rid of 'em no matter what we try.

In the summer I put a fan in the front-room window. This thing is so loud you can't hear yourself think, but at least it drowns out the noise from the mill. Maricel don't mind the heat so much because she's use to it from back home, but she hates the cold like nobody's business.

I'll never forget one time her first winter here. Our street slants down towards the paper mill pretty steep. Maricel slipped

195

on the ice going out the front door and slid pretty near halfway down the block on her rear end. And then she was stuck but good. Because how in hell was she gonna walk back up the same froze-over sidewalk she just got done sliding down?

That's just one example, but anyways I think you'd be pretty safe to say it ain't nothing like the life she pictured for herself.

So by now you're probably asking yourself why in hell do I go ahead and admit all this stuff when it only makes me look like a jerk. Alls I can tell you is I ain't a liar, especially to myself. The truth of it is Maricel come over here with no fucking idea what she was getting into. And not only did I allow her to do it, but I insisted.

She done everything she done because she believed in me. She trusted me to have a plan. It's just too bad I didn't and still don't.

Chapter 10

Carol

Chicago, 1948

One day a few weeks after Jack and I got back from our honeymoon, we took the train out to Arlington Park with my folks. Citation was running that day. He had just got through winning the Triple Crown, and everyone wanted to see him. My dad knows that Jack likes the races, so he was nice enough to borrow a box from a friend of his. I bought Jack a new tie for the occasion, and I must say he looked pretty spiffy.

Jack was like a kid in a candy store when we set out. He had his cigars lined up in his breast pocket. He got his shoes shined at the station and picked up a *Racing Form* to study on the train. He actually offered to buy a *Racing Form* for each of us, which was sort of funny. My mom, God love her, said, "Thank you, dear, but I'm afraid the ink would rub off on my dress."

Jack was intently studying his *Racing Form* when my dad said, "Quite a horse player, are you Jack?" Oh boy, I thought, here we go. But he said it in such a way that allowed Jack to take it as a joke if he wanted.

And that's exactly what Jack did. "Oh, sure," he said. "Why, I might need a hand carrying my bankroll home."

"Is that so? Well, what's your system?"

"Always bet a gray horse," Jack said. "Or never bet a gray horse. I forget which."

"Well, I heard a saying once," Dad said. "He who gambles lives in shambles."

Jack sort of chuckled at that, but didn't say anything.

We weren't the only ones who had the idea to go to the races that day. Far from it. The train was packed like a sardine can. About halfway out to Arlington, around Jefferson Park or Edison Park, my dad jumped up and gave his seat to a woman and her little girl who got on and said they were headed out to a picnic in Crystal Lake. Other women and girls were still standing, but Jack kept his nose buried in the *Racing Form* until I finally gave him a poke in the ribs and he got up.

We glided through suburbs—Park Ridge, Des Plaines, Mt. Prospect, Arlington Heights—that feature tree-lined streets, snug little shops and restaurants, and people going about as if they hadn't a care in the world. At least that's how it struck me. My Lord, their garages are probably nicer than some of the houses in our neighborhood.

I like to think that we can hope to live in one of these towns some day, in a cozy house with a well-kept lawn in front and a patio in back, and send our kids happily off to school a couple blocks away. The ads in the paper for new developments out that way always say GRACIOUS SUBURBAN LIVING IN A PARK-LIKE SETTING, or something to that effect, and have drawings of smiling people barbecuing or playing badminton or just relaxing. It works on me. I love those ads and the whole idea they represent.

When you sit in a box at the racetrack, they bring your drinks and all right to you. The first time the girl came to take our order, Jack reached into his pocket, but my dad stopped him. "You don't have to do that, Jack," he said. "I'll just run a tab and then take care of it at the end."

"That's right, sir," the girl said. "We can do that."

"Then you need to let me buy dinner," Jack said to my dad.

My dad said, "We'll see."

"Well, anyhow, keep 'em coming," Jack told the girl. Then he gave her a dollar.

It seemed that Jack knew of a guy who worked for one of the stables and was going to give him some hot tips. As soon as the national anthem was over, he ran downstairs to look for this guy, who he said was the son of Erv Something-or-Other from work.

While Jack was gone, my folks and I worked out a plan whereby each of us would pick a horse. Dad would bet his to win, Mom would bet hers to place, and I would bet mine to show. The next race we would mix it up, and so on. That way we could kind of root for each other, and it was possible for all three of us to win at the same time. We were your garden-variety two-dollar bettors, mind you. Neither the track nor our fellow spectators was likely to acquire too much of our money. Nor were we likely to acquire much of theirs.

The first two races were already over by the time we saw Jack again. In the first race, Mom's horse won, but she had bet it to place. Even so, it paid fourteen or fifteen bucks. In the second, she won a show bet that paid four dollars and change. She was absolutely tickled. Two for two.

We were all in high spirits when Jack came back to the box. "How'd you make out?" I asked.

"I couldn't find him," he said. "I don't understand it. Erv said he'd be right there by the tunnel waiting for me." He meant the tunnel where the horses and jockeys go under the grandstand to come out to the track.

"We missed you, hon," I said very sweetly. "Why don't you just stay here with us?"

"This guy is supposed to have some good information," he said, more to himself than to me.

"Why don't you sit next to Mom," I said, "and see if any of her luck rubs off."

Then the girl showed up with our second round of drinks. "Jack," my dad said, "I hope you don't mind, we took the liberty of ordering you one."

"Mind, hell," Jack replied. Then he turned to my mom and said, "Pardon the expression."

Jack sat with us for the third race and downed his scotch and soda. When the race was over, he didn't comment on the result one way or the other. He just excused himself and ran downstairs again to look for the guy with the tips, who, we had learned by now, was named Kenny. I wasn't sure if Jack had ever met this Kenny before, or knew anything about him, or could even recognize him, or had just taken Erv's word for everything.

"Listen," my dad said to me. "Suppose this fellow Kenny actually knows something. Why would he go around telling everyone and drive the odds down?"

I had to admit it was a good question.

I didn't say anything to Jack, but I honestly didn't see how he expected to find this Kenny, or anyone else for that matter, in the crowd they had that day. It was the biggest crowd in the history of Arlington Park—almost fifty thousand people. Mom said later that between the train and the racetrack, she'd never been sweated on by so many people of so many different races, creeds, and colors in one day.

For the first six or seven races, Jack continued frantically looking for Kenny. My folks were not terribly impressed, I have to say. Meanwhile Jack kept on betting even without the inside information. When I asked him which horse he liked, he wouldn't tell me. "I'll tell you when he goes to the winner's circle and not before," he said. "Otherwise, I'd be jinxing myself."

Jack was miserable when he lost, and—I kid you not—almost equally miserable when he won. He finally had a winner in the fifth or sixth race, and all he did was beat himself up for not betting more.

My folks and I did okay with our modest little bets. Almost every race at least one of us cashed a ticket, even if it wasn't for very much. One race, I had a win bet that paid twelve bucks. As I turned to Jack, expecting some kudos, he was muttering about a horse that ran out of the money. "Goddamn Arcaro," he said. My folks pretended not to hear him swear. "He went too soon and his filly ran out of gas. Stupid."

I was getting a bit impatient with him by then. "Isn't Arcaro the most famous jockey in the world?" I asked, playing dumb.

"Yes, but he's overrated in my book."

"Then why'd you bet him?"

"I didn't bet the jockey, sweetie. I bet the horse. I bet her for you, because of the name. Mystery Lady. Reminds me of you."

So then I wondered whether it was supposed to be my fault he lost the bet! Regardless, I took the path of least resistance. "That was sweet, darling," I cooed. "I appreciate it. You'll win the next one for sure."

"Wait till I see that Erv," he said. "Honey, I swear I'll tell him a thing or two."

When Citation's race came along, we all went down to the paddock to see him. The people were lined up around the fence three or four deep, buzzing. Jack offered my dad a cigar. When Dad declined, Jack offered it to Mom and me as well, just being funny. Then he lit it up himself.

As the horses clopped around the walking ring, an older lady next to us said, "Which one is Citation?"

"Why doesn't she look at the damn program?" Jack said to me. Then he turned to her and pointed with his cigar. "There he is."

"The greatest racehorse since Man o' War!" the lady's husband announced.

The lady said, "You can see the class dripping off of him."

"Hell's bells," Jack said to me quietly. "Ten seconds ago she didn't even know which horse it was."

Then he said, more loudly, "Lady, you wouldn't know class if it bit you on the rear end."

I tried not to, but I had to laugh.

Naturally, the lady's husband took offense. "I beg your pardon," he huffed, stepping between his wife and Jack.

Jack smiled disarmingly. "Just joshing," he said.

The man stood there for a moment, not sure whether he should let it go at that. He gave Jack a dirty look and seemed satisfied that, by doing so, he had done enough. He slowly turned around and went back to looking at the horses.

Then it was "riders up," and the horses went once more around the ring, this time with their jockeys aboard. As Citation passed by us, Jack had a few words of friendly advice for the jockey, who was none other than Arcaro. "Hey Eddie!" he yelled. "Don't ride him like you rode that last race. You'll put us all in the poorhouse."

Arcaro didn't bat an eye.

For this race only, my folks and I threw caution to the wind and abandoned our usual strategy of hedging our bets. We each put five bucks on Citation to win. That's a good sum of money, as far as I'm concerned. Dad also bought an extra two-dollar ticket to keep as a souvenir.

"Do you want to come in with us?" I asked Jack.

"I'm not sure," he mumbled. "I'm still deciding."

"Okay, suit yourself."

When the starting gate opened, Citation stayed in the middle of the pack for the first half mile or so, then moved up steadily on the far turn. He took the lead going into the home stretch, and we were on our feet cheering along with everyone else. The roar from the crowd grew louder with each step he took toward the finish line. It was deafening. I swear the grandstand was shaking.

Citation won by two lengths. As he jogged back, the announcer said, "Ladies and gentlemen, Citation has equaled the track record for a mile and one eighth." Another roar went up from the crowd, and Arcaro held his cap in the air as he steered Citation to the winner's circle.

"Well, there's one race we all won," my dad said.

"Congratulations," said Jack.

I looked at Jack and whispered, "Didn't you bet him?"

He just shrugged.

"Jack," Dad said, "I think I'll take you up on one of those cigars." Jack handed one over. Then Dad said, "Well! Arcaro brought him home, didn't he? And tied the track record to boot! If ever there was a lead-pipe cinch. Why, Citation would've won going away even if he fell down and got back up again!"

Dad was uncharacteristically animated, almost giddy. Mom and I got a big kick out of seeing him that way.

We ordered another round of cocktails and then my folks and I went to collect our winnings. Each of our five-dollar bets on Citation to win paid only six-fifty, but we were excited just the same.

My mom said, "Aren't you coming, Jack?" I made a face, and she let it drop. Jack remained in the box to work on the next race. He had finally given up the idea of finding Kenny and being handed some sure-fire winners, but there were a couple races left and he wasn't going to sit them out.

When the girl came back with the drinks, my dad asked for the check. She slid it from her apron and started to hand it to Jack.

Dad intercepted it. "I'll take that, Miss."

"But I was under strict orders to give it to the other gentleman!" she said, giggling.

"Nonsense," Dad said.

The girl looked at Dad and then at Jack, who held up his hands to indicate helplessness. "I guess I know when I'm beat," he said.

On the train back to the city, we reviewed the day's results. Dad, Mom, and I had each made a slight profit. Jack allowed that he "didn't do quite as well" as the rest of us. A few of the people around us were loudly rehashing their victories, but most just sat quietly looking hot, tired, and bedraggled. Jack was in the latter group, staring glumly out the window.

It was almost eight o'clock when we arrived downtown. Dad led us to a restaurant that's walking distance from the station. It's called Mike Fritzel's. I saved the matchbook, which says CHICAGO'S NEWEST AND MOST BEAUTIFUL RESTAURANT on one side and WHERE THERE IS NO COMPROMISE WITH QUALITY on the other.

Dinner was uneventful, the conversation superficial but friendly, and then came time to pay the bill. My dad reflexively reached for it, but I put my hand over his and clamped it down. "Remember, Dad," I said. "You promised you'd let us pay for dinner."

"I said we'd see."

"We insist," I said. "Isn't that right, honey?"

"Of course," said Jack. "Sure. Let me have that."

He took up the check and reached into his jacket for his billfold. He tried one pocket, then another, then his pants pockets, then tried all of them over again—to no avail. "I don't know how to tell you this," he said, "but my billfold's missing."

We looked on the floor under Jack's seat while he frisked himself again.

"It's gone, all right," he said.

"Oh, you poor dear!" Mom said.

My dad slid the check back toward himself and took out his wallet.

"I'm awfully sorry, Ed," Jack said.

"No, no," Dad said. "Don't give it a thought."

"The only thing I can think is some schwarze lifted it at the track. When I went to the john, I hung up my jacket on a hook, and I bet that's when they took it."

"That must be it," Dad said.

The next day on the phone with my mom, I got her to confess that she had made do with soup and oyster crackers and a cup of coffee because she'd assumed Jack was paying. "If I knew your father was going to end up treating," she said, "I'd have gotten the most expensive thing on the menu."

That same evening at supper, I asked Jack if he'd talked to his friend Erv at work. "As a matter of fact, I did," he said. "He swore up and down that Kenny looked for me all afternoon. So I says, 'I guess he didn't look too hard.' And you know what else? He told me the little shit won six hundred dollars! I read him the riot act."

Then I asked if there was any news about his lost billfold. "Oh, that," he said. "It turned up in the lost-and-found at Northwestern station. Empty, of course."

"Of course," I said.

Chapter 11

Jeannie

En route to Port Angeles, Washington, 1949

The whole time we lived in the U.P., Bill kept writing every so often to these other logging companies all over the place. It's nothing against the U.P., but we never figured on staying there forever. From the beginning we always wanted to try somewhere farther away from where we started. After all, it's a big country.

I don't remember exactly what came first, the news I was pregnant again or the offer Bill got to work in Washington. I don't mean Washington, D.C. I mean in the state of Washington, a place called the Olympic Peninsula. When he showed me the letter, we looked at each other and both thought the same thing: This is right up our alley. Because it's about as far as you can get from Birch Lake without going to some foreign country.

We'll miss Calumet, but it's not like I had a girlfriend that came over for coffee every morning or gossiped over the backyard fence. We didn't have a next-door neighbor or a neighbor down the block. There isn't any block like you'd picture with houses in a row on either side of the street. It's just a house here and another house there, with no pattern to it. I bet our nearest neighbor was at least a quarter mile away. There are a few couples we socialized with and said we'd keep in touch with, but I'm not sure if we really will. You know how that goes.

One good thing, Julie and Jerry are still young enough, the idea of moving wasn't too much of a trauma like it would be if they were already in school and that. We told them they'd get to see the ocean. They liked that.

Bill's new boss sent him a picture of a cabin he said we could rent pretty cheap with an option to buy. It's just outside of a town called Port Angeles, real close to where the fellas work. "It don't look like much now," Bill told me, "but after we buy the place we can add on and then fix it up real nice."

Bill went to the library in Houghton and got a bunch of stuff to read about the area. He was so excited. Sometimes he even read certain parts out loud to me. "How about this, hon?" he said one night. "'The Olympic Peninsula contained the last unexplored places in the United States. It remained largely unknown until most of its topography and timber resources were mapped around 1900.' Imagine that. Less than fifty years ago."

The main thing Bill couldn't get over was the idea of salmon fishing. He started ordering all kinds of brochures and maps about it. He was just itching to buy the waders and all the other stuff too, but he said he could wait (barely) until after we moved.

When it was time to go, we went ahead and hired a moving van. It costs a few bucks, but that's just the easiest way to do it. A couple of fellas from Bill's work offered to rent or borrow a truck and do it, and knowing them I'd say they were dead serious. But Bill didn't want to end up owing them a favor and not be able to pay it back if he never saw them again.

The interesting part was, Bill said the only way to get his motorcycle out there was to ride it himself and have me and the kids follow along in the car. Maybe I'm nuts, but I thought that was a good idea. It made the whole thing more of an adventure. I mean, if it's not already enough of an adventure to pick up and move two thousand miles away to a place where you don't know a soul.

Bill said it should come out to two thousand miles exactly. "If we go two thousand and one, we've gone too far," he kidded. He reminded me to write down the mileage on the odometer when we took off and then check it again when we pulled up to the cabin. But as it turned out, I forgot all about it when we got to the

207

other end. You'll understand why when I tell that part of the story.

If you jumped in a car in Calumet and drove straight through to Port Angeles without ever having to stop, it might take you fifty hours or so. But if you have two little kids who need to eat and sleep and pee and poop more often than you ever realized before, it will take you way longer. Then the trick is finding enough decent places to stop. Unless you're lucky enough to come across a Howard Johnson's or a Stuckey's (or a good old A&W!), well then you're taking your chances. I'm talking about your regular stops now. The overnights are something else again. The best you can do is look for someplace with the VACANCY sign on, even if it does look kind of seedy. If you get too persnickety, you might go another hundred miles and then settle for a place that's even worse.

The moving van fell way behind us before we even got out of Michigan. I guess we should've expected that to start with. We never saw it again until Port Angeles. As we went along, I could tell it was practically killing Bill to go slow enough for us to follow him. It must've been maddening. I told him he could go ahead and open it up if he wanted to, and we'd catch up to him at the next stop.

"And leave you and the kids out here on your own?" he said. "What do you take me for?"

The way I'm telling it, you might think he really put me in my place there. But actually his tone was friendlier than it probably sounds. I also appreciated the feelings behind it.

All in all, we went through a teeny slice of Wisconsin and then across Minnesota, North Dakota, Montana, Idaho, and finally Washington. You'd think you'd go through more states going that far, but those are some pretty wide states.

The weather held up as good as you could hope for, thank God. I don't know how Bill would've made any progress at all otherwise. It was dry the whole entire time until we got past Seattle and headed up the peninsula. Then it started misting. Not exactly an unusual occurrence around here, as we came to find out. We pulled off to the side of the road to talk it over.

As much as we wanted to get there, we decided to grab a bite first—because when we finally did get to the cabin we'd still have to unpack the car and then go back out for groceries. I can only imagine how fussy the kids would've been after all that.

We stopped in at a place called the Klallam Kafe. There was a giant totem pole in the parking lot. I wanted to get a picture of Julie and Jerry in front of it, but they weren't in the mood so I thought maybe we'd try again on the way out. I remember thinking I should learn more about totem poles and what they mean.

Bill is a big guy, in case I didn't mention that before. He was in his motorcycle garb, hadn't shaved since we left Calumet, and was looking pretty wild after all that time on the road. Everybody in the diner gave him the same look he got practically everywhere we stopped, like he was some kind of crazy outlaw biker about to smash up the place, rob them all, and kidnap the waitress. But when they noticed he had a wife and two kids with him, they changed their mind. I think they were disappointed, in a weird sort of way.

Actually, just being honest, the waitress was kind of plain. Not really the type to be kidnapped and thrown on the back of the motorcycle even if Bill was a crazy outlaw biker with no wife and kids.

"Your children are just darling," she said when we sat down.

"I'll bet you'll never guess where we came from," Bill said.

"Oh, gosh," she said. "I'm no good at guessing."

"Michigan," Bill said.

"Michigan! Well, I've never been, but I'm sure it's quite a long way to come on a motor-sickle."

"It is at that," Bill said. "We made good time, too, all things considered."

209

"Isn't that great? More power to you."

"And my wife here, Jeannie, drove the car all that way and took care of the kids on top of it."

It was just small talk, but you really had to get a kick out of Bill. He was pleased with himself and proud of his little family.

By the time we finished lunch, the mist had turned into a more of a drizzle.

Bill held out his hand and let the rain fall on it. "A little weather ain't gonna slow us down any," he said. "Not after we came nineteen hundred and fifty miles and don't have but fifty more to go." He kissed me and Julie and Jerry—not just for the heck of it like people often do, but for real.

Then we were on our way again, and only an hour or so from our new home. I was feeling sort of emotional, thinking about how far we came and how much nerve it took. I already realized there wouldn't be too many things in my life to equal that trip. It was an unbelievable, once-in-a-lifetime experience. You couldn't repeat something like that even if you wanted to try. Which you wouldn't.

The rain picked up a little more. Not enough to where you'd call it a downpour, but more steady than a drizzle. After we went ten or twelve miles, Bill got stuck behind a slow-moving truck and there was nothing he could do about it. The road is only two lanes, and it's way too curvy and hilly to think about trying to pass a truck you can't see around. Especially in the rain.

What happened next—well, I hope I can tell it correctly. The road curves hard to the right. It isn't quite a hairpin turn, but it's darn close to it. I'd say about the shape of a "C." At the same time you're going around this curve, the road is sloping down pretty steep. And to top it off, at the bottom of the slope is a railroad crossing! Whoever designed that whole thing was having a bad day.

So this truck in front of Bill came out of the curve and was still on the decline as it approached the crossing. I'm sure I could see more than Bill because I was further back. The truck wasn't blocking my view as much as it must've been blocking his.

I heard something. It sounded like a train horn, but I wasn't sure. I don't know if the truck driver heard the same thing and overreacted or if he actually saw the train, but I'll swear on a stack of Bibles he had plenty of time to get through. The lights were not flashing yet and the gates were still up.

The truck driver must've jumped on the brakes with both feet, because the truck screeched to a stop all at once and ended up with its front end practically hanging over the tracks. Bill saw this and tried to stop too, but there wasn't nearly enough time or room. The bike went down onto its right side, sliding on the wet pavement. Then Bill and the bike both disappeared under the back of truck.

Chapter 12

Carol

Chicago, 1948–1951

Jack and I found an apartment in St. Gregory's, not too far from my folks. It's on Farragut Avenue between Ashland and Ravenswood. A typical two-flat with a tiny patch of lawn in front and a narrow gangway that goes through to the back. There are pretty red finish bricks on the front and plain tan bricks on the other three sides. There's a back yard as tiny as the front, and behind that a garage facing the alley. If you're standing in the gangway, you can touch our building with one hand and the building next door with your other hand.

The building is only eighteen or twenty feet wide, but about three times as deep. If you go up the steps, through the exterior door, and into the vestibule, you'll face two doors. The door on the left opens to a narrow flight of stairs leading to the second floor, where Mrs. Scanlon lives. She's our landlady. The door on the right opens to our apartment.

When you come in, you'll be in the front room. If you keep going straight ahead, you'll come to the dining room and then the bathroom on your right, one bedroom and then the other on your left, and the kitchen at the back. Beyond that, a drafty little porch and the back stairs, which are outside the building itself.

They call the neighborhood Andersonville or Lakeview, depending on where you think the boundary lies. But we usually just call it St. Gregory's.

I can tell you this. Going in, I had absolutely no clue what to expect from married life.

I don't mean sex, necessarily. Despite my lack of previous experience, that part seems pretty straightforward. It doesn't seem to require too much analysis. Isn't it just a matter of figuring out where the puzzle pieces are supposed to go?

I mean the simple fact of living together. Accommodating each other's presence day in and day out. Living in a place that is neither his nor mine, but ours. Amidst belongings that are neither his nor mine, but ours. Paid for with money that is neither his nor mine, but ours.

There's so much to work through between us in order to keep our marriage on the right track, and ninety-nine percent of it is never discussed. I suppose Jack would think I was nuts if I sat him down to talk about every little thing that crossed my mind. Doesn't Popeye say, "I am what I am"? That could be Jack's motto, too. He is what he is, and he isn't the type to spend much time contemplating his navel. I guess I do enough of that for the both of us.

I've worked at getting used to the sight and sound and smell and touch of him, in all their various iterations—clothed or naked, awake or asleep, sober or not, before or after he showered and shaved and combed his hair, etc., etc. The way he snores like a buzzsaw (especially after a night out), or the way he sometimes cuts my calf with the nail on his big toe, or the way he'll end up with all the covers when he rolls over. The way he puts salt on literally everything, even including bacon. The way he chews certain foods a little too loudly. The way he reaches into the icebox and drinks milk or juice right out of the bottle. The way he leaves the toilet seat up as often as not.

I love Jack and I want to be a good wife. I've done my level best to adjust to his habits, and I refuse to admit to myself that any of them can be considered annoying. And meanwhile I've done all I can think of to please him and to answer the long list of questions that spring from my own insecurity and self-consciousness.

How to fill up all the hours? What to talk about? When to talk and when to be silent? Who gets up first in the morning? What to do for fun? How much time should he reasonably expect (or want) to spend with his friends, without me? How much time should I reasonably expect (or want) to spend with my friends, without him? How many Saturday nights should we spend with other couples, and how many by ourselves?

How to interact with our families? Should we have my folks over one Sunday and his the next, or both sets of parents together? What about holidays? How to try and please both families at the risk of pleasing neither? That's a tough one. You can't be in two places at once. After some trial and error, we seem to have settled into a pattern which somehow became agreed upon without ever being negotiated. Easter Sunday at our place with both sets of parents. Thanksgiving dinner at my folks' place, and then across town for dessert and coffee with Jack's folks. Christmas Eve with my folks, either at our place or theirs. Christmas Day with Jack's folks, at their place.

What should I feed him? That one can keep me up at night. I know full well that Jack is used to being waited on hand and foot at home. That's just his mom's way. Not that I'm knocking it, but I'm not going to try to compete with that. I have been hoping, though, that Jack will like my cooking well enough and that the variety of offerings will be such that he can't predict too surely what's likely to turn up on his plate from one night to the next.

I'll never forget one time I tried a little experiment. Filet of sole almondine. Jack isn't much for fish to start with, but I saw the recipe in *Good Housekeeping* and thought I'd give it a try. I was feeling adventurous, and besides I always liked fish. So I served it, and Jack took a few bites. Then set down his fork and said, "I trust we won't be having this again." Can you imagine? It sounded like the kind of thing he'd probably heard his dad say to his mom a time or two and saved it up for the day he could use it on his own wife. But knowing Mike, if he ever said something like that to Elizabeth, he would've done so with a twinkle in his eye. I trust she wouldn't have felt the need to run into the bathroom sobbing and lock the door like I did.

The filet-of-sole-almondine incident was typical in one way. We hadn't been married too long when I realized that Jack tends to define himself in terms of what he dislikes, rather than in terms of what he likes. I'm sure he's not even aware of it, but he rarely talks about people or things he likes, whereas he often goes on at length about those he dislikes. I can't help but laugh when he talks about the latter. I know it's childish to egg him on, but he really can be funny when you get him going.

Jack likes cowboy movies and detective movies, especially ones that feature a sexy femme fatale. He dismisses almost all war movies as hooey. He dislikes virtually all of the most popular actors, singers, and comedians. Frankly, I think he resents the idea that they are richer and more famous than the rest of us. He makes an exception for Jimmy Stewart. "He didn't while away the war in Hollywood dating starlets," Jack told me. "He flew bombers right in the thick of it. What do you think of that?"

I don't have anything against Jimmy Stewart, but you can give me Gregory Peck any time.

Jack loves all sports, especially baseball. He likes any kind of gambling. He plays poker with his buddies the second Friday of every month, goes to the races several times a summer, and buys chances in every raffle and sweepstakes he can find. From time to time I gently remind him not to overdo it.

He has no use for what he calls talking people, those who talk a good game but never seem to accomplish much of anything. He dislikes Negroes and Jewish people in general, but then again he likes some of them well enough as individuals, which I take to mean his attitude is evolving in that area.

Men whom Jack dislikes seem to fall into one of three categories: punks, phonies, and queers. As nearly as I can figure out the definitions, a punk is someone younger than Jack who needs to be taken down a peg, a phony is someone older than Jack who needs to be taken down a peg, and a queer—well, I guess that's self-explanatory. Jack often refers to his "book," as in "So-and-so's a phony in my book." A fellow who is none of the above, not a punk or phony or queer, is probably all right in Jack's book.

Women whom Jack dislikes generally are classified as biddies or (forgive me) bitches. To his credit, he seldom uses the latter term in front of me. Then there are the ninnies, busybodies, and fussbudgets. Those terms are basically interchangeable. And let's not forget the hens. That is Jack's name for the girls I play bridge with every so often.

There's a saying in Chicago: "We don't want nobody nobody sent." That means if you want a job with the city, you might as well forget it unless you come recommended by someone who has connections.

My dad's firm does a lot of business with the city, and he was good enough to recommend Jack for a job.

Jack dragged his feet. He didn't want to feel beholden to my dad, which I could understand to an extent. But talk about looking a gift horse in the mouth. My Lord, even the lowliest city job pays more than what he was making. I have to admit I was shocked that he hesitated at all.

"Don't get me wrong," he said. "It's not that I don't appreciate it."

"But?"

"Plastering's a good trade. Nothing to be ashamed of."

"Absolutely!" I said sweetly. "But this way you'll have opportunities for advancement."

"I don't know."

"And you'll have benefits, health insurance and all, which you don't have now, and a pension."

"Yeah."

"And you wouldn't have to break your back doing such hard work, especially when you're a little older."

"You got all the answers, don't you?"

"Okay," I said, as evenly as I could. "I'm not going to fight you over it. You think about it and decide what you want to do. I won't bring it up again."

I kept my word. For two full days and nights not one word about the city job passed between us. Meanwhile my dad kept calling me to ask what was going on. He was fit to be tied. He'd gone out on a limb and used up a favor by getting Jack the job offer, never dreaming there'd be any question about its being accepted.

On the third day, Jack came home from work and said, "I called your dad today and told him thanks for offering to help us out."

"But?"

"But nothing."

After all the hemming and hawing, he couldn't come up with a reason not to take the job that made any sense, even to himself.

Jack started out on a garbage truck, which he considered beneath his dignity but was a start anyway. After that, he was put on a crew that trimmed trees, plowed snow, filled potholes, that kind of stuff.

This was a plum job, mind you. All these city jobs are. People would practically kill for them. I'm not sure Jack quite realizes how good he has it. These crews are overstaffed, to say the least, and no one has to work too hard. If someone has a hangover or what have you and doesn't come in on time (or at all), his buddies punch his time card for him, and nobody says a word about it.

In addition to working for the city, Jack and most of the other guys also work for the Democratic party. Technically the city government and the party organization are separate entities, of course, but you'd be hard pressed to tell the difference most of the time. If someone is doing party work on city time, that's just par for the course. Anyone who'd think to complain about it would be viewed as some sort of a crank or a crackpot or something.

I kept on working at the CTA for quite a while after we were married. Jack would have had me quit as soon as we walked down the aisle, but I persuaded him that we could use the extra money. I liked my job and I was good at it, so I stayed on as long as was practicable. (Isn't that a good word—"practicable"?) Anyhow, as soon as I got pregnant with Ray, that was that.

Actually I didn't quit as soon as I got pregnant. I quit when I started showing. That was a given. They'd have shown me the door at that point even if I planned on staying.

When our dear son Ray came along, he was almost four weeks early. I woke up in the middle of the night all wet and got Jack up. I had dreamt over and over that Jack turned up missing when the time came, out playing poker or who knows what, and in the dream I got more and more panicky as the baby was coming, actually starting to fall out between my legs and me trying to hold it in with my hands, as I lurched around the house looking for Jack. But this dream or nightmare turned out to be wrong, because Jack was there after all. He came through like a champ. He threw some clothes on and drove me to St. Joseph's like a bat out of hell.

I was in labor for an awfully long while and seemingly making no progress. All the while I was in excruciating pain—but how was I to know how much pain should be regarded as normal and how much beyond that indicated a serious problem? I had never given birth before.

Finally Dr. Murphy, bless his heart, insisted that they do a Caesarean. He's been our family doctor for years, a good old-fashioned general practitioner, and he has more sense than the rest of them put together. He saved Ray's life and mine too.

They did the Caesarean, and that's when they discovered Ray was turned sideways at the top of the birth canal, and no matter how long and hard I pushed, he wasn't coming out. This was all explained to me later. At the time I had no idea what was going on.

Ray was in a bad way for the first couple days, and so was I. Poor Jack didn't know whether he'd lose his son or his wife or both. He told me later they even called for a priest during the worst of it.

After I was out of the woods and had come back to my senses, I held Ray in my arms and I knew then and there that the good Lord had shown me the meaning and purpose of my life from that point forward. There was nothing under Heaven that ever would or could mean as much to me as that precious, precious little baby.

Ray had to stay in the hospital for a few extra days before they let us take him home. He had to be fattened up. I went over there every day and held him for as long as they'd let me. Jack stopped in most evenings after work. He was really good through the whole thing. I hated the idea that Ray had to stay in the hospital, but of course it was for the best because he was right as rain by the time we brought him home. There were some other babies in there with him who didn't fare as well. Or didn't survive at all. I don't know how those parents could stand it. There but for the grace of God went Jack and I.

My mom and dad asked if they could come along when we went to pick up Ray. Here again, I have to give Jack credit. He didn't roll his eyes or anything of that sort when I told him. He just said, "The more the merrier." So Mom and Dad came to our place, and we had a little breakfast, and then the four of us rode over to St. Joseph's together.

After we filled out all the forms and waited around a while, they brought Ray down and handed him over to us. He was up to a little over six pounds, having gained almost two pounds since coming into this world. They had him tightly swaddled in baby-blue blankets. He was still wearing his little wristband with his name and what have you on it.

Jack drove, and I rode in the front seat beside him. My folks sat in the back. I gave Ray to my mom because she wanted to hold him, naturally—and because I assumed he'd be safer in the back seat in any case.

It was a gorgeous day. Jack was driving with one hand while I held the other in both of mine. I remember thinking no matter what fate has in store for me down the road, I will have lived this moment, and no one can ever take it away from me. I guess my mom felt the same way, because when I glanced back at her over my shoulder, Ray was sleeping with his head nestled in the crook of her elbow. She was looking at him with an expression that I can't adequately describe, and the tears were streaming down her cheeks.

Chapter 13

Don

Birch Lake, 1952

Give Maricel her credit. She wanted to love me. She really wished she could. But when it come right down to brass tacks, she found out she couldn't. She chose me out of all the guys she met up with during the war, and then she come halfway around the world to be with me. But after while she unchose me. The only girl who would of even given a thought to marrying me, much less actually done it. But pretty soon she wished she didn't.

So what does that tell you? I wasn't the man she thought I was. Or maybe I wasn't the man she wished I was. If I died in the war I'd of been a hero to her forever. The guy who was gonna take her to the States. Instead of that I was the husband she wound up hating.

I never realized how bad it was until one day when she told me she was gonna go ahead and move in with this cousin of hers from the old country! It was spose to be someplace near Los Angeles. You can bet your bloomers I tried to talk her out of it every which way you could think of, but her mind was made up. There wasn't nothing more to talk about or hope for or wish for.

You know what she done? She put her ring back in the little box it come in and left it on top of her dresser. I never noticed it until she was already gone. I don't mind telling you, that made me feel pretty near as low as you can get. But what are you gonna do?

After Maricel up and left, whenever somebody asked me about her, I use to try and make a joke out of it. I'd say, "Well, she couldn't stand the weather around here." And then I would pause and say, "Not to mention the company." Or sometimes Jack would say that last part if he was around. But really there wasn't nothing funny about it.

I never knew if she got sick of me and sick of the whole situation little by little or pretty much all at once.

I know this much. I don't care who it is, everybody in this world wants to be loved, and everybody wants to have somebody to love. Maricel give me both of those, for a while anyways. So I gotta tip my hat to her for that. And if I wanted to give myself some credit, I'd have to say that she could of done worse. Anybody could always do worse, right? I mean, at least I never smacked her around or nothing like that. I'll say this for myself anyways. I can look in the mirror and tell myself I always treated her as nice as I knew how.

Of course, after she left I thought about what I could of or should of done different. I thought about that an awful lot. What in hell else was there to think about? Every time you turn around, it's staring you in the face. Or kicking you in the balls. Maybe you notice something you remember buying together, or something she give you for a present—well, I don't want to get started down that road. Let's just say she left me with lots of time to think and lots to think about.

You know what bothers me the most? I can't remember what it felt like when we was happy together. We was happy for a few years there. At least I think we was. I couldn't read her mind, but you'd of thought she was happy from the way she acted. But I just can't remember exactly what them days was like. What did we do? What did we say to each other? What did we laugh about? What was there between us that there wasn't later?

No matter how hard I try, it won't come back to me. That's really too bad.

I wonder what would happen if a guy could see it coming. You know what I mean? What if you could say to yourself this is the last time we're gonna have the marital relations. Or this is the last time we're gonna go to a movie together. This is the last time she's gonna nibble on my ear. This is the last time she's gonna pack a lunch for me. This is the last time I'm gonna cop a feel on my way out in the morning. This is the last time she's gonna kiss me with her mouth open. This is the last time she's gonna kiss me with her mouth closed. This is the first time she's gonna turn her head when I go to kiss her. And this is the first time I'm gonna know for sure she done it on purpose.

Man, you could drive yourself loony real quick.

You want to know something else? Even after Maricel was gone, the idea of going out with some other gal didn't set right. I couldn't picture doing it. It felt like I'd be cheating on her. That don't make any sense, does it?

Everybody laughed and laughed when they found out I drove her to the Greyhound station in Eau Claire. They'd say, Who in hell would go ahead and give their wife a ride just so she can leave him? They'd say I should of started a chauffeur service and at least charged her a fee while I was at it. Or if she had herself a boyfriend, maybe I could of dropped her off at his place.

They can make fun all they want, but I don't know what else I should of done instead. Should I of made her walk there? Or hitchhike? If you want to call me a sap, then go right ahead. Be my guest. As a matter of fact, I offered to drive her all the way to Chicago to get her more of a head start, but she said no thanks. Shit, I would of drove her all the way to L.A. if she'd of let me. I would of done anything I could for her, even then. I felt like I owed her. But she didn't take me up on it. So I took her as far as Eau Claire, and that's all she wrote. She was on her own after that.

And so was I. On the way back from the bus station, I stopped in at some joint and got smashed. That seemed like the right thing to do, if you ask me.

Chapter 14

Carol

Chicago, 1952–1955

Jack and I haven't had any more children after Ray. I had a pretty tough time of it with him, and even though everything turned out all right, maybe the next time it wouldn't. That's what Dr. Murphy told me. He said he was almost certain that for me, a second pregnancy would be more difficult than the first, and a third more difficult than the second, and so on and so forth. "It's my duty to warn you," he said, "so if you decide to go ahead you'll know what you're up against."

When it came time to discuss all this with Jack, I was terrified. I'm rather ashamed of myself for this, but I truly had no idea how he might react. I must admit he took it very well. Actually, he took it better than very well. He put his arms around me and said, "That's okay, sweetie. We've got each other and we've got Ray." That meant an awful lot to me. I suppose as an only child himself, Jack didn't believe it would be too strange or traumatic for Ray to be one.

I would have to say Jack was right, because Ray is as happy and sweet a child as you'd ever wish for. You can sit him down with a set of blocks or a coloring book, and he'll amuse himself for hours. You'll hardly hear a peep out of him. He's so calm and quiet, always smiling, and he has big, expressive eyes that captivate everyone. If we're out somewhere, total strangers come up to us and say, "My, what an adorable child!" Seriously. They say it's not bragging if you're just stating the facts.

I'll see other kids throwing tantrums, in a store or a restaurant or even in church, and the parents mortified and trying to enforce some discipline without overdoing it in front of everyone. The child will be screaming bloody murder and thrashing about and literally punching or kicking the mom and dad. It's scary to see how out of control some of these kids get.

I can honestly say that Ray has never once behaved like that. The only time he became what you might call inconsolable was on Jack's thirtieth birthday, of all things. I had wrapped Jack's presents and put them on the kitchen table the night before, so he'd find them at breakfast in the morning. Ray saw all the presents, and we told them they were for Daddy's birthday, so he set about looking for his own birthday. He went through the closets, under the beds, all the possible hiding places—but, alas, he didn't find his birthday.

I call Ray my little ray of sunshine. I'd like to take the credit for that one, but actually it was my mom who came up with it first.

Jack is very good with Ray. The three of us do practically everything together. We take Ray to Winnemac Park or to the little playground on Ashland. Sometimes we put him in his stroller and walk around Rosehill Cemetery. I know some people might think it morbid, but it's very pleasant, really, what with the manicured lawns and the trees and the birds chirping.

There are some famous people buried there. Frances Willard, for one, and the original Mr. Sears from Sears Roebuck, and Charles Dawes, who was Vice President of the United States when I was born. And let's not forget the hot-dog king Oscar Mayer. He was a recent arrival.

Maybe it's just me, but I find it very interesting.

Every time we go to the cemetery, Jack will say, "You know what, Ray?" And then comes the punch line: "People are just dying to get in here!" It's gotten to the point where he'll ask the question and Ray will answer it for him.

On nice weekends we might go to Lincoln Park Zoo or the beach or the Cubs game. My family are all dyed-in-the-wool Sox fans, but I'm learning to accommodate Jack's allegiance to the Cubs. And besides, we're almost walking distance from the ballpark. We never have to worry about getting tickets. People joke that if you call over there and ask what time the game is, the fellow on the phone will say, "What time can you get here?"

There are also the museums, an occasional movie that is suitable for little kids, and the trip downtown at Christmas time to look at the department store windows and visit Santa Claus at Field's. My folks join us for some of these excursions. And, of course, Jack, Ray, and I go back to Birch Lake for a week with Jack's folks every summer.

You know those comedy programs on TV about married life? In a typical situation, the wife serves coffee that looks and tastes like tar, and her husband and their guests are making faces at each other and trying to force the stuff down, and of course no one has the heart to tell the poor dear that her coffee stinks. For good measure, she also serves cake that's as gummy and gooey as wallpaper paste. And no wonder—because through an uncanny but hilarious series of missteps, she actually put wallpaper paste into the mixing bowl! And if they have a dog or a child (which are pretty much interchangeable for the purposes of these shows), you can be sure that the dog or the child or both will come in and track mud all over the carpet and the furniture at precisely the worst possible time. And then the only thing the wife can think to do about it is to stand there in the middle of her company and sob hysterically.

I can assure you that nothing of the kind has ever happened at our house. I can't speak for all the housewives out there, but I've served better meals than what you'd get in most restaurants. Everyone says so, especially my father-in-law. He's my biggest fan.

I enjoy cooking and I appreciate the compliments. I can also see that Jack is quite proud of me on these occasions—but then again I've started asking myself whether being a good cook and housekeeper is the limit of my potential. Isn't there something more in this world that I can aspire to?

I'm ashamed to say it now, but I didn't seriously consider going to college. Nor did my parents encourage me to do so. At any rate, I wasn't sure if I wanted to go into teaching or nursing. Those were the only two fields I pictured a woman going into, even with a degree. Imagine nearly all of the most intelligent, capable women being funneled into just two professions. Believe you me, this country must have the best schoolteachers and the best nurses in the world.

Have you ever heard this one? There is a terrible automobile accident in which a man is killed outright and his young son is critically injured. The boy is rushed to the hospital and taken into the operating room. Upon seeing him, the surgeon exclaims, "I can't operate on this boy; he's my own son!" That really stumps them. How in the world could the doctor say that when we know the boy's father is already dead? The idea that the doctor could be the boy's mother just doesn't occur to people.

The first time I heard that riddle or whatever you'd call it, I didn't get the answer either. That really started me thinking. If we women can't imagine ourselves as doctors and what have you, how in Heaven's name can we ever expect the men to do so? I haven't mentioned this to anyone yet, even my mom. She would say that I'm only going to make myself miserable by pursuing this line of thinking. So would the housewives on TV.

There is one situation on these silly shows that seems somewhat realistic to me. It's the one where the husband comes home with flowers and/or a box of chocolates and presents it to the wife. He's all smiles, patting himself on the back and expecting the little missus to go into spasms of gratitude. But she is unimpressed, to say the least. She stands there with hands on hips, glaring at him, and barks, "What have you gone and done this time?"

That got me to wondering whether Jack has ever had something to feel guilty about or to make up for. I really don't think so. I want to trust him, and I believe that I should. I don't want to see myself as the suspicious or jealous type—a shrew or harpy (aren't those funny words?). But I'll never forget this one night I went out with a few of the girls, and over the second or third glass of wine my friend Nancy said, "Don't kid yourselves. Any husband would cheat if only he had enough imagination and initiative."

I started to laugh, but somewhere along the way I noticed no one else did, so I changed it to clearing my throat.

Chapter 15

Carol

Chicago, 1955

When Martin Kennelly went before the Cook County Democratic Central Committee to seek its endorsement for a third term as mayor of Chicago, he did so unsuspectingly, like a steer goes down the chute to be turned into beef. Kennelly was regarded by the press and by most of the voters as an honest and effective public servant. Under the circumstances, he assumed that asking for the party's endorsement was a mere formality.

Imagine Kennelly's dismay, then, when he was informed that the endorsement would not be forthcoming. The committee had decided instead to back Richard J. Daley, who happened to be its chairman.

"It is certainly a great honor," Daley told the newspapers. "I never dreamed it could happen to me." Naturally, he was not so ungrateful as to reject the endorsement once it had been offered to him. His mother and dad hadn't raised him that way. Therefore he agreed to run, even though he had not sought the opportunity and was as surprised as anyone by it.

Well, maybe as surprised as anyone except Kennelly. Daley and Kennelly had been friends and allies for years, and Kennelly had had no inkling that such would not be the case in the future. "A guy like Kennelly, a gentleman, why, he is way out of his league against this fellow," my dad said.

Kennelly put on a brave face and announced that he planned to be re-elected without the support of the party organization—or the "machine," as he was now free to call it. That's what all its

230

opponents call it. He also declared that any city employee who campaigned against him in the Democratic primary would be fired.

He showed some gumption there, but he probably sealed his fate at the same time. Because what did that mean for Jack, his buddies, and thousands of others just like them? Well, Kennelly could follow through on his threat only if he were re-elected. So the army of patronage workers who owed their jobs to the organization and who wanted to stay in those jobs knew what had to be done. Kennelly had to be defeated at all costs.

The rank-and-file party worker, such as Jack, might be sent out to shovel an older person's sidewalk, drive someone to church or to the doctor, distribute holiday turkeys or canned hams, or do anything else his precinct captain can think of to advance the cause.

One thing I've always found curious is that Jack and the other guys who work for the party have no interest at all in politics in the larger sense. Which of Daley's policy positions attracted their support? Which of Kennelly's offended their sensibilities? Which candidate's vision for the future of Chicago was the most promising for our children and grandchildren?

There probably isn't one out of a hundred ward committeemen, precinct captains, or party workers who could give a coherent answer to any of those questions. These aren't stupid people, mind you. They might be rough around the edges, but they aren't stupid. They can't answer questions of that kind for the simple reason that the questions are irrelevant. Questions that the idealists among us might ask in deciding whom to vote for have almost nothing to do with the actual business of winning and losing elections.

Daley knows this better than anyone. He wouldn't allow himself to be pinned down as to what specific actions he would take if elected. He spoke in the vaguest platitudes, often seasoned with malapropisms. He was for "good, honest, hard-working, God-fearing people and families." He was for "sound education of the youngsters." He was against "crime, filth, degeneracy, and Communism." Beyond that, it was anyone's guess.

Poor Kennelly kept trying to turn the voters' attention toward the issues, but the people who paid any attention to the issues were already for him, and there weren't enough of them to win an election anyway. There never are.

Jack and his friends have a role in the political process that isn't covered in civics class. They worked for Daley, but they worked with even greater vigor *against* Kennelly. Working against something or someone, of course, requires less imagination and can be a lot more fun. And so Jack and the guys merrily pursued their anti-Kennelly agenda. They turned out and heckled Kennelly whenever he made an appearance in the neighborhood. They harassed Kennelly campaign workers who attempted to hand out flyers at L stops, on street corners, or (most daringly) door-to-door. And they went out after dark to pull Kennelly placards down from telephone poles and fire-alarm boxes, to egg shop windows in which Kennelly posters were displayed, and to "confiscate" Kennelly yard signs.

On the afternoon of St. Valentine's Day, the organization threw a party for children twelve and under and their moms in the fieldhouse at Winnemac Park. If I wanted to be witty, I'd say the party threw the party.

The primary election was about a week away. I took Ray, and Jack was there too because he was one of the guys running the event. They had cake and cookies and popcorn and games for the kids—leapfrog, pin the tail on the donkey, musical chairs, and what have you. We moms each got a red rose with a tag tied to the stem that said COMPLIMENTS OF 40TH WARD REGULAR DEMOCRATIC ORGANIZATION. The kids each got a box of those little heart-shaped candies with messages on them, such as BE MINE,

DEAREST, LOVE YOU, etc., and a valentine signed by Richard J. Daley himself (or so it was said).

One of Jack's cronies had the idea that it would be a riot to spike the punch bowl with vodka or something and watch the moms get a little tipsy. Boys will be boys. I'm not sure what was supposed to happen in the event that the plan succeeded. They probably didn't think that far ahead. At any rate, it might have worked better if the guys didn't give it away by elbowing each other and snickering every time one of us went near the punch bowl.

I wiggled my finger at Jack to come over to me and then I said, "Is there something in the punch bowl besides punch?"

"Don't look at me," he said. So he didn't deny that someone had spiked the punch bowl, only that he personally hadn't done it. He seemed to believe this was an important distinction.

We spread the word amongst the gals to steer clear of the punch, and after that the guys just stood around sullenly drinking it themselves.

All along, the newspaper polls showed Daley trailing Kennelly rather badly, but my dad told Jack there was nothing to worry about.

"Nothing for you to worry about," Jack said, a little more sharply than I wished. "You'll make out all right either way."

My dad made a face at me, just barely. "I mean for you, Jack," he said. Lots of people claimed to be on the fence or leaning toward Kennelly, he said, and maybe they even believed it. But when push came to shove they would vote with the organization. "They'd probably be embarrassed to tell one of these newspapermen they're voting for Daley," he said. "Or maybe they're just pulling their leg on purpose. But they know where their bread is buttered."

"I sure hope you're right," Jack said.

Dad was right. Daley won by some 100,000 votes out of the 750,000 that were cast. "I shall conduct myself in the spirit of St. Francis of Assisi," Daley said. "'Lord, make me an instrument of Thy peace.'"

Daley was opposed in the general election by Robert Merriam, a liberal Democrat from Hyde Park who was nominated by the Republicans because they had nobody of their own to run. Merriam is young, handsome, suave, clever, and articulate—the very same things Daley is not. He's also a war hero who distinguished himself in the Battle of the Bulge. He might as well have been sent by Central Casting.

Merriam did an interesting thing to kick off his campaign. He mailed postcards to all registered voters in the wards that invariably produced the most lopsided majorities for the organization. As he expected, thousands of them came back stamped by the post office NO SUCH ADDRESS, ADDRESSEE UNKNOWN, or ADDRESSEE DECEASED.

The newspapers were all for Merriam, and they played it up pretty big. And do you know what came of it? Nothing. People just yawned and said, "So what else is new?" Some even held it against Merriam on the grounds that he was being a smart aleck.

A lot of people saw Merriam's polish and erudition as signs that he was putting on airs. When they referred to him as a college boy, it wasn't meant as a compliment. Daley, on the other hand, is an earthy, plain-talking son of the stockyards. And that wasn't all. The party also reminded voters that Daley has been married to the same woman for twenty years, that he is the devoted father of seven fine children, and that he attends Mass and takes Holy Communion every day of his life—whereas Merriam has been divorced and remarried, and *might* have lived with his second wife (who is possibly of mixed blood and definitely foreign) before his divorce was final. I'm not kidding. Jack and the guys said this stuff to people with straight faces.

234

One day I found a flyer in our mailbox. The letterhead said AMERICAN NEGRO CIVIC ASSOCIATION, and the text said:

> Do your part on election day! Remember that a vote for Merriam is a vote for fair, open, integrated housing and schools all throughout the city!

You can guess how something like that goes over in all-white neighborhoods like ours. I showed it to Jack when he got home. "What do you think of this?" I asked.

He glanced at it and said, "I don't much like it."

"No," I said. "I mean do you think it's genuine? Who do you suppose put it out?"

He took the paper and knitted his brow as if he were studying it very carefully. "I assume this"—he paused for effect—"'American Negro Civic Association' put it out." Then he handed it back to me. He didn't laugh, but I could tell he was sorely tempted.

"You guys are really something," I said.

Daley got slightly more than 700,000 votes, Merriam a little less than 600,000. It was an excellent showing by Merriam when you think about it, but he was not destined to be mayor of Chicago.

The man who was so destined did not become mayor because he is charismatic, or because he is an inspiring orator, or because he imagines creative solutions to sticky problems. In fact, the opposite is true on all counts. But as leader of the so-called machine, Daley could have installed himself or anyone else as mayor. My mom said he could put a chimpanzee in if he wanted to.

It is no exaggeration at all to say that no Illinois Democrat can hope to be elected governor, or to the House or Senate, or to the state legislature, or to one of hundreds of local offices, without Daley's explicit approval. He is a wholly unimpressive man on the face of it, but there must be a lot more to him than meets the eye.

"Daley is a dog with some big nuts," my dad told Jack, quoting someone else who had said that to him. Dad wouldn't have repeated it to me in those exact words, but Jack did.

The organization's reason for existing is to reward its friends and punish its enemies. It has the means to do both in spades. Most sensible people see this quite clearly and therefore prefer to be among its friends. There is little comfort on the other side.

And so after Daley's victory came the reckoning. Men who had supported Kennelly and/or Merriam were purged from the city payroll and from the party organization. Men who were judged to have worked only half-heartedly for Daley were purged. And men who had busted their tails for Daley but had nonetheless failed to deliver enough votes were purged right along with the others.

As a result of this reshuffling, Jack found himself moving up in the world. A few days after Daley was sworn in, Jack came home and said, "How 'bout a nice kiss for the party's newest precinct captain?" And it was no mere coincidence that a week or so after that, he came home and said, "How 'bout a nice kiss for the city's newest building inspector?"

The next time we had Jack's folks over, we all drank a toast to Jack and his twin promotions. Later, while we were having dessert, Mike said, "Of course I'm glad Daley won, Jack, for your sake. And Carol's and Ray's too, for that matter. But one thing sort of bothered me."

"What's that, Dad?" Jack asked.

"Well, this business about Merriam's wife." The same rumors we'd heard, of course, had made their way into Mike and Elizabeth's neighborhood as well. "I realize politics is a pretty rough sport, but to knock a man's wife? I don't know."

What a man.

Chapter 16

Don

Birch Lake, 1957

One time we was having a couple pops and Jack says to me, "Now here's something that has perplexed scientists since the dawn of time." He'll talk like that sometimes when he has a few. "When does a gal decide she's gonna sleep with you? Or, more to the point, when does she decide she wouldn't rule it out? Is it the first time she lays eyes on you? The first time you talk to her? The first time you touch her shoulder or her elbow or her hand? Or doesn't she make up her mind until you're just about to stick it in? They can shoot a rocket into space but they can't figure this stuff out."

When we was younger, Jack used to talk about women all the time. He never talked about one specific girlfriend or the other, just about women in general. It seemed like he was always trying to figure 'em out. Far as I could tell, he done a lot better job of it than your average Tom, Dick, or Harry. One thing's for damn sure. He done a lot better at it than me.

He always said when it come right down to brass tacks, all the women in the whole wide world could go in three categories: in a heartbeat, in a pinch, or not in a million years.

You can take my word for this. His wife Carol would have to go in the first group. What a peach.

I always wondered what it would be like to be Jack. Well, maybe I shouldn't say to *be* Jack, but anyways to be a guy like Jack. What would that feel like? I wouldn't mind finding out, even if they said it was only for a while and then I'd have to go back to being myself again.

Here's a guy who grew up with a ma and pa that loved him and was able to give him pretty near anything you'd want. And then he was a star athalete, with the looks to go along with it. He had to beat the girls off with a stick. Then he went ahead and married one who's just as cute and sweet as you could ask for. And don't forget he's a big shot down in Chicago with a swell job and a nice place and all. Finally, if you're still with me, he's got a real nice little boy who anybody'd be proud to have for a son. I tell you that Ray is a chip off the old block, all right. He's just as handsome and athaletic as his old man, and smart as a whip to boot.

Don't get me wrong. I wouldn't want nobody to think I'm jealous of Jack or nothing like that. He's been square to me all the while I've known him. There ain't no sense moaning and groaning about what the next fella has that you ain't. That won't get you nowhere. Anyways, let's not forget there's always somebody worse off. For all I know, maybe there's some poor sap out there somewheres who's looking at me and wishing he had my life. I might go ahead and leave him have it.

I try not to, but sometimes in the middle of the night I'll stare at the ceiling and get to wondering what Maricel's up to and how she's doing. I hope she's okay. She ain't a bad kid when you come right down to it.

Did you ever see a bunch of people at a ballgame or riding on a bus or shopping in a store, and wonder how many of 'em are gonna go home that night to somebody that loves 'em? I mean somebody that really loves them and can't wait for them to get home. I bet there's a lot less than you think. Of course, if you're looking around at a bunch of guys in a bar, then you don't even have to wonder about it. You pretty much know the answer already.

Chapter 17

Carol

Chicago, 1958–1959

Am I happily married? Is Jack? Those are good questions. I've always believed that if you go around looking for things to be unhappy about, you can find them easily enough. I don't look too hard. Sometimes, though, when I'm feeling more pensive than usual, I wonder whether Jack and I have grown to like the idea of being together more than the actual fact of it. I'm sure a lot of couples fall into that trap eventually, and it might be years and years before they realize it—if they ever do.

I don't think I'm going out on a limb too far when I say that Jack is a tough nut to crack. Even after all these years, he remains rather elusive. I don't believe he is keeping any secrets from me, consciously hiding something—but here's what I am starting to believe. Maybe I can't get to know him as thoroughly as I'd like because he isn't entirely sure himself who he really is, deep down, and who he wants to be.

I wonder if the person Jack imagines himself to be is the same one the rest of us see. How's that for amateur psychology?

I'll say this for myself. I'm not a kid anymore, and I've seen enough of the world to know that no wife or husband or marriage is perfect. To think otherwise is to set yourself up for nothing but disappointment and heartache. If our relationship isn't quite the same as it once was, I tell myself, that's only to be expected. Snap out of it, dearie. Count your blessings.

I'm sincerely proud of Jack's progress through the ranks, both in his day job with the city and in his role with the party. To show you how naïve I was at first, I didn't understand why people always chuckled or arched their eyebrows when I told them what Jack's occupation was. Sure, I knew Jack was fortunate to have a well-paying job with a pension plan and all, but beyond that I didn't get what everyone was smirking at.

I mentioned it to my dad, and I must admit he was incredulous. "You really don't know?" he asked.

I confessed that I didn't.

"How to say this?" Dad said. He scratched at the back of his neck. "Well, there are all sorts of rumors out there that people in these particular jobs—building inspector, electrical inspector, fire inspector, and what have you—might occasionally receive, uh, inducements, you might say, in the performance of their duties. Does that help?"

"You mean bribes?"

"Well, I think they call them goodwill offerings."

"Oh, good Lord," I said. "Do I feel dumb. Won't it be interesting to see what Jack has to say about this."

"No, no," Dad said. "I wouldn't mention it to Jack. I think this stuff is highly exaggerated anyway. You know how people are. I'd put it in the category of an old wives' tale."

I had the distinct impression that my dad was being more tactful on the subject than he would have been with anyone else on this Earth—with the possible exception of his own bride, my dear mother, who goes through life happily seeing, hearing, and speaking no evil.

I didn't say anything to Jack, per my dad's advice, but I did file that conversation away and have thought about it often ever since.

And then too I learned that my own status in the neighborhood has markedly improved now that I'm known as the wife of a precinct captain and building inspector. I might not have noticed the first few times they called my number at the bakery or the butcher shop before it was my turn, in front of people who'd been waiting longer. But then it became more and more obvious, and I also realized that no one complained or even looked at me sideways. And then I discovered I was being given more than I had ordered or paid for.

"Look, you don't have to do this," I told the butcher one day. "I'll wait my turn like everyone else. And I'll pay my own way."

"Right, right," he said, smiling and nodding. "Sure. Whatever you say, Missus." And since then the routine hasn't changed one bit.

Having only one child is decidedly the exception rather than the rule in our neighborhood. Many of the couples have a baby every year or eighteen months, and they end up with four, five, or six kids before they know it. There are so many kids in the neighborhood all around the same age that when you look out and see a bunch of them playing kick the can or wiffle ball or whatever, you can hardly keep straight which one is which.

Even if you get it narrowed down to where you can say to yourself, "Okay, now those three are the Drummond boys," you might not know for sure which one is Patrick and which is Brian and which is Kevin.

At any rate, even as an only child Ray never has any shortage of other kids to play with. Quite the contrary. There's always someone knocking on the door asking, "Can Ray come out?"

The other gals around my age—the gals who produce all these children and show no signs of slowing down any time soon—have no trouble figuring out how to spend their time. For those few priceless hours when they aren't feeding their kids and their husbands, doing laundry, cleaning house, shopping for groceries or clothes, running miscellaneous errands, or performing their wifely duties, they aren't pursuing any hobbies. They are sleeping.

My case is different, of course. Ever since Ray became old enough for school, I've been on my own during the daytime with little to do. That's a problem most of my friends can hardly imagine. Most of the moms with kids in Ray's class still have toddlers and/or babies at home, but not me. I don't even have a dog to keep me company during the day.

We always had dogs when I was growing up, and I thought it would be fun to get one—but whenever I brought it up, Jack would change the subject or even walk right out of the room and pretend he hadn't heard me. I never understood it until I mentioned it to Elizabeth one Sunday while we were doing the dishes.

"I hope you don't mind my asking," I said, "but do you happen to know why Jack doesn't like dogs?"

"He loves dogs, dear," she said.

"But he won't even let me talk about getting one."

"You mean he never told you about Queenie?"

It turned out that Queenie was a little border collie the Webers had when Jack was a kid. One day she disappeared. She was three or four years old at the time, and, as Elizabeth told it, "the most precious thing in the world to Jack." Either Jack himself left the back gate open on the way to school and she got out, or someone came down the alley and snatched her. (There had been been rumors in the neighborhood that dognappers were afoot.) Mike and Jack searched for her ceaselessly, they posted signs, they offered a reward for her return. They ran themselves ragged, but Queenie was never seen again.

I thanked Elizabeth for telling me that horrible story, and I put the idea of getting a dog on the back burner.

I needed to find something to do with myself during the day. I thought (briefly) about going back to work, but I knew very well what Jack's attitude was on that subject. I thought I'd wait and have that argument some other time, like maybe when Ray is in high school. So, looking for any kind of outlet for whatever energy and intelligence I could contribute, I signed on as a den mother for Ray's Cub Scout pack.

I also joined the Ladies' Auxiliary at St. Gregory's. The Holy Name Society has its golf outings, bingo nights, Cubs games and Bears games, New Year's Eve dinner dance, and what have you. The Ladies' Auxiliary has what's left over: bake sales, pot-luck suppers, sales of art works by parishioners, lectures on subjects of interest (I know!), and the twice-yearly plays, which give the would-be actors and actresses of the parish their chance to shine in productions such as *Our Town*, *Oklahoma*, and *The King and I.*

I threw myself like a fiend into all these activities, and I also volunteered at the school three days a week. My first assignment was to help Sister Dorothy, the school librarian, recover some semblance of order in her domain. She had been retired from the classroom for umpteen years, but she was still living in the convent and had been put in charge of the library so as to make her feel useful. But she wasn't up to the job, God love her. There was no rhyme or reason to how the books were shelved or how the card catalog was organized. It seemed that when books were returned, they were put back on the shelves willy-nilly or just stacked in a corner. I fixed all that, which was no mean feat. It took weeks. And I made it my business to go back every so often, maybe one afternoon a week, and straighten up again.

I'm not sure Sister Dorothy ever knew the difference, but the principal, Sister Mary Ernest, most certainly did. She took a liking to me, and ever since then she's wanted me around as much as possible.

When I was in school, I never would have guessed that I'd be friends with one of the sisters someday. But lo and behold, Sister Ernest and I have become fairly close. It's gotten to the point where she'll even call me at home to ask for my advice on this, that, or the other thing. Sometimes I feel my opinion is truly of value to her as she struggles with a certain decision, but as often as not I think she just wants another adult to talk to. That is, aside from the other sisters.

I never gave a thought to what the sisters did between the time one school day ended at 3:15 in the afternoon and another began at 8:30 the next morning. For all I knew (or cared), they went into suspended animation overnight and came back to life when the morning bell rang. That they eat, sleep, go to the bathroom, laugh, cry, that they are outgoing, shy, confident, afraid, and all the other adjectives that could apply to any of us, never dawned on me. Isn't that shameful?

In talking to Sister Ernest, I learned that almost all the nuns in Chicago are from Detroit and vice versa. When I asked why that should be, Sister explained that it was to keep them from being distracted by having their parents and other relatives nearby. And the nuns are not only denied the comfort of their own family ties. They also have practically no opportunities to associate with the families whose children they teach day in and day out, year in and year out. Meanwhile, the priests who officiate at christenings, first communions, confirmations, weddings, and funerals are invariably invited to the banquets that accompany these ceremonies, and they make the rounds of other social events as well.

Something occurred to me that hadn't before. Why is it that a man who finds his vocation in the church is a Father, while a woman who does so is only a Sister? The women who live only to educate our children, to do good works of all kinds, and to serve our lord Jesus Christ get up and go to work every day knowing full well that they are second-class citizens in the church to which they devote their every breath. Since I came to understand that, my admiration for the sisters has known no bounds. I've promised myself to do anything I can for them.

I agreed to take over as president of the parish Home-School Association, our equivalent to the public schools' PTA, simply because Sister Ernest asked me. "I need you, dear," she said. "I mean it." And then she badgered Father Fahey "morning, noon, and night," in his words, until he appointed me to the position—for that was his prerogative, of course, not hers.

Not too long afterwards, we received a letter from school in the mail. It was strictly routine, just a recitation of the holidays, dress code, and rules of conduct for the coming year. What struck me was the letterhead:

ARCHDIOCESE OF CHICAGO

ALBERT CARDINAL MEYER, Archbishop

ST. GREGORY THE GREAT PARISH SCHOOL

REVEREND LEO P. FAHEY, Pastor

SISTER MARY ERNEST OSTROWICZ, Principal

MRS. JOHN R. WEBER, President of the Home-School Association

Thanks to Sister Ernest's faith in my abilities, I have outgrown that august body, the Ladies' Auxiliary—but not under my own name.

Chapter 18

Jeannie

Port Angeles, Washington, 1959

I'm embarrassed to say I wasn't very brave when I saw Bill and his motorcycle go under that truck on our way out here. First I let out one of the all-time banshee screams, which caused Julie and Jerry to do the same. When a child sees their mom or dad acting hysterical, what are they supposed to think? And then I jumped to conclusions and assumed Bill was dead, even though it was just as likely he wasn't.

I actually said this out loud: "After coming all this way and putting up with everything, he'll never set foot in Port Angeles and he'll never see our new baby."

Well, I'm glad to tell you I couldn't have been more wrong. I should've known Bill wouldn't go out in a little fender bender, as he called it. He ended up with a twisted ankle, a broken bone in his foot, scrapes and bruises all down the right side of his body, and a deep cut behind his ear. That wasn't too bad, when you think about what might've happened.

Bill took it real good. He didn't have to beat himself up, because he knew he didn't do anything wrong. It was just bad luck the darn truck stopped short in front of him, and it was good luck he wasn't hurt worse. He was sorry he didn't make it all the way to Port Angeles under his own steam, but he kept his sense of humor about it. "They say there's only two kinds of motorcyclists," he told me in the hospital. "The ones that been in a wreck, and the ones that are liars."

246

Bill slept a lot those first couple days, and he was kind of loopy from the pain medicine when he was awake, so he didn't really understand what was going on when I went into labor. It was a few weeks early, but I guess the baby didn't have a calendar. Anyways, if you're going into labor, you might as well do it in a hospital, right?

When they took me down to the delivery room, I kept asking what happened to Julie and Jerry. The orderly said a nurse named Barbara was minding them.

Let me tell you about this gal Barbara. Her shift was over, and she stayed on her own time to take care of two children she never saw before. She played with them, got them fed, and even found a place for them to get some shuteye. She never went home at all that night. She stayed with those kids until her shift started the next day. What the heck can you say about a person like that? I'm sure everybody wants to think they'd help out if somebody really needed it, but I don't know if they really would. I don't know if I would.

Barbara's the first friend we made in Washington and the best. She was the one who wheeled us into Bill's room so he could meet our daughter Debbie.

All that seems like only yesterday, but now Debbie is ten years old, and Jerry's thirteen, and Julie's fifteen—not much younger than I was when I started waitressing. When you add up all the pluses and minuses, we've had a pretty good life out here.

For one thing, you never saw a place like this for an outdoorsman like Bill. There's as many woods and waters as they have in Wisconsin, probably even more, but without all the snow and ice to put up with. Bill was like a kid in a candy store from the day we moved in. He learned how to do salmon fishing, and he won a few contests out on the local rivers. That annoyed the fellas who've been here their whole life like you wouldn't believe, but I guess you can't please everybody.

Around the same time they learned to walk and talk, our kids started learning about the great outdoors. Bill taught each of them how to hunt, fish, and hike just like he taught me when we started dating. He never assumed the girls would be any less interested than Jerry.

Bill bought an old second-hand canoe, and we took the kids out with their little life jackets on as often as we could. We only tipped over once, and it was my fault. Jerry reached out to try and pick up a leaf or something in the water, and when I went to grab him, that screwed up our weight distribution and the canoe rolled onto its side. Luckily the water was only about two feet deep, so nobody drowned. But everybody's lips turned blue by the time we got back on dry land.

I don't want to get too deep on you, but I guess everybody already knows life will give you both good and bad—and not always equally. For example, Bill got promoted at work and ended up in charge of a crew of eight or ten guys. He got a raise, so we were able to buy the cabin and start fixing it up. Just about the same time, though, we lost my mom. It turned out she had cancer and never even knew it till it was way too late. That was just like her. I never heard her complain about one single thing in her whole life, even though she had plenty of reasons to.

After Mom left this world, God rest her soul, I figured maybe it was my turn to have some good times coming to me. Sure enough, everything went just fine for quite a while. Life went on, and it seemed like every day was a teeny bit better than the last. Things were moving forward, and our arrow was pointing up. If you ever find yourself in that same situation, don't forget to enjoy it.

Everything was just hunky-dory until I got the phone call that still doesn't seem real.

"Hello, Mrs. Anderson?" the person said. Our name's not Anderson, but it's a common mistake. "I'm sorry to tell you there's been an accident."

I remember being surprised that Bill went out on his bike that day because it was very hot, and he usually likes to go out when it's cooler. But he said he was only going out for forty-five minutes or an hour, and then we'd all go swimming or something together.

Did you ever hear what happened to James Dean, the movie star? It was almost the same exact thing that happened to Bill. He was clipping along, minding his own business and not bothering anybody, when some yahoo came off a side road at a goofy sort of intersection, didn't yield, and entered his path diagonally from the left—about ten o'clock if that helps you picture it.

James Dean and Bill have this much in common. They both broadsided the car that came into their path. In James Dean's case, he was killed then and there. In Bill's case, he flew over the car and was still alive, barely.

At first they didn't know if Bill was gonna make it or not. "I'm not going to deceive you, Mrs. Anderson," the doctor told me when I got to the hospital. "I wish I could be more optimistic, but he's going to be touch and go for a while. We'll just have to wait and see."

I don't know what else to tell you about those first few days. I can't remember much. I guess you could just call it a nightmare and leave it at that.

For a while all there was to wonder about was whether Bill was gonna live or not. Then, after they knew he was gonna live, they had to figure out how bad he was crippled. First off they said he might be paralyzed from the neck down and not even able to breathe on his own. Then they said, "Good news! His breathing is going to be okay after all, and what's more he might be paralyzed only from the chest down, not the neck. That would mean he could use his arms, at least."

I guess it's easy to say these things when it's somebody else that has to actually live their life in that condition. I'm glad to say Bill is a little better off than they predicted, for whatever it's worth. He is paralyzed only from the waist down (not the neck or the chest), and he's trying to make the best of it.

Of course, whatever kind of future we pictured for ourselves and our kids is out the window. Bill's days as a logger are over with, and we don't see how we can stay out here, two thousand miles from his folks and anybody else who might be able to help us out. Because we're gonna need all the help we can get, and then some.

PART FOUR

When sorrows come, they come not single spies, but in battalions.

                         – William Shakespeare, *Hamlet*

Chapter 1

Carol

Chicago, January 1961

The Christmas season produced a fresh set of memories (and snapshots) to stack upon those of previous years. We had a lovely time with Ray and with both sets of parents. I'm thirty-four, so I now have some thirty years' worth of holiday memories that swirl around together to form my own personal mythology of hearth and home and familial feeling.

As Jack and I clinked glasses to welcome 1961, I took a look around and this is what I saw: We have a roof over our heads, clothes on our backs, food in the fridge, money in the bank (maybe not as much as we'd like, but more than nothing), and, most importantly, we have our health. I mean not only Jack, Ray, and myself, but our extended family as well.

And what about our larger family, by which I mean the whole country? We've elected as our President a handsome, charismatic, and capable young man who has a lovely wife and children and who also happens to share our Catholic faith.

JFK said two things in his inaugural address that gave me goosebumps. First, "The torch has been passed to a new generation of Americans," and second, "Ask not what your country can do for you; ask what you can do for your country."

I've been thinking a lot about those two lines. To me, the first one means that those of us under forty-five or so have waited in the wings long enough. Now it's our turn to take charge and see if we can't build upon what our parents and grandparents and great-grandparents have already bequeathed us.

The second line is closely related to the first, of course, but it's even more interesting. For example, let's suppose that instead of "country," JFK had said "spouse"? That would've gotten your attention, wouldn't it? Or you could swap in any number of other words such as household, family, friends, parish, neighborhood, town, etc. If that doesn't clarify your sense of accountability to something other than yourself, then I don't know what to tell you.

Jack has been out of sorts lately—not for a couple hours or a day here and there, but pretty much all the time.

At first I tried to be patient and hope the problem, whatever it was, would go away. I also wracked my brain trying to remember if I had said or done anything that might've rubbed him the wrong way. Finally I couldn't stand it any longer. I just came right out and asked him what was wrong. If you knew Jack, you'd realize that was a big step. Yes, I'm his wife, and yes, a wife should be able to ask her husband an honest, sincere question like that whenever she pleases. But it's not so straightforward where this particular husband is concerned. He's always been less than eager to share his thoughts, especially under "interrogation," as he's inclined to call the asking of even a single innocuous question.

"What do you mean?" Jack said when I asked him the question over breakfast one morning.

"I don't know, hon," I said. "You just don't seem quite yourself lately. Is there something wrong?"

"Like what?"

"Oh, I don't know. Anything at all. If there's something wrong I'd like to help you with it."

He bit into a strip of bacon. "Well," he said, "nothing comes to mind."

So the interrogation was not a success. I let it go for the time being and promised myself to push harder the next time.

That weekend Jack took Ray to the hardware store. They bought some wood panels to make signs for the names of the cabins at Larry's. We had decided to name the cabins Whispering Winds, Pine Bough, Sunset View, and Autumn Leaves. Ray was going to make the signs with his new wood-burning kit.

They were spreading out some newspapers on the kitchen table when I headed off to the Jewel. "I can't wait to see your work when I get back," I said, after reminding them once again how to spell "bough."

When I returned, I parked in the garage and came up the back stairs with two bags of groceries. I was going to ask Jack to run down and fetch the other two, but when I came in the back door no one was there. The newspapers and the wood panels were on the kitchen table, and the wood-burning stylus or whatever you call it was there too, still plugged in and burning into the table.

Then I heard a commotion in the bathroom. I went in there to find Ray with a nasty burn across the palm of his hand, to which Jack was attempting to apply Neosporin with little cooperation from the patient.

It turned out that Ray had somehow grabbed the hot part of the wood-burning thing, rather than the cork handle.

Ray finally stopped squirming long enough to allow Jack to get the ointment on. Then Jack wrapped gauze around Ray's hand and taped the whole thing up. All in all, he did a darn good job of it.

We sort of spoiled Ray for the rest of that day and night. We ordered pizza and then we had ice cream. After that we made popcorn and curled up on the sofa to watch TV, and we let Ray pick the shows to watch. He chose Lassie, Dennis the Menace, and Red Skelton. Red's not really my cup of tea, but what can you do?

When Ray went to bed, Jack and I stayed in the front room and had a cocktail. I wondered to what extent Jack felt responsible for Ray's accident, but there was nothing to gain by asking. At any rate, it seemed likely that Ray would be fine in a few days.

Then, all of a sudden Jack volunteered the information I had attempted to pry loose several days earlier. That was a surprise. It must have been bugging him quite a bit. "Remember the other day when you asked me if anything was wrong?" he said. "Well, you're damn right there is. I'm on the shit list."

"Oh, honey," I said. "Whatever for?"

"I didn't bring the votes in."

"That's crazy," I said. "How can you say that when Kennedy won, Kerner won, Douglas won, and Adamowski lost?"

Jack polished off his drink and crushed a stray ice cube between his molars. "It's very simple," he said. "I did 66-34 for Kennedy, which met my quota, just barely. But I only did 57-43 for Ward against Adamowski. That won't cut it."

The Republicans have been screaming bloody murder that Daley and the machine stole the election, and the papers pointed out that certain precincts recorded ninety-eight or ninety-nine percent turnouts with (of course) overwhelming majorities for the Democrats. It reminds me of something my dad said one time: "If you don't have the votes, you'd better have the vote counters." I like to believe that Jack allowed honest counts in his precinct on purpose, and not because he simply neglected to cheat.

"Well," I said pleasantly, "Ward won anyway, so there's no harm done."

"It don't matter," he said. "I had x-number of jerkoffs that voted for Kennedy like they promised me and then turned around and voted for Adamowski, just to spite me. So that proves I can't control my people."

"But honey," I said. "The election was almost three months ago. They would've done something by now, if they were going to."

He took out a cigarette and lit up. "They'd never do anything before Christmas."

"I guess that wouldn't be nice, would it?"

"It wouldn't be nice and they wouldn't have gotten my holiday donation."

"Oh, Jack," I said and touched his cheek. "What do you think they'll do?"

He had a look in his eyes that I've never seen before. I don't know if it was fear, exactly, but it sure scared the heck out of me.

"Damned if I know," he said. "But I'm liable to lose the captain job. And if I do, the city job might go down the drain along with it."

He got up from the sofa with his glass in hand. "Do you want another drink?"

"No thanks, honey."

"Listen," he said. "Don't be too alarmed. We'll figure something out."

That didn't sound good at all. We're off to a flying start in the new year, aren't we?

Chapter 2

Ray

Chicago, January 1961

The Hanlons' dog Oliver got run over by a car today. It was a pretty nice day out, not too cold, and we were playing street hockey after school. We saw the car coming down the block and we all moved over to the curb when suddenly Oliver got out and came running right into the street. He is the type of dog who runs all over the place and tries to get you to chase him. He almost got hit lots of times, but today he really did.

The man who hit Oliver got out of the car and put his hands up on top of his head. He was an older man with white hair and a mustache. Oliver was laying in the street. He wasn't whimpering or anything, but just breathing kind of rough. He sounded like he was snoring.

Mr. Hanlon was at work, but Pam was home and so was Mrs. Hanlon. They were inside the house and didn't know what was going on until Peter Cullen rang the doorbell and told them. Pam came running out the front door screaming and then her mom came out too. Pam is about sixteen years old, I would say.

The man who hit Oliver kept on apologizing to Pam and Mrs. Hanlon over and over. I never saw a man cry before. Everybody was standing there looking down at Oliver. Then Mrs. Hanlon said to me, "Ray dear, would you go over and see if Mr. Horvath across the street is home?"

She wanted Mr. Horvath because he grew up on a farm in Minnesota and he is used to this kind of a thing.

I went and got Mr. Horvath. He came out and said, "Oh, this is no good. His back is broke." He took his cigar out of his mouth and tossed it away. It was one of those skinny cigars with a plastic mouthpiece on the end, not like the fat ones my Grandpa Mike smokes even though he's not supposed to.

Mr. Horvath picked up Oliver with two feet in each hand and carried him out of the street upside down. Then he said, "I'll take this guy in back and put him out of his misery."

Pam screamed again. Mrs. Hanlon said, "Thanks all the same, Andy, but maybe you shouldn't."

Then they talked a while. Mrs. Hanlon decided to take Oliver to the vet instead of letting Mr. Horvath hit him over the head with a hammer. So she pulled the car around and Pam got in with her. Then Mr. Horvath put Oliver in the back seat on top of an old blanket.

When Pam and Mrs. Hanlon came back a while later, Oliver wasn't with them. He was put to sleep.

That was about the worst thing ever.

Chapter 3

Don

Birch Lake, February 1961

So this one Friday night Jack was spose to be coming up, Mike and Mrs. Weber invited me to have dinner with 'em. They didn't have to ask twice. If you ever ate Mrs. Weber's cooking, you'd know what I mean. She served up round steak with onion rings baked on top of it, mashed potatoes with gravy, and green beans. It was delicious.

The only problem is I don't want to get spoiled by eating over there too often. I don't want to abuse the privilege, as the saying goes.

After dinner and dessert (homemade apple pie), Mike says, "Let's have a libation or two and wait for Jack." I was always a beer man myself, but being around Mike so much lately I decided to go ahead and give bourbon a try. I'm still getting the hang of drinking that stuff. If you don't watch yourself, it'll jump up and bite you but good. If you think you're gonna down a dozen or so like you would with beers, you better guess again.

Mrs. Weber went in the front room to watch TV. She likes all them cowboy shows they have on, especially Marshal Dillon. I don't know if he was on or it was one of the others. Mike and I set down at the kitchen table to go over our list of projects for Larry's.

There's lots of different kinds of jobs. Some need to be done every year before winter sets in and some need to be done every spring before we open up again. These are your basic jobs like taking the pier out of the water, putting it back in, and what have you. Then there's a whole list of other jobs which are the big improvement projects, like re-roofing all the cabins, expanding the beach area, putting in a swing set and slide for the kiddies, re-grading and repaving the boat launch, stuff like that. And then there's the regular maintenance type stuff, which you wouldn't bother to write down on the list but still needs to get done anyways.

I couldn't tell you how many times we been over the list together, making little changes here and there. I don't mind at all. You can tell Mike gets a big kick out of it, and that's good enough for me. If he wants to go over that list every day and twice on Sunday, you'll never hear no complaints from me.

So we worked on the list, and meanwhile Mike poured a few, and we sort of lost track of time. Finally Mrs. Weber come in from the other room and says to Mike, "Pardon the interruption, dear, but didn't you say we should expect Jack around eight or nine o'clock?"

"That sounds about right," Mike says.

"Well, it's eleven now," she says. "Do you think we ought to be worried?"

Mike took off his reading glasses and looked up at Mrs. Weber. "Well," he says, "maybe he just got a later start than he figured. That could be. Maybe he got stuck at work."

"Do you think we should call Carol and ask her what time he left?" Mrs. Weber says.

"No, let's not do that just yet. I'd hate to alarm Carol for no reason."

"But maybe it isn't for no reason."

"Jack's a smart boy," Mike says. "He'd call us if he needed any help, right?"

"If he could," Mrs. Weber says.

"Don't worry, dear," Mike says. "I'm sure he'll turn up real soon."

Finally midnight rolled around. I didn't want to turn into a pumpkin so I headed out. I was already a little tipsy from the bourbons anyways. Mike always says you should only pour two fingers and go ahead and nurse that for forty-five minutes or an hour before pouring another one, but I can't do it. I ain't gonna lie to you. I don't care if it's water or iced tea or beer or paint thinner, if it's setting there in a glass in front of me I'm gonna down it. It wouldn't take me no forty-five minutes or an hour unless my hands was tied behind my back and I didn't have no straw.

When I went back the next day, sure enough Jack was there safe and sound. Mrs. Weber told me to come in the kitchen and have a cup of coffee with the boys—which is what she always calls Mike and Jack, in case you don't know. I took her up on it. I went and set down next to Jack, acrossed from Mike.

Jack had a cigarette going. He wasn't really smoking it, just holding it out there like people do sometimes when they're bored or whatever. So here's the interesting part. There was a matchbook on the table in front of him, and it said STAR LITE TAP. I ain't no detective or nothing, but ain't that the place Jeannie works at?

Chapter 4

Jeannie

Birch Lake, February 1961

You can tell a lot about somebody when they're smashed out of their gourd. Their true nature comes out, doesn't it? If they are a mean, hateful person to begin with, they'll be that much worse when they're bombed.

I don't really mind waiting on drunks at all, if they're at least nice about it. I guess you wouldn't be cut out for a cocktail waitress if you couldn't stand drunk people. Some of these folks are three sheets to the wind and sweet as can be. But being drunk and belligerent is something else again.

Anybody who passes the time bending their elbow has seen a few bar fights. Maybe even been in a few. You don't even need a full moon. You just put some fellas together, add alcohol, stir, and there you go.

You want to know something? Whenever a fight breaks out at the Star Lite, nine times out of ten it's about the pool table—not over some chicky like you'd think. I guess that's because we don't have too many chickies in there anyways.

A fight at the pool table pretty much has to be about one of two things. One is whether somebody's shot went in as called or was slop. The other is who's next in line to take on the winners. Goodness, you wouldn't think it could be so confusing. Of course, the more the fellas drink, the more confusing it gets.

I never saw somebody break a bottle and threaten another fella with the skinny end like they do in the movies. I also never saw anybody punch a guy with a billiard ball or throw it at him. And I never saw anybody swing a pool cue at someone like a baseball bat. I guess that stuff is against the rules, like pulling a guy's hair or kicking him in the walnuts. One time I did see somebody jabbing at a guy with the butt end of the cue, but that just seemed sort of ridiculous.

Now this one night we ended up having a general brawl. I don't really know how to explain it, and I bet you the guys involved don't either. Here's what I do know. Jack and Don were there, and some way or another Don got into a big argument with a guy I don't know about who was cuter, Marilyn Monroe or Audrey Hepburn.

I recall at one point somebody called Marilyn a cheap slut, but I'm not sure who. After a while you couldn't tell which side of the argument was which. When they finally asked me to settle it, I just said, "I really couldn't say. They're both very attractive in their own way."

Just between us, I like Audrey better. It's strange because I'm blonde and curvy and she's the exact opposite. I wonder if the brunettes like Marilyn.

So anyways, the night went along just like you'd expect in a crowded bar. The talking got louder, the gesturing got exaggerated, and everything sort of heated up. And then a fight broke out at the pool table. Just like clockwork. I didn't see how it started, but this little guy that was arguing with Don about Audrey and Marilyn was in the middle of it, along with two or three other guys I didn't know. Our regulars are pretty harmless, but we had lots of other guys in there that night who we never saw before, and they were harder to control. These guys went from pushing and shoving to throwing a few punches to finally wrestling around on the floor.

I wish we had a bouncer, some giant football player type fella to keep everybody in line. Come to think of it, that would've been a good job for Bill before his accident. He'd have been perfect for it. As it is, our bartender Keith has to break up the fights. By himself. He's a big tall guy, strong enough I guess, but sort of thin and lanky like a basketball player.

Anyways, as soon as Keith hopped over the bar and waded into the fight, Jack and Don went right in after him. I'm not sure if they jumped in to help Keith break it up or to try and get some licks in for themselves. But after it was all said and done, the troublemakers got tossed out on their ear.

Keith couldn't thank Jack and Don enough. He told them, "Your money's no good the rest of the night." It was maybe an hour and a half before closing time, and let me tell you those fellas took full advantage of Keith's offer. Especially Don. He seemed to be doing a shot and a beer for every beer Jack had.

"Don's not used to bartenders offering him freebies," Jack told me. "He thinks he died and went to Heaven."

Exactly ten minutes after last call, Keith yelled out, "Okay, drink 'em up, folks! You don't have to go home, but you can't stay here!" He always says that at closing time.

Jack and Don started to leave with the rest of them. "Sit back down," Keith said. "That don't apply to you two."

After he locked the door behind the last few stragglers he said, "Let's just sit tight. Maybe them guys are still outside laying for us. Let's relax a while. You too, Jeannie."

I figured what the heck, you only live once. I called Bill and told him I'd be later than usual. "I'm so sorry to wake you," I said. "Just wanted to let you know." I don't think he minded. I bet he was asleep again before he hung up the phone. At least I hope so.

The four of us played pool for a while and drank a bit more than we should've. I'm the first one to admit I got a little carried away. I don't get out much these days, if that's any excuse. Plus it was kind of exciting to spend some time with Jack again, just sort of goofing off, almost like we were kids again.

I'm not that much of a drinker to begin with, and I've hardly drank at all since Bill's accident, for fear I'll be passed out the one time he really needs help in the middle of the night. God forbid, he might roll over the wrong way and end up where he couldn't breathe or something. I know something could just as easily happen to him when I'm not home, but there'd be no excuse at all if it happened with me sawing logs right next to him.

Jack and I beat Don and Keith two out of three. Maybe I should say Jack beat them and I watched. I didn't need to shoot very often, since Jack cleared the table without much help from me. Then we agreed to have one more drink apiece. "The final and ultimate nightcap," Jack announced, and we all shook on it. But we ended up having another round after that and yet another after that. If you think it was getting stupid, you won't get any argument from my end.

Finally Keith went outside and took a look around. He came back and said we could all make it to our cars without anybody jumping us. So this is where it got complicated. Don couldn't have driven once around the building, much less all the way home. These roads around here are very dark and very curvy. Even sober people get in wrecks all the time.

"I'll drive you home," Jack said to Don. "We'll come back for your truck in the morning."

"Like hell," Don said.

To make a long story short, Don swore there was no way he could leave his truck at the Star Lite overnight and come back for it the next day—because all that chasing around would take way too much time, and he had some very important things to do in the morning, and this and that. "Now, I ain't fooling," he said.

Jack took me aside. "I hate to take advantage," he said, "but could you possibly help me get our friend here home in one piece?"

"Of course," I said, but I didn't really mean it. I was anxious to get home myself by this time.

Jack said he'd drive Don home in Don's truck while I followed in Jack's car. (I don't know how to drive a truck, and I wasn't about to learn just then.) After we got Don tucked in, Jack would drive me back to the Star Lite so I could get my own car and head on home.

We finally got Don to agree to the plan, rather than trying to drive himself, but we weren't two steps out the door when he threw a wrench in the works. He said it'd be an awful cold day in hell when he'd ride with Jack when he could ride with me instead. "I mean come on," he said. "What do you take me for?"

At first I was worried Don might try something in the car, but all he did was say some very sweet things. He said he thought about me lots of times and always wondered how I was doing and hoped the world was giving me a fair shake. He said when he was overseas in the service he imagined him and the rest of the guys were fighting for me, to keep me safe. Just me and nobody else. Can you beat that? Of course it was the booze talking, but it wasn't only booze talking. I think there was something more behind it. I don't picture Don as a guy who could make up something like that on the spur of the moment just to hear himself talk.

Anyways, after a few minutes he ran out of steam. His chin dropped onto his chest and he started snoring. I wondered if he'd remember any of those nice things he told me.

Jack and I got Don as far as the sofa in his living room. Dragging him all the way to the bedroom would've been a little much. We left his truck in the driveway and the keys on the kitchen counter, and we were off.

I don't know how to describe the feeling I had, riding in a car with Jack again after so many years, cruising along in the dead of night like we did way back when. He palmed the wheel the same way. He whistled no particular tune the same way. He lit his cigarette and clenched it between his teeth the same way. It was eerie.

You could never tell what goes on in Jack's mind, but I have to believe he felt it too. Neither of us said much. We got about half-way back to the Star Lite before he pulled off into a little picnic grove. There was snow on the ground, but not enough for us to get stuck. He parked next to a row of pine trees with snow on the branches. It was real nice there. Is there any place quieter and more private than a picnic grove late at night in the dead of winter? I doubt it.

What happened then, we did the whole shebang right there in the car. Unbelievable. I should have my head examined.

Chapter 5

Carol

Chicago, March 1961

Ray won't touch the wood-burning kit since he burned himself with it, so the signs for the cabins at Larry's remain an idea rather than actual objects that Mike can use and point to with pride. I don't know what we're going to do about that. I think we owe it to Mike to get that project done as we said we would. I can't really blame Ray for feeling the way he does, but I wonder if Jack couldn't nudge him along a bit more forcefully.

As for Jack himself, the touching vulnerability and uncertainty I saw during our heart-to-heart after Ray's accident has given way to a sort of ironic detachment and world-weary cynicism. He has indeed lost the precinct captain's job, as he predicted. He hasn't lost the city job, at least not yet, but he's expected to work for the party as an ordinary foot soldier in order to keep it—albeit with his hours reduced, overtime eliminated, and other slights and indignities tossed his way more or less randomly.

There isn't enough money. I know, even Rockefeller probably says the same thing, but if he offered to switch places with us we'd have to consider it.

Now I'm going to a rather dark place. As a person with eyes and ears and whatever sense the good Lord has given me, I can't help it. Of course, it's no secret that Jack likes to play the ponies from time to time and that he plays poker with his buddies twice a month—but now I wonder if there isn't something more ominous afoot. For some time now, I've been getting the occasional phone call where I say "Hello," and the person on the other end

269

doesn't say anything, just stays on the line for a few seconds and then hangs up. Now what do you suppose that could be about?

I've been thinking back to one Sunday last fall when Jack, Ray, and I were watching the Bears against the Green Bay Packers on TV. By the way, you'll never guess what Jack calls the Packers. It's not very nice. He calls them the Fudge Packers. Can you imagine? Thankfully, he's never said that in front of Ray—at least to my knowledge.

At any rate, the Packers were leading this game 14-0 after three quarters. Then, in the fourth quarter, Galimore scored a touchdown and Casares scored another one to tie the score. When the Bears kicked a field goal to win 17-14, Ray was overjoyed. He and I were cheering, and we couldn't understand why Jack was so subdued. Finally Jack said, "Sure, it's swell the Bears won, but I'd be that much happier with another touchdown instead of the field goal." Then he stalked out of the room muttering to himself.

Okay. So what do we understand from that anecdote? We understand, or can reasonably suppose, that Jack had a wager on the game, and he needed the Bears to win by more than the three points. Right? But what we don't know is how much he wagered on that game, how much he wagered on other games, and how much he has won or (perhaps more likely) lost in the recent past.

I'll grant you that a man is entitled to blow off steam every now and then, in whatever way does the trick for him, as long as it's fairly harmless. But if it precludes him from paying the bills, then you have an issue on your hands.

I married Jack willingly, even eagerly, and I love him. I wish only the best for him. At the same time, I don't feel obliged to defer to him in everything. I have a right to my own opinions, even when they differ from his, and I have a right to voice them for his own good.

Love bears all things, believes all things, hopes all things, endures all things. "We're in this together," I told Jack recently. "I'm

270

here, and I'm not going anywhere. I'll do whatever I can for you. Whatever difficulties come along, we'll get through them together."

I was feeling strong and buoyant and even heroic when I went so far as to suggest I could go back to work if it would further the cause. Of course, I sent up that balloon fully expecting Jack to puncture it.

Imagine my surprise when he blandly said, "Maybe that's not such a bad idea." Will wonders never cease?

Chapter 6

Don

Birch Lake, March 1961

Mike never misses nothing. He wants everything to be just right. The thing about him, he'll do twice as much work as me or anybody else, where back in his day Larry would just set there sucking on a beer and barking out orders.

One of the chores every year is to get the pier ready. Of course you gotta wait until it's pretty near spring so there's no more chances for the lake to get froze over solid. When the time come, Mike and me pulled the tarp off and unstacked the sections, and then we put 'em on the sawhorses one by one and painted 'em. I mean I sanded 'em on one pair of sawhorses and Mike painted 'em on the other.

Jack wasn't around. He supposably come up that weekend especially to help us out with the pier, but he was off somewheres while most of the work was going on. Mike didn't say nothing, and I didn't neither. It wasn't my place to say nothing if Mike didn't. Later on, when Jack got back, he told me he rode out to Lake Wissota to talk to Orville Warnecke again about the pontoon boat. I don't know.

Mike had the idea to use this redwood stain instead of the regular white paint we always used before. I had to hand it to him. I wasn't sold right off when he suggested it, but soon as he put on the first brush full, you could see he was right as usual. It looked real sharp.

"Let 'em dry," Mike says, "and we'll reconvene at nine tomorrow morning. Then we'll carry 'em down to the beach and screw 'em onto the frame."

Well sir, if Mike tells me to show up at nine o'clock, you can bet your buttonhole he'll be on the job himself by eight at the latest. But I didn't push it because I know he likes to work by himself sometimes anyways. Sure as shit, when I showed up at half past eight he was already at it. And how. He had his waders on, and he had the first three or four sections already laid in place. The rest of 'em was setting right there on the shore.

Keep in mind each one of them sections is about six foot long and four foot wide, and pretty heavy to boot. Carrying one by yourself ain't the easiest thing you ever thought of, much less carrying a dozen of 'em all the way from the shed down to the beach one after the other. What a tough old bird.

I walked down there and I says, "How you doing?" to Mike.

Now, normally he would say, "What do you think?" as sort of a joke. But this time he says, "Just fine, thanks." I never heard him say that before in my life. And then, where he usually would say, "And how's everything in Hono-loola?" or Timbuktu or Sheepshead Bay or Constantinople (just anyplace he thought sounded kinda funny), he didn't say nothing else. I realized right off it was strange, but I just let it slide. Why in hell did I do that?

"I don't know if you need me," I says to him. "Looks like you're doing fine on your own."

"Oh, I always need you, Jack," he says. "I mean Don." Then he says, "Why don't you go get yourself a cup of coffee and then come back. I'll hold down the fort."

So I went up to the house and said hello to Mrs. Weber. She set me down to have a cup of coffee with her. We talked about the weather and whatnot for a few minutes, and then she had a question for me. "Listen, Don," she says, making believe she was kidding but actually serious. "What did you do to Jack last night?

Lord knows what time he got in. He hasn't even stirred this morning."

I guess I was a likely enough one to blame, but I didn't do nothing to Jack. I never even seen him the night before.

"Well," I says, "I'm sure he'll be up and at 'em soon. Just as good as new."

For some reason, I happened to look out the window just then, and I couldn't believe what I seen. Mike had the can of stain out, and he was on his hands and knees touching up the sections he already had in place. But here's the thing. You'd never start doing the touchups until you had all the planks screwed down, and even then you'd start from the far end and work toward the shore. He was doing it the other way around. I couldn't imagine what he was thinking. I figured he must be pretty mixed up for some reason and I better get out there.

I went to put my cup in the sink, and by the time I done that and got out the door (maybe ten seconds, tops), I seen we had a man down. Mike was laying face first on the pier.

Of course I thought of a million different things. What if I didn't go in for coffee but stayed there with him instead? What if I got there earlier to help him carry all them sections down to the beach? What if Jack rolled out of bed in time to help out? Who knows? Maybe it wasn't nobody's fault. Maybe when your time comes it just comes, and there ain't nothing nobody can do about it.

One thing I noticed, Mike was always wheezing lately. He kept making kind of a whistling sound when he breathed. And he would get dizzy. He wouldn't admit it, but you could see him wobble every so often, especially when he got up from squatting down or kneeling. Then he would kind of tilt his head forward and hold it in his hand a minute till he got squared away.

I wish I had a buck for every time I says to him, "When's the last time you seen a doctor?"

"You sound just like Betty," he'd say. "Are you two in cahoots together?" He just laughed it off. Some people just don't have no use for doctors.

I hightailed it down to the pier, and when I got there—well, I'm not gonna kid you. It was bad. Very bad. The can of stain was setting on the bottom of the lake, about three foot down, and the stain was billowing up and spreading out over the surface.

Mike wasn't showing no signs of life. I turned him over. I talked to him and patted his cheeks and shook him by the shoulders, but I didn't get no reaction from him at all. He was just staring right on past me—into Heaven, you might say.

Knowing the type of guy he was, he just kept going no matter what and didn't give a damn about nothing. I figure he was already gone by the time I got to him. Maybe even before he keeled over. That was really the only way for him to go out, if you ask me. God bless him, he went out with his boots on. Well, his waders anyways.

He was the best man I'll ever know. That's for damn sure.

Chapter 7

Carol

Chicago, April 1961

I talked to Mike just the day before he died.

I called up north wanting to speak to Jack, who wasn't around, and Mike said, "How's my girl?" He said he'd have Jack call me back first thing, and then he said, "Now, don't let Elizabeth find out we talked. You know, she's liable to be jealous."

He was as alive to me then as I was to myself. More, actually, because he was always more full of life than I consider myself to be. And less than twenty-four hours later he was every bit as dead as Lincoln or Shakespeare or Jesus Christ. I mean in this world. None of us can speak for the next, but I take it as a good omen that he left this life on Good Friday.

Mike was a man in every old-fashioned sense of the word. He was honest and dignified. Strong as an ox and tough as nails (use whatever clichés you want), and yet as gentle and tender as could be. If you ever saw him holding hands with Elizabeth or with his arm around Ray, you'd know what I mean.

There was nothing fake or affected about him. He hated pretense of any kind. He was nobody's fool. At the same time, he wanted to think the best of everyone. He gladly gave people the benefit of the doubt. He'd meet you halfway, or more than halfway—but if you crossed him, he'd have no further use for you. (I'm afraid Jack has inherited a somewhat distorted version of his dad's approach. He goes in expecting the worst from people, and yet when they oblige him by conforming to his expectations, he is still surprised and disappointed.)

I always had the feeling that Mike never had to wonder how he should behave in a given situation, because he already knew. Deep down, in his bones, he just knew.

He could not have been kinder or more generous to me. I have to admit I was scared to death of Elizabeth at first, and only slightly less so as the years went by. I suppose she liked me well enough in her own way, but I always felt I needed to tiptoe around her. Mike, though, went out of his way to make me feel welcome from our very first meeting. He told me I'd have to give him a quarter every time I called him Mr. Weber or Sir, rather than Mike. "If we keep going at this rate," he said one time shortly after Jack and I got married, "we'll soon have enough for you kids to put a down payment on a house."

He used to make little inside jokes that were just for the two of us. He'd wink at me or tap the back of my hand, and then say something to Elizabeth or Jack that they could interpret one way, but which was understood to have a different meaning for me. We weren't keeping any real secrets from the other two. It was just silly stuff, but it was Mike's way of making me feel as though I really belonged—that I was an actual member of the family from his point of view, not a visitor.

I adored him for that.

Mike's passing was a sickening loss for me, but I had to concern myself with consoling the others.

My heart went out to Elizabeth, of course. I don't think she and Mike spent more than a handful of nights apart in forty-one years of marriage. My word, what would you do if all of a sudden you turned around one day and that person was gone?

Jack was simply numb. He wasn't terribly demonstrative about it, but he's always idolized Mike. Anyone could see that.

I felt the worst for Ray. When we sat him down and told him we'd lost his grandpa, he didn't understand at first. "Where do you think he went?" he asked. "Don't you think we can find him?"

The afternoon of Mike's wake, we family members went in before the doors opened to the public. My stomach was in my throat, I was so afraid for Ray to see his grandpa in the casket. I held his hand as we walked in. I was trembling. And do you know what he did, my precious boy? He looked up at me and said, "It'll be okay, Mom." A nine-year-old child who was suffering through the greatest loss of his young life trying to console someone else!

I always thought that Mike looked less like himself in a business suit, unlike my own dad, who seems as if he was born in one. Mike much preferred a weathered fedora or baseball cap, a flannel shirt, a pair of khaki pants or corduroys, and some old clodhopper work boots. But I hope he'd be glad to know that he looked splendid in his new navy-blue suit, white shirt, and sky-blue tie. Maybe it's morbid, but he really did look good under the circumstances.

I bought the clothes for Mike, and I picked out the casket, and I worked out everything with the undertaker and the church because neither Elizabeth nor Jack was up to it. In their grief they were unable to focus on the various things that required *someone's* attention, and I didn't mind helping out. I was quite glad to do it, in fact. I saw myself as doing it for Mike, my buddy, as much as for them. I was a little afraid they'd resent it later and decide that I had been presumptuous. If that were to happen, I told myself, well, sometimes you just can't win.

I also ordered the mass cards, and by a pure fluke I happened to remember a little epigraph I'd read somewhere.

MICHAEL JOHN WEBER

Born into life - January 24, 1895

Born into eternal life - March 31, 1961

Funeral mass - April 4, 1961, St. Denis Church, Chicago

Interment St. Mary Catholic Cemetery, Evergreen Park

When through one man, a little more love and goodness,

A little more light and truth come into the world,

Then that man's life has had meaning.

To their credit, both Elizabeth and Jack pulled themselves together reasonably well when it counted. They were ready to go when
the doors opened and the people started filing in to pay their re-
spects. They greeted the people graciously, and smiled at their little reminiscences about Mike, and patted some of them on the
shoulder. Jack introduced me indiscriminately to people I hadn't
met before and to those I had, even including some whose homes
we had visited and vice versa.

My dear mom sat with Elizabeth when the latter wasn't otherwise occupied. She held Elizabeth's hand and kept her hankies
at the ready and fetched her coffee or water. She didn't go to the
bathroom *for* her, but she did accompany her to the bathroom
whenever the need arose. My mom, bless her, has always had an
easy way with Elizabeth that I haven't. Maybe I've never tried
hard enough. That is really quite possible.

Ray was stunned, yes, but he comported himself beautifully.
He shook hands with the people to whom he was introduced, and
smiled up at them, and let them tousle his hair or pinch his cheek,
all with his typical self-possession. I was reminded of a greeting
card that I picked up for one of his birthdays and will never forget. On the front it said: WHICH THREE LITTLE WORDS MAKE ME THE
PROUDEST TO SAY? When you opened it up, it said: "THAT'S MY
SON!"

279

You should have seen me bawling right there in the aisle at Walgreens when I found that one.

And then there was Don. It was awfully stupid of me, but I hadn't quite grasped just how much Mike meant to him. I knew that Don looked up to Mike and that Mike had a soft spot for Don, but I didn't totally get it before.

To see Don at Mike's wake, it was pathetic. In the first place, he seemed to have bought himself a new suit for the occasion, but unfortunately it didn't fit properly. He'd obviously gotten it off the rack and just wore it as-is or, worse yet, had it altered by someone who didn't know what they were doing. Don is barrel-chested but not very tall, an unfortunate combination when it comes to the fit of a suit. His sleeves covered most of his hands, leaving the fingers sticking out somewhat comically. He had on a grayish shirt that had probably been white at one time and was frayed at the collar and cuffs. His necktie and shoes—well, I probably shouldn't go on about what the poor thing was wearing, but it contributed to the overall impression I got. It was truly heartbreaking.

He stayed around the margins, constantly asking the rest of us if we needed anything, while trying at the same time to make sure he wasn't in the way. Toward the end of the evening, after most of the people had gone, I saw him go over to the casket. He got down on the kneeler, made the sign of the cross, and clasped his hands together as if to pray. But suddenly he pressed the back of his hand to his mouth, and his chin dropped toward his chest, and his shoulders shook from sobbing. I should have gone over and put my arm around him, but I didn't for whatever reason. I could kick myself for that. Finally, he grabbed one of Mike's forearms and squeezed it for a while before composing himself and getting back up.

There's more. I had ordered floral arrangements to be placed near the casket. You know the kind—sort of an oversized wreath that rests on an easel-type stand and has a large blue, red, or green ribbon with gold letters on it. We had three of these arrangements, which said BELOVED HUSBAND, DEAREST DAD, and CHERISHED GRANDPA, respectively. When I stopped by the undertaker's a few days after the funeral to write a check for our remaining balance, the man told me to subtract the cost of the wreaths. He said, "They were paid for by a friend who wishes to remain anonymous."

I still didn't get it. Come on, Carol! I went home and called my dad to find out if he had paid for them. "You know me better than that," he said. And he was right. He wouldn't have done something like that anonymously. He would have marched right up with his checkbook in hand and said, "How much do you need?"

So it wasn't my dad, and it wasn't anyone else I could think of. But when I mentioned it to Jack, he knew the answer right off. "Oh, that sounds just like Don," he said. "Who else would go and pull something like that?"

If it were up to me, we would've sent Don a gift, also anonymously, to acknowledge his kindness. I thought that would've been a nice touch, the anonymous part—responding in kind but not letting on. I bet Don would've gotten a kick out of that. But when I suggested the idea to Jack, he wasn't too enthused. "Just hold your horses a while and I'll think about it," he said. "And I'll check and see what my ma has to say." That was the last I ever heard of it.

Maybe Jack did end up doing something for Don that he didn't tell me about. Maybe he did nothing on purpose, on the theory that Don made the gesture anonymously and wished it to remain that way. Most likely, though, he meant to do something and just didn't get around to it. That would be my best guess.

I gave Jack a sort of gag gift one time. It was a little wooden disk, about the size of a poker chip. On one side it said: ROUND TUIT, and on the other side it said: NOW YOU CAN'T SAY YOU NEVER GOT A ROUND TUIT! It was a silly joke, obviously, and Jack wasn't much amused by it. There was a serious point behind it, though, because I had already admitted to myself that Jack's intentions and his actions are often not very well aligned. But it seems the point was made too subtly. I can tell you without fear of contradiction that if there was a lesson to be taken from the "round tuit," Jack did not receive it.

Mike's wake and funeral were as nice as events of that kind can be, I guess. We were fairly well satisfied that we had done justice to his memory. There was a heartening turnout from Mike and Elizabeth's old neighborhood, from Mike's American Legion buddies and bowling buddies (those two groups overlapped a good deal), and even from people who knew Mike and Elizabeth up north.

But such is Jack's status, or lack thereof, that almost none of his colleagues from work or from the party showed up. I wasn't going to mention it, but on the way home from the funeral luncheon Jack brought it up himself. "These people from up north drove 350 miles to get here," he said, "and the ones who live right around the corner couldn't be bothered. Screw 'em."

He seems to have concluded by now that if Chicago has turned its back on him, then he is prepared to turn his back on Chicago.

Chapter 8

Ray

Chicago, April 1961

People must die all the time. Otherwise there wouldn't be so many undertakers and cemeteries.

Before my Grandpa Mike, I never knew anyone that passed away—except Mr. Weinschenk down the block, who died of old age, and Tommy Barton from school.

Tommy was my age, but he wasn't in my class. He had Sister Mary Frances and I had Sister Constance. This was last year, in third grade. I didn't know him too well, but he always seemed pretty nice. They said he died from a disease called meningitis.

Then there are some famous people that passed away and were in the newspaper, like Clark Gable and Roger Hammerstein.

I never pictured somebody in our own family passing away. I couldn't believe it at first, but Mom explained it to me. She said, "It's terrible, but we must put our faith in the good Lord. He chose this time to call Grandpa Mike into the Kingdom of Heaven, and when He calls each of us in turn, we'll all be together again."

Lots of bad things can happen to people.

The Great Chicago Fire killed about 300 people and destroyed almost the entire city. It started in Mrs. O'Leary's barn at 137 DeKoven Street, which is not there anymore. If it was still there it would be about ten miles from our house.

The Peshtigo fire in Wisconsin was the worst fire ever in the United States. If you can believe this, it happened the same night

283

as the Great Chicago Fire. Nobody knows how many people died, but they think it was around 1,500 or 2,000. The fire destroyed a dozen villages and more than a million acres of forest. Peshtigo is about 190 miles from Birch Lake.

Over 600 people lost their life in the Iroquois Theatre fire. The Iroquois was located at 24 W. Randolph, about nine miles from our house.

Way back in 1905, eleven local men from Birch Lake drownded when they tried to clear a log jam in front of the dam but ended up getting swept over the falls.

About 850 people on their way to a picnic drownded when a boat called the *Eastland* rolled over onto its side in the Chicago River. These people got trapped inside the boat and couldn't get out. This happened about eight miles from our house.

The St. Valentine's Day massacre happened in a garage at 2122 N. Clark Street, which is five miles from our house.

The two Schuessler brothers and their friend Bobby Peterson went downtown to see a movie and were never heard from again. Their dead bodies were found in Robinson Woods two days later. Robinson Woods is only three and a half miles from our house.

Ed Gein was arrested in Plainfield, Wisconsin, for killing a lady who owned the local hardware store. When the police went to his house, they found out he killed many other ladies over the years and did the most unbelievable things with their bodies. He was put in the insane asylum. I hope he never escapes. Plainfield is about 140 miles from Birch Lake.

The Grimes sisters went to see an Elvis Presley movie one night and disappeared. Elvis himself made an announcement asking for the girls to be returned home safe and sound, but it didn't do any good. Barbara and Patricia were found dead alongside of a creek in Willow Springs. They lived at 3624 S. Damen, which is about twelve miles from our house.

Ninety-two school children and three Sisters perished in a terrible fire at Our Lady of the Angels School. I can remember when that happened, because I was old enough. My mom cried something awful, and she wouldn't stop hugging me. Our Lady of the Angels is located at 932 N. Kostner, about nine miles from St. Gregory's.

I bet all these people never thought those horrible things would happen to them.

After Grandpa Mike's funeral, Grandma Elizabeth and Grandma and Grandpa Foley and Mom and Dad and me all came back to our house. Mom went in the kitchen to make some coffee, and then all of a sudden she yelled for me.

She pointed out the back window. "Look, Ray," she said. There was a bright red cardinal standing on the wire that runs from the house to the telephone pole in the alley.

"You know what they say," Mom said. "A cardinal appears when an angel is near."

Chapter 9

Jeannie

Birch Lake, May 1961

Lots of people do stupid things. God knows I've done my share. But fucking Jack again after all those years pretty much takes the cake.

You know what's weird? I would never use a word like "fucking" when I was younger, but I guess I've gotten a little rougher since life did the same. Anyways, after we did it in the car that one night, I didn't see Jack for a while—maybe two or three weeks. When he finally stopped in at the Star Lite again, he brought Don with him and he acted pretty sheepish. So did I. We didn't make eye contact right away. Then I finally got a chance to talk to him one-to-one, and I told him I didn't blame him and these kind of things happen and blah, blah, blah. I also told him it couldn't happen again, and he agreed. He was almost apologetic.

I could blame the booze, or Bill's situation, or a hundred other things—but what would be the point? All the excuses in the world wouldn't change anything. Facts are facts. I betrayed my husband and lowered myself to the level of a common tramp. Or maybe I should say a floozy. What's worse, a tramp or a floozy?

To give you an idea how carried away I got that night, Jack and me ended up doing it in the same picnic grove where Bill and Julie and me spent lots of time way back when. While Jack and me were going at it, do you think I even realized it was the exact same place? If you guessed no, you are correct. Sure, the place is out of the way and it was a long time since I was there, but still. That's pretty weak. When the cobwebs cleared, I thought to my-

286

self the least I could've done for Bill was not cheat on him at the same exact place we used to go to together.

Bill's been a real handful for some time now. He hates the pink store and everything about it with a passion. Except the color, which is the one thing about the place everybody else hates! Everybody always asks why on Earth would you paint the pink store white. Bill just looks at these people and doesn't give them the satisfaction of answering.

When he knocks off, he goes home and parks in front of the TV and downs half a case of beer or so before passing out. Then I get home from the Star Lite and turn off the TV and pick up the empties and get him into bed. Lately I haven't had the energy to get him into his pajamas, so he usually sleeps in his skivvies. Not that he knows or cares one way or the other.

What happened to Bill, you'd never wish on your worst enemy. He's still trying to figure out how to handle it. I hope he figures it out pretty soon, because if he doesn't we might not survive. The kids and myself can't manage without him. We're practically all the way to the edge already. I don't mean just money. We can get by money-wise at least a while longer, but we can't make it without Bill getting back to being himself again. I'm trying to be as sympathetic and patient as can be, but something's gotta give one of these days.

Here's something to think about. Whenever people are going through a bad time they always tell theirself it'll get better if they just keep their chin up and muddle through. But what if our situation isn't gonna get better? What if we haven't already seen the worst of it? What if we aren't even close to the worst of it yet? What if it's just gonna keep on getting worse tomorrow, next week, next year, and every day until hell freezes over?

As far as Jack goes, seeing him again after all those years did set off some sparks on my side. It probably wouldn't shock anybody to hear that. He's still very attractive—actually more so, now that he's a man who knows more about life than a cocky high-school boy. I guess he's had an easier go of it than lots of people, but you can't really blame him for that. I don't begrudge anybody for being more fortunate, unless they go around rubbing your nose in it all the time.

Seeing Jack again hasn't made me feel the same way I did before, but it has made me *remember* how I felt in those days. That counts for something, anyways.

I meant it when I told him the little episode at the picnic grounds wasn't gonna happen again. It wouldn't be fair to Bill. It wouldn't fair to Jack's wife, who I'm sure is perfectly nice. And it wouldn't be fair to the kids, who have a right to expect better from their folks. But the main thing, it wouldn't be fair to Jack and me to get mixed up in something that couldn't possibly go anywhere but someplace bad.

I told Jack all this stuff right to his face, and he took it well enough. Then I reminded myself about it over and over. Sometimes we really are better off to deny ourself something we want, aren't we? It's good for the soul, right?

Jack was around a lot this spring, helping his dad out at Larry's, and he came into the Star Lite a few times. Sometimes he came by himself and sometimes with Don, but we never misbehaved. Well, one time we came out from the back together—me from the kitchen and Jack from the men's room—and Don said to Jack, "Your barn door's open there, bud." I don't know if he thought I had something to do with it, but believe me I didn't!

Mostly we just talked about this and that and the other thing, and I really enjoyed it. It made me feel a little better about myself. I was thinking maybe we could end up being friends without any strange sexual-type stuff getting in the way.

Then, out of the blue, Jack lost his dad. That's just the kind of a thing that can change everything.

Chapter 10

Don

Birch Lake, June 1961

I'm ain't gonna lie to you. Everything is different since we lost Mike. We might as well get use to it, because that's the way it's gonna be from now on. You can't just go around making believe it never happened.

We had all these great plans for Larry's. I don't know if they're all gonna go down the drain or what. I figure the list of projects we was working from must be around here somewheres, but I ain't seen it. I also ain't about to go up to the house and rummage around looking for it. I wouldn't mind hanging onto that piece of paper, if I ever get ahold of it. I'd keep it for a souvenir even if we didn't wind up finishing none of the projects.

I been wondering if maybe Jack knows where it is, but I don't hardly have the heart to ask him about it.

Jack is totally lost. Why, Helen Keller could see that. I feel sorry for him, but at the same time I don't know exactly what he feels like. My old man beat feet when I was so young I couldn't hardly remember him no matter how hard I tried. Jack at least had an old man he can mourn over. And not just any old fartknocker neither, but the best guy you'd be liable to come acrossed. The kinda guy that when he was around, it seemed like nothing much could go wrong.

I know how bad I feel about Mike, but I can only guess how much worse Jack must feel. I figure the only thing I can do about it is hang around with him when he wants me to and leave him be when he don't.

Carol and Ray are still in Chicago, but they're spose to come up as soon as Ray's baseball season is over with. Maybe that'll help Jack get squared away. I don't know. Meantime I'm trying to pick up some extra hours at the Sinclair station, because there ain't been much doing here.

The other day I was just puttering around the grounds, doing busy work, when Jack come along and says I should knock off. I guess he just got back from somewheres or other, but only the Shadow knows where.

"Let's go fishing over by the dam," he says. Well sir, that one really come out of left field. We use to do that sometimes, but not lately.

It was about four o'clock or so, kind of a strange time to go fishing—especially if it's a pretty warm day. But I didn't say nothing about that. I just says, "Sure. Why not?"

We took the speedboat, which isn't really spose to be for fishing, but Jack likes to drive it and it's more comfortable than a regular rowboat with a little outboard on the back. To get to the dam, you go straight out from Larry's dock for a ways, swing to the left of a pretty big island, and then under the bridge County M runs acrossed.

The bridge is so low, you can reach up with your hand and touch the underside of the road. I'm not kidding you. They say it's good luck to put an empty beer on one of the I-beams when you go by, so that's what we done. Me and Jack brought one of them styrofoam coolers with us, and we each had a dead soldier to put up on the I-beam.

Once you go under the bridge, there's a marshy area on the left, so you angle to the right until you see the sign that says NORTHERN STATES POWER COMPANY. That's the dam.

Jack shifted to low gear once we seen the dam, and then we puttered along for a bit until he cut the engine altogether. "This seems a likely spot," he says. We was maybe a hunnerd yards from the drop.

We each cracked a beer and clinked our bottles together. "Here's how," Jack says, and took himself a good swig. I done the same.

Jack always use to say the dam will pull the fish towards it, which makes as much sense as anything anybody says about fishing. We got our gear out. Jack started casting off of one side of the boat and I took the other side. We wasn't at it for too long before Jack says to me, "You know, I got a bone to pick with you."

"What'd I do this time?" I says, just sort of fooling with him.

"Why didn't you tell me Jeannie's married to the guy from the pink store?" he says. "The crippled guy. Bill or whatever his name is."

"What?" I says. I swear I never had no idea. "How in hell would I know who she's married to?"

Jack took a drag on his cigarette. "It must be common knowledge among the locals," he says.

"Well, it's news to me," I says. "I knew she was married and I knew he was married, but I didn't know they was married to each other."

He flicked his butt into the water. He always flicks his butts with his thumb and the back of his middle finger, and let me tell you I never seen anybody shoot one farther.

"Don't fuck with me, Don," he says.

"I ain't fucking with nobody," I says. "I never asked neither one of 'em who they was married to. Why would I?"

Jack looked right into my face and didn't say nothing. He can actually be kind of scary when he looks at you a certain way, especially if he doesn't say nothing.

I reached for another beer. "It never come up," I says to him. "Anyways, what difference does it make?"

"No difference at all," he says.

"Want a beer?" I says.

"Don't mind if I do," he says.

You don't have to knock me over the head with a sledgehammer. I figure I know what that discussion was really about.

See, Jack disappears every now and then and says he's going off to run an errand. It's really none of my beeswax, but still you have to wonder what he does on them errands of his. What kind of errands would a guy be doing when he comes back empty-handed nine times out of ten? That means he ain't going off to buy nothing, which most people mean when they say running errands.

I guess you could go to the bank or the library (like hell) or the driving range and not come back with nothing—but between us, I'd say he probably goes over to the Star Lite Tap where Jeannie works. We stopped in there together a few times when we first found out she was working there, but we ain't done that again since before Mike passed on.

I never pegged Jack for the kinda guy to carry on with another woman. But on the other hand, if the opportunity is right in front of you, being offered to you, it must be awful tough to turn it down. I'm only just guessing now. I wouldn't know nothing about that from firsthand experience one way or the other.

Just for the hell of it, let's say Jack and Jeannie do get together once in a while when nobody else is looking. And let's also say they don't spend the time playing tiddlywinks. If that turned out to be the case, then I'd wonder why Jack would want to go ahead and do that. Why would a guy with a perfectly nice wife, and gorgeous to boot, need to go ahead and mess with somebody else's? Why would you go out of your way to make trouble for yourself? Why would you need two gals when lots of guys don't even have one?

If I had a few under my belt and it was a full moon or some damn thing, I might even ask Jack some of them questions. And then what? What if he admitted to it? Suppose he was to say something like, Well that's just the way it is, and I don't give a hot steaming shit if you like it or not!

If Jack said that to me, then I would tell him, Then you just go right ahead and do what you need to do, but don't get caught at it.

By the time we was ready to call it a day, Jack had two real keepers in his basket. First he landed a nice northern that was about two foot long and maybe four pounds or so. Then he got a walleye that was a little bigger yet. He also tossed back a few that most people would of gladly kept.

Meanwhile, I got a couple little bluegills you could of used for bait but not much else. Then this one time my rod bent almost into a circle, so you know that's a pretty big fish. I yelled, "I got something!" Well sir, you'll never guess what it was. A carp. The worst goddamn fish in the lake.

I guess you could say it wasn't my day. That's nothing unusual, but what happened next was. After we pulled in the anchor, Jack couldn't get the engine started right away. He kept trying to turn the key and fiddling with this switch and that switch, and there wasn't nothing doing except us drifting toward the drop the whole while. Jack didn't seem to notice. He just kept on mumbling to himself and trying to turn the key even harder. It's a wonder it didn't break off in his hand.

This drop or falls or whatever you want to call it is about sixty foot high. I don't know if we would of really gone over it without an underwater grate or something stopping us, but I'd rather not find out. Even if we didn't go over, we'd get all tangled up in the works for sure. That wouldn't of been much better.

"Jack," I says. "Watch yourself, watch yourself." At first I said it sort of quietly and then I got to hollering louder and louder. Finally I just grabbed the anchor and tossed it in. We was maybe fifty foot from the edge by then.

"Oh shit," Jack says. "The ignition got locked somehow. No wonder the key wouldn't turn." Then he tried again and she started right up. I don't know if he ever seen how close we was getting to the drop.

On the way back to Larry's, I had a little buzz on, and all this stuff about Mike and Jack and Carol and Jeannie was running through my head, not to mention the idea of almost going over the falls, and I forgot to put an empty bottle up on the I-beam. I never even thought of it until after I seen Jack put his up there. By then it was too late. We was already coming out the other side. Even if I'd of realized it sooner, I didn't have a dead soldier handy anyways when we went under the bridge.

That did sort of bother me. I wished I'd of remembered. Maybe it's a silly superstition in the first place, but I'll take all the good luck I can get. Who knows? Going along with it might not help, but it can't hurt any, right?

Chapter 11

Carol

Chicago, June 1961

With his career prospects at a low ebb in terms of both the party and the city, Jack doesn't seem to want to show his face in Chicago at all. Even before his dad passed away, he was making insinuations about telling them all where to go and taking his chances in some other line of work. I thought he meant going back to plastering or something like that. At the same time, he allowed that the idea of my going to work was not quite as egregious an affront to everything sacred as he'd previously believed.

As soon as we lost Mike, though, all bets were off. Since then Jack has spent more and more time helping out at Birch Lake, mostly on weekends but also by using some of his vacation days and sick days from the city job—which he still has, but just barely.

He's not coaching Ray's baseball team this year. He said he didn't have time, and I let it go at that. So did Ray, bless his heart. But I think the real reason is that Jack viewed coaching the team as obligatory for a precinct captain, and now he feels he's not obliged to do that or anything else for the people of this neighborhood. I'm sure he would love to see his successor as precinct captain and his successor as the Little League coach fall flat on their faces.

Since we lost his dad, Jack has even been talking about chucking everything here in Chicago and moving to Birch Lake! I mean year-round. Honestly, it would be impossible to list all the reasons why that wouldn't work.

First, Chicago is our home in every sense of that word. It's where our friends and relatives are, where our parish is, and where Ray feels comfortable. It's where we *belong*.

Second, these remote outposts in the north woods are charming in their way, but unless I miss my guess they don't have a school or a library or a hospital or even a grocery store worthy of the name. Don't even think about museums, concerts, plays, zoos, and a hundred other things.

Third, and this is a good one, what kind of a living could we expect to make for ourselves in Birch Lake, even with me working? Well, we could start with thirty-five bucks a week times the four cabins at Larry's, times however many weeks there are in the season. That's assuming all four cabins are rented every single week. How much does that add up to? Five thousand bucks or so for the year, minus expenses? It was fine for Jack's mom and dad because they were retired and running the place as sort of a hobby. But to think for one second that this amount, whatever it comes out to, could begin to support not only Jack and Ray and me, but also Jack's mom, not to mention Don?

I won't go on. I think you get the idea.

I say if we're so bound and determined to leave Chicago for whatever reasons, why not move to the suburbs? That would most likely improve our situation in any number of ways. I'm sure my dad would help us get started if we asked him. Maybe Jack could become a precinct captain for the Republicans! He'd probably like that. I've always thought of myself as a city girl, but I can certainly see myself fitting in the suburbs better than I would in the wilderness. At least I wouldn't get hopelessly lost on my way home from the market. (Well, maybe I would the first time or two, but not thereafter.)

The other thing that I've been pondering is the future of Larry's and all the old-fashioned resorts at all the myriad lakes in Wisconsin and Minnesota and Michigan. To my way of thinking, the various improvements that Mike and Don were planning would make very little difference, except insofar as they would've served to keep Mike and Don occupied and entertained. Larry's can be the nicest resort on Birch Lake, but the competition isn't really Hellstrom's or Vogel's across the lake. It's Fort Lauderdale and places like that—because in this day and age, people from Chicago or Milwaukee can fly to Fort Lauderdale, check into the hotel, and be on the beach in about half the time it takes to drive to Birch Lake.

I trust Jack to recognize all this in due time. Maybe he already does, deep down, but he's adrift right now. All these points and many others will need to be discussed, but I don't know that this is the time. I want to respect the fact that Jack needs time and space to grieve in his own way. If this idea of moving to Birch Lake is simply a fantasy that he needs for the short term, then I'm all for it. My goal for now is to get through the summer without any new disasters and with as little disruption as humanly possible for Ray. If we can do that, I think we'll be back on the right track before too long.

Do you know the song "Somewhere," from *West Side Story?* I love that song more than I can tell you. I hum or sing it to myself all the time. I usually don't even realize I'm doing it. The whole song is tremendous, but the last verse is the one that really gets me. It says everything you need to know. Jack and Ray and I are on our way somewhere, but we know not where just yet. Lord willing, the three of us will get there together, and all in one piece.

There's a place for us,
A time and place for us.
Hold my hand and we're halfway there,
Hold my hand and I'll take you there
Somehow,
Someday,
Somewhere.

Chapter 12

Ray

Birch Lake, July 1961

I didn't sleep much the night before Dad was going to take me golfing. I could've gotten up any time, but I waited till I saw some light coming in. The birds were chirping outside the window, but there wasn't any sound from inside the house except a clock ticking. I got dressed and tiptoed downstairs. Then I went through the kitchen and the breezeway to the sunroom, which I thought would be a good place to wait for Dad.

When I went in there, I found out Dad was already there. He was sitting on the couch smoking a cigarette. At first I thought it was Don, because he sleeps there sometimes when he doesn't feel up to driving home. But then I got closer and saw it was Dad.

"Look at you, up and at 'em at the crack of dawn," he said.

"I couldn't sleep," I said. "I'm too excited."

"Well, this is a special occasion, so we're going out for breakfast. If you're ready, we might as well head out."

Dad said we were going to have breakfast at a place called Dot's Diner. As we went across the bridge into town, the water and the sky were getting to be pretty light, and Dad said exactly what I was thinking.

"Looks like we're gonna have a nice day."

Most of the buildings on Main Street are two stories with some kind of a business on the ground floor and an apartment or two on the second floor. Dot's is in one of these same buildings, and it was the only place open.

There are stools along the counter and a few tables in the middle and booths in front of the window. The walls and the counter and the booths are all yellow. A couple of farmers in overalls were sitting at the counter and some guys from the paper mill were at one of the tables. They all had on a navy blue shirt, navy blue pants, and work boots. They had the name of the company on the back of their shirt and their own name on a little patch in front.

We sat down at the counter. The lady said hello and poured Dad a cup of coffee. "Long time no see," she said. She looked around forty-five or fifty, with sort of purplish hair and lipstick about the same color. Her outfit looked like a nurse's, except it was yellow instead of white. I thought she must be Dot, but her name badge said Peggy.

"And who's this handsome stranger?" she said.

"This is my son Ray," Dad said. "You met him before, when he was just a little guy."

"I guess the apple don't fall far from the tree," Peggy said. "Well, you better keep him hidden unless you want all the girls in town bothering you morning, noon, and night." She winked at me and then she said, "You gentlemen ready to order?"

"Not just yet," Dad said. "We're gonna be one more. Ray, I don't know if I told you Don is joining us."

"At this hour?" Peggy asked. "I better get a full pot ready." She went to put on some more coffee and then she came back and gave me an orange juice. "Here you go, sweetie."

"He ought to here by now," Dad said.

"Maybe he overslept," Peggy said. "He might've been out late."

"He might've at that."

Then the little bell on the door jingled, and it was Don.

"Oh, speak of the devil," Peggy said. "Look what the cat drug in. So he's not lost, strayed, or stolen after all."

Don said hello to us and sat down. "Jeez, Don," Dad said. "Don't anybody light a match. The whole place is liable to go up."

"Maybe you ain't heard," Don said. "I don't drink no more."

"Is that a fact?" Dad asked.

"Yep! And I don't drink no less, neither."

Peggy poured Don a cup of coffee. "What are you doing up and about?" she asked him.

"Ask this one," he said and pointed his thumb at Dad.

"We're going to try Ray's hand at golf today," Dad said.

"Why, that's swell!" Peggy said. "I knew it had to be something pretty big to get this here one up so early."

"I wouldn't miss it," Don said. "I'm gonna tell my grandkids all about it."

Dad looked at Don, and then he said, "Gave your razor the day off, did you?"

"Sure did. I might go ahead and give it the whole week off."

After we ordered, I noticed there was a photo on the wall of Peggy shaking hands with President Kennedy.

"Dad, is that for real?" I asked.

"Hey Peg," Dad said. "Ray wants to know about this picture over here."

Peggy came over smoothing her apron. "Isn't that something?" she said. "He was here for the election. Not the election. You know."

"The primary," one of the farmers said.

"That's right, the primary. He came in with all these newspapermen and photographers and all trailing behind him. It was exciting!"

"I hope he spent some money, at least," Dad said.

"Couldn't have been nicer," Peggy said. "And good looking? I should say."

Then Dad said, "You've got something in common with my wife, Peg. You both met Kennedy and you both—"

"Want to screw him," Don mumbled to the farmers.

"—have a crush on him," Dad said.

"Myself, I voted for Nixon," Don said.

"Well, I didn't," Peggy said. "Not on your life!" Then she laughed.

It's about half an hour from Birch Lake to the golf course in Ladysmith. Dad and I rode together and Don drove separately in his pickup truck. Mom says Don has a new truck just about every year. She means a different used one, not really a new one. But you can always tell Don's truck by the bumper sticker on the back that says PROUD TO BE A PACKER BACKER. I don't know if he has a whole stack of those bumper stickers or what, but he always has the same one even when his truck is different.

When we got to the golf course, Dad told the man there, "This young man is making his debut today."

"His first time out?"

"Yes sir," Dad said and slapped his hand on top of my shoulder.

"He'll never forgive you," the man said and smiled.

Dad laughed a little.

Then the man said, "Well, there's worse things you could do to your kid."

"What's that?"

The man pointed to my cap. "Letting him be a Cubs fan," he said and laughed.

Dad didn't laugh. He paid the man and then the man told us good luck. We went out to the first tee but there was still no sign of Don.

"Where is Don?" I said.

"Who knows?" Dad said. "I thought he was right behind us. Anyway, let's go ahead and get loosened up while we wait." Dad took out his driver and used it to stretch out his shoulders and back, kind of like a batter does in the on-deck circle. I took out my driver and tried to imitate whatever Dad did.

After a few more minutes, Don showed up.

"Where you been?" Dad asked.

"I had to stop a minute. Not quite a hundred percent this morning," Don said.

"You don't say," Dad said.

Don reached into his pocket and started walking towards the clubhouse. "You're too late," Dad said. "It's already taken care of."

"Like hell," Don said. "You already paid for breakfast."

"Your money's no good today," Dad said.

Dad already took me to the driving range a few times, and I can hit the ball pretty good off the tee. They let me go first and I hit a good drive. Don said, "Look at that. Straight as a string. What do we have, a ringer here?"

Dad slapped me on the back and said, "Nice shot, bud."

"Beginner's luck," I said.

"Beginner's luck, my eye," Don said. "We're up against a live one, Jack."

Then it was Don's turn. He sliced his drive over the barb wire fence and into a cow pasture. "Aw, shit," he said.

Dad put his drive right down the middle, about twice as far as mine.

"Showoff," Don said.

Don went to look for his ball while I walked up the fairway with Dad. He took a cigar out of his pocket and lit it up. I asked him, "Dad, what does 'on the wagon' mean?"

"What?" Dad said. "Where'd you hear that?"

"Grandma said Don was on the wagon and then Mom said it was too bad he fell off."

"Is that right? Your mom said that? Well, never mind. It's just a silly expression."

Don found his ball in the cow pasture. It was behind a giant stump. "Don't hit it from there," Dad said. "Just toss it back over here."

But Don shot from where he was. The ball hit the stump and ricocheted right back over his head.

"Shit!" Don said. Then he went and got his ball and lobbed it toward us. It rolled up pretty close to my ball.

"All right, you're back on the golf course anyhow," Dad said.

But there was one more thing. As Don was coming back from the cow pasture, he tried to duck between the top strand of barb wire and the middle one, but he got his pant leg snagged. He lost his balance and ended up ripping his pants and cutting his arm. He swore again, worse than before, and then he said, "Pardon my French, ladies."

Dad puffed on his cigar and said, "We're off to a flying start."

"I'm a pretty fair golfer myself," Grandpa Mike told me one time, "but your dad is something else again." I was actually amazed to see how good Dad is. He made it look easy. Not every shot of his was perfect, but even the shots he called bad looked pretty good.

Seeing Dad play so well seemed to make me play worse. I knew he wanted me to be good and expected me to be good, and knowing that made me a little nervous. I wanted to impress him, but wanting something and really having it happen are two different things. Maybe I tried too hard.

The third hole is a par three, only about a hundred yards. Dad's tee shot came down from a mile high, landed behind the flag, and then spun backwards towards the hole. He could've made the birdie putt with his eyes closed. I topped my tee shot and it only dribbled a few yards. I could've kicked it farther than that. On my second shot I hit behind the ball, and the divot went farther than the ball.

"Relax, bud," Dad said. "Take your time." So I took a deep breath and planted my feet and lined up my next shot very carefully. This time I hit it square, but too square. It was a line drive that sailed over the green and into the woods.

Dad got frustrated. "Come on, Ray! Concentrate. Think about what you're doing."

Then I did the very last thing I wanted to do, which was to start bawling. I couldn't help it.

Don wasn't really as bad as it seemed at the beginning. He was better than me, but way worse than Dad. You could tell he didn't take it seriously.

This one time Don was trying to hit his ball out of the sand. He took three or four whacks at it and still didn't get it out. So he just picked the ball up and threw it on the green.

"That's one way to do it," Dad said. "But aren't you forgetting something?"

"What's that?"

"You gotta rake the trap, Don."

"Oh, silly me," Don said. He went back and raked the sand trap real quick, but there were still quite a few footprints after he got done.

Dad looked at me and made a face.

When we got to the eighth tee, Don took a little camera out of his bag and offered to take a picture of Dad and I. That hole is a par three. The tee is on top of a hill with the green way down below. It's a very nice view from the tee looking out at the Flambeau River behind the green, so that's where Don took a picture with Dad's arm around me.

"Hey Ray," Don said, "did your old man ever tell you he aced this hole one time?"

"Pardon?" I said. I didn't know what he meant.

"A hole in one. Your dad shot a hole in one right here. True story."

I said, "That's great, Dad." And I meant it.

Don said to Dad, "You never told him? You are really something." Then he said to me, "We were playing with your Grandpa Mike, God rest his soul. Man, did he get a kick out of that."

Dad said, "That was a long time ago."

For the next few holes Dad was pretty quiet. He told us "nice shot" once in a while, but other than that he didn't say much.

The ninth fairway runs along the edge of the river. When we were getting ready to tee off, Dad told us, "Make sure you land your ball left, up on the slope a ways, or else it will roll into the drink."

I didn't need to worry about my drive rolling into the water, because I hit it in on the fly. So did Don. Dad's drive landed halfway up the slope and then rolled down and stopped in the middle of the fairway.

We were almost done and I hadn't goofed up anything too bad for a while—but when we got to the green and started putting, I did. My ball was the furthest out, so I putted first. It was a pretty good putt. I started maybe forty feet from the hole and ended up five or six feet away. Dad said, "Nice up."

I walked over near my ball feeling proud of myself, and then it was Dad's turn to putt. He squatted down to line it up, got into his stance, and then looked up at me and said, "Ray."

I didn't know what he meant.

"Your shadow's in my line."

I still didn't understand.

"Look at your shadow, Ray."

Don was standing near me. He pointed at the ground and said, "See, your pa is putting through your shadow. Just move back a bit."

I stepped back to where Don was and got my shadow out of the way.

"That's the stuff," Don said.

I still have a lot to learn.

When we totaled up the damages, Dad had 38 for nine holes. He had me down for 67, but I don't think he counted all my shots. Don didn't keep score.

"Let's get a bite," Dad said. We went into the clubhouse and sat down at the bar. There's a Hamm's beer sign behind the bar that says FROM THE LAND OF SKY BLUE WATERS. It has a picture of a lake scene where the water and the clouds look like they're moving. I thought that was pretty neat. Below the sign there were some hot dogs rolling on metal rods underneath an orange heat lamp. Dad ordered three of them and three little bags of potato chips.

"What to drink?" the man said. I ordered a Coke and Dad ordered a bottle of Leinenkugel's, which is a beer from Chippewa Falls. Grandpa Mike took us to see the brewery one day last summer when it was raining.

Don said, "Same here." Then he said to Dad, "A little hair of the dog."

There is a poster on the wall with two cartoon ballplayers shaking hands, and it says WELCOME TO TWINS COUNTRY! The Minnesota Twins are a brand-new team in the American League. Now I guess people around here will need to decide if they are Twins fans or Braves fans, just like people in Chicago have to decide if they are Cubs fans or Sox fans. Anyway they are in different leagues, so they won't have to play against each other unless they both make it to the World Series.

We ate our hot dogs and chips, and the man introduced himself to us. His name is Ralph. He looks like the dad from *My Three Sons*, Steve Douglas. Except he has glasses and a little mustache, which Steve Douglas doesn't.

"Tell me, Ray, how did it feel to watch the master at work?" Don asked.

"Great," I said.

"Thank you Ray," Dad said. "But, as Bobby Jones said, 'No one has ever mastered the game of golf—"

And then Don yelled, "And no one ever will!" at the same time Dad was saying the same thing.

306

Don elbowed me and said, "See, I know your old man so well I can finish his sentences for him."

"Very impressive," Dad said. Then he got up and went over to the pay phone to make a call.

When he came back he said, "Hey listen, Ray. I have to run an errand real quick. I'll meet up with you back here in a bit."

I was going to ask him where he was going, but Don jumped in and said, "You go right ahead, Jack. We'll amuse ourselves for a while."

"You sure you guys will be all right?" Dad said.

"Sure," Don said. "We're going to play poker. Liquor up front and poker in the rear."

"But I don't know how to play poker," I said.

"That's fine," Don said. "I can win some money off of you."

"He's just pulling your leg, Ray," Dad said.

"Am not neither. I'm gonna clean him out. How much you got on you, Ray?"

"Sorry, no gambling on the premises," Ralph said, and smiled a little with his mouth closed.

"Lucky for you, Ray," Don said. "Well, in that case we can play the back nine if you want."

"Where is the back nine?" I asked.

"Same as the front nine. They only have nine holes here."

"That's a good idea," Dad said. "Why don't you go ahead and play nine more, and I'll be back before you know it. Maybe I'll even play the last few with you." He offered Don some money, but Don didn't take it.

Then Dad said, "Are you guys sure you're gonna be okay?"

"Of course," Don said.

"Don, you're sure you'll be all right."

"Absolutely."

"Don?"

"Scout's honor."

"Okay," Dad said. "Anyhow, I'll be back in a flash. You made some good shots out there, Ray. I'm proud of you." Then he gave me a big hug and went out the door. He usually doesn't hug me like that.

Don said, "The Phantom departs, only to reappear when we least expect it."

I didn't really think too much of it, because I'm used to hanging around with Don sometimes. I figured Dad would be back pretty soon, so it didn't seem like a big deal.

"You guys want another nine holes?" Ralph asked. He must've overheard.

"Yes, most likely," Don said. "But I think I'll have me a refill first."

Chapter 13

Carol

Birch Lake, July 1961

A lake, like a forest, is timeless, mysterious, and, depending on your point of view, either magical or frightening. I've always felt like a fish out of water at the lake, no pun intended, and that feeling has only intensified with Mike gone. If I've ever managed to fit in there to any extent at all, the credit would go to him. Of course, everything about the place reminds me of him, and every time I turn around I half expect to see him.

There's a matched pair of old lawn chairs at the lakeside where he and Elizabeth would sit every evening after supper. This went back many years before they ever dreamed of buying the place. As soon as the last dish was in the drainboard, you could find the two of them sitting side by side down there holding hands. It was really sweet. Now I can't walk by those chairs or even look at them without getting a lump in my throat. I can't imagine how Elizabeth can stand it, bless her heart. She won't go anywhere near those chairs.

For his part, Jack has taken to driving Mike's Buick rather than our family car. It still smells vaguely of cigars (having been the only place where Mike could still get away with smoking them), and some miscellaneous belongings of Mike's are still in the glove compartment and the trunk. That must be very comforting for Jack.

On the morning of the big golf outing, Ray's debut (which Mike had so looked forward to), somehow I never heard Jack get up. I went downstairs at sunrise with every intention of making break-fast for him and Ray, but they were already gone.

I've never been the type to go back to bed after I'm already up, so I got myself some toast and coffee and waited for Elizabeth to come down. I've always heard that older people don't sleep much, but Elizabeth seems to sleep a lot.

I finished my toast and had a second cup of coffee and tidied up a bit. There was still no sign of Elizabeth for about an hour. When she finally did come down, she was still in her nightgown and slippers. She didn't even have a robe on. That was a first. In all the years I've been with Jack, all the days and nights we've spent with his folks at the lake, I'd never seen Elizabeth come downstairs without being dressed and having fixed her hair.

It was a strange beginning to what turned out to be a very strange day.

The first thing Elizabeth did upon arriving in the kitchen was to click on the radio. I'll be honest with you. I can't stand the sta-tion we always listen to from Eau Claire or Chippewa Falls or wherever it is. Except for five minutes when they do the national news, there isn't anything worth hearing. I know this isn't very nice, but the announcers' northwoods accents are like fingernails on a chalkboard to me. They drive me batty. Sometimes when Elizabeth is in another part of the house, I try to tune in to good old WGN. You can make it out, just barely, amidst the static. As crazy as it seems, I prefer the static to the local station.

It seemed to be a slow news day in Eau Claire, as usual. If they ever said anything about a giant storm headed our way, I didn't catch it. And neither did Elizabeth, no matter how intently she seemed to be listening. If she had heard anything about bad weather coming, she wouldn't have looked out the window and said, "Well, dear, it looks like a perfectly beautiful day for the boys to have their golf game." But she did say that, and then hav-ing said it, she fell silent and put her chin in her hand—because she had misspoken and she knew it. To Elizabeth, "the boys" could refer to a combination of males including Mike and Jack, or Mike and Jack and Don, or Mike and Jack and Ray, or even Mike and Jack and Don and Ray. But it could not refer to a group that did not include Mike.

Elizabeth and I have known each other for fifteen years. She's been my mother-in-law and I her daughter-in-law for thirteen. She and I have been pretty good to each other, all things considered. But we had never been emotionally close in any way until the moment our eyes locked and I saw in hers what I can only describe as abject terror. Her mask of ladylike (or I could say "haughty," if I was being mean) poise was gone. She was naked before the fact that Mike was really gone forever. I pressed her free hand between both of mine, and neither of us felt the need to say a thing.

Jack had left a note to the effect that he and Ray wouldn't be back for lunch, so Elizabeth and I had ham sandwiches and cole slaw on paper plates at one of the picnic tables. I wish I could say that all traces of awkwardness and guardedness between us had evaporated thanks to our weighty encounter at breakfast, but that would be stretching the point a mite too far. Even so, I can honestly say that we spent the time together as better friends than we'd ever been previously.

Elizabeth even told me a story I'd never heard before.

It seems that when Mike first bought Larry's, the first thing he did was install a hammock between two trees not far from the main house. "For thirty years," Elizabeth told me, "Mike told Larry he should put a hammock there. 'For crying out loud, Larry,' he'd say. 'That spot is just perfect for a hammock.' But every time, Larry just said it was a great idea and then forgot all about it. Gosh, did that aggravate Mike! So, as soon as we bought the place and Larry handed over the keys, why, Mike was out there putting up the hammock. And then he said the only way to test it properly was for the two of us to cuddle up in it together."

311

Forgive me, but I couldn't help wondering whether "cuddle up" was a euphemism for something more intimate. If it was, though, Elizabeth probably wouldn't have quoted it back to me. Or would she? It was a very strange day, as I already mentioned. In any case, the punch line of the story was that when Mike and Elizabeth got in the hammock together, it spun around a time or two and pitched them both to the ground. The next day the hammock was gone, and Mike never said another word about it.

Elizabeth and I were having our dessert, watermelon balls, strawberries, and banana slices all mixed together, when the wind noticeably shifted and the sky darkened.

Even as a little girl, I wasn't afraid of thunderstorms. I loved them. One of my favorite things was to nestle in bed at night with the covers pulled up to my chin while the lightning flashed and the thunder boomed and the raindrops clattered. In the city, the buildings are close together and most of them are made of brick, and the storm doesn't really get in between them. If you get caught outdoors, you might get your umbrella blown inside out and you might wind up soaked. But if you're indoors, you can appreciate the grandeur of Mother Nature's fury while staying snug as a bug in a rug, as they say.

At the lake, you can see the squall line rolling toward you from miles away. It's awe-inspiring, and not necessarily in a good way. You see the water turn gray to match the sky, and then you see it churning and roiling. Around the same time the trees will look fluffed up, swollen, and the treetops will start whirling. Sometimes, in the more extreme cases, the sky goes from gray to a sickening shade of green and finally to black. As dark as night. Then the rains come pelting down in sheets, often with hail sprinkled in as well. And being indoors is little consolation, given the rather flimsy construction of the cabins and even the main house. Lord knows, if a big enough tree were to fall on one of these buildings, there'd be nothing left except kindling.

In the country, you are part of the storm, not a casual observer of it as in the city.

So here came the weather. That's the expression we always use, as in "I wonder if we'll get some weather later." Well, by now there was no question that we had some real honest-to-goodness weather on the way. Elizabeth and I gathered up the remnants of our little picnic and scurried back to the house. Elizabeth, bless her heart, ran with one hand covering her head for fear her hair would get "mussed," in her words.

Whenever there's a crazy wind howling away, I always think of a saying Ray came up with: "The wind must be in an awful hurry to get wherever it's going." He's such a clever boy.

The radio was still on in the kitchen. It's always on during Elizabeth's waking hours, as I mentioned before, simply to kill the quiet inside the house. I usually ignore it as best I can, but not this time. The announcers were discussing several funnel clouds that had been sighted in the area, including one that was believed to have touched down near Rice Lake.

The Rice Lake funnel cloud was said to be headed east-southeast. If it stayed on that path, it would pass right over Highway 27 somewhere between Ladysmith and Birch Lake. Would Jack and Ray be on that road when it did? While I was pondering that question, our local tornado siren went off.

That would've been thanks to Bill, the crippled man over at the pink store. The siren is located right behind the store, so it's Bill's job to activate it. He must have gotten a call from the weather service and then, the poor thing, he'd have wheeled himself out the back door, around the propane tank and the garbage cans, and set the siren off.

I got out the phone book and called the golf course in Ladysmith. The man who answered identified himself as Ralph, and when I asked about our guys he knew exactly who I meant. "They left here some time ago, ma'am," he said. "Jack took off a bit earlier, and then after while Don and Ray took off. If you're over at

313

Birch Lake, why, they should've—I mean they should be home any time now."

Naturally, I assumed he just mixed up the names, and it was Don who left by himself and Jack and Ray who left together. "Thank you kindly," I said. "Of course, I'm a little worried about the weather and all."

"Well," this fellow Ralph said, "maybe I was mistaken about how long they've been gone. I'm sure they'll turn up soon."

I didn't know what to think. I tried to make myself believe that Jack had pulled over somewhere and that he and Ray were inside a gas station or some other likely place of refuge waiting the storm out. I tried to imagine Ray having a candy bar from the vending machine. But then again, I know Jack too well to picture him playing it safe like that. He isn't one to recognize discretion as the better part of valor. As I grew more and more frantic, the weather deteriorated at about the same rate as my mental state. I was literally walking around in circles for lack of any better ideas when Elizabeth looked out the window and said, "The boat."

Of course. The speedboat. Mike's pride and joy. We needed to get it out of the water, didn't we? Otherwise it might be swamped and end up on the bottom. Either that or dashed to smithereens against the pier.

"Oh, dear," Elizabeth cried. "Where *are* those fellas?"

"Probably up to some foolishness," I said, without meaning to. Honestly, I didn't realize I had said it aloud until Elizabeth wrinkled her brow.

"I mean Don," I added, lamely attempting to cover myself.

At any rate, Elizabeth and I were on our own. Two frontier women without our menfolk around to look after us. For that matter, I don't know where the rest of the men were either. I mean the men who'd rented the cabins with their families. They might have gone off on some day trips. Who knows? All I know is that we didn't see them around.

"I'll go and get the boat," I announced.

"Not by yourself, you won't," Elizabeth said. "I'm coming with you." I'm sure that she'd ever been in a situation like this before without Mike there to take care of it for her, but she was determined to pitch in and do what she could. As it turned out, she proved to be tougher than I had ever given her credit for and probably tougher than she herself had suspected.

We put on the most suitable clothes we could find for the task at hand. For Elizabeth, that meant an old brown oilskin of Mike's and some rubber boots that he must've used for duck hunting or some such thing. Both the coat and the boots were far too big for her. The get-up was rather comical, but that was entirely beside the point. I admired her enthusiasm.

As we were preparing to head out, I got the idea to call Don's place and see if he had any news. But when I picked up the phone, it was dead. No dial tone, no nothing. The lines must have been down—just like in the movies. Only this wasn't a movie; it was our real life.

Elizabeth and I ventured out into the maelstrom.

The first order of business, before moving the boat, was to haul the trailer down to the landing and maneuver it into position. In a perfect world, someone else could have handled that job while I was bringing the boat over. But Elizabeth has never driven a car in her life, and this didn't seem an opportune time for her to learn how. (This is no knock against Elizabeth, mind you. My mom doesn't drive either. As far as I know, neither of them has ever given it a thought.)

The trailer is kept behind the garage. When we went back there to fetch it, we were dismayed to find it sitting in knee-high grass. More evidence that Mike was gone, as if we needed any. He used to move the trailer out of the way, mow the grass there, and then put the trailer back. And so did Don. Both subscribed to the motto "Do the job right or don't do it at all." Don says it all the time, as if to remind himself.

It wasn't easy, but eventually we managed to drag the trailer out of the high grass and then roll it out into the open. Elizabeth really was a trouper.

This whole time I'd been trying to visualize getting the boat started, driving it over to the landing ramp, and steering it onto the trailer—all in the middle of a monsoon. It would be a tall order for anyone, let alone someone like me who's never driven the boat before. But even though neither Elizabeth nor I have ever been granted the privilege of driving the boat, we've heard about what to do and what not to do countless times over the years.

Gas tank full, or at least not empty. Check.

Fuel line connected to gas tank. Check.

Fuel line open. Check.

Choke engaged. Check.

Start ignition, but go easy and don't flood the engine. Check.

I went over that list in my head while I ran to get the car. I jumped in the car and started her up. And then, all at once, did I feel stupid—because it was our family car, the Chevy, when of course the trailer hitch is on Mike's car, which Jack and Ray had taken to the golf course.

"Where *are* those guys?" I said to myself.

I pulled the car into the garage, and while doing so I noticed the canvas cover that goes with the boat. I went back and told Elizabeth that I had goofed about the car and trailer, but there was something we could do after all. I thought if we put the cover on the boat, we'd have done as much as we could under the circumstances. Elizabeth was game.

The walk down to the boat was scary. There was stuff like leaves and twigs and even small branches flying everywhere. It was lucky that neither of us got knocked on the head by some airborne object. Also, about this time it started hailing. Now you've probably heard people talk about hail the size of golf balls or even baseballs. I don't want to exaggerate. I don't think our hail was quite that big, but I'll say this. Even if it was only marble-sized, the pellets (or whatever you call them) came down so fast and so close together that they reminded me of beaded curtains. We practically had to push our way through them.

When we finally got to the pier, we literally got down on all fours and crawled forward. It was the only way we could stay on the pier and not be blown into the water. When we came abreast of the boat, I tossed the rolled-up canvas in and the two of us sort of tumbled onto the seats in the rear. This entailed a drop of a foot or two from the pier, but we had made it to the boat. So far so good.

You've probably seen the kind of canvas boat cover we're talking about. It's the same size and shape as the top of the boat, and when you pull it taut, you can snap it into place. I know for a fact a child can do it, because I've seen Ray do it many times. Not to make excuses, but in our case the job was made more difficult by the gale-force winds that kept flipping the cover this way and that even as we were trying to hold it down and get the snaps to line up.

It took some trial and error, but eventually we got the hang of it. (I started to say it took patience, but patience is hard to come by when all you can think about is getting done and getting the heck out of there.) We got all the snaps snapped from inside the boat except the last few along the pier. We could've fastened those from inside the boat, too, but then we'd have been under the cover. That would have been an oops. So we crawled out of the boat and back onto the pier, and then Elizabeth held onto the pier for dear life while I snapped the last few snaps on my hands and knees.

Heading back to the house, I noticed that the flag was sticking straight out as if it were made of sheet metal rather than cloth. This was yet another reminder of Mike, for his first official act after taking over the place (not counting the ill-fated hammock)

317

was to go out with Don one day and erect a much taller flagpole than the little one Larry had. "By God," he'd said, "they'll be able to see the Stars and Stripes from pretty near anywhere on the lake."

The flag was snapping in the wind just like a whip cracking, and the lanyard was banging against the flagpole like a bell. I was taking this in, sort of objectively, when just then a bolt of lightning hit the ball on top of the flagpole! At least I thought it hit there, because that's where I saw the flash. I put my arms over my head and ducked. But at the very same instant, a large branch cracked off a tree behind the third cabin and fell to earth in slow motion—so maybe the lightning actually hit the tree and not the flagpole. Or maybe it hit both at the same time. Or maybe it hit the flagpole as I thought, and it was only a coincidence that the wind tore the branch off the tree just then. I guess we'll never know. Fortunately, the branch fell parallel to the back wall of the cabin and landed on the ground rather than falling through the roof.

When we got back to the house I said, "You were just great, Elizabeth!" and gave her a bear hug. That was the first time I ever called my mother-in-law by her first name to her face.

Neither Elizabeth nor I had stopped to ask why we should have gone out of our way to try and protect an inanimate object—albeit a dearly beloved one to both her husband and mine. We just saw something that needed to be done, and we did it. Did we literally risk our lives? I don't want to overdramatize, but we do know this much. A funnel cloud unequivocally touched down near Rice Lake, fifty miles away, and was reported to be traveling in a direction that might have taken it right over our heads. The Rice Lake tornado lifted a moving car off the road, carried it a quarter mile, and dropped it into a scrubby field. The driver, poor man, was pronounced dead at the scene. A storm that could do that could certainly have picked us up off the lake and tossed us who knows where.

I'll say this. If it was ill-advised, foolhardy, or even unnecessary, our mission still accomplished something. It kept Elizabeth and me occupied for forty-five minutes or an hour that would otherwise have been spent wringing our hands and wondering what had become of my husband and son, a.k.a. her son and grandson. It distracted us at least in part from that nerve-wracking set of questions. It also enabled the two of us to prove something to ourselves and to each other. We took on a task that was difficult and even dangerous, we didn't panic, we worked together, and we came through just fine, if not exactly with flying colors.

I like to think that Mike would've been proud of us.

Chapter 14

Don

Birch Lake, July 1961

Jack asked me to tag along on this golf outing with him and Ray, so I did. To tell you the truth, I never was much of a golfer, and when you play with Jack (and the same went for Mike, may he rest in peace), it's more business than pleasure. There isn't any goofing off or joking around out on the golf course. No sir. I'm not quite sure where the fun is spose to come in, the way they go about it. It's just the same with fishing and everything else. There's always a right way and a wrong way to do everything, and you can bet your buttons if you do something the wrong way, you'll hear about it. And how.

Don't get me wrong. If Jack or Mike or the both of 'em was nice enough to invite me, I was gonna be there come hell or high water. That was the fun of it for me, just the idea of being included.

"You know this golf outing?" Jack says to me. "We were spose to be a foursome, you know—my dad, you, Ray, and me. My dad couldn't wait to get Ray out there. So now we're down to three, but we'll play in honor of my dad's memory."

What in hell could you say to that? I was in.

Jack shot like a pro, which you could of easily predicted, and I shot terrible, which you could of predicted even easier. But the thing I really got a kick out of was having Ray out there with us. So would of Mike. Man, he would have been in his glory, as they say. Ray held his own just fine for a kid that never played before, even though you could tell Jack was making him nervous. A couple times I made a funny face at him or slipped in a little wisecrack, just to lighten things up a little. But like I say, he come through like a champ. I think he probably outshot me, if you really want to know.

We played nine holes and then we stopped in the clubhouse for a quick snack. I thought the plan was to play another nine after that—but the next thing you know, Jack made a phone call and said he needed to run an errand. At first I thought he was pulling our leg. Here we are having our big golf outing, the first annual Mike Weber Memorial Invitational, and he makes a phone call and needs to run an errand right then and there? At eleven o'clock or whatever it was in the morning? With Ray setting there? He's going to duck out and run the errand, and he doesn't think Ray is going to wonder about it?

I figured Jack was gonna take a break from the errands after Carol and Ray come up north, but I figured wrong. I don't know. Maybe he can't help himself. If he was hell bent on running the errand, then there wasn't nothing I could say that was gonna stop him. Besides, it was no trouble for me to keep Ray company for an hour or whatever. It was actually a pleasure. You wouldn't have to twist my arm none to get me to spend time with that kid.

So Jack took off, and me and Ray was spose to bide our time till he got back. We shared a bowl of pretzels and I had another beer. Then Ray started getting antsy and asked if we was gonna head back out. "You betcha," I says. "Just wait till I finish my beer first."

He asked if he could go out and practice putting while I was finishing my beer. "Fine with me," I says. You could see the practice green right outside the window behind the bar, so that way I could keep an eye on Ray while he was at it. He looked in from time to time and we waved back and forth.

I got the idea we should stop in and see my ma if we had the time. The old folks' home ain't no more than a mile from the golf course. I figured she'd enjoy seeing Ray, even though she'd probably think he was Jack.

Then the Braves game come on TV, and I felt like watching an inning or two and having a couple more beers. This barkeep kept giving me a dirty look every time I asked for a refill. I don't know what his problem was.

After while Ray come back in and set down next to me. "I thought you were coming out," he says.

"Oh shit," I says. "Pardon my French. I'm sorry, Ray." And I meant it, because I just plain forgot. "Let's head out now."

The barkeep, being a busybody, was listening in on our conversation, and he chimed in. "I don't know if you fellows want to go out now," he says. "There's a bad storm brewing."

I never seen it coming. The window behind the bar faces south and the weather was coming from the west. I leaned forward and hunched over the bar and cricked my neck sideways so I could see more out the window. What can I say? The barkeep was right, the son of a bitch. The treetops was spinning but good, and there was dark clouds swirling around in all different directions.

"Listen, Ray," I says. "Let's take a rain check. We'll watch the ballgame for a while and I bet your pa will be back any time now."

"Okay," he says. Really, he's the nicest kid you'd ever hope for.

Then Hank Aaron come up to bat on the TV. "Did you know Hank Aaron started out over in Eau Claire?" I says to Ray. "Did I ever tell you about the time me and your pa and your grandpa, rest his soul, went and seen him play?"

He looked at me sort of funny. "You mean today?" he says.

"Hey, barkeep," I says. "How's about another Coke for my buddy and another Leinenkugel's for me."

Right away this barkeep got a little snippy. "The name's Ralph," he says. "Like I already told you."

This guy was really something.

"Excuse me. Another Coke and another Leinenkugel's. If you please, Ralph."

This Ralph stood there and looked at me like he was trying to think of something smart to say. I thought maybe I should stand up myself and see how he liked it. But then he just went back and got the drinks. When he put 'em down he says, "Own stock in Leinenkugel's, do you?"

"Come again?"

"I'd say you must be one of their best customers."

"What's it to you?" I says. "It's a local beer made by local guys. In fact, I got a cousin works there. So why in hell shouldn't I support 'em?"

"No reason at all," he says. "But you don't have to keep them in business single-handed."

Honest to God, if Ray wasn't there I would of socked this guy right in the Adam's apple. "You're very funny," I says. "You oughta go on TV." I took a giant swig of my beer and went, "Ahh."

Then Ralph says, "Why don't you just slow down a little?"

"Why don't you mind your own business?" I says.

"It is my business," he says. "I'll be out of a job if it's anything like the last time you were here."

"I don't know what in hell you're talking about," I says. "I don't remember nothing."

"I can believe that all right," he says with a little smirk on his puss.

He wiped at the top of the bar with his rag, then he leaned over towards Ray and says, "Is your dad coming back soon, sonny?"

"He said he was," Ray says.

"Just running a little errand," I says.

Then it started raining cats and dogs. I mean a real downpour. There was giant drops clanging on the roof, and out the window you could see the sky was a greenish-gray color. You don't see that every day. And then the wind picked up, and I swear the building started creaking. For a while there all the golfers who got caught out in it come slinking in three or four at a time like drowned rats. And finally, for the topper, the tornado siren went off. That means an actual tornado was seen in the area.

We probably should of gone down in the storm cellar, but nobody else said nothing about it, so I didn't neither. I was just wondering if I should switch from beer to something that would put a little more hair on my chest when the phone rang and Ralph answered it. "For you," he says and give it to me.

It was Jack. "What's up?" he says.

"What's up yourself?" I says.

"Is it raining there yet? Did you guys get caught out in it?"

"No, we've been watching the ballgame and chewing the fat."

"Good," Jack says. "I'm glad you guys didn't get struck by lightning or something."

"That makes two of us," I says. "We're fine. Except my friend Ralph here's been giving me the business the whole while." I looked over at Ralph, but I guess he didn't hear me.

"Have you been antagonizing him?"

"I would say he started it."

"Yeah, I'm sure you would," he says. "Is Ray okay?"

"Just great."

"Okay. Thanks for taking care of him. He gets a kick out of seeing you."

"Likewise, I'm sure."

"Listen," he says. "Would you mind if I met you guys at your place instead of coming back there? That way I don't have to drive all the way there and back again in a monsoon, and Ray and I can get home that much sooner."

He had a point there. He could save at least half an hour by not coming back out to Ladysmith to pick Ray up. Not to mention he'd have a little extra time to finish doing whatever he was doing. And then I thought to myself, Holy shit, Carol and Elizabeth are over at Larry's by theirself and God knows what they got to deal with. They might of had trees falling down on 'em or anything you could think of.

"You know what?" I says. "You're right. We'll meet you at my place in thirty minutes. Don't be late. Let's scrutinize our watches."

"Are you all right?" he says. "Seriously. You gave me scout's honor, Don. You sure you're all right?"

"Never better."

"You sound a little funny."

"Aw, what do you want to go and get on me for? Who's the one helping who out?"

I explained the new plan to Ray, and he was agreeable as always. He hopped off of his bar stool and was ready to go. Such a damn nice kid. I mean the absolute best. Then I told Ralph I was ready to settle up, and he wasn't so agreeable. "Wouldn't it be better to wait for the boy's dad?" he says.

"We got our marching orders *from* his dad," I says.

And then he put both palms flat on the bar and leaned forward to talk right in my ear, like you would with a gal when you want to whisper sweet nothings. "I wonder if he knows how many beers you had," he says. "I wonder if you're fit to drive a vehicle with somebody else's kid in it."

"You can wonder all you want," I says. "But it won't do you no good."

This Ralph looked at me for a second, and then at Ray, and then back at me. At first he didn't say nothing. He just scrunched up his face and let a long breath out of his big fat nose. Then he says, "How'd you like some hard-boiled eggs? On the house. Might do you some good."

"No, I don't want no hard-boiled eggs."

"Why don't you have a coffee at least?" When he turned around to go get it, I tossed a few bucks on the bar (probably more than I owed anyways), and we was out of there.

We was just pulling out of the parking lot when I realized I forgot my golf clubs. Actually it was Ray realized it and told me, because I forgot his too.

Okay. Maybe I was a little tipsy after all. If I wasn't, how could I of forgot the sticks? Mine are twenty-some years old, so I wasn't too worried about nobody swiping 'em, but they was hand-me-downs from Mike. I sure as shit didn't want to lose 'em. They have sentimental value. And trust me on this one. I damn sure didn't want to be to blame for Ray losing his clubs, because they're brand-new and also a gift from Mike.

If I just said the hell with it, I'll come back and get 'em in a day or two, I'd of been worried about it the whole time. So we pulled a U-turn back into the lot and found the clubs just where they should of been, leaning up against the side of the building under the eaves.

Then we was on our way again.

I probably wouldn't even mention it, except going back for the clubs cost us a few minutes that sure would of came in handy later. Because we wasn't hardly out of the lot the second time before I realized I had to pee.

Whoever said you don't really buy beer, you just rent it—man, did that guy hit the nail on the head. I had a good number of beers under my belt. If somebody was to ask me how many, I'd of probably told 'em three or four, but when you really get down to it I don't know for sure how many I had. Alls I know is I had to pee like nobody's business.

Everybody knows there ain't nothing worse than needing to pee so bad it hurts and having no place to do it. There isn't a gas station or nothing between Ladysmith and Birch Lake. Not even a little side road to duck onto, far as I know. That being the case, normally you'd just pull off to the shoulder and look for a likely bush to stand behind. But you can't do that when it's raining sideways and you can't see past your hood ornament. You might misjudge where the shoulder is and go right down the embank-

326

ment. Or you might pull off on the shoulder just fine and then some yahoo rear-ends you. I couldn't take no chances like that with Ray.

I started asking Ray questions about school and sports and whatnot to try and take my mind off of my situation. I don't know if it helped or not.

We were still about five miles out from the intersection of 27 and County M, where Hardt's roadhouse is located. That's what I was shooting for. I've darkened their door many times. I even remember most of 'em.

This one time they tossed me out for going in the ladies' john, even though I did it on accident. I mean, come on. It's dark in the corridor back there and there's two doors right next to each other, and I happened to go in the wrong one. Everybody makes a mistake now and again. You wouldn't believe the fuss this one little ninny kicked up about it. I never did nothing to her. I never touched her with my pinky finger, even. You wouldn't neither if you seen her. Alls I done was turn around and beat feet out of the ladies'. And then the old man, Mr. Hardt, says, "Don, I'm awful sorry but I'm gonna have to ask you to leave." I respect that. He's nice about it even when he's throwing you out.

Well sir, after while I could tell for damn sure it was gonna be tough making it to Hardt's without peeing my pants. I grabbed the wheel as tight as I could and squirmed around in my seat and tried to grin and bear it. And here's the sad thing. I always keep an old mason jar under the seat for spitting tobacco juice into. That would of served the purpose just fine, if it wasn't too full already, but not with Ray setting right next to me. What if he was to tell his ma, You'll never believe what I seen Don do on the way back from Ladysmith.

While I was thinking about what Carol might say to that, the intersection we was looking for sorta snuck up on me. Don't ask me why, but for a second I forgot where we was spose to be going. Having to pee as bad as I did, and being in a goddamn hurry to get *somewheres*, I kept on going straight ahead like I was going to my place. It was just force of habit. But then I realized I needed to stop at Hardt's.

I was almost to the intersection already, and still doing sixty-five or so, when I tried to swing into Hardt's.

It was too late. Instead of staying straight on 27 towards my place or making a ninety-degree turn into Hardt's, we ended up headed to the right at about forty-five degrees. I could of sworn I was braking the whole while, but the road was wet and my tires are bald and you know how that goes.

We slid right acrossed County M and into Hardt's parking lot at a pretty good clip. The next thing you know, there was a loud thud, and then all this glass shattering. We was wrapped around the sign post. Then Ray went, "Oh!" Just exactly like that. "Oh" and nothing else. After that he clapped his hand over his eye and started moaning, sort of.

Chapter 15

Jeannie

Birch Lake, July 1961

Isn't it supposed to be fun when you're getting away with some-thing? Then why am I so miserable?

Jack is a very attractive man. There's no use denying that. I know damn well everything about this situation with him is as wrong as wrong can be, but still I keep going on with it in spite of myself. I've been telling myself if your life really and truly is go-ing to hell in a handcart, or whatever the expression is, then maybe you're better off to just relax and enjoy the ride. At least you can try and have some fun before you crash into the concrete wall or whatever comes at the end.

Sex is fun. I guess most people would agree with that, along with the animals that get to do it. Otherwise humans and all the other species wouldn't have survived this long, would they? May-be the good Lord gave us sex to enjoy just for the fun of it, with-out having to feel guilty about it and without worrying about marriage and monogamy and that. I've been telling myself that over and over, but I don't really believe it.

One day Jack and me were chit-chatting about this and that, and we got on the subject of our kids. Jack told me a few things about his son Ray. You can tell he's very proud of that little guy.

Then he asked, "How old are yours again?"

I swear I already told him any number of times before, but oh well. "Julie, the oldest, is seventeen," I said. "Jerry is fifteen, and Debbie is twelve."

"Seventeen," he said. Now I could see his wheels turning. I knew exactly where he was headed. "I don't guess she—"

"Could be your daughter?" I said. "Are you serious?"

"I don't know. I just wondered, is all."

"No, your math is a little off there. Julie was born in May of '44, and I hadn't seen you since August of '42."

"Oh, yeah. I guess that's right. Well, anyhow."

Truth be told, Jack is sort of maddening. Did he really think I would've brought a child of his into the world and not told him? If I told him Julie was his daughter, he'd wish to God she wasn't—but since I told him she wasn't, he seemed to wish she was. That's just the way he is.

Here's the main thing to keep in mind about all this. Whatever goes on between Jack and me, there isn't a snowball's chance in hell he would ever leave his wife or I would ever leave Bill. It just ain't gonna happen, ladies and gentlemen.

If Bill is suspicious at all, he hasn't let on. He's never said a word to imply anything of the sort. He just keeps crawling further into the shell he's built for himself.

That's probably the saddest, most pathetic part of this whole state of affairs. The old Bill, the one I fell in love with, would tell you exactly where you could go if he didn't like something. This Bill we have on our hands now, I can't tell if he really doesn't suspect anything or if he suspects everything and just doesn't care enough to comment.

I almost wish he'd confront me, accuse me right to my face, and go over the whole list of everything I've done wrong line for line. If he did that, I'd throw myself on the floor in front of him and beg for his forgiveness.

Chapter 16

Ray

Birch Lake, July 1961

I don't remember much about the accident. I remember us sliding sideways on the wet pavement and Don yelling, "Look out, Ray!"

I don't remember Don's truck actually smashing into the sign-post, and I don't remember the ambulance ride to the hospital, but I do remember the doctor coming in and looking me over with a light strapped to his forehead. "You're a very lucky young man," he said. "Why, you might've lost your eye or even worse."

It turned out the passenger side mirror snapped off and hit me in the face. There's nothing wrong with my eye or eyelid. I just ended up with a nasty gash from my eyebrow almost to my scalp and a few scrapes and scratches in other places where little pieces of the windshield landed. The doctor said he would put the stitches real close together so the scar won't be too bad.

Mom and Dad were there when I got wheeled into the other room to get the stitches, and they were there when I got back. I had to be blindfolded during the stitches to keep from squirming around. "Don't feel bad," the doctor said. "I never met anybody yet who doesn't flinch when they see a needle coming at their eye."

The doctor put a patch over my eye, just like a pirate wears. "His buddies will be impressed with this," he told Mom and Dad. "Just keep it on for a week or so, until everything quiets down. Change the dressing and ointment under there every day."

Then I found out I had to stay overnight in the hospital. "Pure-ly precautionary," the doctor said. "We just want to watch out for any signs of concussion or anything strange while he's sleeping." Mom and Dad promised to stay with me for as long as they were allowed to. I remember Dad said he was going to read *The Sporting News* to me, but I don't know if he really did or not because I fell asleep right away.

When I woke up the next morning, Mom and Dad were already there. They couldn't sign me out of the hospital until the doctor came by and gave his permission, so in the meantime I had breakfast in my room. Mom realized I didn't much care for it, so she said we could have another breakfast when we got back to Larry's.

I was feeling okay. They gave me some pills to control the pain. While we were waiting for the doctor, I asked Dad about Don. I never heard if he got hurt in the crash or not. "Don is pretty near indestructible," Dad said. "He got away without a scratch. He just needs to make sure your mom doesn't get her hands on him."

Dad sort of chuckled and then looked at Mom to see if she was going to laugh, but she didn't.

"The main thing is that you're going to be all right, Ray," Mom said. "Thank Heaven."

Nobody said much on the ride to Larry's. Dad was driving and Mom kept looking out the window on her side. They said I could lay down in the backseat and take it easy, but that started to make me dizzy so I sat up instead.

When we got to Larry's, Mom and Grandma Elizabeth fixed me a real nice breakfast just like Mom said. I didn't eat it all because I already ate some of the hospital breakfast, and they didn't make me clean my plate.

Then Mom sat down next to me. "Ray dear," she said, "you and I are going on a vacation from this vacation. We're going back home first thing tomorrow morning. We need to have you see a doctor and get a clean bill of health."

"But the doctor at the hospital already said—"

"Ray," Mom said, "these doctors up here..." But she didn't finish.

"Is Dad coming?" I asked.

"No. Your dad is going to stay on here and help Grandma and Don with running the place."

"Are we coming back if the doctor says it's okay?"

Mom took a sip of her coffee. "Good question," she said. "First we're going to get you some rest. Then we might do some fun stuff together for a few days—that's the vacation part. After that, if you feel like it, maybe we'll come back up here. How does that sound?"

"That sounds swell," I said.

It was cool and cloudy when we got ready to leave the next morning. Dad carried my suitcase to the car for me. He offered to carry Mom's too, but she said, "I'll manage myself, thank you."

After we got in the car and Mom started the engine, Dad reached in through the open window and ran his hand through my hair. Then he leaned over and kissed me on the cheek. I can't remember him ever doing that before. "You take good care of yourself," he said, "and don't forget to mind your mom. We'll see you real soon."

When we started moving, Dad said, "Sorry for all the trouble." Then he held up his hand and waved to us until we went around a curve and we couldn't see him anymore.

It was kind of odd that I didn't see him and Mom kiss goodbye. They must've done that beforehand.

I've always meant to make a list of all the different towns we go through between Birch Lake and Chicago, but then I would forget when the time came. This time Mom reminded me, and she even brought a pencil and a notepad. "I don't want you straining your eyes and giving yourself a headache," she said. "So why don't you just call out the names of the towns and I'll write them down for you. Today is Be-Nice-to-Ray Day."

I already knew the first three by heart: Crescent, Cadott, and Ludington. But I waited until we got to each place before calling it out. Then came Augusta, Fairchild, Humbird, and Merrillan. By then we'd been on the road about an hour and a half.

We were almost to Black River Falls when Mom pulled over to pick up a hitchhiker. She said, "Aw, look at this poor kid."

He was a young guy, kind of scruffy looking, with a tan jacket and blue jeans and a guitar case strapped on his back. He put his guitar in the back seat and then he got in. "Howdy," he said. "I sure do appreciate you stoppin' for me."

"It looks like rain," Mom said. "I'd hate to drive by you and have it open up five minutes later."

"Well, that's mighty nice of you."

"Don't mention it," Mom said. She turned around to look at him, and so did I. "Are you all settled in back there?"

"Yes, ma'am."

"I guess we should introduce ourselves," Mom said. "My name is Mrs. Web—uh—Carol, and my son here is Ray."

"I'm Bob," he said.

"Where you headed, Bob?"

"I'm on my way to New York City, but right now I just need to get to Madison." He scratched the side of his face. "I gotta see about a girl I know."

"Well, we can get you to Madison all right," Mom said. "But you're on your own with the girl."

She pulled off the shoulder and back onto the highway. "Mom," I said. "Black River Falls."

Bob asked what I was talking about, so I explained it to him.

"That's very interesting," he said. "Mind if I help?"

"Sure," I said.

Bob asked what happened to me, so I told him, and then Mom asked him to tell us some more about himself. He said he was originally from the Iron Range in Minnesota, but lately he's been working on a dude ranch out west, traveling with a carnival, shoveling coal on a tramp steamer, riding the rails, and playing music all around the world. "Not all at the same time, of course."

"My!" Mom said. "You've certainly had an eventful life. May I ask how old you are?"

"Twenty." (He pronounced it "twunny.")

While we were listening to Bob, we almost missed Sheppard, Millston, and Kirby. Some of these towns go by pretty quick.

Then Mom asked Bob who his favorite musicians are, and he started telling her, but I didn't recognize any of the names. I dozed off and didn't wake up until we were past Madison and Bob was already gone.

"We didn't have the heart to wake you," Mom said. "Bob asked me to say so long for him. He said maybe he'll write a song for you someday and call it 'Ray of Hope.'"

"That would be nice," I said.

"He also wanted me to show you this." Mom handed me the notepad. After Kirby, which was in Mom's handwriting, there was Tomah, Oakdale, Camp Douglas, New Lisbon, Mauston, Lyndon Station, Wisconsin Dells, Lake Delton, West Baraboo, Bluffview, Sauk City, Springfield Corners, Middleton, Shorewood Hills, and Madison. Bob must have written all those down.

Madison was in capital letters with a star next to it. "That's because it's the capital," Mom said. "Or, on second thought, maybe it's because that's where the girl he's looking for is!" She laughed. "What a strange, fascinating little fellow. I wonder what will become of him."

Chapter 17

Carol

Chicago, July 1961

Just after my big death-defying adventure with Elizabeth, and at roughly the same time as a giant rainbow appeared across the lake, Jack showed up at Larry's and said that Ray had been in an accident. I didn't understand at first. Jack was obviously no worse for wear (I mean physically, because he was clearly shaken) and neither was Mike's car.

My initial reaction was absolute panic and terror. Lots of histrionics. For a few horrifying seconds, I was convinced that my most nightmarish visions from earlier had come true. And that's not all. I also allowed myself to believe that whatever had happened to Ray had actually been *caused* by my having imagined it in advance. Only after I calmed down slightly did Jack get a chance to explain that Ray was injured, but not gravely.

Then he told me that Ray was riding with Don when the accident occurred and that he (Jack) had come upon the scene some five or ten minutes after the fact, just as the police and all were arriving.

Why was Ray riding in a rickety rust-bucket of a pickup truck *in the middle of a hurricane* with a driver who's been known to drink, rather than with his own dad in a comfortable, stylish 1959 Buick that still smells faintly of Old Spice and cigars, just like his late and beloved grandpa?

Don is Don. He has his good points and not-so-good points— but when push comes to shove, he wasn't responsible for Ray's safety. Jack was.

Jack told me that Ray had opted to ride with Don for a change and that he (Jack) had stopped for gas on the way out of Ladysmith. This would explain his being a few minutes behind Ray and Don. It sounded plausible, and it might even be true. But then again, the man at the golf course, whose name escapes me, said that Jack left *before* the other two. At the time I assumed he was simply mistaken, but now I'm not so sure.

I haven't asked Ray for his version, and I probably never will—but Jack doesn't know that.

Let's say for the sake of argument that Jack's explanation is the God's honest truth. Okay, fine. But don't we still have to ask why he didn't have five minutes to spare and call over to Larry's? He could have easily guessed that his mom and I would be worried sick about him and Ray. For that matter, he might have also wondered how we were holding up on our end.

I don't consider myself an unduly suspicious person, but I think we need to allow for the possibility that Jack left the golf course first, as the man told me on the phone, and was coming from somewhere else when he came upon the accident scene at Hardt's by happenstance. And then the question becomes, where in the world was he coming from? Where might he have gone that was so gosh-darn important that he'd leave our son behind and entrust him to Don's care at the height of what they called a once-in-a-decade storm?

Right now my top priority is to focus on Ray and make sure he's going to be okay. We can peel that other onion later. Who knows where that will lead?

Trust is very precious. When you lose it, you lose everything.

I'm glad to report that Ray and I managed to list all the towns we went through on the way home from Birch Lake. That has always been a goal of Ray's. We couldn't have done it without some help from an odd little hitchhiker we picked up, a troubadour (as he called himself) named Bob. He wrote down all the towns between

337

Black River Falls and Madison, while Ray was napping. After he hopped out at the university, Ray and I handled the rest.

From Birch Lake to the Illinois border we passed through Crescent, Cadott, Ludington, Augusta, Fairchild, Humbird, Merrillan, Black River Falls, Sheppard, Millston, Kirby, Tomah, Oakdale, Camp Douglas, New Lisbon, Mauston, Lyndon Station, Wisconsin Dells, Lake Delton, West Baraboo, Bluffview, Sauk City, Springfield Corners, Middleton, Shorewood Hills, Madison, Rutland, Union, Evansville, Leyden, Janesville, Emerald Grove, Fairfield, Darien, and Walworth.

A lot of these are one-stoplight towns, of course. You might go down the main street at high noon and not see a soul. There's one thing that has always struck me about these little country towns and their environs. You see quite a few abandoned houses and farms, overgrown, in various states of age and decrepitude. When I notice one, I can't help wondering about the first day the first family moved in. When was that? Eighty years ago? A hundred? A hundred and twenty? What were the people like? Were they happy on their modest little farm? Were they able to make a go of it? I'd like to think so.

What about the other side of the coin? What was it like when it became obvious that the future, if there was one, lay elsewhere? When it came time to call it quits because the bank foreclosed or because place and the people were just worn out, what did it feel like to close the front door for the last time and head off to someplace better or someplace worse, never to return?

Thinking about that actually makes me shiver.

On the Illinois side, we went through Harvard, Woodstock, Crystal Lake, Cary, Fox River Grove, Barrington, Palatine, Arlington Heights, Mt. Prospect, Des Plaines, and Park Ridge before entering the city limits. I was working on my mental checklist of things to do with Ray over the next few days. The first day was already spoken for, with Ray due to see a specialist about his injury. If all went well, I planned to take Ray someplace fun every day thereafter.

As soon as we got home, before we even used the bathroom, the doorbell buzzed and it was Mrs. Scanlon, the landlady. She must have been peering through her curtains watching for us—or watching for something, at any rate.

"I'm so sorry to disturb you, Carol," she said.

"I wish I could invite you in," I said, "but we just got back and—"

"Hello, Ray dear." Then she noticed his eye patch. "Goodness! What on Earth happened to you?"

"He was in a little fender bender up north," I said. Then I touched Ray's shoulder, "Weren't you, hon?" I shouldn't answer for Ray (after all, he's ten years old now), but I wanted to keep it short and get Mrs. Scanlon out of our hair as soon as possible.

"My word."

"He'll be just fine," I said.

"Well, he's a brave boy," Mrs. Scanlon said. "That's for sure."

"Yes, he certainly is." I said. "I'm very proud of him. Now what can we do for you, Mrs. Scanlon?"

"I almost hate to mention it, dear," she said in a stage whisper, "but it's about the rent. See, I haven't received July's, and now the first of August is Tuesday, so—"

I interrupted her. "Ray, sweetie," I said, "why don't you go in your room and rest a few minutes, and then I'll fix you something to eat as soon as I'm through visiting with Mrs. Scanlon."

Ray did as he was told. "Such a good boy," Mrs. Scanlon said. "Now as I was saying."

"You never received the rent for July, and next week is August, so we'll owe you two months by then."

"That's about the size of it, dear."

"I can't imagine what happened," I said. "I'm sure Jack must've sent it, but I better speak with him and see what's what."

"Thank you, dear. I wouldn't say anything if I didn't need the money myself."

"Don't be silly," I said. "Of course you've got every right to your money. I apologize for the confusion. We'll get it figured out."

"I take it Jack didn't come back with you and Ray?"

"That's right, but he's got our checkbook and I'm going to call him just as soon as—"

Mrs. Scanlon stepped closer to me, so that our shoes were almost touching. "There's one more thing," she whispered, "which I didn't want to mention in front of Ray. A couple of plainclothesmen were here the other day asking for Jack."

Well now. This was getting curioser and curioser. "Plainclothesmen?" I said. "Whatever did they want?"

"I'm sure I don't know, dear. They just asked if Jack was around, and when I said no they said they'd come back another time."

Suddenly I thought about those phone calls I've been getting where the person just hangs up without saying anything. "Did they show their badges?" I asked.

"Oh, golly," Mrs. Scanlon said. "Come to think of it, I don't think I asked them to."

That night after Ray went to bed, I called up to Larry's and got Jack on the first attempt. That was unusual, and so was the fact that he answered the phone himself, rather than being called to it by Elizabeth.

"Hello Jack," I said. I immediately realized how strange that sounded. I couldn't remember the last time I called him Jack and not "honey" or "hon" on the phone. It was probably only a couple months after our first date. A long time ago.

"Oh!" he said, like he was surprised to hear my voice. "Hello. How's Ray holding up?"

340

"He was fine today. He's sleeping now. He'll see the doctor tomorrow, you know, and then we'll have a better idea. I'll keep you posted."

"I appreciate it."

What an awkward, stilted conversation!

"Listen," I said. "I'll come right to the point, Jack. Mrs. Scanlon is saying she never got the rent this month. Do you know what's going on?"

"Shit," he said.

"Okay, well if you forgot to send it, it's not the end of the world. Just go ahead and send it tomorrow, and you might as well include August while you're at it. You can save a stamp."

"Well, see, the checking account's a little short right now."

I didn't say anything to that right away. I just held the phone to my chest and sort of sighed. I'm sure I rolled my eyes, too, but there was no one around to see that.

"All right," I said. "I guess I'll ask my dad to help us out, unless you have a better idea."

"What are you going to tell your dad?"

"What am I going to tell my dad," I said. "I don't know. I'll think of something."

"Oh, well," he said. "Just do it your way then. Whatever you think is best."

"Thanks," I said. "I'll do that. Good night and send my best to your mom."

There was nothing more to say. I didn't mention the so-called plainclothesmen. I also didn't ask how we can be out of money when we haven't bought anything that would account for the absence of the money. I don't know what all Jack has gotten himself into this time, but it's pretty scary.

I cried myself to sleep. Whatever has been broken between Jack and me is going to be awfully hard to fix.

Chapter 18

Don

Birch Lake, August 1961

If anybody had to get hurt in the wreck, I wish to God it would of been me instead of Ray. I love that kid. They say he's gonna be okay. That's the best news I heard in quite a while. If he wasn't, I don't know what I would do. Maybe I'd just shoot myself and do everybody a favor.

When the cops got there, they never said nothing about drunk driving. You know, somebody who is use to drinking, why, sometimes they can be three sheets to the wind and nobody else can even tell. That must of been what happened. I figured they'd take me in for sure, but nobody said nothing. They just called for the ambulance to come and get Ray.

Anyways, I learned my lesson. You better believe it, brother. I ain't touched a drop of nothing stronger than orange juice since, and I ain't planning to.

I know lots of people say never again when something bad happens, and then they forget all about it a while later. I might of even done that myself a few times. But this time I really mean it. I'm done drinking for good.

My truck is setting in the weeds back behind the Sinclair station, right where the tow truck left it. I don't think it's going nowhere. At first I figured I could go over there and work on her every so often, but now I think that's a lost cause. It's gonna take an awful lot of body work before you could even think about trying to get her running again. Then you'd probably need a whole new motor and a bunch of other stuff to boot. I guess my best bet is to try and find some other piece-of-shit truck for less than it will cost to fix the one I wrecked.

Jack's been pretty good about helping me out until I figure out what to do. Sometimes lately he goes fishing by himself for hours at a time, and he says, "You can go ahead and use the car if you want." He means Mike's Buick. Carol and Ray took the family car, the Chevy, back to Chicago.

I don't know if Jack is still running his errands since Carol and Ray left. He hasn't said nothing about it and I ain't asked him. But get a load of what happened the other day.

I ducked into the pink store to pick up a few odds and ends, and when I went to pay for the stuff, Bill didn't start ringing nothing up. He just set there in his wheelchair looking at me. "You know what I heard?" he says. "I heard some guy in a big black Buick's been bird-doggin' my wife. You know my wife, don't you?"

"Yeah," I says, "I've met her a time or two."

"No need to be so modest," he says. "I understand yous go way back."

I didn't really like where this was headed. "I guess you could say that," I says.

"I thought so. Well, anyways, I heard this guy in the Buick even had the gall to stop by the house when I wasn't home."

I had drove the same Buick he was talking about to the store, but there wasn't no way he could see it, parked off to the side like it was, without wheeling hisself all the way out the front door and halfway around the building.

"Afraid I can't help you," I says.

"You see we got this neighbor," he says, "name of Mrs. Krause, next door from us. She's sort of sickly and don't get out much, and she likes to poke her nose in everybody else's business. You with me so far?"

"Yep."

343

"So anyhow, I'll be damned if she don't sit and gape out her front window morning, noon, and night. She don't miss a thing that goes on around there."

"Is that a fact?"

"You betcha. For instance, this one time I had a couple too many and started in hollering at the wife about this or that, and you know what the old gal did? She called us up on the phone and asked if everything was all right. Can you beat that? I would've told her to pound sand, but the wife answered, and she said, 'Everything is fine, Mrs. Krause. We were just watching a movie on TV, and the people were quarreling. I guess we had it turned up too loud. You were very nice to call.' The wife's more polite than me."

I didn't say nothing. I just kind of looked down at the stuff I meant to buy.

Bill kept on talking. "Well, anyhow," he says. "To make a long story short, this busybody Mrs. Krause was at her post the other day and do you know what happened? I got this straight from the horse's mouth. This black Buick pulled up in our driveway right in the middle of the day. She could probably give me the exact time and the license number if I asked her for it. Some guy got out and went in the house, and then he came out after an hour or so and took off again. That doesn't sound too good, does it?"

I still didn't say nothing. I figured if I agreed with him, he might take it like I was insulting Jeannie some way or another.

"Here's the part that tickled me," he says. "You know what the old biddy said to me? She said she didn't mean to be nosy, she just thought I'd like to know about it since she figured it must've been a friend from out of town looking for me. Because why else would a man stop by the house in the middle of the day like that when everybody and their uncle knows I'd be here at the store?"

I still didn't say nothing.

"So then I put my thinking cap on, and the only guy I know of with a car like that is Mr. Weber, Mike Weber—and I don't guess it could be him unless he came back from the other side, rest his soul. Anyways, I never figured him for the type, did you?"

"Nope," I says. "Never did."

"I wonder who it could be then. I don't guess you'd happen to know anything, would you?"

Now what in hell what I spose to say to that?

Bill finally started ringing up the stuff I wanted to buy. "What it really boils down to," he says, "I don't like anybody to think they can play me for a fool. You know?"

"Can't blame you there," I says.

Chapter 19

Ray

Chicago, August 1961

Dr. Wagstaff is what they call a specialist, so he knows lots more than some country doctor up north. Mom said he darn well ought to, when you consider how much he charges.

After Dr. Wagstaff gave me a clean bill of health, they call it, Mom and I did something fun every day. We went to Riverview one day, the Cubs game the next day, and the Museum of Science and Industry the day after that.

Riverview is great. If you've never been there, you probably have heard of it at least. It's a very famous amusement park located at Western and Belmont, which is only about three miles from our house. We decided to take the bus from Foster and Ravenswood because Mom thought it would be easier than having to worry about parking the car and all.

There are tons of great things at Riverview, but I would have to say my favorite is the Bobs, which is supposed to be one of the best roller coasters in the whole wide world. Mom loves the Bobs too, but when we went with Dad last year he didn't go on it. He said, "I'd rather keep my breakfast right where it is, thank you."

We also went through Aladdin's Castle, which is kind of a funhouse-type place with crazy mirrors, slanting walls, a floor that moves around, and all kinds of stuff like that.

Then we went on the Rotor. It is a round room that you go into, and then the whole room starts spinning around faster and faster until the floor drops out and you end up plastered to the wall from centrifickle force. Lots of people screamed when the floor dropped, but Mom and I already knew what to expect. We didn't scream, but we were walking sideways when the ride ended just like everybody else.

We did so many fun things at Riverview, I can't tell about all of them. It was a great day.

The next day we went to the Cubs game against the Cincinnati Reds. Mom invited my friends Peter Cullen and Brian Drummond to come with. We got there early enough for batting practice, and you'll never guess what happened.

We were in the bleachers out in right field, and there weren't too many people around. I had my mitt on, and Peter did too, but Brian forgot his. Billy Williams hit one almost right at us, and I got the ball! Can you believe that? I didn't catch it on the fly, though. I caught it after it bounced off an empty seat a couple rows in front of us. A few people came up and shook my hand.

And that's not all. Even though Cincinnati is in first place and the Cubs are toward the bottom, the Cubs ended up winning 7-6! Billy hit a three-run homer, which landed a few rows behind us—or else maybe we would've gotten another ball. Ernie Banks and Ron Santo also hit home runs for the Cubs.

I wish Dad could've come to the game with us. He would've gotten a kick out of it. I called him on the phone that night and told him all about it. He was really excited. "They found a couple keepers there, Williams and Santo," he said. "But Altman will be the best of the lot, you mark my word." Dad meant George Altman, the Cubs' right fielder.

I'm going to keep that ball on my nightstand and never use it to play catch or anything, for fear it would get all scuffed up or maybe even lost. Dad said the next time we go to a game together, we should try and get Billy Williams to sign it.

We went to the Museum of Science and Industry the day after the Cubs game. I thought it would be hard for anything to be as much fun as the Cubs game, but I was wrong. There are lots of amazing things at the museum, but my favorites are the coal mine and the Nazi submarine.

Just like a real miner, you take a bumpy elevator ride down into the coal mine. When we took the elevator up to Dr. Wagstaff's office, we couldn't tell where we were going except by looking at the floor numbers lighting up. But this elevator is wide open on all four sides, so you can see exactly where you're going. You also need to watch yourself and make sure you don't scrape against the wall of the mine shaft or get stuck between the elevator and the wall. That would be bad.

Even though the elevator ride is pretty dangerous, it's not as dangerous as the rest of a miner's job. Miners dig inside the Earth quite a ways underground, so one thing to worry about is whether everything will cave in on top of you and bury you alive. Or you could suffocate from carbon monoxide and never even know the difference. Did you ever hear of a canary in a coal mine? Well, if the canary passes away, then the miners know it's high time to get out because there's too much carbon monoxide in the mine to breathe.

They say the worst thing of all would be a giant buildup of methane gas or even plain old coal dust, which could blow the whole works to Kingdom Come.

What I learned from all that is I'd rather not be a coal miner.

Being on a submarine probably isn't any better. You have tons of water sitting on top of you, rather than tons of dirt and rock. You also have people dropping depth charges on you, trying to send you to Davy Jones's locker.

The main thing I noticed about the Nazi submarine was how cramped it was. They say the American ones are pretty much the same, except everything is in English instead of German. If there are two people going down the aisle, one guy going one way and one guy going the other way, they can't go past each other unless one of them stands off to the side and gets out of the way as far as

348

he can. You also have to duck your head all the time if you are more than about five and a half feet tall.

Mom and I had so much fun going to all these different places on our vacation from our regular vacation. I always used to say Birch Lake was my all-time favorite place for sure, but now I would have to say it is one of my favorite places, along with Riverview, Wrigley Field, and the Museum of Science and Industry. I might have to add Montrose Avenue Beach, but Mom said that will probably have to wait until next week.

We went back to Dr. Wagstaff the day after the museum. He took my stitches out and told me I could do without the eye patch. The only thing was, I had to stay inside the rest of that day so my eye could get used to letting light in again.

When we got home and checked the mail, we found a get-well card from Don. The writing was kind of hard to read, but we think it said: *Here's hoping your back on the ball field with your buddies real soon.* That was nice of Don, wasn't it?

Then, while we were having supper, Mom said something I never expected. "Ray," she said, "you are such a good and sweet boy, which I've been reminded of over and over the past few days. What would you say to the idea of going and picking out a puppy tomorrow? Maybe a little cocker spaniel like you've been wanting."

I couldn't believe it, because every time I asked before Mom and Dad said we just couldn't get a dog and there wasn't any use arguing over it.

"That would be swell, Mom," I said. "Do you think it will be okay with Dad?"

"Well, maybe we'll surprise him," Mom said.

Chapter 20

Don

Birch Lake, August 1961

There's this ash tree behind the third cabin that dropped a giant branch during the storm last week. After me and Jack looked it over, we realized we might as well take the whole tree down. We worked on the job together. I went up in the tree with the chain saw, and each branch I sawed off, we lowered it to the ground with a rope. Some of the little kids from the families staying here—what we call the paying customers—stood around watching us. After all the branches was off, I come back down to Earth.

Now I don't like to push my nose in other people's business, but I figured I better tell Jack what Bill had to say at the pink store the other day. What kind of a friend would I be if I just let something like that simmer and never said nothing to Jack?

There wasn't nobody else around and I figured it's as good a time as any, so I went ahead and mentioned it to him. And do you know what he done? He looked at me like I was from Mars or some damn thing and then he says, "I don't know what he's talking about."

Okay, I says to myself, if that's the way you wanna play it. It's no sweat off my back one way or the other.

Mrs. Weber fixed us up a pretty nice lunch—bacon, lettuce, and tomato sandwiches with potato salad on the side. When we got done with that, it was time to deal with the trunk and the stump and whatnot. I told Jack I could probably do that part myself if he didn't feel like helping.

"As a matter of fact," he says, "I was thinking about maybe heading out for a while. If you don't need me."

"That's fine," I says. "Just help me make sure the trunk don't fall through a window or something. Then you can go on about your business."

We looped the rope around the top of the trunk. I went at the bottom with the chain saw, and when it started tipping Jack pulled it away from the cabin with the rope. He even yelled, "Timber!" That was a nice touch.

Then I seen there was something carved into the trunk. "Hey Jack," I says. "Look here. Somebody carved a secret message."

Jack looked at it. "Well, I can't make it out." He reached into his pocket and jiggled his car keys. "What do you think?"

Between us four walls, I thought it looked like "J + J" more than anything else. I wonder who in hell that could of meant, don't you?

"Nah," I says. "I can't make it out neither."

I asked Jack if maybe I could take the car out for a while after he got back. I figured I'd go see my ma in the old folks' home. I felt awful guilty for driving right past the place on the way home from the golf outing.

"Fine with me," he says.

"I really appreciate it."

"All right, well," he says. "I'll see you in the funny papers."

Jack went ahead and took off on his errand, and I kept working. There was plenty more to do cutting up that tree into logs for firewood and then figuring out what to do about the stump. To tell you the truth, I didn't mind the idea of working on it by myself, because otherwise me and Jack would of probably been tripping over each other anyways.

I made pretty good progress while Jack was gone. I cut quite a few logs about a foot long each and got 'em stacked behind the garage. Any branches that was too skinny to use for firewood, I just loaded 'em in the wheelbarrow and dumped 'em back in the woods. All the while I was working, of course, the different people staying with us was sunning theirself on the pier, floating on inner tubes, going out in the boats, playing badminton, and whatnot. I always get a kick out of seeing the families enjoy the place, just like Jack and his folks done back in their day.

Jack got back after while, and I told him I was gonna get cleaned up a bit and then head out myself, if he didn't mind.

"Where do you figure on going, again?" he says.

"To see my ma in the home," I says. "And maybe go for a little drive after that. It'll be a nice night for it."

He took out a cigarette and lit up. Then he kind of looked at me but didn't say nothing right away. I always hate that silence he puts out there. It's nerve wracking.

He finally spoke up. "Yes, well," he says. "Don't do anything I wouldn't do."

I felt like saying, I guess that gives me a good deal of leeway.

And then he handed over the keys. It reminded me exactly of how his pa, God rest his soul, use to give us the keys in the old days.

"You got anything planned?" I says.

"I'll probably sit tight in case Carol and Ray try and phone me," he says. "Also my mom wants to watch a rerun of *Perry Mason*. I'll never understand how she can watch a rerun like that when she already knows who the killer is."

"She probably just wants to have the time with you," I says.

"I guess so," Jack says. "If the excitement gets to be too much for me, I might take a walk down to the Black Bear."

It was still pretty early when I signed in at the old folks' home in Ladysmith. In fact, they was just getting ready to serve supper. The lady at the front desk said I should go ahead and surprise my ma in the dining room. I thought to myself, she'll be surprised all right. She'll be surprised to hear she even has a son.

I was trying to be nice, so I played along. I went over to the dining room, and this big fat lady who works there and knows how to handle these folks says, "Hey, Sophie! You'll never guess who come to see you. It's your son!"

I stepped up and give my ma a little kiss.

"What's for supper?" she says.

"It's just wonderful," the fat lady says. "Pecan-crusted wall-eye."

"I should of known," Ma says. "The same old thing."

So I set down next to my ma, and this lady leans down with her bosoms on my shoulder and whispers into my ear, "I think your dear mother is a little confused."

"You got that right," I says.

"You see," the lady says, "we rotate all the meals on a monthly basis. So you could hardly say with any justification that pecan-crusted walleye is 'the same old thing.'"

"Maybe she didn't care for it last month neither," I says.

Did you ever hear the saying "No good deed goes unpunished"? All right, I admit I owe it to my ma to go ahead and visit her in the home even if she thinks I'm the janitor, but at the same time it's hard to see her that way. I been wondering if I might be doing her more harm than good. If alls I'm doing is confusing her and making her worse off, then what in hell is the point?

It was almost dark when I got out of there. So here I was with a nice car (actually, a *very* nice car) and plenty of gas in the tank and plenty of time on my hands. Where in hell should I go?

I know it sounds crazy, but I got the idea to drive out to Orville Warnecke's place in Lake Wissota. Orville is pretty near the most unfriendliest person you'd ever meet, but he almost sold us a pontoon boat just like Mike always wanted. I guess Mike never knew me and Jack was working on that for him—and just as well, since nothing come of it. I'm not sure why, but I figured it would be fun to see that boat one more time.

It's about 25 miles from Ladysmith back to Birch Lake, and another 25 miles from Birch Lake out to Lake Wissota. You go straight south to get from Ladysmith to Birch Lake, and then you wind along the river going southwest to get from Birch Lake to Lake Wissota. There ain't no way in hell to go southwest straight from Ladysmith to Lake Wissota unless you have a helicopter or some damn thing.

During the drive I was thinking about my poor ma and what it must be like to be in her shoes. We lost Mike all at once, and that was pretty rough. We been losing Ma little by little, and that's even worse. By the time she passes away, there won't hardly be anything left of her to lose.

When I finally got to Orville's place, I seen the pontoon boat we almost bought for Mike was gone. Even though we was never gonna buy it anyways, I still felt sorta disappointed. I guess maybe because it was one more pipe dream definitely over with for good. And do you want to know something else? Pretty near all of Orville's inventory of junk or whatever you'd call it was gone. In the middle of the yard there was a sign that said:

HOUSE + LOT FOR SALE.
INQUIRE WITHIN
ONLY IF "SERIOUS" OFFER!!

Well, that was interesting. Orville Warnecke isn't nothing to me, and I'm sure he'd tell you the feeling is mutual. But you can say this much for him, anyways. He don't give a damn what nobody thinks and he's a genuine character. I'd say the world needs all the genuine characters it can get. I hope he's fixing to move by choice and not for some reason he don't have no control over.

Heading back to Birch Lake, I had to go right past the Star Lite Tap—which, if you don't know by now, is where Jeannie works.

354

Come to think of it, I already passed it on the way out to Orville's, but it didn't really register until I started back.

I figured I might as well stop in for an hour or so.

There was a few reasons I had in mind. First off, I wasn't quite in the mood to go home and hit the sack just yet. It was only about eleven o'clock. You can get a little stir crazy when you ain't got your own wheels and you gotta keep asking to borrow somebody else's. I also figured it would be a real good test for me to try and stay on the wagon even while I'm setting in a bar. What do you think of that? And then I thought anybody can stand to see a friendly face every so often, which Jeannie always was and probably always will be, no matter what life throws at her.

When I went in and bellied up, Jeannie seen me right away and come running over.

"Why hello, stranger," she says. She set down her tray on the bar give me a hug around the neck. "What a fabulous surprise!"

Just then, the barkeep, Keith, cracked open a Leinenkugel's and slid it down the bar just like they do in the movies. It was only ten foot or so.

I waved to him. "Hiya, Keith," I says. "I appreciate it, but I'm gonna stick with ginger ale tonight." I slid the beer back down to him. Then he poured a ginger ale over ice and come over to hand it to me.

"I'll give you some credit," Keith says. "I wouldn't of thought you'd remember my name, judging by the last time we seen you. If alls you want is ginger ale, then it's on the house any time."

"Fantastic!" Jeannie says. I guess she meant me being on the wagon. "I take it your partner in crime isn't with you tonight."

Of course, she meant Jack with that one, which was kinda silly because I never was in there with Jack for about the last five or six months anyways. Maybe she couldn't think of nothing else to say.

Well sir, Keith kept them ginger ales coming like nobody's business. I couldn't hardly finish one before he had the next one in front of me. Plus he kept on filling up the plastic basket of peanuts over and over. I figured I'd be good and constipated before he got through.

The Braves was on TV playing a night game out in San Fran. It was a pretty good game, too. They was losing 1-0 when I set down, but Aaron hit a home run in the top of the seventh to tie it up. And wouldn't you know it, old Hammerin' Hank come up again in the ninth, and damned if he didn't hit *another* homer to put the Braves ahead! Spahn handled it from there.

Where in hell do you spose the Braves would be without them two, Aaron and Spahn? Or let's say them two and Mathews. They wouldn't be worth a damn, if you ask me.

Jeannie swung over by me a few times on her way back and forth. She looks as good as ever, which is saying something. "You know," she says, "I think you're doing a very smart thing, quitting drinking. Lots of people would be better off if they did, too. They wouldn't do near as many stupid things."

"Yeah," I says, "like crashing a car into a signpost and nearly getting Jack's boy killed."

"But he's going to be okay, right?"

"No thanks to me," I says. "I don't know what I'd do if..."

She patted my cheek. "Don't beat yourself up too bad," she says. "His guardian angel was watching out for him."

"Maybe you're right," I says.

"Sure I'm right. Too bad my husband's took a day off at just the wrong time."

When last call rolled around, Keith said I could stay and shoot the shit if I wanted to while they was closing up. Then, when it was really time to go, I thought to myself it was the first time I ever walked out of a bar without being shitfaced or pretty near shitfaced. It was kind of a strange feeling.

I was just getting into Mike's car when Jeannie hollered to me from where she was parked, maybe twenty foot away. "Don," she says, "will you come here a second?"

I ran over there, and she was standing next to her car pointing at the left front. "See this?" she says. "Some drunk must have clipped it on the way out. Didn't even leave a note."

The fender was pushed in and sort of bent up inside the wheel well. There wasn't no way in hell the tire could move in there with it like that.

"That don't look good." I says. "It ain't too much damage, but I don't think you can drive it."

Keith stopped his car on the way out and come over to take a look.

"What do you think I should do?" Jeannie says.

"We might be able to pull the fender back out of there," Keith says. "Right, Don?"

"We might," I says. "But not without ruining the fender for good."

"Oh, we better not," Jeannie says. "That might send Bill clear over the edge."

"If we get her to the garage in the morning," I says, "they can probably fix it without tearing everything up. They got the right tools, which we ain't."

"That sounds right," Keith says. "I'll give you a ride home, Jeannie."

"But it's so far out of your way," Jeannie says. If I recall, I think Keith said he lives near Bloomer.

"I can take you, Jeannie," I says. "It's not out of my way at all."

"You're a prince," Jeannie says.

"Isn't this Mr. Weber's car?" Jeannie says when we got in. "I mean Jack's dad."

I was thinking she must know damn well whose car it was, but I didn't say nothing about that.

357

"Yes, it is," I says. "Jack borrowed it to me for the night."

"Well, that was nice of him," Jeannie says. "Jack's a good guy, isn't he?"

"One of the best," I says.

"I guess Mr. Weber must've been quite a Buick man," she says. She was right about that. As far as I know, Mr. Weber always had Buicks, one right after the other.

"When I first met you fellas, he had a sky-blue Buick. You were driving it the first night we met. Remember?"

"I sure do," I says, "but I didn't think you would."

"Oh, I'll never forget it," she says. "Do you want to know something interesting? Well, I don't know if you'll find it interesting or not. Tonight is the twentieth anniversary of the night I first met you fellas at the A&W."

"Is that a fact?" I says. "That's amazing."

"Isn't it?" she says. "I might not've remembered myself, except for my father dumped a big box full of all my old belongings on our front stoop a while back. These little notebooks I used to keep were in there. Kind of like a diary, but not really. Anyways, I wrote something about the night I met you fellas in the sky-blue Buick with Illinois plates. August the fourth, 1941."

"Unbelievable," I says, and I meant it.

I guess we was both thinking the same thing. Twenty years behind us, more than half our life. Just like that.

Then Jeannie went ahead and started the conversation up again. "How are all your projects at Larry's coming along?" she says. "I imagine you guys are really going to town."

I always knew she had one of them bubbly personalities, but here she was talking a blue streak. It was almost like she was nervous or something.

"To be honest with you," I says, "we ain't accomplished much since Jack's pa passed away."

"Oh," she says. "I, um, understood you were making better progress than that. But then I guess losing Jack's dad must've set you fellas back a ways."

"You can say that again."

"It was a terrible thing. You know, I met Mr. Weber once or twice, and he struck me as a very nice, dignified gentleman."

"He was at that."

She fished around in her purse and pulled out a cigarette. "You don't mind if I smoke, do you?"

"I don't know," I says. "I wonder would Jack would say. After all—"

"I don't think he'd mind," she says. "I think he might've smoked in here himself from time to time. Anyways, we've got the windows down."

"Don't let me stop you," I says.

She went ahead and lit up. Then she held the pack out for me to take one, but I said no thanks.

"Listen, Don," she says. "Does Jack ever mention anything to you about me, I wonder?"

I wasn't sure exactly what she was driving at with that one, so I just told the truth. "I can't say he does."

"No, I guess he wouldn't, would he?"

She took a long drag on her cigarette. With the windows down, her hair was kind of flying all around her face. It was what they call a sultry night.

Another thing I noticed, it's way easier driving the back roads in the dark without a buzz on. That was a new experience for me.

"Now Don," Jeannie says. "I don't mean to put you on the spot, but how would you describe Jack's wife?"

So here I was again on some thin ice. "Oh, I'd say about five-five, dark brown hair—"

"No, sweetie. I mean what kind of a person would you say she is?"

"She's great. Terrific. Nicest gal you'd ever meet. Why wouldn't she be?"

"Oh, I don't mean anything by it. Just being nosy, I guess."

Then we rattled across the bridge and into town. I asked Jeannie for her address. I never knew exactly where she lived, but I heard it was spose to be somewheres near the southeast corner of the lake.

"We're almost there now," she says. "So before it's too late, I want to ask you something, Don. Do you happen to remember any of the nice things you told me the last time? I mean that night Keith was talking about."

"The night I was overserved, and you and Jack had to drag me home?"

"Well, if you want to put it that way," she says. "The main thing I remember was you said when you were in the war you pictured yourself fighting for me. To defend me. Not Rita Hayworth or Betty Grable or anybody else, but just me. And I thought that was about the sweetest thing anybody ever told me."

Take my word for it. I wish I could of crawled into a hole underneath the car seat. "Well, I can't say I totally remember all that," I says, "but I can tell you this much. A gal like you shouldn't have to listen to no crap like that from a guy like me. I hope you left it go in one ear and out the other."

"That's ridiculous," she says. "When you say a guy like you, I think you're selling yourself way too short. You can get yourself a nice girl. You just have to find the right one."

I've heard that kinda thing many times before before, from my ma and from my sister Rosemary and from Carol and even from Jeannie herself way back when. When I thought about that, something popped into my head.

"I don't know if you remember," I says, "but back in the old days, you promised to fix me up with a girlfriend of yours named Mary Jo. Maybe you should check your little notebook."

Jeannie laughed, very adorably. Then she took a puff on her cigarette. "Jeepers," she says. "I'm not sure I remember that discussion, but I'll trust you. I don't know if Mary Jo is still around. I haven't heard from her."

"Well, I'm still game."

"Okay," she says. "A deal's a deal. If we can't locate Mary Jo, I'll keep my antennas up. It'll be fun."

And then we were in her driveway. I don't mind telling you, I was starting to feel pretty good about trying to stay sober and maybe meeting a nice gal to boot. If she was anything like Jeannie, she would fit the bill and then some.

"Thank you so much for the ride, Don," Jeannie says. "You're a good man." Then she leaned over and kissed me on the cheek. That was just great.

Chapter 21

Jeannie

Birch Lake, August 1961

After I gave Don a little peck on the cheek, he said, "Wait right there," and hopped out of the car. He wanted to come around and open my door for me like a gentleman.

He was walking around the back of the car when I heard the shot.

Lots of people hear a car backfire or something like that, and right away they dive under the bed thinking they heard a gunshot. Not me. I know a rifle shot when I hear one.

I turned and looked out the back window, and then I knew the worst had happened. Because Don wasn't there.

I didn't scream. I couldn't have screamed even if I tried. I would've needed to get some air before I could think about screaming. I pounded on the dashboard with both fists. I was moaning, "Oh, Bill... oh, Bill... oh, Bill..." over and over.

My whole body was rocking back and forth in the seat, but I couldn't get my legs to lift me out of there. I was obviously a sitting duck, because the passenger side of the car was closest to the house, but I didn't think about getting shot right then. Plus, if I was gonna get shot there wasn't a whole lot I could do about it.

Finally, I did find the strength to push the door open and get out of the car. It seemed like forever, but it was probably less than a minute since I heard the shot and Don disappeared. I went around back of the car, and sure enough Don was gone. There was no doubt about that.

It's a pretty intimate thing, isn't it, to be there when somebody dies—alive one moment and dead the next? To be the first one to ever see that person dead? And then when you consider it was also my fault, well....

I dropped to my knees next to Don and sort of clawed at the gravel. Then I actually wailed, kind of like an animal who's caught in barbed wire or something. "Bill!" I shrieked, "what did you do? What did you do?"

Just then I had a horrible moment of panic about the kids, until I remembered none of them were home. Thank God. Julie was at a slumber party down the street and the younger two were camping out with a church group on Brunet Island. Maybe that explains, in a way, why this was happening when it was.

When I heard the second shot, I ducked—which was just a reflex and completely useless, of course. Because if that shot was meant for me, I would've been dead already. It took me a second or two to realize I wasn't hit, which meant I wasn't the target, which meant I was now a widow.

I knew I'd have to go in the house soon enough and find Bill and call the cops and then figure out how to get the kids back home and break the news to them. Then I'd have to figure out what to tell them about why this all happened. But for the time being I couldn't do anything except kneel on the ground next to Don and work on trying to breathe.

I wonder if Bill realized he had shot the wrong man. I mean before he turned the gun on himself. God, I sure hope not.

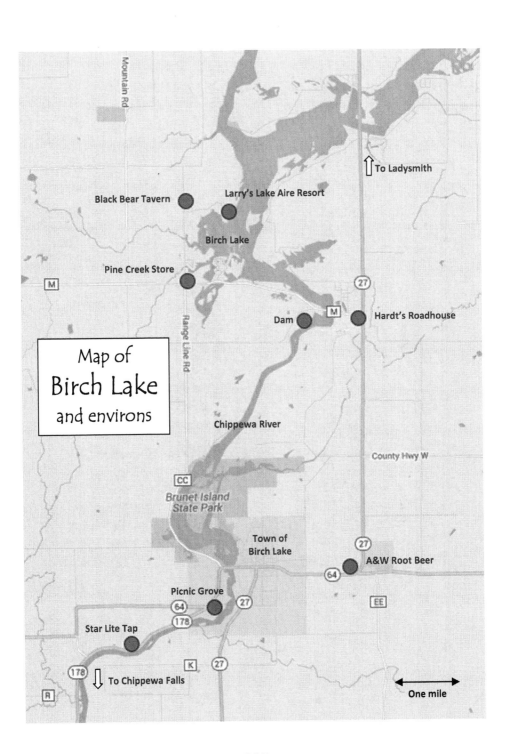

Map of Birch Lake and environs

To Ladysmith

Black Bear Tavern

Larry's Lake Aire Resort

Birch Lake

Pine Creek Store

M

27

Dam

M

Hardt's Roadhouse

Range Line Rd

Mountain Rd

Chippewa River

County Hwy W

CC

Brunet Island State Park

Town of Birch Lake

27

A&W Root Beer

64

EE

Picnic Grove

64

27

Star Lite Tap

178

178

To Chippewa Falls

K

27

R

One mile

34512204R00208

Made in the USA
Middletown, DE
27 August 2016